Right Girl, Wrong Side

GINNY BAIRD

sourcebooks
casablanca

To my late mother, Irma Aboy Turner,
our family's Abuelita and "Abi,"
who is, without a doubt, leading all the angels
in a heavenly Macarena.
Te quiero.

Published by Sourcebooks Casablanca, an imprint of Sourcebooks
P.O. Box 4410, Naperville, Illinois 60567-4410
(630) 961-3900
sourcebooks.com

Printed and bound in the United States of America.
WOZ 10 9 8 7 6 5 4 3 2 1

ONE

EVITA MACHADO COULD TELL A lot about a person by the kind of flowers they ordered. Roses had their own special code. Yellow roses stood for friendship. Pink roses for sweetness. Red roses always said *love*. She placed three pretty red roses in a bud vase then added two sprigs of baby's breath and some greenery. She topped it off by winding a silky red ribbon around the vase and tying it in a lavish bow.

"Last order of the day!" she said, inserting the plastic card holder into the vase. She stood at the workstation at the rear of the shop facing the street. Some florists kept their workstations in back and out of public view, but not Evita. She was too chatty and outgoing to spend hours alone in a gloomy storeroom.

Josie smiled from behind the register by the front window. It was a mild afternoon. Breezy and warm. The perfect summer day. "It's a pickup. I'll wait." She wore her straight blond hair in a ponytail and had bright-blue eyes. Her forest-green shop apron matched Evita's.

"No," Evita said. "You go on home. You've got that wedding of yours to plan." Josie and David were getting married in

September, and the couple couldn't wait. They'd been dating for over a year and were ready to make things official. Evita liked David, who managed an area nursery. He and Josie had connected over plant talk when she'd stopped by to pick up some potting soil. He was a good guy and very well matched with Josie. Evita was pleased to be included in their wedding party as Josie's maid of honor.

The flower-arranging station was a mess with clippings and discarded ribbon remnants covering its woodblock surface. She picked up the small dustpan and handheld broom from nearby and began sweeping up the clutter, depositing it in the waste bin.

One whole wall of the shop was an encased refrigerator section, teeming with gorgeous ready-to-go floral arrangements. The opposite wall housed bins of netting and other supplies along with spools of various ribbons, and a counter with stools and catalogs for customers to browse through when they ordered in person. That happened most often for larger events like weddings.

Josie's eyes sparkled. "Yeah, and you've got your beach week to pack for."

Evita was so ready for this vacation. She hadn't taken more than twenty-four hours off since opening this shop three years ago. Getting her new business launched had been challenging but fun, and now they were finally turning a profit. She was thrilled with the name she'd chosen too: Coming Up Roses. So cute and upbeat. Fitting for Lexington, Massachusetts.

If she stayed solvent a few more years, she'd be able to tackle her long-term goal of starting that community garden in the disadvantaged neighborhood where her grandparents still lived. It would be her way of giving back, and she had so many great ideas about making it work.

Evita finished tidying up and sat on a stool. "Yeah," she said, dreaming of white sands and sunny skies. "Can't wait." Her olive skin rarely burned, but she'd slather on extra SPF as a precaution. Ah, to lie in a lounge chair and breathe in the ocean. Maybe with a tropical drink in her hand. Her dad's piña coladas were amazing, and her mom's cooking put the rest of their efforts to shame.

Her brothers and their wives made up for any culinary deficits with their good humor and warmth, and she loved being auntie to their cute kids. Even when they were being a handful and chasing each other around the house half-naked and screaming. That's usually when her dad cranked up the music. The symphony of Latin music played in her head. Wailing trumpets, rattling maracas—guitars, guiros, and tambourines.

Machado family beach party, yay!

"So?" Josie asked. "Have you told them?"

Evita grimaced. "About Sebastian?" She'd been putting that part off. "Not yet."

Josie's mouth dropped open. "They don't still think he's coming to the beach?"

She'd been working up the nerve to tell her family that she and Sebastian had broken up after he'd accepted a Fulbright scholarship in Mexico and had become involved with someone else. Someone with whom he had so much more in common. He even told Evita her name, Liliana. He'd met her playing tennis, and she sounded like everything Evita wasn't: super athletic and with advanced degrees. Sebastian was all about higher education. He basically fanboyed anyone in academia with a name. But those names meant nothing to her.

"Evita," Josie said. "You guys split up in January." She frowned. "It's June."

"Yes. And…" She licked her lips. "I've been waiting on the right time."

"Which was six months ago." Josie set one hand on her hip. The diamond on her left hand caught the light and shimmered.

If things had gone according to plan, Evita would be wearing an engagement ring of her own right now. Last year, she and Sebastian had talked about making things official this spring, and her parents had been ecstatic. When Sebastian didn't come home over spring break as expected, Evita invented some excuse, and her family assumed their pending engagement was postponed, not cancelled completely.

She was the only one of her parents' kids not married, and they were anxious for her to "settle down"—she supposed so they could stop worrying about her. But they didn't need to worry. She was a twenty-eight-year-old independent woman, not some helpless child.

Although she had felt pretty helpless when Sebastian dumped her. That had been a heartless act to undertake long distance—by text. The jerk. Good thing she was over him. Way over him. Her heart gave a little twist. Totally. And not looking back.

"I was still healing in January."

Josie frowned. "And February?"

"I didn't want to ruin the holiday."

"Which holiday?" Josie smirked. "Valentine's Day?"

"No, seriously," Evita said. "My parents love it! That's the day they got engaged."

"So. What happened with March?"

"Quique broke his arm."

"Quique?"

"Enriquito, my nephew. Chachi's son."

"Oh yeah." Josie surveyed the ceiling like it was all coming back to her. "Chachi—for Carlos, right? He's married to Kendra and their little girl is Nanny."

"For Ana Maria, yes," Evita said. "Your memory's very good."

"That's only because you've talked about your brothers *nonstop* for the past two years." Which was how long Josie had worked here and also the approximate amount of time they'd been best friends. "I know you'll be happy to see them."

"It's been way too long. It will be the first time I've met Robby and Eunice's sweet baby, Luisa." She was only two months old, such a precious age. Practically a newborn.

"What's her nickname?"

"Just Luisa."

Josie shook her head. "At least that's easy."

Evita laughed, and her springy curls bounced.

Sebastian had loved her long hair, but she loved herself this way a lot better, with short hair that didn't need straightening. After years of wasted hours spent with her flat iron, her new look felt like freedom. She was actually glad Sebastian had left her. Otherwise she wouldn't have realized how hard she'd been trying to bend herself to please a man. Her emancipation had come in February, shortly after she saw what he should have seen in her mirror. A dynamic woman, who was good enough as she was.

Scratch that. Not good enough. Great. Fantastic. Strong, accomplished, savvy. And someone who was very skilled with a pair of scissors, thank you very much. She'd never put herself in a position of weakness around a guy again. And now she was going on vacation. Surrounding herself with love and family, so she could completely let down her guard. Recover. Breathe. Forget about guys for a bit.

Josie carefully scanned her eyes. "You still didn't answer my question."

"Yes, I did." She started counting on her fingers. "Quique broke his arm in March, and my parents went to help Chachi and Kendra with things in Brooklyn."

"I thought that was just for a few days?"

"No need to heap bad news upon family tragedy." Evita lowered her eyebrows and kept counting. "Luisa was born in April."

"Which was a *happy* occasion, yeah?" contested Josie.

"So you wanted what?" Evita frowned. "Me to rain on their new-baby parade?"

"Evita, I hardly think your family—"

Evita held up her hand with her counting fingers. "My parents flew out to LA for a week, and Mom was a wreck, conducting real estate closings virtually."

"I thought she did that all the time?"

"Yeah, but not while holding a colicky baby."

"Luisa's colicky?" Josie winced. "Oh, sorry. My brother's kid was that way."

Evita rolled her eyes. "I'm sure it's not as bad as they say."

Josie blew out a breath. "So May?"

"That's the start of our wedding season! On top of Mother's Day and college graduations, we got so busy at work I couldn't prompt a big family drama. You know how Mom adored Sebastian. Dad too."

"But—it wasn't your fault."

"No." Evita set her chin. "And that's what I'm going to tell them. The moment we get to the beach." She added slyly, "With my brothers and their kids serving as distractions, that will take the spotlight off of me." Plus, her parents would understand. They loved her. Once her family learned about Sebastian, they would love him less. Especially her brothers.

Josie's forehead rose. "Sounds like you have yourself a plan."

"I do. And the beach house is dreamy. One of those shake-sided, rose-covered deals."

Josie smiled. "Nice."

"Best part! I get to have my own suite. With an ocean view and everything. There are four en suites so my brothers and their wives, and my parents, will have theirs too. And Quique and Nanny will have separate rooms so they won't fight." Those two were always antagonizing each other, despite Chachi being a school counselor and Kendra a child psychologist. Oh well. They were only seven and five. They'd grow out of it. She hoped.

"Ooh. Lux accommodations. Good thing your mom won that silent auction of hers. Places like that go for a fortune, I hear. Nantucket's not cheap."

"Yeah. Mrs. Hatfield was determined to outbid Mom, but she

didn't. Apparently, the bidding was neck and neck till the end. My mom was *not* going to lose to Daneen Hatfield." She rolled her eyes. "Of all people."

Josie tsked. "Their competition's still going strong, huh?"

Evita crossed her arms. "I'm sure you've seen their competing billboards with each of them claiming to be the top commercial real estate agent in the area."

"There can't be two tops."

"Exactly."

"Which one of them do you think it is?"

"No clue, but I'm guessing it's very close."

"Well, at least you won't have to worry about that rivalry while you're away. Or anything else stressful really." She was glad about that. Having her mom and Ryan's mom at odds during their high school years had been bad enough.

He'd been a cute guy. Brainy. She'd majorly crushed on him in high school, when they'd been chemistry lab partners in the eleventh grade. He'd rocked memorizing that periodic table. Near genius level. They'd been on friendly terms before that but grew a lot closer during the semester, and a part of her had hoped for more. The thought of dating him had seemed dangerous, verboten—so totally against her family's wishes that she'd almost been tempted to try it—but he'd never been interested in her in that way. He'd only seen her as a friend.

He'd had his own crowd and extracurriculars, anyway, while she'd been into foreign languages and art. Then she discovered horticulture, and it had been love at first frond. She got a part-time job at a garden center, determined to learn everything about plants that she could. And Ryan started dating someone else, Layla Petroski, homecoming queen. He'd gone on to grad school to do something or another. Her mom probably knew because she knew everything about the Hatfields, but Evita wouldn't dare ask her.

Speaking the Hatfield name was akin to blasphemy in their house.

Josie sighed dreamily. "I hear Nantucket's beautiful. Bet you're looking forward to the peace and quiet."

Evita laughed, considering the concept of a staid family reunion.

"The Machados don't do quiet, but I'm sure we'll have a great time."

Ryan Hatfield's mom threw open the front door to the seaside cottage. Its front porch faced a parking area and a sandy stretch dotted with seagrass. The gray shake-sided building and its weathered picket fence were covered with pink climbing roses.

"Well, isn't this lovely!"

Her eyes gave the vaulted-ceiling room an appreciative sweep. Enormous windows framed an ocean panorama straight ahead of them, and French doors opened onto a covered porch. Beyond that, the expansive deck held a stone firepit surrounded by Adirondack chairs and connected to wooden steps with railings descending to a private beach.

Ryan's dad adjusted his tie. "It is stunning, yes." Typically, he'd go into his office before leaving on vacation, even though it was Saturday. His tax accountant job kept him on a rigorous schedule.

There was always an end-of-the-quarter crunch, a mid-quarter crunch, a start-of-the-quarter—something or another. Ryan's eyes glazed over at the details.

Ryan was more into historical dates than hard cash numbers, but his mom was also big on the bottom line. She'd stayed glued to her computer up until the very last minute this morning, negotiating a mega shopping complex deal that simply couldn't wait. None of her corporate real estate deals could wait. All were perpetually urgent.

Ryan and his teenage sister, Maddy, had done the brunt of the legwork loading up the SUV. He'd stayed over at his parents' house last night so they could get on the road early. But he might as well have driven over this morning, given that his folks' business preoccupations had caused departure delays. They didn't get away until after two, so wound up having lunch at home then eating the sandwiches they'd prepared for the road on the ferry as an early supper. It was nearly seven now, but there was plenty of daylight left to enjoy the scenery.

The great room before them led to a dining area on the left and a kitchen on the right. The kitchen gleamed with high-end stainless steel appliances and polished stone countertops, and had an island in its center flanked by high bar stools. The dining area contained a long table with seating for ten and extra chairs pushed up against the wall. Separate spiral staircases on either side of the entryway led upstairs to an open loft adjoining narrow hallways. Ryan noted the loft was some kind of library with packed bookshelves and comfy furnishings scattered about.

Maddy pulled the earbuds from her ears and glanced around,

holding her phone. She stared out the French doors at the deck and the broad swath of the ocean. "Where's the pool?"

"Don't think there is one," her mom answered.

Maddy puffed out her pale cheeks, her face turning pink. "I thought you said 'luxury,' Mom?" She goggled at the open floor plan, staring at the wide foyer's four closed doors. From the photos he'd seen of the house, Ryan knew one led to a half bath and another to a coat closet. The others, on opposite sides, opened into large, ground-floor suites. There was a laundry room off the kitchen.

None of the online pics did this place justice. It could double as a Hollywood set.

"This is very high end," his mom told Maddy. "I won't have you complaining. Each of us gets our own suite with a wonderful view."

At least that was something. Ryan had been about as thrilled as Maddy about taking this forced family trip. But their mom had eventually beaten everyone down with her relentless insistence that this vacation was going to be different. During their previous vacations, they'd barely said two words to each other and had kept themselves apart.

As her broker's top-selling agent, she'd earned tons of ritzy incentive trips to various fancy locales, but she'd won this place in a charity auction. Therefore, this week was bound to be special in her eyes. More focused on downtime and relaxing than adventuring at some glam resort. A chance for all of them to truly connect for once, *bond*.

Which generally meant making awkward conversation during

cocktail hour and at mealtimes while Maddy played on her phone and Ryan self-consciously avoided pesky questions from his parents about his career and love life.

Boy, this was going to be fun. Maybe he should have attended that revolutionary period history conference instead. He checked his phone. Registration had closed. It was too late.

Not that he could get out of this now.

He was in it for the next seven days.

"Go on then," Ryan's dad encouraged his kid sister. "Why don't you check out the upstairs and see which suite you'd like?"

Maddy lugged her backpack and duffle bag along, lumbering up the spiral steps. "Oh wow," she said, glancing out at the sea and their desolate surroundings. "It's like we're the only people on this planet. There's no tiki bar or anything? Jet Ski rentals? Parasailing?"

"This isn't Cancún, sweetheart," their dad said.

Their mom shook her head, and her blond pageboy wobbled from side to side. She held part of it back with a beige headband that matched her short-sleeved beige cardigan sweater. She always dressed in pearls like she was expecting a surprise photo op. Ryan didn't think he'd ever seen her in shorts. Just capris like she wore now. With a tangerine-fruit-patterned orange top.

"Or Barbados either," she told Maddy. "But there's a small town close by called 'Sconset Village. Looks sweet. Maybe we can go there exploring? Get ice cream?"

"Ice cream?" Maddy sighed and rolled her eyes so hard they nearly got sucked back into her head. "I'm not eight, Mom. I'm fifteen. Sixteen next month."

Ryan felt sorry for his little sister. She was so determined not to be seen as a kid that she was making herself miserable. He guessed she had other things going on, but he didn't know what. With the age difference between them, they'd never been super close. He worried about her and wished he could help. Maybe this vacation would be good for them. Without the distractions of Jet Skis and visiting Mayan ruins. Although he'd loved Tulum.

Their dad ran a hand through his cropped brown hair. "The whole island's very small," he said cajolingly. "Only fourteen miles long and three-and-a-half miles wide. This house comes with some bikes, so maybe we can—"

Maddy gawped at him. "Exercise? On vacation? Ugh. No thanks." She turned and continued up the stairs, her long blond hair swinging behind her. She was a little heavier set than the rest of them and shorter than their mom. Ryan was on the tall side like his dad.

He wore his sandy-colored hair short and shaggy in no particular style. The casual vibe suited his role as a professor. His mom would have preferred it more if he'd taken a job at a nameplate university. But no, that wasn't him. Community college was what he wanted because it was a population he badly wanted to reach. He loved his students, and they loved him. He didn't care about prestige or his paycheck, as long as he could pay his bills and set some aside for that piece of property he hoped to purchase someday.

He had this romanticized notion of buying a historic farmhouse and refurbishing it on his own. It would take some muscle, but he was handy. Something his parents never gave him credit for, along with pretty much everything else.

His mom watched Maddy disappear down an upstairs

hallway. "I don't know what she's so grumpy about. School's out for summer."

"And her cello schedule's much lighter now," his dad said.

"Yes, but she has her summer orchestra performances coming up," his mom said. "She can't afford to slip."

There'd been a minor scuffle this morning about his mom wanting Maddy to bring her cello to the beach, saying she couldn't risk having any practice lapses. Not if she still wanted to get into Julliard. Maddy had claimed she wanted a break. Ultimately, the SUV's trunk area had had the final say. There was no room for a cello once everything else had been packed.

His mom threw up her hands. "Oh well! I'm determined to have fun. Just look at this place." She turned to Ryan. "Let your dad and me take a peek at the two suites downstairs. After we pick, you can have the other one." She whispered when Maddy crossed through the loft above them. "The first-floor suites are larger." She squealed. "Plus, they have Jacuzzi tubs."

They heard Maddy opening and closing doors, then she reappeared. "I'll take the one over the kitchen."

"What else is up there?" her dad asked her.

"A couple of small rooms with bunk beds and a big bathroom behind the loft." She thumbed over her shoulder. "Between the bookcases back there. The suites have their own bathrooms."

As Ryan explored the house with his parents, his dad said, "Very nice work winning this place, Daneen. It's fabulous."

"I agree, Kirk." Her mouth twitched. "And to think Lissette Machado thought she was going to snatch it right out from under me."

His dad shook his head. "I'm sure she didn't stand a chance."

"No. I kept my eye on that ball. Every bid she placed, I topped it."

Ryan's shoulders sank. Really? After all these years? The two of them were still at it? His mom and Mrs. Machado had had some huge fight in high school when they'd both run for class president, with Mrs. Machado ultimately winning and his mom questioning the fairness of her defeat. Their unhealthy animosity was so strong it still carried through to this day. And the Machados weren't a bad family.

He'd had a thing for their daughter once, way back when he'd been in high school himself. Not that their parents would have let them come within ten feet of each other socially. His mom had totally flipped when she'd learned at parents' night that Ryan and Evita had been assigned as lab partners in chem class their junior year. Well. That was the story Ryan told her afterward. The truth was that he and Evita had assigned themselves as lab partners, because the teacher had let the kids choose who they wanted to work with, and Evita had approached him first. He'd seen her around school and thought she was cute and outgoing. They'd even shared the same lunch table a few times with their respective groups. Just because their parents didn't like one another, that didn't mean that he and Evita couldn't get along. And they did get along—pretty great, as it turned out. But neither set of parents was too keen on the idea.

Her folks even tried to get their teacher to have them "reassigned" to different lab partners during parents' night. Mr. Amberly was cool though, and he held his ground, telling Mr. and

Mrs. Machado that the semester was already under way and that no changes could be made. Evita and Ryan loved Mr. Amberly. He had them do free-writing exercises to clear their minds during the first ten minutes of class, saying it paid to think creatively in science. He wasn't that much older than any of his students, being a newly minted teacher out of college himself.

Ryan could still see Evita's wide, dark eyes when she shared the news about her parents' reaction the next day during class. They had a substitute, who was boring them all senseless. Which made Evita more inclined to misbehave. Nobody ever acted up around Mr. Amberly.

"You should have heard my mom." She leaned toward Ryan, her long hair cascading over her shoulder. "She forbade me from being friends with you."

His eyebrows rose at the term. "Forbade?"

"I know, right?" She imitated her mom's light Spanish accent. Evita's mom had mostly grown up here, but she'd lived in Puerto Rico as a kid, until her parents moved their family. Evita's dad's family was still in Puerto Rico. He'd come to college in Massachusetts and stayed. "Evita Machado." She mimicked her mom in hushed tones. "I forbid you from seeing that boy."

Ryan laughed. "Does she think we come to class blindfolded?"

"Who's talking?" Mr. Pinkerton turned from making notes on the whiteboard, his intense gray eyebrows knitted together. A few students shook their heads, but most of them shrugged.

Evita's deep dimples settled as she grinned at their substitute teacher, the picture of innocence. Yeah, right. She was such a little troublemaker. That was part of what made her so much fun. They were at their table in the back, which was convenient for passing notes without being detected. Not that Mr. Amberly really cared, as long as they got their work done. He was basically pretty awesome in every way.

Mr. Pinkerton droned on in humorless tones. "Marie Curie," he said, writing her name on the whiteboard with a green marker. "Was key among women scientists because those are so rare."

"You mean, were rare," Evita called out. "Back in the day."

Mr. Pinkerton lowered his tortoise-shell glasses. "I believe you'll find those statistics still hold."

Evita blinked. "Are you saying women aren't as scientifically minded as men?"

Pinkerton straightened his yellow bowtie. "You can follow the data, Miss—"

"Ms. Machado."

His lips twisted wryly. "From Einstein to Galileo. Think Darwin! Newton! The vast majority of all the great scientists have been male."

"Yes, but!" Evita contested. "There are more women than men enrolled in colleges these days—"

Mr. Pinkerton capped his marker. "Not in the hard sciences, I believe."

Evita leaned forward. "How do you know? Have you followed the data?"

"She's right!" Jax squared their shoulders in the second row. "You're genderizing!"

Pinkerton scratched his head. "Gender what?"

A low murmur circulated around the room along with muted chuckles.

Layla Petroski sat up ahead of them. She leaned over and whispered to the girl beside her, Emily Rivers. "Why are we talking about this here?"

Emily whispered back. "Amberly probably left no sub plans, so this guy's winging it."

Pinkerton glared at the back of the room. "You're being very impertinent, Miss Machado. I'd encourage you to watch your step."

He turned toward the whiteboard, and Evita fumed. Ryan laid a hand on her arm. She had a right to be ticked. Pinkerton was being a pig. Ryan just hoped Evita wouldn't say anything else. This sub really wasn't worth getting into trouble over. He'd be gone tomorrow. Ryan cut Evita a side-eye, seeing her dander was definitely up. She was so fierce and brainy, with a sharp tongue and a quick wit. He was glad she was on his side.

He'd always take her side, no matter what.

"Einstein, as you know..." Pinkerton said, starting to write again. "...developed the Theory of Relativity..."

Evita's jaw tensed. The twitching muscle in her cheek said she was holding back a scream, and Evita had a loud one. She spread her hands out on their table, quietly grating out the words. "Pinkerton's got another thing coming if he thinks he can diss women here." The lines surrounding her frown deepened, as she glanced at Jax. "Or anyone really, of any identity." Ryan saw her hand on the beaker, guessing what was coming next.

"Evita," he urged. "Don't—"

But it was too late to stop her. She pushed the glass structure off their table and it crashed to floor, startling Pinkerton, who instantly straightened his spine. Students spun on their stools, scanning the back of the room, and Layla winked at him, probably thinking he'd done it. Evita was always claiming Layla had a crush on him, but he didn't buy it. Or maybe he did and didn't care. The only girl he cared about in chem class was Evita.

Mr. Pinkerton removed his glasses, storming toward them in his rumpled plaid slacks and worn penny loafers. They actually had coins in them. "Who did this?" he demanded, staring down at the shattered glass on the floor.

Ryan shifted in his seat. "It was an accident."

"An accident?" Pinkerton asked, like he doubted that. He shook his head and tsked. "Then clean it up."

"Yes, sir." Ryan hopped off his stool and Evita got up to help him.

"Not you, miss," Pinkerton said, whirling around. "You're coming with me."

Evita crossed her arms, not budging. "Where?"

"I'm writing you a pass to go to the principal's office."

She gasped, her hand fluttering to her Notre Dame sweatshirt. Her oldest brother, Robby, went there, and he kept lobbying for Evita and her other brother, Chachi, to join him. Although Chachi, a senior, had pinned his hopes on Penn. Evita didn't know where she wanted to go to college, but she thought it was sweet her brother cared. It was sweet. So was Evita deep on the inside, but she hid it well with her toughness. "Me?" she asked, incredulous. Man, she was good, but Pinkerton was wise to her game.

Ryan held out his hand. "Look, Mr. Pinkerton. There's been a mistake. Evita didn't knock that beaker over, I did." Evita's eyebrows arched before she set them in straight lines, resuming her poker face.

"You don't have to cover for her, son," Pinkerton said.

"I'm not covering." Ryan cleared his throat. "I hit it with my elbow."

"With your elbow? Right." Pinkerton clucked his tongue and studied them both. "If that's how you want to play it," he said, "fine." He motioned Ryan along, leading him toward Amberly's desk. Ryan received a stern lecture from the principal about respecting substitute teachers after that, and a short stint in detention, but he hadn't minded one bit.

He'd have done anything for Evita.

"Ryan," his mom said, traipsing through the dining area of the fancy Nantucket cottage. "You're lagging behind."

"Right." He picked up his pace, shaking off all thoughts of Pinkerton. Memories of Evita clung to him though. He hadn't thought much about her until lately, when his mom had started making such a big deal out of besting Evita's mom in winning this place. He couldn't help but wonder about Evita's life now. He didn't know much, and the details were sketchy. One of his friends said she'd opened her own flower shop in Lexington. Good for her. She'd been big into plants in high school, especially their senior year.

He trailed his parents into one ground-floor suite and then the other, before they all went upstairs. Maddy was busy settling into her space by strewing her clothing and hair products everywhere.

It was cool how the downstairs suites ran the width of the house, providing them with seaside ocean views and a scenic landscape out front.

The two upstairs suites were smaller, owing to their attached ocean-front balconies. They also had their own bathrooms and sitting areas overlooking the drive, which could be separated from the bedrooms by pocket doors.

His parents picked the suite closest to the kitchen, and he deposited his stuff in the one near the dining room. It had double doors leading directly to the deck. He stepped through them, absorbing the warm ocean breeze. His jaw muscles relaxed, tension seeping from his body. It would be okay. He'd weather this. It was only a week with his parents and Maddy.

The views were great, and the house was large. They'd have all kinds of room to spread out from each other. It wasn't like they were crammed together like they'd been in the stateroom of that cruise ship back when he'd been thirteen and Maddy a newborn. That had been a nightmare. But not this. The ocean crashed and roared, sending curtains of foam raining down onto the beach, and gulls combed through an azure sky. It was beautiful here. How bad could things get?

His parents walked onto the deck from their room at exactly the same time. "One whole week of glorious serenity," his mom chirped. "Just us four Hatfields together. Enjoying each other's company." Her blue eyes lit up. "I think this calls for a martini."

A drink did sound good. Maybe he'd have a double.

Maddy leaned over one of the balconies upstairs and hollered, "I want one!"

"*No-ooo,*" his mom replied in lilting tones.

"I'll fix her a Shirley Temple," his dad said.

"I'm. Not. A kid!" Maddy groaned from above.

"Let's grab the rest of our things from the SUV," his dad suggested. "I'll tend bar after we set up the kitchen."

"Maddy!" Ryan called as he walked back through the great room. "Come help!"

She scampered down the spiral staircase closest to her room, finally seeming excited. Maybe the enormous flat-screen TV in her room had helped her mood. Along with the fact that she had a whole floor to herself. "Guys!" Her face was flush with wonder. "I saw a whale!"

"What?" her dad asked. "How?"

She waved the pair of binoculars in her hand. "These were in my room on the dresser."

Their mom took away the binoculars, setting them on a side table. "It was probably just a dolphin, hon."

Maddy's cheerful expression waned. "No. It was a whale."

"Wouldn't that be something?" Their dad grinned. "A sighting on our first day."

"I'm sure you'll see another one. Come and get me next time." Ryan smiled in an attempt to be brotherly, but Mads just grumbled and stepped away. It was so hard to connect with her. At some point, she'd have to meet him halfway.

He'd been out of the house and off to college by the time she was five, but they'd seen each other plenty during vacations and over holidays. He frowned. Those gatherings hadn't exactly proved stellar for relationship building, if he was being honest.

Not with each member of his family always doing their own thing.

He looked up at the wall between the spiral staircases, the one below the loft. With the openness of the design and the ocean-facing windows, it was the only logical spot in the great room to mount a television. But it contained a large-framed painting instead. It had to be a copy or a print, but it was a stunning rendering of Monet's *Water Lilies*.

"It's interesting that there's no common-area TV. You'd think they'd have a gigantic one out here. Given that this house has everything else." He'd seen speakers for an expensive sound system that could be controlled through a phone app. His mom had told him there was an instruction manual in the house, and they were welcome to use it. So the owners weren't tech Luddites by any stretch.

"Every room's outfitted for TV here," their dad said informatively. "Even this one." He picked up a remote and clicked it on. Monet's *Water Lilies* morphed into a gigantic television screen loaded with streaming apps.

Ryan blinked. "How did you know about that?"

"Guy at the office got one for his bedroom. Told me all about it." His dad shrugged, seeming pleased to be in the know about something. "It was also in the house check-in information. I couldn't wait to see one for myself."

Their mom nodded happily. "No shortage of entertainment choices around here. Maybe we can all watch something together on PBS?"

Maddy blanched. "I'm good with the TV in my room, thanks."

The sun was partway down and evening starting to bloom, settling in with a purplish haze. "When can we go down to the beach?"

Their mom waved her hand with a flourish. "As soon as we have our welcome drinks."

TWO

BABY LUISA WAILED IN HER car seat, her face the color of a very ripe eggplant.

Her normal complexion was a sunny amber like her mom, Eunice's.

Evita sat beside the baby in the third row of her parents' Suburban, her heart pounding. The little bundle of "joy" looked positively volcanic. Like she could blow at any second.

"Um. Does she need a pacifier or something?"

"Won't take them," Eunice said over her shoulder.

Robby turned and his dark eyes met Evita's. His shock of dark curls spilled off the top of his head, shorter on the sides and higher on top. He had a mustache like their dad, although their dad's hair was straight and salt-and-pepper gray. "She's wound up from the flight, I think. The altitude bothered her ears."

"Right." Evita's ears were splitting now, but she couldn't say so. "It's okay, little Luisa." She patted the baby's foot and the child gurgled, then exploded in a rage, shaking her tiny fists and cramming one in her mouth. Very hard. Ow. That seemed to alarm her and make her cry louder. Okay. That didn't look like fun. Poor baby.

Evita hoped Robby and Eunice's room wouldn't be near hers. She'd take pains to avoid it. She was looking forward to catching up on her sleep here, and relaxing. Not that she didn't love her niece.

Robby must have nerves of steel to be able to work around a screaming baby. He did his screenwriting at home while Eunice's job as a film editor kept her busy at a studio, so at least she had some professional distance from family life during her work day.

Evita's mom was at the wheel, and her dad sat in the passenger seat, fiddling with the radio dial. Audio speakers crackled and hissed, spitting out broken-up sound blips of music and official-sounding announcements. He was too polite to mention Luisa's screaming so was likely trying to drown it out.

"Poor reception," he said. "Maybe I should plug in my phone?" Her dad had a gazillion playlists on his smartphone, and subscribed to tons of music streaming services.

"No time." Her mom glanced in the rearview mirror. "We're almost there!"

The GPS said: "In 500 feet, take the next right."

Thank goodness. She couldn't wait to get out of this SUV.

Chachi and Kendra were directly behind them with their two kids. They'd met up in town after Robby and Eunice's flight finally arrived from LA via Newark. Chachi and Kendra had driven directly to Hyannis from Brooklyn to catch the car ferry to Nantucket, like Evita and her parents had. She'd spent three boring hours waiting on the delayed flight with her folks at the airport while Chachi and Kendra had had fun in town with their kids.

They'd toured the Whaling Museum and had gotten lunch and then coffee, visiting the dock area and ogling the big yachts. Chachi had updated her and her parents with texts and photos, each one making Evita greener with envy. But she couldn't abandon her parents when Robby's plane was due in at any minute. Until its ETA changed again—and again. Cooling her heels at the miniscule airport was not her idea of a great start to a vacation. But these things happened. What could you do?

By the time they all met up in the historic district, everyone was travel-weary and cranky. So they decided on an early dinner in town rather than having to fuss with preparing something back at the cottage with them arriving so late.

Evita drew in a calming breath, soothing her jangled nerves.

It wasn't Luisa's fault she was unhappy. Being on the road was undoubtedly making it worse. She'd do better once she was freed from her car-seat prison.

Another ear piercing cry. That jailbreak couldn't come soon enough. How did new parents handle this? She questioned her mom's sanity in having three. Must be some form of infanthood amnesia? You forget all the bad parts when they grow older and cute. Like Quique and Nanny.

No. Wait. Bad example.

Nanny had stomped on her foot instead of saying hello outside the restaurant. On purpose. Because Evita hadn't noticed she'd gotten her ears pierced. To be fair, Nanny was shorter than everyone else—with the exception of Luisa—so often overlooked in adult conversation. She'd been vying for Evita's attention before she'd finally gotten it with that foot stomp. Immediately after,

Quique had asked her for money, saying she'd forgotten his birthday. Which she had. It was in January.

"Oh cool, is that it?" Eunice gave a happy gasp. "Look at all those pretty roses!"

"What's with the Lexus?" Robby asked.

Evita stared at the luxury SUV in the driveway. Her parents leaned forward to peer through the windshield too.

"Could be the cleaners?" her mom ventured. "Marylin said the house would get freshened up before our arrival."

Marylin had been one of the two people running the silent auction. After she'd called to congratulate Evita's mom on winning the week, she'd provided the particulars by email, including directions to the house and the entry code for the front-door keypad.

The owners were on a rustic camera safari in Kenya and well out of touch. They'd arranged everything about the house before their trip. All that had to happen was for the auctioning group to appoint their winner. Which they had in Lissette Machado.

Evita's mom had glowed when she'd shared the good news with Evita over lunch. Evita was excited too. With everyone's busy lives, it had been harder and harder to get the family together for more than brief visits over the holidays. A whole week at the beach was like a gift from the gods! Evita's mom knew that none of her brood would turn down Nantucket.

Who would?

"Pretty fancy wheels for a cleaning crew," her dad said. "Maybe it's Sebastian's ride?"

Evita's stomach clenched. She'd had plenty of time to fill them in on the truth earlier, but everyone had been so absorbed talking about their travel woes while trying to corral the children, Sebastian hadn't even come up. Nobody was expecting him until tomorrow anyway.

"Yeah." Eunice spun in her seat, her chin-length black hair framing her roundish face. "Maybe he came early to surprise you?"

"Ah. I don't think he could have gotten into the house." *All the way from Mexico City.* Her skin burned hot. Okay. She had to tell them, and she would. Once they'd unpacked and settled in. With glasses of wine. Big glasses. Huge.

Hers would be the hugest.

"So, no. No," she said. "I don't think that's Sebastian's."

"She's right, Pablo," her mom answered. "Sebastian's not coming until after lunchtime tomorrow. Isn't that right, Evita?" Evita held her breath.

"I'm sure it's the cleaners like you said."

"It's pretty late for cleaners to be here, isn't it?" Eunice chimed in.

Her mom strummed her fingers on the steering wheel. "Hmm, yes. Maybe they got delayed."

"It's a day for delays." Eunice sighed.

"Well, if it's the cleaners," her dad said, "they must pay them *very well* out here."

Robby shrugged. "It's Nantucket."

A strange sound filled the vehicle: silence. Except for tiny gurgling noises coming from the baby. Evita was scared to guess from which end. Although she didn't smell anything.

"Looks like someone's settled down," her mom said, smiling.

"Should we wait on the cleaners to finish up?" Robby asked. "Or?"

Their dad popped open his door. "We should let them know we're here and ask how much longer they'll be. This is ridiculous. It's after eight o'clock."

"Yes." Evita's mom checked her watch. "They've got to be nearly done by now."

Chachi's SUV pulled up behind them and soon everyone was climbing out onto the sandy drive. Warm gusts of wind wrapped around them as seagulls dove through the sky. The views of the sea ahead of the house were outstanding. Evita sighed. "Some place."

Eunice had her shoulders ladened down with canvas bags, a diaper bag and her purse, and her arms embraced a package of disposable diapers. Robby had his hands full too, grabbing their luggage and a suitcase of their mom's.

"Evita?" Eunice asked with a weary smile. "Would you mind bringing Luisa?"

She glanced in the SUV at the infant who cooed sweetly. She'd just had a moment, that's all. As people do. Even babies of course.

"Sure." Evita reached for the car seat, unhitching its breastplate. She'd done plenty of babysitting as a teen and had looked after Quique and Nanny some when they'd been younger and slightly better behaved. Giving this precious bundle a lift into the cottage should be no problem at all. She'd return afterward to grab her things.

"Come to your Auntie Evita," she said, gently lifting the kid out of the SUV and into the open air.

Luisa gurgled and grinned. How cute!

"Look everyone!" Evita lifted Luisa in her arms. "She's smiling!"

The volcano erupted, spewing from the mouth.

A warm sludge hit Evita in the face running down the bridge of her nose.

And the smell. Ew.

Her stomach roiled.

But she instinctively held on to the baby, propping her against her shoulder.

"Evita!" Eunice called. "Oh no." She dropped her things and hurried over with a burp cloth to wipe at Evita's face. The goo was warm and sticky. Like rotten oatmeal but worse.

Her stomach roiled again, and Evita steeled herself. She could *not* retch.

One instance of projectile vomiting was enough.

Robby set down his load and reached for his daughter. "Here. Let me take her."

Evita gratefully passed Luisa to him. "Sorry, sis." He frowned. "You don't want to see your face." His lips twitched. "Or hair. Or clothes."

"Very funny." She tried to make light of it, but the experience was seriously gross. She ran a hand through her hair and her fingers came back covered in pasty barf. Oof. The side of her head where she wore a pretty daisy clip had taken a direct hit, along with her face.

How did babies do that? She thought that was only in horror flicks.

She couldn't wait to get inside and shower. She wiped her

fingers on the burp cloth. She'd have to toss it in the wash. Great. She hadn't expected to do laundry on arrival. She glanced down at the snug green top and white shorts that hugged her curvy figure. Those were puke-splattered and would need washing too. So would her cute shoes.

Her dad owned a designer athletic footwear business and had custom made this pair just for her when she'd opened her shop. They were flat white sneakers with pretty rose buds on them. The buds had green stems and were now all coated in ick.

Chachi's chubby cheeks hung in a frown. "Happens to the best of us, sis." He sighed and turned up his palms. "Kids." He was stocky like their dad but thicker around the middle.

The curly hair came from their mom, who'd not yet parted with her flat iron. Silky caramel-colored tresses graced her shoulders. She'd been at her office this morning and still wore her bright-yellow skirt with a scoop-necked blouse showcasing papayas, mangos, and pineapples. It matched her dangly fruit earrings and fun yellow sandals with heels.

Her deep golden tan came from a bottle.

"I want to see the beach!" Nanny said, dashing to the front door.

Quique raced past her, rudely pushing her aside. "Me first!"

"Kids!" Kendra called in embarrassed tones. One of the pins in her bun slipped loose, releasing a wisp of coarse, dark hair. "Stop!" Her warm brown cheeks deepened a hue, as she scurried after them, hauling grocery sacks, and wearing a T-shirt, jeans and sneakers. She probably needed running shoes to keep up with them.

"You'll want to earn your stickers today!" Chachi urged. He grumbled something to himself about a reward-system failure, catching up with his wife.

Their pleas fell on deaf ears.

The kids were already pounding on the door and repeatedly punching the doorbell.

Bang! Bang! Bang!

Ding-dong, ding-dong, ding-dong.

"Children!" Evita's mom shrieked. "*Por favor.*" She set her hands on her hips, arms akimbo. "You'll scare the cleaners."

Evita's head throbbed.

Her dad made his way to the porch and shot Quique and Nanny stern looks. "No manners, no ice cream after dinner, eh?" he said with lowered dark eyebrows.

Quique was the first to hang his short-shorn head. "Sorry, Tito."

Nanny followed suit, looking adorable in her first set of earrings and braids. "Sorry."

"Apologize to your grandmother too. She's our host this week."

"Sorry, Tita!" the kids crooned together.

Her mom folded her arms and smiled. "That's better."

Nanny slowly looked up and asked softly, "What kind of ice cream?" Her eyebrows arched adorably, and Evita's heart warmed.

They weren't so bad. Quique and Nanny. They were just kids. Evita and her brothers had caused their share of trouble too. Back in the day.

Their Tito tousled the tops of their heads. "You see?" He winked at Chachi. "*Incentivos* can work."

Robby smirked, jostling Luisa on his shoulder. "You mean bribes."

Chachi shook his finger at his brother. "Just wait till she's older."

Evita's mom read out the number sequence from her phone and her dad worked the keypad. The door lock slid open. "Ta-da!" He grinned at his grandkids. "Magic."

They squealed and raced into the house.

"Don't touch anything!" Kendra called, slogging after them with her grocery bags. She stared around the open interior and out the front windows. The sky had gone magenta and looming shadows cloaked the room. "Gorgeous."

Robby nodded toward the right, while holding the baby. "Kitchen's over there."

Quique and Nanny raced around the sofas then their eyes lit on the stairs.

"Two sets!" Quique cried. "Cool!"

Nanny darted for the stairs closest to her. "This one's mine."

Kendra grimaced. "Careful on those!" But they'd already scampered to the top, crossed each other in the loft, and were racing each other back down dueling steps.

Evita's mom found a light switch and flipped it on. Four lamps on either side of the two facing sofas illuminated. The lamps' bases were brass and shaped like anchors, and each sofa was flanked by two comfy swivel armchairs creating two individual seating groups complete with a coffee table and end tables, or one very large group area when taken all together.

The color scheme was various shades of blue and white, with

lots of throw pillows. The walls were all whitewashed. The vaulted ceiling too. Beachy-themed paintings and accent pieces throughout the space spoke to a professional interior decorator's touch. The cottage was absolutely beautiful.

The kids raced up the stairs again and darted down a hall.

Evita's mom pointed to a spot beside the French doors. The color drained from her face. "Look over there! What's that?" A pair of men's dress shoes sat on the polished oak floor, which was covered in places with simple but elegant rugs. Black socks were jammed inside the shoes. Her eyes widened as she stared around. "And that!" She jumped like she'd seen a snake. "*Ay!*" But it was just a red-and-blue striped necktie draped over the back of a dining room chair.

"And this?" Chachi picked up the empty soda can on a coffee table. He peeked into it, rattled it, then set it back down.

Evita's dad opened doors in the foyer, scanning darkened rooms. He didn't enter any of them though. "Oh!" he said shutting a door. "This one's a closet." He stared at his family. "Where are the cleaners?"

"Looks like they missed a few things." Robby nodded at the dining room table and the four small plates with food remnants on them. Crackers and cheeses, pretzels, nuts. Someone had been enjoying snacks. And drinks! Judging by the three drained martini glasses.

Kendra set her grocery bags on the kitchen counter and displayed a martini shaker. "Looks like they had a party."

Eunice gasped. "Maybe they're squatters?"

"Squatters?" Evita clutched her barf rag, then grimaced.

Where should she put this thing? She wasn't sure. Robby noted her expression and took it from her, shoving it into a section of his diaper bag. He'd grabbed the multi-pocketed bag along with the baby after the upchuck incident in the drive. She supposed that's where the dirty stuff went.

Robby nodded, agreeing with Eunice. "That happens sometimes in LA too. People find an empty house and take advantage. Move right in."

"Very high-end squatters." Their dad picked up a martini glass and studied it. He sniffed the dregs of the liquid inside. "Considering their taste in gin. This smells like Hendrick's."

Evita's dad knew his liquor, that was true.

"Hmm, yeah." Robby glanced toward the drive. "And the Lexus."

Kendra lifted a bottle off the kitchen island. Evita's dad was right. The label did say Hendrick's. "Maybe the liquor was already here?"

"I don't like the sound of this," Eunice said.

Evita's mom frowned. "Me either."

Evita's pulse raced. What kind of people would undertake something so brazen? Just break into—and take over—a stranger's cottage? Maybe they were dangerous?

"Ahhhh!" Shrieks came from upstairs.

Nanny and Quique!

The adults darted for the spiral staircases, nearly trampling over one another in their haste. Kendra reached the children first. They were in an upstairs bedroom over the kitchen.

"It's a monster!" Quique shouted, pointing to the bed. His small chin trembled.

Nanny leapt at her mom's legs, wrapping her arms around them. "With scary green eyes!"

Chachi flipped on the light and they saw what it was. A gel mask of some kind lay at the head of the queen-size bed. It had glowed iridescently, eerily catching the dim light. "Here is your monster," he said, indicating the gel mask on the pillow with a sweep of his hand.

Nanny released her hold on Kendra's legs. "That's silly."

"Yeah." Quique snatched it up, pressing it over his eyes. "I'm Zorro! Or. Or. The Green Lantern!"

Evita's dad took it away. "Let's not go touching other people's things, *hijito*."

"Yeah." Kendra pulled a face. "Might be germy."

Evita's mom placed a hand on her heart. "Look at this mess!"

Jeans and shorts were everywhere along with sparkly tops. Hair supplies. A bathing suit. A curling iron. Discarded flip-flops and sneakers. An open backpack on the floor revealed a laptop inside it.

Robby set his chin. "Definitely squatters." Miraculously, Luisa had passed out on his shoulder and was sleeping like a lamb.

Their dad shook his head. "We'd better check the rest of the house to see what other damage they've done."

"Wait." Her mom looked petrified. "Do you think they're still here?"

"The house feels empty," her dad answered.

"Yeah," Chachi said. "Creepily so."

"But that Lexus is here," Robby reminded them.

"Maybe they're hiding?" Eunice whispered.

Chachi called out as they cautiously climbed down the stairs. "Hello?"

"We know that you're here!" their dad yelled gruffly. "Show yourselves, please!"

Her mom touched his shoulder. "Pablo, wait. Maybe we should phone the police?"

"Not until we know what's going on," he said in low tones.

They reached the first floor, and Evita's dad held them back with his arm.

"Nobody move! There's someone outdoors."

THREE

EVITA'S PULSE RACED. IT WAS a man on the youngish side with shaggy golden-brown hair. He wore khaki shorts and a T-shirt and had his hands in his pockets. Sauntering along barefoot like he hadn't a care in the world and striding toward the house like he owned it.

But he didn't own it.

The owners were in Kenya, and the Machados had been told that this cottage was theirs.

"Okay enough." Chachi yanked his cell from his pocket. "I'm dialing 9-1-1."

"Wait," Kendra said. "Maybe there's been some mistake?"

Evita's mom huffed. "What kind of mistake?"

Eunice nodded. "An accidental double booking? I mean…" She glanced around and nodded at the gin bottle then at the approaching guy. "They don't seem like the sort to squat. Do they? Just look at him."

"He does look kind of preppy," Robby said.

"Shh!" Chachi warned. "He's coming closer." And he was. He'd just passed the firepit and was almost to the covered porch.

Her sisters-in-law were making sense. The civilized thing to do would be to confront these people first and discuss the situation. Maybe there really had been some sort of mix-up? Once the Machados explained they had the week, surely the other group would understand. Might even apologize for getting the dates wrong on their calendars. Then they'd pack up and go, and problem solved! Her parents had been looking forward to this week so much, and so had she. "Let me handle this."

"Evita, no," her mom said. But she was halfway to the French doors.

"Excuse me!" she said when the guy was almost to her.

He stared at her long and hard. Then blinked.

"Evita?" he asked.

Wait. How did he—

"Evita Machado?"

Her heart pounded like a kettle drum. His voice was deeper. Richer. Now a smooth baritone. Tiny shivers raced down her spine. It couldn't really be him, could it? Part of her wanted it to be, but another part was terrified. For his sake, mostly. Her parents would freak first, and then toss him out on his ear. They'd never liked the idea of Evita being around Ryan, even when they weren't together romantically. No fault of hers. She would have seized that opportunity in a heartbeat. "Ryan?" she asked uncertainly. "Ryan Hatfield?"

"Yeah," he said with an air of confusion. "That's me." Her head spun and her world went topsy turvy. He was so much better looking than she remembered. All grown up but with those same amazing brown eyes and that heart-melting grin. Her stomach flipped, memories flooding her. They used to sneak off campus for coffee in high school. They'd quickly go through the drive-through, then arrive back at their school parking lot, chuckling about their sneaky deed.

"Come on," she said, nudging him. "You know you want your java."

He laughed, unaware she was flirting. Darn it. He never picked up on that. "My java, right," he said, drawing out the word. "Like you don't need your fix?"

"Guilty as charged," she responded, grinning. "But at least our addiction's legal."

"All right." Ryan raked a hand through his hair, and it flopped back down in sexy waves. "I'll drive." He sat behind the wheel and glanced her way. "I want you to know you're corrupting me."

"Am I?" she asked, pleased. She buckled her seat belt. "Good." She only wished she could corrupt him more. By covering him with kisses...

She stared down at her clothes, remembering she was in Nantucket and covered in baby vomit. *Nooo.* She probably reeked too. Her hand shot to the side of her head, hiding the barrette and the biggest blotch of nasty.

Ryan's face registered concern. "Are you all right? You look a little—"

"Oh, yeah. Yeah. Ha-ha. My niece, she..." She winced. "She had a little accident."

"I see that," he said, like he couldn't. Or maybe he could? His sister was several years younger, so maybe he remembered some baby stuff. Like about how unpredictable they could be. Also terribly embarrassing. And it was hard to imagine being much more embarrassed than she felt now. Running into her old high school crush all these years later. Looking—and smelling—like this.

"I'm kind of surprised to see you," he said. "What are you doing here?"

Her face flushed hot. "I, uh. I'm here with my family."

He gave her a dazed look. "Funny. So am I."

The Hatfields arrived on cue, traipsing up the wooden steps from the beach. Mr. Hatfield stopped walking when he saw Evita. He wore a white button-down shirt cuffed at the sleeves. His business slacks were rolled up at the ankles. Those had to be his shoes and socks in the house. His tie, too, more than likely.

Ryan's teenage sister yelped like she'd seen an alien. "Ahh! Who's that?"

Evita startled and dropped the hand shielding her hair.

Maddy shrieked again. "Is that our maid?" she asked in horror.

"No." Ryan's mom covered her mouth, looking like she might faint. "It's a Machado."

Evita's family flooded the deck surrounding her and she was glad for the reinforcements. Nobody messed with the Machados when they were en masse.

"You!" Her mom locked on Mrs. Hatfield's gaze. "I should have known!"

"What?"

"You didn't win this week, so you decided to take it anyway."

Shocking, but probably true. At least from the evidence. The Hatfields were here, weren't they? Encroaching.

"I did not take anything." Mrs. Hatfield tugged on her pearl necklace. "I won this week in the auction." She appeared to be dressed for a ladies' brunch and not the beach. That was so Mrs. Hatfield. She never changed.

Then again, Evita's mom was dressed up too, given that she was in her work clothes.

"No you didn't. I did."

Evita stared helplessly at Ryan, who appeared just as lost as she was. The two of them had to do something, but what? A small and selfish part of her wished she hadn't run into him again for the first time like this, surrounded by their warring families. She had so many questions. Where did he live? Did he have a good life? Was he still seeing Layla Petroski? Grrr. But she couldn't ask any of that now. They'd both have to survive this first.

Quique and Nanny glanced back and forth between Ryan's mom and Evita's like they were watching a tennis match, then Nanny started crying. Loudly.

"Wah! That lady's being mean to my Tita!"

"Shh, shh," Kendra soothed Nanny. "It's all right."

"No it isn't." Her voice warbled. "I want to stomp her."

Quique took a giant step toward the Hatfields, but Chachi held him back by his collar.

Mrs. Hatfield gasped. "So this is how you play, Lissette? You bring in your whole family? To what? Chase us out? Like a band of bandits?"

Her mom set her hand on her hip. "I'm offended by your language, Daneen."

Mrs. Hatfield's face tensed. "And I'm offended by your actions, Lissette."

"Hang on!" Chachi held up one hand. "Nobody's chasing anyone! I'm sure there's been an honest mistake." Leave it to Chachi to mediate.

All the shouting woke Luisa, and she started whining. Robby patted the baby's back. "I... I'd better go and change her."

"And feed her." Eunice scrambled after him. "I'm coming."

Chachi sent Kendra a look. "We'll take our kids inside too." They latched on to Quique and Nanny's hands, tugging them along.

Now Chachi and Kendra were abandoning ship.

Nanny sniffed and peered over her shoulder. "I want to stay with Tita and protect her."

"Your Tita can take care of herself," Chachi whispered.

Mrs. Hatfield addressed Maddy. "I think you should go inside too."

"Uh." She gave her mom the side-eye. "With *them*?"

Ryan raked a hand through his hair and it flopped back down in waves. Evita's pulse hummed. That habit of his hadn't changed, and it had the very same effect on her. Even in the midst of this madness, her heart went a little swoony.

But wait. There was real shellfire going on. *What* was that noise in the house? The kids began shouting and chasing each other around the downstairs again. The closed French doors served as a very poor sound buffer for the internal commotion.

"Quique!" Kendra said. "Put your shirt back on!" She groaned. "Nanny! You too!"

"But we're at the beach!" the boy said.

Something clattered in the house, and everyone jumped.

Evita winced seeing Ryan's eyes on her. Who knows what he was thinking? That her family was out of control? He cocked his chin and she remembered that move from high school as well. He wasn't judging her. He was commiserating. His look said, *How did we get here, and how do we get out of it?* Evita had no idea.

Mr. Hatfield glanced at Mrs. Hatfield with an expression like *We have to solve this now.*

Evita's parents shared the same look.

Luisa broke into a roar. She had a serious set of lungs.

"I thought you packed the breast pump!" Eunice hollered.

"Me?" Robby shouted. "I don't have breasts!"

Ryan's face reddened. That was probably a little much, even for him. And the old Ryan she knew wasn't flustered by much of anything.

Maddy shuddered, but her dad said gently, "Your mom's right, sweetheart. We adults need a moment to"—he cleared his throat—"talk. Why don't you wait upstairs in your room?"

Maddy's shoulders sank. "Whatever."

"Quique! No!" Chachi called. "Do *not* hang from that railing!"

"You won't earn your gold star!" Kendra tempted.

Chachi added with a desperate growl, "Or your Tito's ice cream either!"

Glass shattered. "Oh, Nanny!" Kendra wailed. "Nooo."

Evita folded her face in her hands.

"What was that?" Eunice yelped.

"Martini glass!" Robby answered.

Evita peeked out between her fingers to see Mrs. Hatfield giving her husband a disapproving look. "Go on then," she said to Maddy, like she was sending her daughter into a war zone. "Carefully."

She dropped her hands, and Ryan stared her wide-eyed. This was really tricky territory. You couldn't have thrown two families together who were more different, or more historically at odds. They were in deep trouble here, and both of them knew it.

They glanced at the French doors then back at each other, each waiting on some genius solution to occur. Evita could tell Ryan was thinking. He had to know she was too. Spinning her wheels around and around hunting for answers to this impossible situation.

One thing was clear. She and Ryan couldn't leave their moms out here alone. Even with their dads present. Those men were helpless in the face of their steamroller wives. Once Mrs. Hatfield got going, there was no stopping her. Evita's mom was even worse.

"I have evidence!" her mom said, defending her position with a swagger. "Right here on my phone." She pulled up the email and defiantly walked toward the Hatfields. "You see? Here's confirmation that I won the week."

Mrs. Hatfield paled and pulled out her phone. She tightened her slim fingers around its case, forcing her hand to stay steady. She swiped open an email, displaying it to Evita's parents. "And here's mine."

"Unbelievable," Evita's dad said, goggling at the message.

Mr. Hatfield scratched his head. "How is that possible?" He turned to his wife. "You said yours was the final bid?"

Mrs. Hatfield nodded. "At the bottom of the last page before they picked up the bid sheets."

"Wait." Evita's mom frowned. "I saw your bid, and I topped it at the start of a new page."

Mrs. Hatfield's face tinged pink. "What new page?"

Evita's mom checked her phone again. "There were two coordinators for the auction. Each was contacting half the winners. I heard from Marylin." She addressed Mrs. Hatfield. "You?"

"Drake." Mrs. Hatfield's mouth fell open. "So each of them somehow—"

"—got mixed up over assigning this prize, with both of them doing the honors. Only Drake didn't get the final bid sheet."

"What happened to it?" Evita's dad asked.

Mr. Hatfield rubbed his cheek. "Dropped? Lost? Two pages stuck together?"

"Well." Evita's mom sighed. "I guess that settles it. The week was technically supposed to be ours." She arched her eyebrows at Daneen. "So."

"Not so fast, Lissette." Mrs. Hatfield adjusted her cardigan. Each of its tiny buttons looked like a pearl. "We were told that *we* won. Not only that, we arrived at the cottage first. So we have squatter's' rights."

"Squatters! Ha! Hahaha!" Evita's mom laughed and then she laughed some more, harder and harder. Evita bit her lip and shrugged at Ryan, who clearly thought her mom had lost it. Evita's dad sent her a glance. At least he got the inside joke. He pursed his lips, trying very hard not to chuckle along with his wife.

The Hatfields didn't seem to find it funny though.

Lissette pulled herself together with a steely, "Sorry, Daneen. You'll have to pack up."

Mrs. Hatfield crossed her arms. "We're not packing up."

Evita's dad stepped forward. "Neither are we. Our son flew all the way here from Los Angeles. The other one came from Brooklyn. Both brought their families a very long way."

Mr. Hatfield moved toward him, his "business casual" in stark contrast to her dad's flower-covered guayabera shirt, which was hot pink actually, and cargo shorts. "Then we're at an impasse, aren't we?"

"Let's be reasonable," Mrs. Hatfield said. "I received my email first. Two hours ahead of yours, Lissette. So I was the first declared the winner. The second designation was a mistake."

"No. I paid my bid already."

"What?" Mrs. Hatfield's cheeks reddened. "So did I." Their entire family had a pale palette, except for Ryan, who had a tawnier look, more peaches than cream. His nose was a little crooked because he'd broken it playing soccer. When it healed, giving him a young Owen Wilson look, the high school girls had all been after him, including Layla Petroski. She'd had ambitions of becoming a movie star herself. She looked like one too. Evita couldn't compete.

"I suppose it was a good day for the animal rescue then," Evita's mom said, since the charity in question was called Pets and Paws.

Mrs. Hatfield raised her chin. "Which is a worthy cause."

With each exchange, their tones grew more combative.

"Uh." Evita sent Ryan a panicked glance, and the two of them inserted themselves in front of their parents, so they were face to face. His scent washed over her, all spicy and shower-washy fresh, like cypress and cedar. Ooh, with a splash of citrus and lemon peel.

She hoped he wouldn't get a whiff of her *eau du baby barf*.

His nose twitched. Uh-oh.

She casually put space between them.

Ryan turn up his palms in a placating way, "I'm sure we can arrive at some compromise." He fixed his gaze on Evita and she tried to read his eyes. Compromise? What compromise? Not all of them in the one house? The Hatfields and the Machados? No. They'd never survive the night. Okay. Maybe if everyone cooperated. Which seemed like a long shot.

"Hey," Ryan whispered. "What other choice do we have?"

He was right. The alternatives were worse. If one family got booted out, it would totally ruin their vacation. And each family had counted on this getaway, planned for it, with both moms believing they'd won. The mistake wasn't the Hatfields' or the Machados' fault.

He nodded and raised his eyebrows. Her knees went distractingly weak. If it were just the two of them... Which was a stupid, stupid thought. It would never be just the two of them. There were—she added quickly—fourteen people here, counting the baby. And they were all going to drive each other nuts. It wasn't like that with her and Ryan anyway. There was no kind of romantic vibe between them. The fire of deceit tore through her. Okay she might have *once* felt a—totally unreciprocated and gut-wrenching—attraction. But that was ages ago, and they were kids. That didn't mean they couldn't share the same goal as grown-ups now.

Ryan was right. This was the only way. Otherwise, neither of them would ever hear the end of it, and their moms' rivalry would only get worse. Maybe they were naïve to think having them all share the same house wouldn't do just that: drive the wedge deeper between the two families. But. She exhaled sharply. They were working with what they had. Taking a stab in the dark. And maybe. Just maybe they'd come out of this week two big happy families.

No. One big happy family. And one happy little one.

A breeze lifted off the water, blowing across the deck, and someone turned on the outside porch lights. "Yeah," Evita said. "Just look at this house." She stared up at the second story and then down at the beach which was covered in darkness with the moon rising over the water. It would be a terrible time to force someone to go. Everyone was exhausted and had traveled for hours. It was no small feat to get to Nantucket. "It's really nice. And huge!"

"Big enough. Maybe." Ryan swallowed hard. "For both families?"

"Are you kidding me?" his mom asked.

Evita's mom snapped, "No way."

"Mom and Dad," Evita said. The weight of disappointment hung in her voice. "We have to consider it."

Ryan's gaze swept over his parents. "Us too. It's only fair."

Mr. Hatfield shook his head, and so did Evita's dad, but Evita could tell her father was rolling the proposal around in that sharp mind of his. Then he gave a grumpy frown, evidently not liking the mental pictures he'd conjured.

"I don't know how we could do that," Evita's mom said. "Without all of us bumping into each other. The house is decently sized, yes, but not enormous."

"We'll just make a schedule," Evita said. "And a plan."

"Right." Ryan nodded. "To divide the house."

"Divide?" her mom said, like the idea was ridiculous. "No." Still, she tapped one foot, which meant she was thinking about it. She crossed her arms, and Mrs. Hatfield did too, both of them acting bullish. Neither prepared to back down.

Evita stared at her mother. "Mom, please."

Her mom sighed. "Okay fine. I'll do it." She threw up both hands, then narrowed her eyes at Daneen. "If she will."

Mrs. Hatfield relented. "Only if we get half."

"Half?" Her mom's temper flared, and her dad laid a hand on her arm.

"One half of the house, Lissette. Take it or leave."

"Don't be ridiculous, Daneen. Our family's much bigger than yours."

Her mom had a point. Ryan looked like he agreed. He opened his mouth to talk, but his mom interceded. "I paid just as much as you did for the privilege."

"No," Evita's mom said. "There was a last page. I paid more." She was sure her mom had. They should settle this. Evita tried to speak, but both moms held up their hands.

Mrs. Hatfield's eyebrows arched at her mom. "How much more?"

Evita's mom stood very still. Too still. Uh-oh. Something was up.

"How much more, Lissette?" Mrs. Hatfield asked in a bullheaded way. "I'll match it."

Evita's mom hesitated then murmured, "Five dollars." She spoke so softly, Evita barely heard her. She glanced at Ryan who raised his brow. He hadn't heard clearly either.

"What?" Mrs. Hatfield leaned toward her. "Five hundred?"

Evita's mom grumbled. "Five dollars, I said."

Evita and Ryan locked gazes. What now?

Mrs. Hatfield smiled coolly. "No problem," she said. "It's yours. Let me grab my purse."

Evita's mom stopped her. "I don't need your handouts, Daneen."

Evita stepped forward and so did Ryan, but their moms held them aside.

"Good," Mrs. Hatfield smirked. "We're in agreement. We'll split the cottage fifty-fifty."

Sweat beaded Evita's hairline, and Ryan's Adam's apple rose and fell.

Hopefully, that was a *good* thing.

FOUR

A SHORT TIME LATER, THE families gathered in the great room. The Machados had unpacked their vehicles, and their luggage and coolers piled in the foyer. The groups faced off in the living area, each commandeering a sofa and two armchairs with their own separate coffee table. Evita's oldest brother, Robby, sat on an ottoman next to his wife, Eunice, and she held their baby. Evita's parents, Chachi, and his wife, Kendra, and their kids squished onto a sofa with their little girl sitting on Kendra's lap. The adults sipped wine with the exception of Eunice, who had a water bottle beside her. Kendra had passed too, opting for ginger ale.

Ryan's parents were on their second round of martinis. He'd decided to skip the booze for now. He needed a clear head to see this through. The moment they'd stepped inside, both moms had phoned their contacts at the auction, demanding assistance in getting the situation rectified. But neither had offered much more than a heartfelt apology, plus encouragement about the two families finding ways to work things out.

Maddy tapped on her phone, pivoting in her swivel armchair. Ryan had a whiteboard on his knees and held a marker, which he'd dug out of a game box he'd found in a laundry room cupboard. He'd created a rudimentary scheme of the cottage with special attention to its six bedrooms. He wasn't the most skilled artist, but he was good enough. He drew occasional illustrations while teaching his courses.

"Okay! As soon as Evita's back, we'll get started."

"I'm here!" She came down a spiral staircase, and his heart skipped a beat. He almost hadn't recognized her when he'd first spotted her on the deck all covered in baby goo, but then he'd caught a glimpse of her amazing dark eyes. She was gorgeous, her face still flush from her shower. Then he got what it was. He'd known there'd been something different about her, apart from her being older.

"Aha! That's what it is!" Ryan playfully shook his finger at her, putting it together. "Your hair. You've cut it." In high school she'd worn it long and straight.

"Yeah." She ran a hand through her damp curls. "Just this year."

"Looks nice." Her shorter hair suited her bubbly personality. It was a no-fuss look. Casual, and she wore it really well.

"Thanks!" She grinned and her dimples settled.

Warmth spread through his chest. He'd spent a lot of time thinking about those dimples back in high school. Too much time probably, given that he and Evita never stood a chance. He'd been dying to ask her to the prom their junior year, and might have braved it, had their moms not been standing in between them like two staunch sentinels.

"Ryan?" his mom prodded, and he realized he'd been lost

in a fog. She and Mrs. Machado gave him and Evita suspicious looks, probably thinking about that lab partner blowup. Evita's parents weren't the only ones who'd tried to get Mr. Amberly to reassign the pair. Ryan's mom had showed up at the high school with Ryan's grandpa the next day, demanding the same thing. But Amberly was tougher than he looked, even though he was extremely chill.

"Uh. Right." He pulled his gaze off Evita. She wore jeans and a clingy purple top and large lilac hoop earrings that glittered. She walked past him leaving a cloud of her perfume and shampoo in her wake, which was definitely a lighter and fresher scent than before. Babies. Ha. One minute they could be such sweet little nuggets, and the next turn into outraged ogres. He'd spent lots of late nights walking while holding Maddy when she was tiny, not that she remembered.

"Have a seat, Evita," her mom said. She gestured to the empty armchair, looking askance at Ryan. A weird feeling prickled through him. Like she was sizing him up. Not trusting him. With who? Evita? That was absurd. Evita sent him a quick glance, and his pulse thrummed. Totally absurd. Wasn't it?

He'd only seen her around town once or twice since they'd graduated high school. They'd both gone on to college, then he'd moved away for grad school before returning to his home state to take up his teaching career. He'd heard through the grapevine that she'd been dating different people, and so had he.

A curious niggle coursed through him, and he wondered if she was seeing anyone now. Which was 100 percent none of his business. It wasn't like he was going to ask her out. His parents would flip, and so would hers. There was also the very good chance she'd turn him down.

Evita found her spot in the other armchair on the Machados' side. Chachi leaned forward and passed her a full wineglass from the coffee table. She nodded in thanks and stared expectantly at Ryan.

Okay. Time to put his mind back on business and helping both families survive the week.

He hoped this worked.

"So," he said. "Here's what I'm thinking." He pointed to his boxy diagram of the house. "This cottage is big enough for all of us, if we're a little flexible."

Mr. Machado frowned. "Define flexible."

Ryan cleared his throat. He'd always found Evita's dad mildly intimidating. Maybe it was his protective nature about his daughter. Then again. Ryan cut quick glances at Chachi and Robby, who watched him, stone-faced. Her older brothers were kind of intimidating too. "The cottage has four suites. Two upstairs and two down." He pointed to these on the whiteboard. "Since the downstairs suites are larger, those should go to the parents."

Evita's mom nodded. "That seems fair."

Unbelievably, his mom agreed. "Yes." Still, she couldn't bear to meet Mrs. Machado's eyes when she did.

His dad exhaled. "Good. Then we can stay where we are. I've already unpacked."

Ryan glanced around the room when there was brief chatter.

"What about everyone else?" Chachi asked him.

Ryan turned his whiteboard to face the group. "We've got

four couples here and four suites. You and Kendra and Robby and Eunice should each get one of those bigger bedrooms upstairs."

Maddy yanked out her earbuds. "What?"

"I'm sorry, Mads." Ryan frowned. "But I've got you in this room." He tapped on the small one at the top of the stairs and to the right.

"But it's got *bunk beds*," she said, like it was contaminated with some highly toxic chemical agent.

"Yes, and anyway," Ryan's mom quipped, "shouldn't she be on our side? Our suite is next to the kitchen."

"That bunk bed room is next to the suite where Chachi and Kendra are staying, so I thought their kids could stay there closer to their suite."

"I'm not sharing a room with Nanny," Quique said.

"I hate my brother!"

"Shh, shh." Kendra jostled her in her arms. "You don't mean that. Hate is a very strong word."

Ryan's mom hoisted her martini glass. "Sacrifices must be made."

Mrs. Machado's eyes were cold, dark embers as she glared at his mom.

Okay. So she was a bit intimidating too.

Ryan turned the whiteboard around, studying it. "I guess we could move Maddy to that room, and have Robby and Eunice stay above the kitchen."

Ryan's mom set down her martini glass. "With the baby?" she asked, sounding horrified at the prospect of having a screaming infant located directly above her room. Luisa sputtered out a cry, growing louder by the instant. She arched her eyebrows at Ryan as if to say, *surely, you appreciate my concern.*

Mrs. Machado tsked. "Now you've hurt her feelings."

"She's just a few weeks old!"

"Two months," Eunice said.

Robby stood and reached for the baby.

"I'll take her." His eyebrows arched then he spoke with a dismissive air. "Eunice and I would prefer to stay on our side of the house anyway." He patted Luisa's back, doing a daddy bouncy walk to calm her.

Ryan grimaced. "There can't be 'sides' technically. I mean, we'll do the best we can, but certain things like the kitchen are hard to divide."

"We'll make up a schedule then," Evita said. "And assign pantry space and refrigerator shelves."

"A schedule?" Evita's mom sighed. "*Ay.*"

Mr. Machado chewed on his cheek. "We have a problem with the suites," he said, waving his hand. "We're forgetting about Sebastian."

"Sebastian?" Ryan's parents said. They glanced at each other and then at the Machados. "Who's Sebastian?"

"Evita's boyfriend," Mr. Machado said.

"Almost fiancé." Evita's mom's eyes twinkled. "He's coming from Mexico tomorrow."

A small knife twisted in Ryan's gut. Of course she had a boyfriend. Why wouldn't she? She was smart and funny and beautiful. So it all made sense. Maybe that was much safer for him anyway. What had he been thinking? Clearly not that he and

Evita…? After all these years. No. "Oh. Well." Ryan stared at his diagram. "That does complicate things. Somewhat."

Evita sank down in her chair, sipping her wine with her eyebrows lowered. For whatever reason, she didn't seem thrilled about her boyfriend coming. Which was odd. Maybe he didn't get along with her family? The Machados were a tough crowd.

Ryan rubbed his cheek, considering their options. "There's a pull-out sofa in each of the upstairs suites. In separate sitting areas with pocket doors."

"Evita and Sebastian can stay with us," Robby offered generously.

"Yeah, sure." Eunice smiled at Evita. "We don't mind."

Evita's eyes widened. "Oh no. I don't want to be a bother. Your family's so new. You—"

"Nonsense," Eunice said. "We insist."

Luisa sputtered a cry and Robby rocked her.

Evita sank lower in her chair hiding behind her wineglass.

Mrs. Machado nodded, speaking to the crowd. "Everyone *loves* Sebastian," he said proudly, like she was personally responsible for having him associated with their family. "He has a PhD in Latin American Studies."

There went that theory.

Sebastian was apparently some kind of god, and they all idolized him.

Except for maybe Evita? Her jaw clenched, but Ryan appeared to be the only one who noticed. She seemed super tense about something. Then again, this wasn't the most comfortable situation. Two archenemy families having to live together in the same house.

Even for just a week.

"Er. Great," she finally said. Maybe it was more about Sebastian and how he got along with her family? They loved him, but was it mutual?

Ryan's dad spoke up, addressing Chachi and Kendra. "Why can't your two kids stay with you in your suite? Then Ryan can take the other bunk bed room?"

Kendra and Chachi got bug-eyed. "In the same bed? No," Chachi said. "We tried that at Kendra's parents' house in Atlanta, and they kicked each other all night long."

Ryan's mom whispered to his dad, but not quietly enough. "Maybe if they were better behaved," she said, sounding all judgy.

Kendra's mouth hung open. "Excuse me?"

Mrs. Machado leaned forward, but Mr. Machado waved her back down.

Ryan stared at Quique and Nanny, who both wore angelic grins. For once they weren't racing around and shouting. Maybe they'd worn themselves out. Nanny yawned, and so did Quique. It was after nine o'clock, so probably past their bedtimes.

He tried to stay on task. He had almost everyone in place now.

"So. Evita and Sebastian will stay with Robby and—"

"Wait!" Evita sat up in her chair, and the color drained from her face. "I have something to say." She meekly glanced at her parents. Then at her brothers and their wives. "Everybody. Listen. I'm sorry, but..." She frowned. "Sebastian's not coming." She let out a shaky breath. "He and I broke up."

"What?" Mrs. Machado pressed her palms to her cheeks. "No."

Mr. Machado's forehead furrowed. "When?"

The whole group stared at her, and she took a gulp of wine. "In January."

"This *past* January?" her mom asked, appearing gobsmacked.

The air whooshed back into Ryan's lungs. So she wasn't involved with anyone. Which was just basic information and a sad admission for her. He didn't feel glad about it. Just oddly relieved. He hated that she looked so down though. "I'm sorry, Evita," he said, meaning it.

"Yeah," Chachi echoed. "We all are."

"We'll talk about this later," her mom said in soothing tones. She observed Ryan's family and added, "In private." She sent Evita a silent signal, sharing a sympathetic pout.

"It really is too bad," Ryan's dad said quietly to his mom. "Breakups are so hard."

She elbowed him. "Kirk. Shh."

Maddy groaned and fell back in her chair. "Can we please just end this?"

Evita's mom stared at Ryan's. "It's a shame your daughter's not better behaved."

"Oh. How dare—"

"Mom, please." Ryan shot her a pained look.

Maddy folded her face in her hands. "Okay," she said, getting up. "I'm done." She glanced at a spiral staircase. "So my room's—?"

"Yeah." Ryan nodded. "That one."

Maddy trudged up the steps then not-so-quietly shut her door.

Evita drew in a breath. "So. The parents are on the ground floor. The kids are in the bunk bed rooms—"

A door upstairs cracked open. "I'm not a kid!"

Evita gasped as Maddy crossed through the loft, presumably to grab her belongings from her former suite. "How thin are the walls in this house?"

Mr. Machado frowned. "Not too thin. I hope."

Evita turned to Ryan, who set down the whiteboard, leaning it against his chair. "Where will you sleep?"

He shrugged. "One of these sofas looks fine."

"You are not sleeping on a sofa," his mom told him.

Mrs. Machado shook her head. "Everyone needs their own bed. What if you want to sleep in?" Here? He couldn't imagine that luxury. "Or someone wants to stay up late?"

"I think it's good for Ryan and Evita to keep their distance," his mom said. She'd been extra relieved when he and Evita hadn't had any classes together their senior year, and happy as a clam when he began officially dating Layla.

Heat swamped through him. "Mom." She surveyed him, searching her memory and probably thinking about that prom. He'd gone out on a limb even broaching the topic with her, which had been a big risk. She'd shut that subject down summarily, and—when he'd turned to his dad for help—his dad had backed up his mom. Per usual.

"I agree," Chachi said when Mrs. Machado sent him a pointed look. "Evita and Ryan should each have their own space." Ryan sighed. There was a time when Chachi had seemed cool about him and Evita. He was just one year older than them and had tried to intervene with her folks about their friendship back in high school, but the Machados wouldn't hear it.

"A separate space," Robby added, causing Evita's blush to deepen. "Very separate. Opposite ends of the house." He caught his brother's eye and Chachi took the hint, understanding they needed to present a unified front. Whatever her brothers believed previously, they were backing up their parents now, in the interest of family harmony, he supposed.

"No problem." Chachi crossed his arms. "Ryan can stay with us."

Mr. Machado cut Ryan a glance, indicating he should watch his step. No sneaking out for hanky-panky with his daughter. As if. Ryan wasn't like that. He didn't even hanky-panky. Much. At least, not much lately. And he wouldn't dare try pulling any fast moves here.

Kendra murmured, "*Cha-chi.*" Like she wasn't so wild about the idea. Neither was Ryan. He'd have to what? Knock and ask permission each time he wanted to exit his part of the room? That was tantamount to needing a hall pass. No. He couldn't see that working.

"It's fine. Fine." Ryan held up his hands. "I don't mind roughing it for a few nights. Maybe I can sleep in the loft?"

"The sofas up there are short," his mom said. "Two-seaters. You're too tall. Just like you're too tall for those bunk beds in either room. They're kid-size."

Ryan's dad frowned. "This is all getting very complicated."

Chachi nudged Kendra who inhaled deeply. They exchanged some kind of private communication with their eyes before she said, "Chachi's right. I'm sorry, Ryan. You should stay with us. With those pocket doors, it will be like having your own room."

Ryan shifted in his seat. That sounded really awkward, but he couldn't very well throw a monkey wrench into things when they were finally coming together. "I'd… I'd hate to impose."

"You won't be imposing," Chachi said. "We Machados are used to big family get-togethers." He raised his wineglass toward Ryan's mom. "And making sacrifices."

She picked up her martini glass and took a swig.

Ryan's dad rested his hands on his knees. "Well, if that's all settled," he said, preparing to stand. "I've had a long day. I think all of us have."

"Yes," Ryan's mom said. "We've got the bedrooms sorted out, and tomorrow we'll divvy the kitchen and set a schedule."

Mrs. Machado glanced over her shoulder. "Okay. But we get the dining room table."

Ryan's mom gaped at her. "What?"

"We are ten people, Daneen. You're only four. You can eat in the kitchen at the island."

Ryan's mom bristled. "We're not the help."

"Neither are we," Mrs. Machado said firmly. "The dining room table is ours."

"Wait!" Evita got to her feet. She blew out a breath. "My family probably eats later than yours," she said to Ryan. She glanced at his folks. "When do you all normally have dinner?"

"Sixish," Ryan's dad said.

"Great," Evita said. "We're lucky to eat before eight. So maybe we can share—"

Her mom shook her head. "No sharing. This is our side of the house. We eat over here."

"Fine," Ryan's mom said. "We'll make a 'sacrifice' and eat in the kitchen."

"There's also a picnic table!" Evita pointed out. Ryan's mom shot her down with a stare. She gulped, then said softly, "Outside on the porch."

"Hang on," her mom said. "I have a question about scheduling the kitchen. What if I'm making a dish that takes a while?"

Evita shook her head at Ryan, and he knew what she was thinking. Would this never end?

"We'll work those schedules out too," he said to Mrs. Machado. "Maybe you should let Evita and I—"

"No," Evita's mom said firmly. "There is no you and Evita."

"Right," his mom said. "Now that we've settled most of it. It's not like you'll have much need to spend time together."

Mrs. Machado set her chin. "My thoughts exactly. When we're not sleeping, we'll each keep to our own sides of the cottage. Evita will stick with us, and Ryan will stay with you."

"But—it's not *totally* worked out," Ryan told the moms.

"Then let's work on it," Mrs. Machado said efficiently. She stood up and grabbed Ryan's whiteboard, scribbling down a schedule. "We'll be in the kitchen at these times, and you all can be in during these."

Ryan's mom stood and looked it over. "Fine." She took away the whiteboard. "How about the porch and the deck?"

"Split down the middle."

Ryan's mom drew a thick line with the marker. "The beach?" she asked.

"Same."

"Daneen," Evita's mom said. "I think we've got ourselves a plan. Now, you and your family try not to blow it."

Ryan's mom smirked. "Me and my family will do just fine. Maybe you should worry about yours."

"We Machados play by the rules," she said gruffly. "Unlike certain others in the room."

"That was years ago, Lissette! And it was you—not me—"

Ryan and Evita both shot to their feet and shouted, "Stop!"

For an instant their moms looked abashed, although they were still fuming.

Evita licked her lips. "I think we should try very hard to get along."

"Yeah," Ryan said. "For everyone's sake." He glanced at Evita, and she locked on his gaze. He fell into those heady dark eyes of hers, and for an instant the rest of the world slipped away. There were no warring factions. It was just the two of them. Like they'd been as lab partners. On great terms and having fun. Sharing one lame joke after the other. Maybe he should have stood up to his mother and asked Evita to the prom. What if she'd said yes? Their entire realities could be different now. They'd also likely both be ostracized from their families.

Evita's mom stepped forward and latched on to her elbow. "Evita, why don't you come with me. I'll help you settle into your room."

"But I don't need—"

"Of course you do. Don't argue with your mother."

"Mo-om." Evita forced a pleasant face but talked through gritted teeth. "I'll settle in later *by myself*."

Ryan's mom caught his eye, and he just said, "No."

"Ryan—"

"Thanks, Mom. But I can handle moving my things."

Evita's mom shook her head at Evita before addressing the group. "Tomorrow!" She gestured around the room. "It's us over here and you over there."

Ryan's mom met her eyes. "I wouldn't cross that line if you paid me, Lissette." She gave Ryan an extra-long look. "None of us would."

Oh boy. "Okay, everyone." Ryan nodded in parting and scooped up the whiteboard. "Good night."

"Good night!" Evita raised her eyebrows at him, and his heart pinged. It was just a little ping. Nothing consequential. He hoped. Otherwise, he was in very big trouble.

———

Evita's mom stopped her when she was about to climb the stairs. "*Mija?* Can we talk?" The rest of her family had retreated to their rooms after putting their wineglasses in the dishwasher beside the Hatfields' martini glasses. The Hatfields had bailed out first, with Ryan looking slightly overwhelmed by the situation. Evita knew just how he felt.

She glanced at her mom. "Sure. What's up?"

Her mom sat down on a sofa and patted a cushion.

Evita's stomach tightened because there were only two options for topics of conversation: Sebastian and Ryan. "If this is about Ryan and the Hatfields—"

Her mom shook her head. "No, sweetheart. It's about you." She lowered her voice. "And Sebastian."

Evita frowned and sat beside her. "Oh."

Her mom lightly rubbed Evita's forearm. "Since January, Evita?" Her eyes shone with understanding, and Evita felt embraced in her motherly love. "I wish you'd told us sooner."

Evita swallowed past the burn in her throat. "I needed a minute. I was dealing."

"Dealing? Ahh. I see." She took Evita's hand and squeezed it. "Did he hurt you, *mija*?"

Evita turned to her. "Physically? No. Emotionally?" She exhaled a shallow breath. "Maybe he hurt my pride." She blinked and turned away when her eyes burned hot. "But I'm better now," she said, meeting her mom's eyes and believing it. It had been a rough road, but she'd made it to that light at the end of the tunnel. That bright light that spoke of self-confidence and learning to stand on her own.

Her mom cocked her head and said sweetly, "I would have been here for you, you know. All of us would have. We're your family."

"Would you have?" Evita sniffed. "Given how much you all loved Sebastian?"

"Sebastian, ha!" She held Evita's chin. "You have to know I've always loved you more. *We've* always loved you more." She frowned. "Was it another woman?"

Evita ducked her head. "Yes. Liliana."

Her mom crossed her arms. "Well, she couldn't have been worth it. Not half as great as you."

Evita looked up. "Thanks, Mom."

"I mean it," her mom said, her fierce loyalty shining through. "Sebastian didn't know what he was losing."

"Maybe not," Evita said. "But that's done now."

"I'm sorry."

Evita thought on this. "You know what?" she asked, the realization filling her. "I'm not." She sat up straighter. "I think I'm better off without him."

"If he couldn't appreciate what a gem you are, then I'm sure that's true."

"I don't really want to rehash this with the others," Evita said, knowing at least a few of them would probably ask.

"I'll talk to your father tonight," she offered. "And the boys, Chachi and Robby, tomorrow. Tell them you don't want to talk about it."

Evita sighed gratefully. "I'd appreciate that."

She glanced at the stairs, then issued a word of caution. "But Evita, just because you're single now —"

Evita huffed. "Mom, please. Don't make this about Ryan."

Her mom's eyes opened wide. "I'm not making anything about anyone. I'm just saying." She licked her lips. "Let's not make this vacation any more complicated than it already is."

"I wasn't planning on adding any complications," Evita said maybe a tad more defensively than she should have. She knew her mom's intentions were good. She was only looking out for her daughter, in her mind. But inwardly, Evita worried that she and Ryan had made a mistake in encouraging the two families to stay here together.

"Well," her mom said on a sigh. "That's good to hear." She held out her arms. "Come here. Let me give you a hug." Evita's mom wrapped her arms around her, smelling all fresh and flowery. "I love you, Evita."

"I know you do." She hugged her mom, never having doubted that for a moment. "I love you too."

"Now," her mom said, pulling back with a soft smile. "Let's go to bed."

FIVE

EVITA WOKE UP THE NEXT morning, bright sunlight shining in her eyes. The blinds. She'd been so dead tired she'd neglected to close them fully. She sat up on the sofa bed, fluffing the pillows behind her. It hadn't been that uncomfortable—once she'd gotten to sleep, which had to have been who knows when in the morning.

She climbed out from under the covers, desperately needing coffee.

Everything was quiet in Robby and Eunice's room. She didn't want to wake them.

She made up the sofa bed and threw on some shorts and a top, changing out of her comfy pj's. If the Hatfields weren't here, she'd go down to breakfast in those. But no. That would feel weird. Especially with Ryan around.

He'd done such a great job with that whiteboard; she could only imagine the fantastic teacher he made. His students must crush on him wildly. With his easy manner and nice looks, it would be hard not to be attracted to him were she in his class. Her cheeks burned hot. Her parents would freak if she became interested in Ryan now, especially her mom, after their little chat on the sofa. But beyond a few intense looks, nothing indicated that Ryan wanted to go there. He could be involved with someone else as far as Evita knew. Just because she was single, that didn't mean he was. And anyway, what was all that talk by their moms about them staying on opposite sides of the house? How embarrassing!

What did their parents think? That she and Ryan were Maddy's age and could have their actions dictated like they were still teenagers? She sighed, realizing that's exactly what had happened, and neither she nor Ryan had fought back. Likely because neither had had the energy. It had taken everything they had to get their families to cooperate on the cottage division. Now that that was established, maybe each group could find a way to enjoy their vacation peaceably.

A girl could dream.

She knocked lightly on the pocket doors but didn't hear anything on the other side. She tentatively slid them open just an inch. A rumbling met her ears. She opened them further.

It was Robby snoring. Eunice was nowhere in sight, and their portable crib for Luisa was empty. Eunice must have taken the baby downstairs so Robby could sleep in, which was a good thing. Since Robby spent most of his time at home, he was essentially a stay-at-home dad.

He also worked very hard as a screenwriter. It was a tough field, though, and highly competitive. In LA, supposedly everyone had a script in their glove box. Even cab drivers. He'd had a handful of projects optioned, but none ultimately produced. Meanwhile, Eunice's film editing career was going phenomenally.

She'd worked on several recognizable films with high-profile actors and had achieved some kudos and big awards.

Evita tiptoed past the bed and out into the upstairs hall.

Ryan was across the way, coming out of Chachi and Kendra's bedroom at the same time, dressed in swim trunks and a T-shirt and wearing flip-flops. Her heart stuttered. He was adorable, all sleepy-eyed and disheveled.

"Oh hi," she said awkwardly. "Good morning."

He raked a hand through his sticking-out hair. "Hi there."

"Evita!" Her mom stared up at the loft from where she sat on a sofa drinking coffee and reading her laptop. "You're up."

"Hi, Mom," she called over the railing. "Good morning."

"Coffee's on and it's our turn in the kitchen."

Evita grimaced at Ryan. "I'm sure it's okay if you—"

"Our turn," her mom reiterated.

"Fine," Evita said before whispering to Ryan. "Don't worry. I'll fix you a coffee."

His eyes glimmered gratefully. "No seriously. You don't have—"

She stared at him like it was settled, and he relented. "All right then. That would be nice."

"Still take yours with milk?" she asked quietly.

"Yeah." His husky breath raked over her and her pulse quickened. "Same as back then."

So, he hadn't forgotten about that either.

Evita's mom cleared her throat to remind them of her presence, and Evita held her finger in front of her lips in a shush sign. Ryan nodded, repressing a grin. They could do this, the two of them.

Get through this week with their families, especially since they had each other, and it was pretty clear that they did.

Evita scanned the great room, but it was mostly empty. Where was everyone else? She headed down the stairs, speaking to her mom. "Is Dad up?"

Her mom nodded, her eyes on her device. "In the shower. Chachi and Kendra took their kids down to the beach."

She heard the microwave beep, then saw Eunice with Luisa in the kitchen. "Oh hi, Evita," Eunice said, taking a seat at the island and stirring a spoon in her mug. "How did you sleep?"

Evita walked toward the coffee maker. "Like a rock." Eventually. She wasn't going to complain about the baby's fussing to her sister-in-law or Robby. They were well aware of it themselves and looking haggard enough. She didn't need to make anyone feel guilty for keeping her up. That's clearly not what Eunice or Robby would have wanted. Fact was, they would have likely loved to get a bit more rest themselves.

"Yeah." Eunice said. "Robby too. He's been working really hard these past few weeks. Going through rounds of revisions on a major project, so I decided to get up with Luisa this morning." The baby's combo car seat and carrier rested on the island, and the infant was sound asleep. She appeared to have two modes. Wide awake and fussing or completely passed out and looking like an angel.

Evita opened a cupboard, hunting for coffee mugs. Someone had taken masking tape and tagged certain shelves of dishes "Machado" and others "Hatfield," dividing everything neatly in stacks. She sighed and grabbed a mug from each section, one for her and the other for Ryan.

The French doors closed, and she looked over her shoulder, seeing him join his parents and Maddy at a picnic table on the Hatfield side of the porch, which was just outside the kitchen window with an ocean view. The laundry room was on the other side of the kitchen facing the drive, and under Ryan's sleeping area. The Hatfields had breakfast plates and were munching on bagels while drinking coffee. Maddy had orange juice.

Evita poured both coffees and opened the refrigerator hunting for milk.

There were two cartons. A large gallon size of 2% on the Machado shelf and a smaller half gallon size of skim milk on the shelf for the Hatfields. Someone had been busy with the masking tape this morning. The meat drawer was Hatfield. The crisper Machado. Each section in the door was marked off too. Okay. There'd be no mistaking who'd brought what. Including in the pantry, which was duly organized as well, down to the division of liquor bottles.

"Who did all the labeling?" she asked Eunice, who sipped from her mug. She saw from the box on the counter that Eunice drank herbal tea, probably remaining cautious about caffeine since she was breastfeeding.

"That was your dad. He got up early, saying he was trying to prevent more shellfire."

Evita chuckled. "Maybe that was a good idea." Everything should go much more smoothly now. The house was divided, the kitchen apportioned out, and both families had agreed to a schedule. Now all they had to do was enjoy the beach.

Luisa cooed softly in her sleep, and her lips twitched like she was having a happy dream about nursing. She was precious with her little wisps of dark hair and pudgy dumpling cheeks.

"She's a beautiful baby."

"Thanks." Eunice gazed adoringly at the infant. "We think so."

"Think you'll have any more?"

Eunice's eyes flashed with surprise. "Not for a long time. Long, long time." She shook her head and laughed. "If ever."

Evita understood. "Sorry. I know it's early days. I probably shouldn't have asked."

Eunice shrugged, considering Luisa. "It's all right. I'm just not sure. Neither is Robby. We adore her, but she's honestly a handful. I mean, lots of babies are, and they outgrow it. But work is so busy—"

"Hey, hey, congrats on that Oscar."

Eunice flushed. "I was part of a team."

"An award-winning team."

"Yeah." Eunice shook her head. "At first we thought we'd lost the award, since the announcer got the wrong card."

"I know your heart must have stopped when you heard the real news."

Eunice grinned hugely. "It was an amazing turnabout. One second the guys and I were all deflated, thinking, well, we lost, but we gave it our best shot. And the other film was really good, taking all the prizes anyway. Then, *zing*!" Her face brightened at the happy memory. "We learned the prior announcement was a mistake. It was such a surprise. We felt like phoenixes rising up from the ashes."

"I'll bet." Evita smiled at her sister-in-law. "I know Robby is so proud of you. We're all proud."

"Thanks." She took a sip of tea. "Robby's going to make it too, you know. He just has to hit upon the right project." Evita loved Eunice for who she was, and for the way she supported Robby. Kendra was an awesome wife to Chachi too. Evita was really happy for her brothers.

"I'm sure you're right." Evita finished making coffee for herself and Ryan and put away the milk.

"I'm really sorry about Sebastian, by the way. What happened?"

"He decided I wasn't the woman for him," Evita said. "But somebody else was."

"Jerk." Eunice frowned. "I never did like him."

"What?"

"There was just something about him." She shrugged. "Too self-important. You know? Showy."

She'd never looked at it that way specifically, but now that Eunice had said it, maybe Sebastian was a little full of himself. Pretentious. Always kicking around big, fancy words, then pausing to ask if she knew what they meant. Of course she did. She just didn't feel the need to talk like a walking dictionary all the time. People could be smart and not flaunt it. Just look at Ryan. He had a PhD, but she doubted very seriously he'd shove that in anyone's face the way Sebastian repeatedly touted his advanced degree.

"His loss, you know?" Eunice shared a warm smile. "There are other fish in the sea." She stared down at Evita's two coffee mugs. "Who's the other one for?" she asked in lilting tones.

Evita felt immediately called out, although she shouldn't have. It was only coffee.

She lifted a shoulder. "Ryan."

Eunice's eyebrows arched. "I see."

Evita tsked and chided her. "It's not like that, come on. Ha!" she said like the idea of her and Ryan getting together was the farthest thing from her mind.

"All right," Eunice said. "If you say so." Still, she wore this impish grin like she knew better.

Her mom heard her heading toward the door and looked up from her computer.

"Where are you going?"

"Outdoors. To sit on the deck."

"On our side, okay?"

Evita huffed out a breath. "Yeah. Fine."

Her mom arched an eyebrow. "Evita. Why do you have two mugs?"

"I'll be back in a bit!"

Ryan saw her and leapt to his feet, holding open the French door.

"Thanks. Here's your coffee." She shut the door behind her before her mom could complain. She got enough disapproval from Mrs. Hatfield's frown. She wore a floppy beach hat and sunglasses and had a cover-up on while Maddy sat there in her swimsuit and shorts. Mr. Hatfield wore shorts and an informal shirt with a collar.

"Appreciate it," Ryan said in a husky whisper.

"No problem."

"Hope today goes better than, you know." He nodded back inside the house with his chin.

"Yeah." She sighed. "Me too."

Mrs. Hatfield coughed into her hand, and Evita held back a giggle because it was such an obvious fake cough.

Ryan smirked.

"I guess I'll just go over there." She pointed to a spot by the firepit in the sunshine. "And enjoy my coffee."

He looked like he wanted to join her. Then he stared back at his parents and frowned.

"Yeah, okay." He lifted his mug. "Thanks again."

It was a gorgeous summer day, and Evita couldn't wait to get down to the beach. From her position on the deck, she could see Chachi and Kendra strolling along hand in hand while their kids raced ahead of them, shouting and spreading their arms out like wings as they darted in and out of the shallows and danced into the waves.

It was hard to believe that she and Sebastian had talked about having a family. She'd honestly believed that was going to happen. That they were going to happen. A tender spot welled in her throat. But she wasn't crying over spilt milk. Those days and expectations were long gone. Eunice had surprised her by admitting that she hadn't liked Sebastian. She'd believed his fan club was unanimous in her family. Now she wondered if anyone else felt the way Eunice did. Ryan walked up beside her, and she turned in surprise. "Oh hi!" She stared back at the empty picnic table. "Where's the rest of your family?"

"They went inside to grab their stuff for the beach." He pulled up a chair and sat down beside her with his coffee.

"Well, if they won't be too long, you'd better be careful," she teased.

"Yeah." He sipped from his coffee. "I could lose my beach privileges."

"What beach privileges?"

He shrugged. "No swimming before lunch?"

"Ryan," she said, rolling her eyes.

He leaned toward her with a husky whisper. "Evita." He said it low and smooth, and tiny crackles of electricity hummed through her. She lightly shoved his arm. "What?"

His gaze washed over her, and she caught her breath. "You're so much like I remember."

"Yeah?" She licked her lips. "You are too." Sweet, funny, and *superhot*.

"Ryan!" his mom commanded, emerging from the house. "What are you doing over there? You're supposed to be grabbing our umbrellas?"

He got to his feet, raising his eyebrows at Evita. "Sorry," he whispered. "Duty calls." He stared down at his empty coffee mug, and Evita reached for it.

"I can take that inside."

"You sure?"

"Sure I'm sure, big guy. I brought it out to you, didn't I?" Her tone slipped out a little flirty, and she bit her lip.

He gave her a slow perusal and handed her his mug. "Yeah, you did. Thanks."

"Ryan!" his mom called.

"Yes, son," his dad chimed in. "Come on and give us a hand."

He scowled playfully with his back turned to them, and Evita held in a giggle. Ryan always had a way to make her laugh. Still, his family was waiting, casting suspicious gazes their way and appearing antsy.

She leaned toward him and whispered. "Looks like you'd better go."

"Yeah." He nodded toward his coffee mug. "Thanks for the java."

"It can be a serious addiction, you know."

He cracked a lopsided grin, and her heart thumped. "That's what I hear."

He turned and walked away, leaving her heart hammering. The more she was around him, the more it felt like yesterday, only better. And worse. Given that they were sharing this beach house with their archenemy families. Evita sighed and set both coffee mugs on the table beside her, leaning back in her chair and closing her eyes. Sunshine warmed her face and ocean breezes rifled through her hair.

Maybe she should just relax and try to enjoy this vacation as much as possible? Things seemed to have calmed down between the parents, and she and Ryan were getting along. That should be more than good enough for now. She didn't need to go getting greedy by hoping for more, like she'd done in high school. That had never gone anywhere then anyway, so the odds of her and Ryan getting together now seemed slim to none. Especially here in Nantucket with both of their families tugging them apart.

She was just settling into her sunbathing tranquility when she heard scuttling behind her and turned around. The Hatfields lugged loads of beach gear down the steps, including two large umbrellas.

"Where did you find all that?" she asked Ryan as they passed by.

He thumbed over his shoulder. "There's a storage closet next to the outdoor shower. There's one on either side."

"Thanks," she said lightly, trying to ignore her pounding heart. "Good tip."

He lagged behind his group. "Come on, Ryan," his mom said.

He rolled his eyes, and she couldn't help but adore him. Ryan was a guy who never took himself too seriously, even though in many ways he was a very serious guy. Educated. Intelligent. Comfortable with who he was. Those things about him hadn't changed. Neither had his overpowering effect on her.

"You going down?" he asked.

She fluffed her hair with her fingers. "I thought I might."

"Okay then." He winked, and she went all fluttery inside. "See ya on the beach."

An hour later, the Machados clustered seaside with their own cache of beach chairs and umbrellas. Unfortunately, the two umbrellas they tried were broken with bent spindly frames that bowed downward instead of holding the canvas sheath up.

Robby gave up wrestling with the second one and frowned at Eunice. "I'm afraid if we can't get one up, we'll have to take her back inside." He glanced down at the beach towel where they'd temporarily set Luisa's carrier.

Eunice sighed, knowing that was true. They couldn't expose their newborn baby to the UV rays, which meant one of them would have to stay back with her in the house, and that would be a bummer. They'd flown all this way to be with family.

"I can go back inside with her." Evita's dad stretched out his arms toward the baby. "Wouldn't you like to come sit with your Tito?" Luisa gurgled and then gave a small choking cough.

"Dad! Step back!" Robby jerked him away just in time.

A greenish-gray spray arced onto the beach towel, then she whimpered.

"Poor baby." Evita's mom unbuckled her carrier. "Here, I'll take her." Eunice passed her a burp cloth and she settled Luisa on her shoulder. "Your Tita's not afraid of a little mess," she said for the benefit of Robby and Evita. "All of you children were messy."

Evita hated to think that's what she had in store. Someday. In the very distant future. Being covered in baby barf for the majority of her days didn't exactly sound like the dream domestic scenario.

She caught a glimpse of Kendra and Chachi frolicking with their kids in the waves, understanding that they'd weathered babyhood. Two times. She loved seeing her brothers as dads. They were so good at it.

"Pick up the carrier," her dad said. "I'll take that towel in and go get more fresh ones."

Evita's mom cradled Luisa in her arms, and Luisa sagged into her, molding up against her Tita. Now that she'd gotten over her tummy upset, she seemed a lot more content.

Her mom's gaze snagged on the pile of beach stuff the Hatfields had lying beside their open umbrella. Maddy sat listening to music on her earbuds while Ryan's parents both read books, and Ryan flipped through electronic pages on a reading device. "Look! Over there! The Hatfields have an extra umbrella."

It was true. They did. Plus, they weren't using it.

Her mom's eyes gleamed suspiciously. "You don't think they swapped their umbrellas out for ours?"

"No, Mom," Evita said. "I was right there when they went down to the beach. They got their umbrellas from the storage closet on their side of the cottage."

"Just rotten luck," her dad said, holding the wadded-up beach towel.

Her mom passed Luisa to Eunice. "They certainly don't need two."

Evita's heart pounded. "Mom, wait."

Her eyebrows twitched. "Their second one's not even in use."

"You should probably ask first," Robby suggested as she trudged through the sand.

"Excuse me!" Evita's mom said loudly. The Hatfields turned toward her, and Mrs. Hatfield lowered her sunglasses. "Do you mind if we borrow this?" She picked up one end of the long umbrella and Mrs. Hatfield gasped.

"We most certainly do. That came from our storage closet. On our side of the cottage."

"Daneen, please." Evita's mom sighed. "We have the baby."

Mrs. Hatfield stared at Evita's dad clutching the wadded-up beach towel. "Is that what I smell?"

Evita's mom scowled. "You're a very rude woman."

"It takes one to know one, doesn't it, Lissette?"

Evita's mom huffed. "All I'm asking is to borrow this umbrella, which you and your family clearly aren't using."

"And I said no."

"Okay." Evita's mom glanced over her shoulder at her family.

"I'm done with asking politely." She hefted the heavy beach umbrella into her arms and began carting it off.

"*Querida,* let me help you." Evita's dad set down the beach towel and stepped toward his wife. Mrs. Hatfield shot to her feet. "Kirk!" she complained. "They're stealing our umbrella!"

"Honestly, Daneen. We weren't exactly—"

She huffed and stomped after Lissette. "We will be using it later to shield our coolers from the sun when we bring them down for lunch."

"Oh no you won't," Evita's mom said, tugging it away. "We need this—right—now!"

Mrs. Hatfield latched on to its pole. "Give it back, Lissette."

Evita's mom leaned into her effort. "No way!"

Mrs. Hatfield yanked on her end, and Evita's mom stumbled.

"Now, wait just one minute," Evita's dad said. He took two giant steps toward her mom and gripped the top of the umbrella. "My wife is right. We need this more than you do. Let's be reasonable here. You all are not being fair."

This spurred Mr. Hatfield into action. He clambered to his feet and took up his position behind Ryan's mom, pulling the umbrella toward him. "I believe we set some ground rules." He tugged and grimaced. "Last night."

"Rules that can be amended," Evita's dad groaned, pulling harder. "When necessary."

Mr. Hatfield gritted his teeth. "I. Don't. Think. So."

Ryan scrambled out of his chair and Evita raced toward them. This was not going to end well. Ryan tried to intercede. "Mom. Dad. Please. That's enough." But they completely ignored him, yanking harder and harder—at last gaining ground.

"Argh!" Evita's mom growled and threw back her head. Digging her bare heels into the sand and bending her body in a sideways V with her ample butt sticking out behind her.

Her dad broke a sweat. Muscles strained in his arms. "This. Umbrella. Comes with us!"

Now the umbrella swung their way, and the Hatfields jerked forward in the sand.

Evita gawked at Ryan. "Somebody's going to get hurt."

"Folks! Please! Stop!" he said in commanding tones. But the tug-of-war was full-on.

"Stop fighting, Daneen!" Evita's mom called. "Let us have what is rightly ours!"

"It was in our storage closet!" Mrs. Hatfield contested with a sharp tug.

"But I." Yank. Yank. "Technically won the week!"

"No." Tug. Tug. "We settled that!"

Maddy sat on her side with her eyes closed like she was meditating, or trying to drown everything out. "I'm going for a walk," she said suddenly, standing.

Her combative parents didn't seem to notice.

"Give us that umbrella," Evita's folks said.

"Nothing doing! It's ours!"

Evita's dad lowered his eyebrows. "Not for much longer."

"Hey!" Mr. Hatfield shouted. "It's on our side of the beach!"

"Is it?" Evita's mom asked with another hard yank.

This had to stop.

Evita pressed two fingers inside her mouth and blew—hard.

A shrill whistle tore down the beach, startling wandering gulls into flight.

Maddy quit walking and turned around, then she kept going, picking up her pace like she couldn't wait to get out of there. Evita didn't blame her. If she could have run, she might have too. But no. She had to stay here with Ryan and face the music.

Ryan blinked at her, clearly impressed by her whistle. "I forgot that you could do that."

"Mom. Dad," Evita said, breathless. "Please. Enough is enough!"

Ryan stared down his parents. "I could say the same of you." He cocked his chin toward Luisa. "For crying out loud, they've got a baby. Give them the umbrella."

His mom threw up her hands. "Fine. Okay. Whatever."

His dad let go too, and Evita's parents lugged the umbrella to where they'd set their other belongings in the sand. Both perspired heavily. The Hatfields were flushed too.

"That was really not cool," Ryan said under his breath to his parents.

Evita's mom smirked. "You see. Even their son is embarrassed."

"He's not the only one who's embarrassed," Evita told her. "Gee."

Her dad inhaled deeply. "Well, anyway. Let's put this up."

Robby helped him and they moaned. "This one is bent too," her dad grumbled.

"Yeah, but not as badly as the others." Robby pressed at the bowed frame. "Maybe we can fix it."

Eunice strode back toward the house carrying the baby.

"Wait," Robby said. "Where are you going?"

"I'm exhausted from all that." Her face hung in a frown. "I think I'll go inside and rest with Luisa."

Chachi and Kendra came back with their kids, all dripping wet. He grabbed a beach towel off the ground. It was the nasty one. He scrunched up his face. "What? Ew."

"Sorry, Chachi," Robby said. He tossed him a few clean towels, and Chachi passed one to Kendra.

"Thanks!" Kendra said, dabbing at her glistening torso with a towel. She was the only one in a bikini, and she wore it super well. Evita couldn't imagine looking like that after having two kids. She hadn't had any and didn't look that good now. Kendra's glistening brown stomach was nearly flat again, with just a little rise in it below her belly button, a barely noticeable bump. "Nice going," she said. "You got the umbrella up!"

SIX

RYAN PUT HIS PARENTS' BEACH umbrella and the four folding chairs away in the storage closet. The shower beside it was occupied, and so was the one on the Machado side. His dad had gone indoors, and his mom had taken off down the beach to hunt for Maddy, who'd gone on another walk. He didn't blame her. If he'd been able to escape the melee, he would have too. He closed the storage room door, and the Machado side shower shut off. Now that he thought about it, the shower on his side wasn't running. Maybe someone was toweling off? For a long time. Wait. It could only be his dad, but no. His dad had gone inside.

Evita emerged across the way with her hair in damp curls and wearing her emerald-colored swimsuit with a halter top hugging her soft curves. She was a super attractive woman, so feminine and sexy in a way that made his heart pound and heat coil in his belly. She flushed and wrapped her towel around herself, covering her thighs, but not quite concealing her cleavage. He found it cute that she seemed modest now.

She hadn't appeared self-conscious down on the beach when she'd been having a great time playing in the sand with her niece and nephew. He'd loved watching her build that sandcastle, carefully molding its turrets and then decorating them with seashells on top. "Ta-da! It's perfect!" Quique and Nanny had giggled and started splashing her with water from the moat. She hadn't minded. She'd splashed them right back. She'd been so happy and carefree, joking around with the kids, and they'd been captivated by her.

Ryan knew how they felt. It was hard not to become enthralled by her warm brown eyes and dazzling spirit that sparkled brighter than sunshine. Just the same way it had back in high school. He heaved a breath, still embarrassed by his parents' behavior. "That was some scene down there."

"With the umbrella?" She gritted her teeth. "Yeah." She tightened her towel around her as moisture dripped from her hair, clinging to her shoulders. Each tiny droplet glimmered like a diamond in the sun.

Ryan shifted on his feet, instinctively inching closer. "Maybe that was the worst of it?"

She winced, peering up at him. "Hope so."

He nodded. "Thanks for helping break it up."

She rolled her eyes and chuckled. "That took *two* referees."

He laughed. "No kidding. Evita—" Oh how he wanted to tell her. What? That she was unique? Charming? The only person he couldn't stop thinking about? No, he couldn't do that. The week was just getting started, and they were trying to keep their families from fighting. There wasn't time to think about them romancing each other.

Ryan swallowed hard. And he was *not* thinking about that. Even though she was single and available, apparently. That didn't mean she'd want anything to do with him in that way. And what about their parents? His mom would blow a gasket.

"Hmm?"

His shoulders sagged. "It's just been good seeing you again, that's all." He wanted to say more, but then he stopped himself from blubbering needlessly. "Even under the circumstances."

"Yeah. I know what you mean." She held his gaze, and for an instant he couldn't think straight. Process anything beyond her presence and those really dark eyelashes that matched her arched eyebrows. He was caught up in her scent: the fragrance of her soap and her shampoo. The daring look in her eyes. His pulse thrummed in his ears. Then her smile blew him away.

"There you are!" his mom called.

Evita stepped back, the spell broken, as his mom came up the steps from the beach. She toted a beach chair with her. Maddy held her canvas bag and her beach chair, looking very grumpy about being found.

"Mom." He nodded. "Mads." He shoved his hands into the pockets of his swim trunks, acting like nothing had been going on. Like he hadn't totally lost his head to the Machados' only daughter. Thinking of her in a way that he shouldn't have. A way that made him wonder what it would be like to hold her in his arms. Maybe even kiss her like he'd dreamed about doing once or twice in high school. Okay, more than once or twice. Lots.

"Where's your father?"

"He went inside to shower."

She glanced at Maddy. "You should go and grab yours in the hall bath upstairs."

"Uh," Evita intervened. "I believe Quique's in there."

Mrs. Hatfield sighed. "I suppose there's this shower here." She latched on to its handle.

"Wait!" Ryan called, but not in time to stop her from yanking the shower door open.

Chachi and Kendra were inside it, engaged in an amorous embrace, their slick bathing-suited bodies molded together. They bolted apart at the fresh blast of air from the outside, blinking at the intrusion.

The color drained from Ryan's mom's face, and Maddy pursed her lips.

"Ever hear the word knock?" Chachi asked, tugging at the waistband of his swim trunks.

"Ever hear the word decency?" His mom scoffed. "What in the world are you two doing in our shower?"

Kendra winced, and Chachi slid up the strap of her bikini top, which had slipped just a little. "Sorry." Ryan didn't know Kendra had this mischievous side. Chachi either. Though he suspected it more of Evita's middle brother. "All the others were occupied."

"Well, you're not supposed to be in this one." She placed her hand on Maddy's back and shoved. "This shower is for my family."

Maddy dug in her heels and leaned back. "Ew, Mom. No!"

"Don't mind us!" Chachi scooted out of the shower, grabbing Kendra's hand. "We were *just* leaving."

Ryan's mom blocked their escape. "What were you doing in our shower anyway? What's wrong with the one in your suite?"

"My mom's helping bathe Nanny," Chachi said.

Mrs. Hatfield huffed. "And you couldn't wait?"

Kendra flushed, standing closer to Chachi. "Wait for what?"

"To"—she waved her hands around in the air—"you know."

Kendra gasped and Chachi stood upright. "We were not 'you know,'" he said, his dark eyes glinting.

Kendra scoffed. "We were just kissing!"

"Right!" Chachi moved around Mrs. Hatfield, pulling Kendra along. "Grabbing some couple time."

Mrs. Hatfield stared at them, incredulous. "Why out here?" She covered Maddy's eyes, then her ears with her hands, but Maddy had already seen and heard everything. "You have a whole suite to yourselves, for goodness sakes!"

The couple gaped up at her like they'd encountered Godzilla, and Evita's mom stepped onto the deck. "What's going on, people? I thought I heard shouting." Quique and Nanny were behind her, dressed in their pajamas. The sun was already going down.

Ryan's mom spun on her. "What's going on here is that these two *love birds*..." She framed the words in quotation marks with her fingers, nodding at Chachi and Kendra, "couldn't keep their hands off of each other in *our* shower."

Chachi and Kendra slunk past the moms, creeping indoors. Maddy followed them.

"Right," Ryan said. "We should all go back in the house."

His mom raised her hand. "Not until we discuss this."

"What?" Evita's mom asked.

Ryan's mom jutted her chin at the shower. "This violation."

"Oh please, Daneen."

"They were in there making out!"

"And so? They're married."

"What's that supposed to mean?"

Ryan lightly touched her arm. "Mom."

Evita stepped toward her mom. "Maybe we should forget about this?"

"I wasn't making the big deal. Daneen was."

"Because you can't seem to keep your hormonal family under control."

"Hormonal?" She broke out of Evita's grasp like she was ready to take a swing at Ryan's mom. Evita grabbed her. "Spoken like a woman having a hot flash."

"Hot?" Ryan's mom turned beet red. "Unbelievable." She cast a look at her son and then at Evita. "You two," she instructed dogmatically. "Stay away from each other."

"I'm sure they will," Evita's mom said.

Evita looked like she wanted to sink through the floorboards, and Ryan's face steamed.

Evita tugged on her mom's arm. "Come on. Let's go." Before they left, Mrs. Machado sniped, "Maybe if Daneen spent more time in the shower with Kirk, she wouldn't be so cranky."

"I heard that, Lissette!"

Evita's mom shut the door.

Ryan was glad to be sitting down to dinner with his parents because that meant this day was almost over. If only he and Evita could find a way to prevent the near-constant bickering between their moms, this week would go so much more smoothly. But it was hard to see how they could make that happen. He glanced out the kitchen window at the Machado family. They'd gathered around the firepit—on their side—and were all drinking piña coladas. Laughing and joking with one another while Nanny and Quique sat on beach towels playing handheld games.

"Thanks for cooking dinner, Mom." He chewed on his chicken, finding it tough and difficult to swallow. He reached for his water glass, but it was empty.

"Here," she said. "Let me refill that." She frowned. "The chicken might be slightly overcooked." She pressed his glass into the ice dispenser in the freezer door and it made a whirring sound. No ice came out. She tried again and got the same result.

She groaned.

"What's going on?" his dad asked her.

His mom stared sourly toward the deck. "I think Pablo used all the ice for those drinks of his."

"I'm okay with just water," Ryan told her.

Meanwhile, Maddy stabbed at her chicken breast with her knife and fork. She couldn't seem to get leverage, so she flipped it upside down. Then back the other way. She finally gave up, pouting at her brussels sprouts.

"Want me to cut that for you?" Ryan asked.

"No thanks. I'm not hungry." Although she had totally demolished her dinner roll.

Something delicious simmered on the stove in two covered skillets. The scheduled kitchen division gave the Machados time in the kitchen in the late afternoon. So if they wanted to start something for their dinner then, they could. They'd only used two burners, sticking to the half a house rule.

His mom returned to the island and Ryan's dad held up his fork. "Wonder what she's cooking in there?"

His mom shrugged. "I think it's chicken too."

His dad stared at the morsel on his fork then set it down. "Smells really tasty, doesn't it?" he asked his kids.

Maddy's stomach rumbled. "Yeah. Like a restaurant."

Ryan couldn't resist a peek. He hopped off his stool and raised the lid on one of the frying pans.

"Ryan!" his mom chided. "What are you doing?"

"It is chicken—with rice and olives. Oh. And sausage. No. Chorizo." Savory scents wafted into the room, including hints of saffron and smoked paprika.

His dad lifted his nose in the air, catching a whiff of the tantalizing aromas.

Ryan peered in the other saucepan at the caramelized dish. "And plantains." They looked sticky and sweet, and super delicious.

His mouth watered and he replaced the lid. Oh no. Evita was looking inside from out on the deck, and she'd seen him.

He returned to his place and stared down at his food, which somehow didn't look quite as appetizing as those Puerto Rican concoctions. He made an effort eating anyway. He'd burned tons of adrenaline today trying to keep his folks in check. He was famished.

"I'm not so happy with this house division," his mom said. "The Machados seem to be taking it over." Eunice had forgotten her diaper bag in the kitchen, and Nanny had left a stuffed toy in a Hatfield-side armchair. A large beach towel fluttered from the railing beyond their picnic table, hanging out to dry. It was red, white, and blue, sporting the design of the Puerto Rican flag. Red and white stripes with a large blue triangle and a single white star in the center of that.

"It's not that bad, Daneen," his dad said. He motioned with his knife toward the deck. "They appear to be staying on their side for the moment." He stuck his knife into his chicken and sawed. And sawed. Back and forth several times. At last, he achieved a bite.

Ryan's mom's face fell. "I'm sorry it's not as delicious as," she glanced at the stovetop, "all that." She didn't often admit defeat, and her downcast expression moved Ryan. Was she imperfect? Yes. Judgy? Often. Did she sometimes make mistakes? You betcha. But she honestly loved her family deep down underneath.

She'd been a good mom to him and Maddy in many ways. Made their lunches when they were little, volunteered with the PTA. Showed up for school events. Ryan's dad did too. She just wasn't the warm fuzzy type, but she probably couldn't help how she was made.

"No, Mom. It's really good."

"Very tasty," his dad said. He chewed thoughtfully. And hard. "It just might need a little something."

"I know." Maddy shot to her feet. "Ranch dressing!"

"Good thinking," Ryan said as she retrieved a bottle from their shelf in the refrigerator door. It actually helped a lot. Ryan served himself a liberal portion and so did his dad and Maddy. After a pause, his mom did the same.

"I really wanted this week to be special," she said with a discouraged look. "Good for all of us. You know? I'm sorry it's been such a bust."

"It hasn't been a bust," Ryan's dad said.

"Right," Ryan added. "We've only just arrived."

"Tell you what," his dad said. "Tomorrow is another day. How about we get up and start fresh?"

She patted his cheek. "Thank you, Kirk."

His forehead rose. "For what?"

She shared a wan smile. "For putting up with me."

He nodded like he was glad to. Okay, if not glad, at least that he understood his obligation, as well as his vows. Ryan couldn't envision those two at the altar. He'd seen the wedding photos of course, but it had been like staring at a different couple. His dad had worn a full beard back then, and his mom had had longer hair.

"Speaking of starting fresh," Ryan said, seizing the opportunity. "Maybe we can all do better with the Machados tomorrow too?"

His mom set down her fork. "What do you mean?" Her innocent gaze didn't fool him.

"I think you know, Mom. As long as we're here together, we should strive to get along. Otherwise it's going to be rough week."

"I didn't start that thing with the umbrella," she said. "Lissette did."

Ryan's dad turned to her. "Maybe we should have offered them ours when we saw they were having trouble?"

"Kirk! Really. You were out there tugging too."

He frowned. "You don't have to remind me." He glanced at

Ryan. "Maybe he's right, Daneen. Maybe we should try harder with the Machados. After all, we're all stuck here together."

"We don't have to start doing things with them, do we?" his mom asked, aghast. She fiddled with her necklace, brushing her fingertips across its pearls. "After all, this was supposed to be our family vacation."

Kirk leaned toward her and whispered. "No, but being cordial would work."

Ryan shared what he hoped was a placating smile. "It would be so great if we could all at least try."

His mom sat up straighter on her stool and tsked. "I'll do my best." She patted her pearls. "But it's not all up to me—or us."

His dad hung his head, his face ruddy. "I'll try harder too."

They all stared at Maddy, waiting on her to agree.

"What?" she complained with an exasperated look. "I haven't done one thing wrong." Her shoulders sank when Ryan's eyebrows arched. If she could just do this one little thing, it would mean so much. "Okay. Fine," she said on a sigh. "I'll *behave*." She said it in an exaggerated way like they'd requested the moon.

His dad wiped his mouth with his napkin, changing the subject. "So, Ryan, tell us about you. How's work going?"

"Oh. Um. Great. It's been going really great."

"Still at the community college then?"

"Yep."

"Made associate professor?"

"Not yet."

His mom popped a brussels sprout in her mouth and pulled a face. "I hear there's an opening for an associate professor at

Wellesley," she said, continuing to chew behind the back of her hand.

He'd seen the posting and had taken a cursory glance, knowing how much his mom would love for him to apply there, but Wellesley wasn't his style. Still, he'd bookmarked the listing in spite of himself. Just in case he changed his mind. Which he wouldn't. Absolutely wouldn't. He loved his job at Smithburg. "Yeah. Well. Thanks, Mom. But"—he took a sip of water—"I'm not so interested in that." He forced a pleasant smile, and she angled toward him.

"I heard that Clarice Sutton's daughter is back in town. You remember Jocelyn? She's turned into a beauty. Got her MBA from Wharton," she said, like that was the greatest thing on earth. She tittered. "I always knew that girl was brainy." She lowered her voice in an excited fashion. "And now—she's *single*." She actually squealed on that last word. "Recently divorced. Her mom and I were talking and, you know, Lexington's not that far away from—"

Ryan pursed his lips. "Not so interested in that either," he said as lightly as he could. He recalled his former neighbor as being nice enough. But she'd never been "the girl next door" for him.

"Ryan," his mom said seriously. "A nice-looking, eligible man like you should be seeing someone."

"How do you know he's not?" his dad asked her.

Ryan's gaze flitted briefly outdoors where Evita chatted with her family. She threw back her head and laughed in a wholehearted way, and her short curls bounced. Whoa, she was a mesmerizing woman. So in charge of herself. So free but at the same time tough.

"Are you?" His mom followed his gaze out the window and frowned. "Seeing someone?"

"No, Mom." He shook his head. "Not anyone seriously. And I'm good, really good for now." He turned his attention on his little sister, so past ready to stop being the center of these inquiries.

"How about you, Mads?" he asked, turning to her. "Have fun wrapping up your sophomore year?"

She shrugged. "I wouldn't exactly say fun."

His mom sat up straighter. "Maddy placed first chair in the orchestra."

"First? Sweet." Ryan met Maddy's eyes, but she looked away.

"It wasn't hard."

"Not for you maybe," his mom said in proud tones. "But for most people, yes." She addressed Ryan. "Your dad and I believe she's a shoo-in for Julliard."

Ryan whistled. "Nice, Mads. Good for you."

She stood suddenly and picked up her plate. "Can I go upstairs to my room?"

"What? Now?" her mom asked, crestfallen. "But, sweetie. I thought we might play a family game after dinner. Maybe a hand or two of bridge?"

Ryan was sure that was music to a teenager's ears.

Maddy scraped her plate and put it in the dishwasher. "Maybe tomorrow? Okay?"

His mom frowned and glanced at Ryan.

"I can play." What else did he have to do?

"Yes. Well. It's harder without a fourth."

"We can play a dummy hand," his dad suggested.

"Or," Ryan said, "we can just chill and read?"

His dad nodded. "That sounds good."

"To me too," his mom said. "A nice, quiet evening."

A loud burst of laughter erupted from outdoors. Someone had obviously told a joke. Or several of them. Ryan looked up to see Evita watching him again. Warmth buzzed through him. It wasn't just those dimples. It was her.

He and his folks left the kitchen as Evita's family filed indoors.

"Everyone wash up!" her mom said. "Dinner's nearly ready."

Mr. Machado placed his arm around her shoulders, appearing really happy from his piña coladas. "Want help setting the table?"

"Yes, *mi amor*." She sweetly kissed his cheek.

"*Hijos*," he commanded. "Set the table for your mother!"

She nudged him when the others got busy. "And what will you do?"

His eyes twinkled at her, his affection clear. "Help you serve the plates."

Their relationship was very different from the one Ryan's parents shared. More open and expressive. Though his folks loved each other too, they exhibited it in very different ways, by basically not exhibiting it much at all. But that was okay. Every couple was different.

Ryan nabbed an armchair, nearly colliding with Evita as she breezed through the room with two glasses of water. "Oops! Sorry!" Her cheeks held a faint blush.

"No. I—stepped right out in front of you."

"No harm done." He wasn't sure about that. Just being close to her felt risky. Because the closer he got, the closer he wanted to be.

She leaned toward him and whispered, "I saw you peeking at our dinner."

He whispered back, "It looks really good."

"Evita!" her mom called. "The water!"

She bit her lip. "Ah, yeah. I'd better go."

"Your side's over there, dear," Ryan's mom said, looking up from her book. Ryan frowned. "What?" she replied quietly. "I said it nicely."

"Yes. I know." Evita answered. "But I have to walk through here from the kitchen." She strode away sassily swishing her hips, and Ryan held back a chuckle.

"Oh! Well." His mom blinked, then stuck her nose back in her book. Evita sure was something. She didn't let people get to her much. Not even his mom. All of his previous girlfriends had been terrified of her. Evita wasn't though. No. Not even close.

His folks sat on the sofa, ignoring the well-oiled machine that was the Machado family. But Ryan caught glimpses of the action above his e-reader. All of them worked together so seamlessly, even the children. Nanny and Quique had jobs putting napkins and salt and pepper shakers on the table. Robby had Luisa strapped to his chest in a snuggly, so he helped out too. The infant's eyes were alert as she followed the movements of the group.

Evita's dad arrived with a fresh bottle of wine and filled glasses.

"Okay!" Evita's mom announced. "It's time."

Their meal was peppered with laughter and easy conversation. Forks scraping plates clean and hearty compliments.

"Wonderful, Lissette! Delicious!"

"Thanks, Mom! Really good."

"Tita's *plátanos* are the best!" Quique proclaimed.

The adults all agreed.

It was such a congenial group, but he was on the outside looking in. A foreigner getting a glimpse of a strange land. It was the sort of place he longed to visit. Welcoming and warm. Evita caught him watching her, and her cheeks glowed in the candle-light. That was the other thing about her family. They'd packed travel candles to use at dinner. For them, it was an important daily occasion that merited honoring.

His mom staged a yawn, standing. "I think I'll turn in and read in bed." Her pinched expression said she wasn't as much sleepy as she was tired of gazing at the Machados' overt display of camaraderie. Ryan didn't think that she was jealous. More like overwhelmed by a situation that was tough for her to compre-hend. From what Ryan remembered of his mom's parents, they would have considered all that excess wine and laughter frivolous. Ryan wasn't even sure if he'd ever seen his grandpa smile.

His dad cast a sidelong glance at the dining table and got to his feet as well. "Good idea," he said to his wife. "I'm coming too." Apparently, watching the Machados enjoy their evening meal was too much for the two of them to take.

Ryan felt suddenly awkward about sticking around here himself. Seeing Evita and her family together made him feel good about the comfortable relationships they shared. In another way, their expressive warmth made him feel a little lonely too.

He glanced through the window, seeing it was a nice night out and that the moon was full. Maybe he'd get out for a bit and gather his thoughts.

"I think I'll take a walk," he told his folks before they left.

SEVEN

EVITA SAW RYAN SLIP OUT the door when his parents retreated to their bedroom. He'd been sneaking glances at her all night long, but she'd caught on. She was very good at knowing when she had a man's attention, and she had Ryan's. Maybe it wasn't romantic interest. They were comrades in arms, trying to keep the peace between their families. He'd more than likely been thinking about that. Still. When his gaze had roved over her on the deck this afternoon, she'd felt all tingly inside. Like he was evaluating her as a woman and not just a friend.

She helped her folks clean up, and Robby and Eunice took the baby upstairs. Chachi and Kendra disappeared with their kids too, going to tuck them into bed. Nanny and Quique had spent a long day on the beach. They'd probably fall asleep the moment their little heads hit their pillows. No time for fighting with each other or Nanny kicking the underside of Quique's upper bunk like she'd done last night.

Evita had heard all about that while building sandcastles with the kids and had mildly scolded Nanny, telling her that wasn't very nice. The two of them should get along for their family's sake. She wished she could give the same speech to her mom about getting along with Mrs. Hatfield. She'd tried to diplomatically suggest to her parents about everyone being gentler with each other while they were having piña coladas and in a great mood. She hoped she'd made an impression, but she honestly wasn't sure.

"Evita," her mom said, as she walked toward the French doors. "Where are you going?"

"To get some air."

Her mom must not have seen Ryan leave earlier or she might have protested. "Well maybe take a jacket. It's gotten chilly out."

Evita nodded and grabbed her windbreaker from the back of a chair, then she stepped out into the breezy night. She strode to the edge of the deck, watching the ocean curl over itself in the moonlight, one huge wave after the next crashing against the shore.

Then she saw him sitting on a bottom step. Her heart pitter-pattered as she approached him. She hadn't stopped thinking about him all day. Was it too much to hope he'd been thinking about her? He sensed her presence and turned around. "Oh hey." His smile washed over her like a warm ocean wave, and her face heated.

She self-consciously tucked a curly lock behind her ear. "I thought you went for a walk?" she said, easing down the stairs while holding on to the railing.

He shrugged. "I did. But then I came back here. It was too pretty to go inside."

Evita sighed at the gorgeous view, purposely tugging her gaze off his. When he looked at her like that, it was hard to keep her bearings. "Yeah. I see what you mean." She sat down on a step beside him, and his eyebrows arched.

"Does your mom know you're out here?" His tone was light and flirty. He leaned toward her, and their shoulders brushed. Tiny tingles tore through her.

She laughed to conceal her blush. "Yeah, but not with you."

"Maybe we should keep this our little secret?" His soft growl caused warmth to pool in her belly. His face was so close and handsome in the shadows, and all those earlier dreams she'd had of kissing him came rushing back. Evita bit her lip, but that didn't still her hammering heart.

"We should definitely keep it a secret."

He dipped his chin closer, a spark of mischief in his eyes. "Our moms would have our heads."

She sighed, hating to admit the truth. "That would be one way to ruin this vacation."

"Right," he quipped dryly. "Like it's not toast already?"

Evita gaped at him. "It is *not* toast."

His forehead wrinkled. "No? Then what?"

She beamed self-assuredly. "It's a biscuit."

He laughed out loud. "A biscuit?"

"Yeah, you know, the kind that parts in the middle? Divides in two halves?"

He laughed harder. "Let me guess. The Machado half and the Hatfields'?"

She nodded, so happy he got it. Then again, he'd always understood her. "Yes."

He play-frowned, then issued a challenge. "So, what kind of jelly does yours have?"

"What?"

"On your Machado side of the biscuit?"

"Has to be mango. Or wait! Maybe guava?" She turned to him, her eyebrows arched. "How about your side?"

He tapped his chin. "Hmm. I'd have to say orange marmalade."

"What?" She gasped. "But that's so bitter!"

He smirked. "Don't knock it until you try it."

"Same with you and guava."

"I happen to like guava." His mouth tipped up in a grin. "Very much."

When he said it like that, it sounded like he was talking about her, and she was glad. "I'm not opposed to a little marmalade," she lied, because she was. Made with orange peels and everything? Yuck. But Ryan wasn't yuck. He was genuine and funny, and yeah, okay. Maybe a bit yummy in the moonlight, with that shaggy golden hair of his and his swoony dark eyes. "Oh Ryan." She sighed heavily, settling into the moment and his company. "I've missed this."

"I've missed you," he admitted, his voice husky. She ducked her chin when her face burned hot. She'd missed him too. So much more than she knew. It was so easy being around him. Effortless, really.

He stared out at the ocean, evidently searching for something to say. He was an intuitive guy and got that he'd embarrassed her. The tawny patches on his cheeks said he'd also embarrassed himself by admitting his feelings. As good friends as they'd been, there was something slightly awkward in reconnecting, especially given the way they'd drifted apart senior year. They never had a big falling out or anything but, once he'd begun dating Layla, keeping her distance had been easier on her heart.

"Did you know it's three thousand miles to Portugal from here?" he said, scanning the waves. The darkened sea seemed to stretch on forever, endlessly out into oblivion.

"Yeah. That's very cool." She noticed he'd scooted a little closer. Or maybe she'd moved nearer to him. When their shoulders made contact this time, it felt fitting and right. She leaned into him, and he did the same, the heat of their bodies mingling in the moonlight. Though they'd shared snatches of conversation here and there since their arrival, that had been in broad daylight or around the others. Somehow being out here all alone under the stars felt a lot more intimate.

"Almost makes you wonder if there's someone over there staring out at the sea and looking this way."

She blew out a breath. "I hope none of them are in the situation we're in."

"I know, right?" He rubbed his neck. "How crazy is this? Our two families winding up at the same beach cottage in Nantucket."

"Maybe it's fate," she teased.

"Or Karma."

"What do you mean?"

He shrugged. "I'm talking about our moms. Maybe the universe has brought them back around. Landed them here together so they can finally settle things."

Evita sighed. "I wish."

"Yeah. I wish too." He set his elbows on his knees and leaned forward, staring out over the ocean. "That's a long time to hang on to feelings. Since high school." She knew he was talking about their moms, but still her heart pounded. Because part of her had hung on to certain feelings too. Although she hadn't known it until she'd seen him again.

"I'm not even sure what happened to make things so bad between them," she said. "I know about the election, but not why they both wound up so angry about it."

"Yeah, I know about that vaguely too," he said, "but not really any of the specifics. Just that my mom had really wanted to win and that her dad had put extreme pressure on her about it. He was like that, my grandpa. Stiff upper lip and high expectations."

"Oh no."

"Yeah. I wouldn't be surprised if..." His voice trailed off as he turned away.

"Ryan? What is it?"

"Not sure. It's just a feeling I have. I think the way my mom is now might have something to do with that. The way she was raised by my grandparents. She was their only kid, so they pinned all their hopes on her. I'm guessing they didn't cut her much slack."

Which was why Evita supposed Ryan had decided he should. He was mature enough to guess she had her reasons for being who she was, and he allowed her grace for that. Evita's heart swelled with admiration at his forgiveness and understanding.

"My mom's no saint either," she admitted honestly. "But she's been a really good mom to me and my brothers in her own way." Evita's shoulders sank. "It's so hard to believe our two moms are still at odds with each other after so much time."

"Even though they shouldn't be," he told her. "They're both doing so great with their jobs. And well"—He swallowed hard—"with pretty much lots of things."

Evita pursed her lips. "I guess I didn't understand the full level of tension between them until seeing them together here. Whatever happened in high school must have been bigger than we know."

"At least *our* high school days weren't full of drama. Huh?"

"Speak for yourself." Her tone was coy, but she didn't care. It felt good talking with Ryan again. Fun.

He perused her, and her pulse fluttered. "You weren't a drama queen."

"Not me, silly. Others."

"Oh yeah?"

"Like say..." She rolled her eyes. "Layla Petroski." She drew out the words.

"Case in point."

"She was homecoming queen too." Plus, amazingly beautiful and blond, although nobody was entirely sure if that was her natural hair color.

"Yeah. Hard to forget that." He shook his head. "She loved that tiara of hers."

"Whatever happened to her?" Evita asked, the tiniest bit curious. And. Okay. Megawatt jealous. Once Ryan had started dating Layla, there was obviously no chance for her. Not that it could have happened anyway. Her stomach tightened when she remembered how incredible Layla and Ryan had looked together. A golden couple of sorts in high school.

"She moved to LA. Got a bit part in something."

"That's impressive."

"I suppose." He shrugged. "We didn't keep up after high school. We were on different paths."

"You were both very similar though," she joked. "Teachers' pets."

"The teachers liked you."

She shrugged. "Maybe so, but not as much as Layla, because I mouthed off to them."

He didn't disagree. "Only when they deserved it."

Evita sighed at the memories. "Oh gosh. We had so much fun together in chem class."

"We had more fun out of it." He got a playful gleam in his eyes.

She ducked her chin. "Yeah."

"What were we thinking? Sneaking off campus for coffee? We could have gotten suspended. You know that?"

"Wasn't that the fun of it?" she asked with a sassy edge.

"No. The fun of it was in not getting caught."

"Ha ha! Our parents would have freaked."

"No joke. I guess we were lucky." Evita couldn't help but feel lucky now, having the chance to see him again after so many years. The ocean roared, and a rough wind combed through her hair. Then the evening seemed to settle with gentle breezes rippling across the sea. It was nice out here with Ryan. Like old times.

His shoulder brushed hers. "Remember that time we skipped class to hang out at the football stadium?"

"We weren't just hanging," she contested. "We were cramming for our chemistry exam."

"Yeah, but we missed drama class to do it."

Evita smirked. "I told you my high school days were low drama."

Ryan held up a hand. "Not true! You were in that one play."

"I was a stagehand, Ryan."

"Still counts."

"It was a requirement of the class."

He laid a hand on his heart. "But, soft! What light through yonder window breaks? It is the east, and Juliet is the sun."

Evita shut her eyes, taken back. He'd been the very best Romeo. But Layla of course had been his Juliet.

Ryan caught up with Evita backstage. She'd been arranging props, which at the moment meant moving lots of stuff around, including fake daggers and empty vials of supposed poison. He lightly touched her arm. "Hey, how are ya?"

"Um, me? Pretty good." They spoke in hushed whispers while the action continued on stage.

"Dress rehearsal's going well, don't you think?"

"Mm-hmm. You and Layla are doing great."

Ryan rubbed the side of his neck. "Evita? Is something wrong?"

But how could she tell him she was falling when Layla kept inching her way closer? "No. I'm good," she lied. "How about you?"

He shifted on his feet, looking swarthy in his balloon britches, ruffled shirt, and cap. "Yeah. Me too."

She pasted on a brave smile. "Keeping breaking a leg," she said, unable to let him know he was also breaking her heart. And, when she watched him kiss Layla on stage from behind the curtain, her heart cleaved in two, because what was supposed to be a fake kiss looked so real.

Ryan gently stroked her cheek with the back of his hand, his touch silky smooth. Surf crashed against the shore, and waves combed the darkened beach. "Where were you just now?"

Her voice trembled. "Thinking." She was aware of him sitting beside her. So close.

"About 'Romeo and Juliet'?"

"Yeah."

"Huh." He stared back at the ocean. "Some play."

"You and Layla were a hit."

"It wasn't Layla that I cared about." Her face heated when turned to her. "I liked you a lot back then, you know." His husky confession stunned her. "I mean, *a lot, a lot.*"

Wait. Was he saying what she thought he was? He couldn't mean that he'd actually crushed on her too? She caught her breath, hoping the answer was yes. "But you and Layla dated?"

He smiled softly. "Yeah but Layla came after."

"After what?"

He looked at her so intensely it was like gazing into the sun, and oh how she welcomed that warmth. He cupped her cheek with his hand, and her skin tingled at his touch. "After I realized I didn't stand chance with you." The words landed like weighty raindrops, nourishing her parched soul. All that time spent waiting—hoping. "Evita." He searched her eyes. "You had to have known."

"I didn't know," she whispered. "Honestly."

Ryan leaned closer, his spicy scent washing over her. "And if you had?"

She licked her lips. "Then I guess things might have gone differently."

"Because?" he asked, fishing. But the twinkle in his eyes said he suspected he knew.

"Yeah, Ryan," she said, as a blush consumed her. "I liked you too." She practically whimpered. "*A lot, a lot.*" She thought he was about to kiss her—and she wanted that too. But then he pulled back.

"Man." He raked a hand through his hair. "If only I'd known that."

"Then what?" she challenged lightly.

"You're right," he said. "The two of us were stuck."

She leaned against him, laying her head on his shoulder. "It was hopeless, wasn't it?"

"Yeah," he said hoarsely. "Our parents would never have let us date. In fact, your mom forbade it."

Happiness bubbled up inside her. "I can't believe you remember 'forbade.'" She stole a peek at him, and he bent down to look at her.

"I remember everything, Evita."

"You know what?" she said. "So do I."

He settled his arm around her shoulders, and they surveyed the tumbling ocean. Evita snuggled closer, enjoying this moment. Loving how together they seemed. What if they'd found a way to be together back then—just like Romeo and Juliet? Evita's heart sighed, but then it clenched up. No. Bad analogy. That ended tragically.

"I wanted to ask you to the prom, you know. Junior year."

Her heart skipped a beat. She was so flattered and pleased. "Seriously?"

He lowered his eyebrows in a mock-stern expression. "Seriously."

"But what about Layla? You wound up taking her."

"That's only because." He hung his head at the admission. "Our parents were so against it."

"It would have been hard to fight them on that."

"Trust me," he said. "I tried." He glanced back toward the house. "I even brought it up to my mom."

Her eyes widened in shock. "You didn't."

"I did." Ryan's shoulders sank. "You can imagine how that went."

"Yeah. Not good." She sagged against him. "My mom never would have let me go anyway." She paused and then said, "Maybe we're certifiable for believing our two families can share this beach house."

He grimaced. "Seems to be working out so far."

"Yeah, right." She lightly shoved his arm, and he clasped his hand over hers. Her pulse thrummed as she fell into his eyes.

"Evita—?"

"There you are!" It was Chachi at the top of the steps.

Ryan released his grasp and she dropped her hand.

Chachi studied them curiously. "I think Mom's looking for you," he said.

Evita got to her feet. "Right. I'd better go."

Ryan stood. "Yeah. Me too."

"Maybe you should wait and come in later?" Chachi suggested to Ryan. "A few minutes after my sister?" His eyebrows knitted together in a playful fashion. "We can't have my parents thinking she's been fraternizing with the enemy." Wait. Chachi was helping Ryan out now? But what about earlier in the house?

Ryan nodded. "Fair point." He winked at Chachi like he knew he'd won an ally.

Evita spoke to Chachi as they climbed the steps. "Thanks for looking out for me."

He nodded. "No problem."

"Ryan too." She sent Chachi a curious glance. "What changed your mind about him?"

"Changed?"

"Before, when we were dividing the rooms, you were dead set against him staying on the same side of the house as me."

Chachi rubbed his chin. "Moderating, Evita. Like I always do. Saying the right things to calm the situation. Don't think I don't remember. I was still in high school when you were friends with Ryan. I saw you two around, always so chummy together. Until that blond homecoming queen came along." Chachi stopped her by the firepit. "You still like him, don't you?" he asked with a knowing gleam.

"Yeah," she confessed, because it was pretty impossible to lie to Chachi. "A little."

He glanced back toward the steps. "Looks like feeling's mutual."

She shrugged. "Ryan's a nice guy."

Chachi thought on this. "You deserve nice. Nothing but the best for my baby sister." He frowned. "Mom said you don't want to talk about that scumbag Sebastian, but if you do—"

She didn't. She really didn't. Though she appreciated everyone's concern, she was just now wrapping her head around the fact that Sebastian wasn't nearly as "beloved" by her family as she'd supposed. "Thanks, Chachi," she said fondly. "I probably won't."

He grunted and crossed his arms. "Good riddance is all I say. You deserve someone better."

Her eyebrows arched. "And you think that someone's Ryan?"

"Come on, Evita. You can't fool your big brother. I can see it in your eyes. Something changes in you whenever you're around him. In spite of this very weird situation we're in, he seems to make you happier." His mouth twitched. "Plus, Eunice might have said something to Robby who said something to me about"—his voice took on a lilting tone—"fish in the sea."

Evita slapped her forehead, recalling her conversation with Eunice in the kitchen. "I supposed Kendra's in on this too?"

"Of course."

Family. They were all into each other's business. But maybe that was okay in this case. The fewer people at war with the Hatfields in her family, the better. Chachi opened the door for her, and she was glad he had her back. Chachi always had. It was good to know her brothers and their wives weren't opposed to her spending time with Ryan. But her parents? They were another story, especially her mom.

Kendra stood in the great room holding a remote. "Anyone up for a movie?"

Evita stared around the living area but didn't see a TV. Then Kendra nodded toward the loft. Amazing! That giant painting had somehow become an enormous television. It apparently paired with large speakers located on the bookshelves.

"How cool is that?" Chachi said, goggling at the screen.

"Very cool," Evita conceded.

Her folks were finishing something up in the kitchen. They returned, each carrying wine and dessert plates. "*Postre, niños?*" She lifted her plate. "I brought a *tres leches* cake."

Evita, Chachi, and Kendra were in the kitchen before she could ask twice.

Robby trailed Eunice down the stairs. They were baby-free for once and appeared relaxed and happy. "Did we hear dessert?" Robby asked.

Eunice shot a look at the screen. "And a movie?"

This was good, really good. Evita wanted her family around her.

That way she didn't have to think about her rapidly beating heart.

Ryan came through the door, and her heart pounded harder. Their moment in the moonlight had been so telling, almost magical. She'd had no clue he'd felt that way about her in high school. Even though they couldn't change the past, it was sweet to know that now.

Ryan looked around the room. When his gaze briefly flitted over her, his face went all tawny, like he was trying hard not to stare at her too long. "I'm just—on my way upstairs," he said. "I think I'll do some reading and head to bed. I guess I'll see you guys in the morning."

"Okay," Eunice said. "Good night!"

The rest of them followed her lead, offering up good nights and see you tomorrows.

Even her dad joined in with a gruff, "Night."

Her family was far from inhospitable, but they'd been put in a difficult position. She knew them, and they were trying their best. Hopefully tomorrow, the Hatfields would try their best too. In a different world, she might have asked Ryan to stay and watch the movie with them. Maybe even offered him a glass of wine and a slice of *tres leches* cake. Her mom wouldn't like that though. So, no. Not happening.

Her heart hammered at his earlier admission. He'd liked her, really liked her, when they were younger. He'd wanted to ask her to the prom. What if he had, and she'd gone? But no. She wouldn't have done that to her parents. It wouldn't have been worth it to make her mom so unhappy. Despite being an adult and a confident woman, she was still reluctant to disappoint her folks. They asked so little of her normally and had always showered her with love.

She took a seat on the sofa with her parents. "What shall we watch?"

With the Hatfields all having gone to bed, her family decided to spread out, everybody selecting a comfortable spot. "Anything but a rom-com," her dad teased.

"Hey," Robby said. "I'm writing one of those."

Everyone laughed, then Kendra said, "I'll bet it's excellent too."

"It is excellent." Eunice snuggled into the crook of Robby's arm on the other sofa, holding her dessert plate. "And this one's going to sell. I feel it."

"From your lips to God's ears—" he joked.

The rest of them chuckled warmly.

"I'm sure your wife is right." Evita's mom winked at Eunice. "She knows her film."

Eunice nodded and took a bite of cake. "Yes, I do. Mmm. Yummy."

Chachi held hands with Kendra. He'd pushed two of the armchairs together facing the screen. "Why don't we watch something actiony?"

"I heard you were getting some action in the outdoor shower today," Robby teased.

Chachi lobbed a pillow at him, and they all laughed again.

Kendra's color deepened. "It was not nearly as bad as Mrs. Hatfield made it out to be."

"I'm sure that it wasn't." Evita's mom rolled her eyes. "Daneen exaggerates things." She brightened, staring at the television screen and apparently getting an idea. "How about *A Walk in the Clouds*?"

"That's a good pick," Evita's dad said. The rest of them groaned.

Evita was sure her family had seen that movie two dozen times, but her parents never tired of it. "Maybe we can find something new?" Kendra held out the remote, and Robby reached for it, flipping through more options.

But after nearly an hour of viewing multiple trailers and arguing over choices, they settled for their old standby. It was either that or call it a night.

"I've always loved this movie." Their mom sighed, and Chachi chuckled.

"Yes, yes. We know."

Kendra watched the credits roll. "I've always loved Keanu Reeves."

Evita laughed, adoring her family. "Same."

———————

Ryan was glad to have some alone time to process his emotions and also be away from Evita's penetrating gaze. She had a way of seeing through him, all the way straight to his heart. He'd put his high school crush on her aside long ago but had found himself dwelling on it a lot lately. He liked the same things about her now as he did then. Her laugh. Her smile. Those amazing dimples. And the cute way she liked to banter with him. She'd never been afraid of authority and had sometimes even challenged their teachers when she'd believed them to be misinformed or wrong. The grip her parents had on her was different though.

Like he was one to talk. Twenty-eight years old—and PhD proud—and he still hadn't stood up to his folks. He was getting better at it though. Working his way up to a full-fledged—what? Not a confrontation, no. He wasn't a huge fan of those. It was more like a confident assertion. He burned to tell his parents to respect his choices about his job and his dating life too. His mom was more intrusive, but his dad's silence on many matters made him complicit.

He'd dated his share of women and found many of them intriguing, but none of them had clicked with him in a way that spelled commitment. He'd gotten a kick out of Evita rolling her eyes about Layla Petroski. Layla had been pretty high mainte-nance when he thought about it. And Jocelyn Sutton? No. Just no. He couldn't see it. Besides which, he wasn't about to have his girlfriends picked out for him by his mom. Even though she'd tried plenty.

He shut the pocket doors to his assigned space and pulled out the sofa bed. It wasn't the Ritz, but it was cozy enough. Just weird being on the other side of the room from Evita's brother and sister-in-law. Still, Chachi seemed all right. He'd helped them out by giving them that tip earlier about going into the house one at a time. Seeing as how the whole Machado clan was gathered inside, that had been good advice.

Ryan slid a few pillows behind him and switched on a nearby lamp. He selected the music app on his phone and popped in his earbuds, bringing up the scholarly journal he intended to read. He tried to get into the content, but his mind kept flitting back to thoughts of Evita in the moonlight, then earlier on the beach and on the deck after her shower. Before that, during that unexpected moment when he'd first stumbled across her at the cottage. She'd been so surprised to see him and he'd been stunned to see her. But once they'd begun working together, they'd become a unified team.

Just like they'd been in chem class when they'd aced all of their exams together. Ryan hadn't found chemistry particularly interesting, but he had been invested in Evita and impressing her. That's why he worked so hard to get one of the top grades in the class. She'd gotten the other one, and probably could have gone in a number of directions with her life. He supposed, he could have too. He stared down at his e-reader, realizing he'd perused the first page of his article five or six times. This was no good. It was too hard to concentrate on something this dry with thoughts of Evita bombarding his brain. There was a new suspense novel he'd heard about that had gotten raves. Maybe he'd download that to read instead.

But when he went online, one of his bookmarks stared him in the face. It was the one to the job application at Wellesley. While Evita had appreciated who he was as a guy back in high school, would she him value him more now as a man if he got a plum job like that? His mom would be ecstatic. Maybe so ecstatic she'd lay off about other things. Like his dating choices?

At the very least, she'd stop hassling him about his job, and maybe—for once in her life—would actually act proud of him. Pain seared through his chest because he wished he didn't care what his parents thought. He was his own man and free to make his own choices. Still, a little bit of acknowledgement would have been nice. He scanned through the position description, realizing he actually was qualified for this one. He wanted to buy that farmhouse, and this paid more money than his community college job ever could. But no. His applying to Wellesley might appease his mom, but he'd only be betraying himself.

Ryan closed the window on the job posting, going to his favorite online bookstore instead. He purchased the murder mystery he was after and downloaded it to his e-reader. The opening scene was intense, sucking him into the story. Then another clue unfolded and another, with an array of suspects lining up. When he paused to check the time, nearly three hours had gone by. He rubbed his neck and yawned. He should probably get some shut-eye. Who knew what tomorrow would bring?

Hopefully not more beach wars over bent umbrellas. When this week was finally over, maybe both families would look back on it and laugh. Or maybe not.

He removed his earbuds and grabbed his toothpaste, floss,

and toothbrush, tiptoeing to the door. Wait. He thought he heard something, but no. Chachi and Kendra were probably already in bed fast asleep. They'd said it was okay for him to pass through their part of the room after knocking, but he hated the idea of waking them. He knocked very softly but didn't hear anything, so he slid the door open a smidge.

Bed springs squeaked and the headboard thudded against the wall.

He quickly shut the door. Oh boy.

The noises stopped. "Chachi?" Kendra whispered hoarsely. "Did you hear something?"

"No, shh. Shh! Ryan's sleeping."

He grimaced and scrambled for his earbuds, popping them back in. Then he cranked up his music, deciding to finish that novel.

EIGHT

WHEN EVITA WENT OUT ON the deck the next morning, the Hatfields were already there having breakfast at their picnic table. "What a beautiful day," she heard Mrs. Hatfield say. "So peaceful out here."

Ryan rubbed his eyes, looking sleepy. He had to have slept better than she had, between the baby crying half the night and Robby's snoring the other.

Evita sent him a tired smile over the rim of her coffee mug, and he smiled back. Somehow the two of them would fix this. Their families couldn't stay at odds all week. That would take too much emotional energy.

Evita sat in a chair near the firepit, staring up at the brilliant blue sky. Puffy white clouds dotted the horizon and gulls soared through the air. Down at the beach, sea terns swooped into the waves and sandpipers hopped along the shore, plunging their beaks into the wet sand. Her loose peasant top fluttered in the breeze, and sunlight warmed her face. She'd change out of her shorts and into her swimsuit in a bit, but for now this felt great.

Her dad exited the house carrying the large portable speaker that had sat on a charger in the kitchen. It was connected to some kind of high-tech sound system with voice recognition software built in and accessed all sorts of music streaming services through an app he'd downloaded to his phone. Several other speakers in the house could be paired with it, or it could be used alone.

He was prepared for a day on the beach in swim trunks, a tropical shirt, hat, and sunglasses, but he set his music player beside a lounge chair on the deck like he was setting up shop there. "Morning!" he said pleasantly all around.

Evita was extremely proud of him. Just look at how he graciously tipped his hat at the Hatfields. He held a chilled drink in his hand that looked like iced coffee.

"Good morning, Pablo," Mrs. Hatfield said stiffly. She cast her gaze over the short speaker tower with a suspicious gleam.

Mr. Hatfield nodded cordially, and Ryan's eyebrows shot up.

He had to be thinking what Evita was.

Progress. Yay! At least they were talking and not shouting at one another.

Her dad sat back in his chair and sighed. "Ah, beautiful." He inhaled the ocean breeze, then took a sip from his straw before giving a command.

"Delilah, play Latin Music Combo from Tuneify."

An electronic voice boomed, "Playing Latin Music Combo from Tuneify!"

Loud Latin music blared from the speaker, and the Hatfields jumped.

Maddy stared at her folks. "That's really great sound."

Evita's dad overheard her. "It's wonderful, yes? My cousin's in this band." Trumpets blared and maracas shook to the tempo kept by trilling guitars and pounding drums. Then the volume hiked up.

Music poured over the deck and washed out to sea, sailing up into the clouds.

Mrs. Hatfield's mouth fell open, and she lowered her sunglasses.

Evita's dad waved at her, not taking the hint. Or maybe he did and chose to play oblivious. He relaxed in his lounge chair and angled down his hat.

Evita had been enjoying the quiet too, but she didn't mind the more upbeat vibe, which was lively and fun. The Hatfields minded though. A lot.

Mrs. Hatfield nudged her husband, and he stood awkwardly.

He walked across the deck in his slacks and Tommy Bahama shirt.

Ryan shot Evita a wide-eyed gaze, and she nodded. This spelled trouble. They both knew it. The calm before the storm.

"Excuse me," Mr. Hatfield said to her dad. "Would you mind turning that off?"

Her dad placed a hand behind his ear like he couldn't hear him. "Sorry?"

Mr. Hatfield pointed to the speaker.

"Oh, sure, sure. Up?" Her dad feigned misunderstanding. "Of course." He tapped four times on a lighted icon on top of the tower, cranking the music louder. Evita massaged her temples. He was clearly doing this on purpose. Her dad. And just when she thought the two families were starting to find some common ground.

Mr. Hatfield play-plugged his ears. "Pablo, please! A little peace and quiet here?"

"Peace and quiet?" Her dad sat up in his seat and spoke above the music. "We're on vacation, Kirk."

"Exactly!"

"So this is relaxing."

Mr. Hatfield scowled. "Well, it's not relaxing to us. Please turn that *off*."

"Up?" her dad teased again. He started to crank the volume higher, but Mr. Hatfield commanded loudly. "Delilah! Music off!"

A hush fell over the deck. They could have heard a pin drop.

Evita's pulse raced. This was not good.

Evita's dad scowled and adjusted his sunglasses. "Delilah! Resume!"

Ryan got to his feet. Evita did too.

"Delilah off!" Mr. Hatfield shouted. Silence ensued. He frowned at Evita's dad. "A little consideration, Pablo? This beach house is not just occupied by you."

"Consideration?" her dad said. "How's this for consideration? This is my favorite kind of music. And news flash, Kirk! It's my vacation too." He snatched away the speaker when Mr. Hatfield grabbed for it, holding it out of reach. "Delilah. Music on!"

Mr. Hatfield huffed, his face tomato red. "Delilah. Off!"

Her dad hugged the machine to his chest and whispered. "Delilah. On."

"Argh!" Mr. Hatfield lunged at him, wrestling away the speaker.

"Dad, stop!" Ryan said. "You're going to break it!"

"Give that back!" Evita's dad said.

"No, Pablo! Aha!" Mr. Hatfield found the kill switch on rear of the tower and silenced the machine. He reluctantly returned it to Evita's dad. "Now. Let's be sensible about this and enjoy the sunshine—and the breeze."

Her dad's mustache twitched. He held the tower in front of him, positioning his finger above the on button on the back of the tower.

Evita stepped forward. "Dad! Please!"

"What, Evita?" he said like nothing had happened. "I'm just enjoying my music."

"Yeah, but maybe the Hatfields—"

"Don't get to say how I have fun." He stubbornly set his chin, and Evita sighed.

"*Por favor.*" She almost never spoke Spanish, and when she did, he claimed it melted his heart. Her eyebrows rose. "Just until they go down to the beach?"

He sighed, beholding his daughter. His eyes glimmered sadly. "As you wish." He set the speaker tower on the deck beside him. He sat back in his lounge chair and crossed his arms, like he was not fine at all. Then he grumbled, "Grouchy gringos."

"Dad," Evita cautioned. "Shh."

Mr. Hatfield returned to their picnic table, and Mrs. Hatfield let out an exaggerated sigh. "Well. Isn't this better?"

Evita's dad's hand settled on the back of the speaker tower, but Evita pushed it away.

Ryan's mom stretched out her arms, lacing her fingers together. "Nothing but the sound of the waves and the gulls. Absolute tranquility."

Luisa wailed upstairs, her staccato cries escaping from the ocean-facing doors above them. Robby and Eunice's room had its own small balcony like Chachi and Kendra's suite.

"I can't believe she's hungry again," Eunice said wearily. The child yelped louder. "What am I? A nonstop feeding machine?"

"You know I'd help if I could," Robby said.

"But you can't," Eunice answered tersely. "Remember?"

"That is so unfair. I didn't forget to pack it on purpose!"

"No? Maybe you wanted a break?"

"You're just tired and cranky."

"I am. Not! Tired! And cranky!"

The double doors upstairs slammed shut, while the rest of them tried to pretend they hadn't overheard the argument. Being new parents had to be rough. Extra rough. Especially when you traveled. Evita understood that Robby was worn thin from being a stay-at-home dad while trying to write and that Eunice had burnt herself out by dividing her time between the studio and her new family. Things would improve once they all got more sleep. Or Luisa got older. Whichever came first.

"Um." Ryan shifted on his feet. "How about we head down to the beach soon?" he suggested to his folks and Maddy. "I can set up the umbrella for everyone. Chairs too."

"That sounds lovely, Ryan," his mom said. "I'm ready for a change of scenery." She pulled a face as the baby cried and Eunice's and Robby's voices rose behind the closed doors. "Aren't you, Kirk?"

"I'll go change into my swim trunks." He glanced at Maddy.

She had a canvas bag with her. "Whatever," she said, not sounding thrilled about it.

Ryan frowned. "Right. I'll just grab our things from the storage closet."

He passed Evita when she was on her way into the house.

"Psst," he whispered, his back turned to the others. "Want to sneak out for coffee?"

She giggled at the twinkle in his light-brown eyes. Oh man, that sounded good. "What? Now?" Truth was she was very ready to get out of here and away from all the tension. But could they really get away without being noticed? Her pulse fluttered. It was definitely worth a try.

"Meet you around the front of the house in ten?"

"Okay."

———

Evita crouched low as she scurried toward the sandy plain where their vehicles were parked, but Ryan motioned her toward a freestanding shed. She blinked at him in surprise. "What's in there?"

He worked the padlock combination. "Bicycles."

"Awesome." It was such a pretty day, and she hadn't been on a bike in years. Plus it meant they'd be much quieter getting away than in a car.

They located two old-fashioned looking ones with high handlebars and baskets in front. The other two were little kids' bikes. One had training wheels. "These look like they've been here for ages," she said.

He studied the frames of both bikes. "But they're still in decent shape." He squeezed their front and back tires. "Hang on. Let me add some air." He located a bicycle pump in the shed, and Evita shielded herself from the cottage with the open shed door.

"What did you say to your folks?" she asked as he worked. She held in a giggle, feeling as sneaky as she had in high school, when they'd ventured off campus.

"I said I wanted to rest. Didn't get much sleep last night."

She started to laugh, then stopped herself. Maybe he was serious. Her forehead rose. "Didn't you?"

He gave an embarrassed flush. "No. It was…uh, noisy."

"Noisy?" She cupped a hand to her mouth, getting it. "Kendra and Chachi? Oh my gosh."

She blushed too. They were kind of carrying on like newlyweds this trip, although she had no idea why. Maybe it was the freedom of being away from their jobs and day-to-day pressures? Evita sucked in a breath. Or maybe they were always like this now. Including at home. Whatever she'd heard about couples becoming tired old married folks didn't seem to apply in her family. She grimaced at Ryan. "Ooh. Sorry."

"Not your fault," he said. "Or theirs. It's their vacation too, and they were in their own room. Sort of."

Evita rolled her eyes. "As opposed to the shower."

Ryan hooted. "My mom really lost it."

"I know!"

He shook his head. "How'd you sleep?"

"Er. Not too well." She shrugged. "Robby snores, and the baby…"

"Yeah," he said. "I'll bet." He rolled a bike out of the shed, handing it to her. A helmet was suspended from its handlebars.

"Ryan," she said, snapping on her helmet. "Last night, when Chachi interrupted us, what were you about to say?"

He smiled at her and rolled his bike out of the shed. "That maybe we should do something like this?" He shut the shed door, then put on his helmet too. "Go out for coffee."

"It was a good thought!"

They both mounted their bikes and started pedaling away. "What did you tell your parents?" he asked when they reached the end of the drive.

She leaned forward, gripping her handlebars. "Same as you. That I was tired and needed some downtime."

"Let's hope they don't figure out we're taking it together." He winked, and her heart fluttered happily. She liked that they were in on this together: their secret getaway. Even if it was just into a nearby town and for coffee, breaking away from their parents and the others seemed daring and fun. Just like in the old days.

"They won't," she said. "They'll all be preoccupied on the beach. Hopefully not with fighting each other."

"Yeah," he said. "At least they got the umbrella part worked out."

The front door of the cottage popped open, and Maddy walked onto the porch, looking for something. "We'd better get going," Ryan urged quietly.

Evita started pedaling faster when he pulled out ahead of her, going down the road. "Will Maddy tell?" she asked, catching up with him.

He pointed to a bike path up ahead, motioning her along. "This way!"

She pedaled alongside him. "Where are we going?"

"'Sconset Village," he informed her. "I found a great little coffee shop online."

"You're full of surprises, Ryan Hatfield."

His eyes sparkled in the sunlight, and she caught her breath. "Yeah, Evita Machado," he said. "So are you." His words tumbled over her like a sultry ocean breeze, and she was caught up in his spell. They passed others heading into and out of town, and everyone shared friendly greetings and smiles.

With the island being small, the village wasn't far away—a short bike ride. Evita was charmed by the old-fashioned streets and quaint rose-covered cottages that were so classic to Nantucket. The homes here looked old and were smaller than their lux rental, which had been built within the last twenty years, yet modeled to replicate the island standard on its outside. They took a few turns in town, then they pulled up to the café.

"This looks sweet."

"Different from the place we used to go in high school," he joked. "But hopefully the joe is good." The truth was, she didn't care if the coffee tasted like mud. She was just happy to be out having it with Ryan. This felt almost like a date. Sort of, but not really. Then, he stepped forward and held open the café door, letting her walk in ahead of him. That made her feel special, because he was considerate. That was so Ryan. Always putting others first.

They left their bikes outdoors and ordered coffees, grabbing a booth by the window.

Lots of shoppers strolled by. Tourists and locals dressed in hats and sunglasses, some wearing T-shirts with whales on them. "I'll have to get some of those for my family," Evita said.

"What? T-shirts?"

"Yeah," she told him. "It's a thing we do sometimes. Get matching shirts on vacation, then take a group pic of us all dressed alike."

"That sounds fun. I wonder if— No." He shook his head, thinking better of it. "My dad might? But it's hard to see my mom being into that."

They both sipped from their coffee, commenting that it was good.

"How do you and Maddy get along? When we were in high school, she was so small. Just in preschool or something."

"Yeah, the age gap's there. It's almost like we grew up in different families. I just wish—" He frowned, appearing distant for a moment.

She touched his arm. "Wish what?"

His smile held a hint of melancholy. "Just that I knew more about her. She seems really unhappy all the time."

Evita lifted a shoulder. "Maybe it's teenage angst?"

"Hmm. Maybe."

"Have you tried talking to her?"

"She's not very talkative, truthfully. I'm not sure what I'd say?"

"Anything, really. The words aren't so important. What counts is that she knows you're in her corner."

His smiled softly. "Thanks for that."

She heaved a breath. "I've had a lot of experience with family."

"Yeah, and yours seems pretty great. I mean, I'd never seen all of you together. Not until this week. You all seem to mesh. Get along."

She wished she could say the same about him and his parents and Maddy, but she'd noticed the cool distance there. "All families are different," she finally said.

"True." He toyed with his coffee cup. "So tell me about you," he said. "And that flower shop of yours. What's it called?"

She grinned, because this was one of her favorite topics. "Coming Up Roses."

"Love it?" The way he asked, with a sunny smile on his face, indicated he knew she'd say yes.

Warmth filled her soul, because she was liking him so much, and liking his interest *in her*. She set down her cup, beaming contentedly. "Yes, I do."

He crossed his arms and studied her. "I'll have to stop by sometime." If he was hinting he'd like to see her again, she was happy to take the hint.

"Oh. I wish you would." Her mind whirled with excitement at the thought of sharing this special part of herself—*her world*—within. "I'd love to show you around and have you meet Josie."

"Who's Josie?"

"Only my best friend on earth and shop manager."

He cocked his chin, and his sandy hair swished across his forehead. "Then I'd like to meet her for sure."

"You don't live in Lexington anymore, huh?" she asked, thinking she'd heard he'd moved.

He shook his head. "No, in Smithburg. Closer to the community college where I teach."

"Is that called Smithburg too?"

"It is." He was enjoying this conversation and the fact that she was asking about him, she could tell. "I've been there four years, but it only took four minutes to know it was the right fit."

She set her elbows on the table, appreciating his dedicated look. He'd set his jaw the way he always did when he'd firmly decided something. "What do you mean?"

He raked a hand through his hair which spiked high then flopped back down in a buttery golden mess. But it was a sexy mess that framed his rugged face perfectly. "I mean, it's the right place for me, I guess. I love the students and my fellow faculty. I was looking for a post where I could make a difference, and that first day at Smithburg—after my very first lecture—I knew I'd found it.

"I had a student come up to me who said she'd enjoyed my talk but hadn't understood all of it because she was still learning English. I offered to help her during office hours, then another student approached us while we were talking. Before long, we'd made a small lunch-bunch group. I told them I'd leave my office door open, and they could come hang out when they liked while they were doing their studies. If they had questions, then I'd help them if I could." He shrugged, radiant in his memory bubble. "And, if I couldn't help, I'd find someone else who could."

"Oh, Ryan," she gushed, meaning it absolutely. "That's wonderful. How did they do?"

He nodded proudly. "Every single one of them got high marks and graduated."

"Thanks to you."

He chuckled modestly. "Thanks to them and the hard work they put in."

She sat back in her booth, seeing him through new eyes. She always knew he was a giving person, but the fact that he extended this part of himself at work spoke volumes about his character. "How far do you live from Lexington?"

"About forty-five minutes," he said. "Close enough to see my folks when I want to, but not so close they drop in unexpectedly on me a lot either. If you get my drift."

She chuckled, understanding his desire for a little distance and privacy. "Nice." She toasted him with her coffee cup. "Also nice that you've found your passion. History."

His grin said it all. "Absolutely." He took a sip of coffee and so did she. "There's a lot of history to this place, you know. The native people here were the Wampanoags."

"Oh yeah?"

He nodded. "The name 'Sconset comes from the Algonquin word Siasconset, meaning 'Near the Great Bone.' 'Sconset Village started as a fishing village in the 1600s. Later, whaling captains built second homes here to get away from the noise and smell of Nantucket Harbor. By the late 1800s, it caught on as a vacation destination for actors and such from New York City."

"I didn't know any of that." She thought of the museum in the historic district that Chachi and his family had visited. "Nantucket's primary industry was whaling, right?"

"Yep." He smiled. "Maddy loved that part when she found out. Not that she was happy about what happened to those whales back then."

"Yikes. I suppose not."

"They were an important source of oil though, very valuable during the industrial revolution. Not just for lamps. Also used for clocks, typewriters, sewing machines. Stuff that had gears."

"That's fascinating. You know your history."

"I'd better," he joked. "Or I'd be out of a job."

She playfully shoved his arm, and he caught her hand on the table. Butterflies flitted around in her belly. His touch was so reassuring and warm.

"This is nice," he said. "Getting away. Just the two of us."

"Yeah," she agreed. "But we probably shouldn't stay gone too long."

"We won't," he whispered. "Just long enough to catch our breath."

She rolled her eyes. "It does feel like we've been in a boxing ring."

"Ha ha! Twelve rounds!"

"And this is just day three."

"Don't remind me." He gently squeezed her hand, then released it, picking up his coffee. "Coming Up Roses," he said. "Tell me all about it."

So she did, and about how she'd become interested in growing things her senior year in high school. And that she'd majored in horticulture in college, always knowing she wanted to work in the business somehow. At first, she'd thought of opening a garden shop. But then, she settled on flowers, because they made the world extra beautiful and warmed people's hearts.

He sighed as she summed things up. "I think that's amazing. It's really great you're doing what you love."

"Yeah. You too."

He frowned. "My parents wish I'd do a little more. Work at a nameplate university, that kind of thing."

"You probably could if you wanted to."

"Ah. But see," he said. "There's the catch. I can't imagine myself anywhere else. I love the students I serve. It's like opening a window to the world for so many of them. I have adults in my class who've decided to pursue higher education for the first time in their forties. Immigrant students for whom English isn't their first language, like the ones I mentioned... Bright kids coming out of high school who can't afford full-time universities or to live in dorms."

Admiration coursed through her. "You really have your calling."

"I like to look at it that way, yeah."

"Then I'm glad you found your fit."

"You too." He held his coffee cup up to hers in a toast and they both realized their drinks were empty. "Want one more?"

She checked the time on her phone. "I don't believe we'd better. We've been gone a while, and our folks are bound to start looking."

"Right." He stared down at her cell phone. "As long as you've got that out, maybe I can have your number?" Her heart pounded. "I mean, it might be good. In case we need to text or something? You never know when things back at the cottage could get dicey."

She laughed. "Yeah. Sure." She couldn't always be guaranteed to snatch private moments with him. They exchanged phones and each added themselves in as a new contact in the other's cell. Evita glanced out the café's front window. "There's a gift shop across the street. Do you think we can stop in quickly so I can ask about T-shirts?"

"Of course."

"I hope they have all the sizes I need."

He met her eyes. "I guess you can ask?"

A light bulb went off in her brain. Maybe she should buy a lot of them. Not just ten. How about fourteen? That way she could surprise everybody. The Hatfields too. Like it or not. She hoped they'd love it. She giggled at her plan. "I am!" she said, answering Ryan. She got the idea that it would be fun to surprise him too. "You know, the coffee's really good here, maybe we can buy a pound for everyone to try on our last day?"

"Then wouldn't they catch on that we'd—"

She winked at him. "It will be *our last day*."

"Right. What can they say to us then?"

She glanced at the coffee shop counter which now had a short line. "Would you mind staying here to get it while I dash across the street?"

"Yeah, sure." They both slid out of the booth.

"Don't forget to have them grind it."

He nodded and cracked a joke. "After that, we should probably head back to the cottage before someone sets it on fire."

She gasped, but she was cackling. "Bite your tongue!"

NINE

AS RYAN AND EVITA APPROACHED their cottage on their bikes a short time later, he regretted his lame joke. It had seemed harmless enough at the time but now... Smoke poured through the open laundry room window facing the drive and seeped out of windows on the right side of the house. That was the kitchen.

"Oh no!" She jumped off her bike, racing inside, and Ryan was right behind her, his heart pounding. He hoped everyone was safe.

She dropped her shopping package in the foyer and raced into the kitchen, her face creased with worry. The microwave door stood open, and plumes of noxious black smoke were everywhere. "Mom! Dad! What happened?"

Her parents waved damp dish towels in the air, trying to clear the room, coughing and covering their mouths and noses. The cottage's windows and French doors stood open to the deck. The smoke alarm blared, and Robby furiously punched at it with a broom handle.

"Quique and Nanny decided to make microwave popcorn," her mom said.

Her dad shook his head. "While the popcorn packages were still in the box."

"But everyone's okay?" Ryan asked, looking around.

"Yes, yes." Mrs. Machado nodded. "Thank goodness."

Eunice cradled Luisa on the deck oceanside, keeping her away from the smoke. Chachi and Kendra had Nanny and Quique lined up on a lounge chair and were calmly delivering a lecture. Both of them frowned, and the kids appeared squirmy, mostly staring down at their feet and only once in a while peeking up at their parents. They were clearly being scolded.

"And my family?" Ryan asked the Machados.

Evita's dad answered. "Still down on the beach."

Ryan strode through the house and went out on the deck. He spotted his mom and dad under their umbrella. Maddy had moved her chair far away from theirs and was on a separate spot a ways down the beach in her folding chair. She had her sunglasses on and held some kind of craft project on her lap. "Now's your chance," Evita said, standing beside him.

"What?"

"Go on down," she urged gently. "Talk to her. See how's she's doing. I'll put away the bikes."

He really wanted to, but his feet felt rooted in cement. He could deliver a lecture to 150 students no problem, but talk to his little sister who didn't have much use for him most of the time? He wasn't sure. He didn't even know how to approach her. "I have no idea what to say."

"You don't have to say much." Evita met his eyes. "Maybe mostly listen. The important thing is to let her know that you're here."

Ryan walked up beside Maddy and took a seat on the sand. "Hey, Mads. Can I join you?"

She shrugged without looking at him. "I guess."

He studied the project she'd been working on. She had a flat piece of cardboard on her knees and was making lots of tiny knots from thin blue cords. "That's cool. What is it?"

"Macrame."

He'd seen things made from it, but had never seen it in action before.

She held up the small figure. "Like it? It's a whale."

Now that she pointed it out, he could see the shape exactly, with the large humped back and dorsal fin. "That's fun. What do you plan to do with it?"

A smile lit up her face. "I thought it would make a good Christmas tree ornament." She dangled it in the air, holding it by her thumb and forefinger. "What do you think?"

"Yeah. I can see it."

"I'll probably make a few more. Maybe Mom and Dad would like one for a Christmas gift."

"I'd like one too." She glanced at him. "If it's not too much trouble."

"No, yeah. It's fine. I'll make one more." She tried to act cool about it, but he could tell his request pleased her.

"See any more of those guys?" He gestured to the ocean.

"Not yet. Mostly dolphins."

He stared at the waves, watching a glistening arc curve out of the water. "Mads, wait," he said, pointing. "Look! Out there!" They scrambled to their feet, shielding their eyes from the sun with their hands.

"Oh gosh! Is it really?" Maddy bounced up and down on her heels.

He couldn't have been happier for her, or for the two of them. This was a bonding moment. He now saw those couldn't be orchestrated. They just happened.

She grabbed her phone from her canvas bag. "I'm going to try to get a video."

"Hurry then."

She filmed as the creature moved down the shore.

"Mom! Dad!" he called to his parents. "Look out there! A whale!"

But by the time they focused their attention on the sea, it had disappeared, submerging itself in the waves like a big submarine.

Maddy replayed the video. "Got it!" she said, holding up her phone.

"Amazing," he said when she played him the clip. "You enlarged it?"

"Yeah, and sharpened the contrast."

"There will be no parents doubting you now."

She frowned.

"Mads?" he said. "Are you okay?"

She sat back down in her chair. "I'm really sick of playing the cello." Her admission came out of left field. She was a genius at that. He'd been to her concerts. Extremely gifted.

"Wait." He sat down beside her. "What?"

She hung her head and said glumly, "It's all Mom can talk about. Julliard. Dad too. I mean, what's the big deal? Just because the place is famous."

"Maybe they think that's what you want?"

"No. I've tried to tell them." She sighed. "They just never listen to me."

He rested his arms on his bent knees, studying the waves as they rose in regal white crests, then fell with great splashes. "What *do* you want to do?"

"I don't know yet." She motioned to her macrame whale. "This?"

"Work with your hands?"

"It's really fun, you know?" She angled her chin toward the clouds. "Creating stuff."

"Music's creative."

"Not really if you're not writing it."

"What about the greats who perform it? The masters put their own spin on a piece. Sometimes improvise. Think—Yo-Yo Ma."

"That's just it," she said. "I don't want be a great master. Or even a minor one."

He laughed at her joke. "I see."

"Just because you're good at something doesn't mean you should be forced to do it, right?"

"I agree."

"I mean, the cello is easy for me. I don't know why. Just is."

"You're a natural."

She shrugged. "Maybe."

"That doesn't matter so much if it's not what you want to do."

"It's not that I hate playing," she told him. "I like getting things right."

He stared down at her handicraft. She hadn't missed a stitch. "You're very detail-oriented. I can see that. That's an asset. A skill."

"I like other artsy stuff too," she said. "I tried papermaking once in art class. That was cool."

"There are lots of programs where you can explore that. College programs in art, if that's what you want."

"Mom and Dad would never send me."

He frowned because he feared there was some truth to that. "You could always send yourself."

"Doubtful."

"There are scholarships for talented people," he said. "You've still got two years left of high school. There's still time for you to take more art classes. Feel out what you'd like."

She gave a resigned pout. "Mom and Dad make my schedule. I never even have a say."

"Yeah. But." He waited until she met his eyes. "What if they didn't?"

"Are you kidding? They'd never listen to me. They think I'm just a kid."

"What if I talked to them?"

Moisture glistened in her eyes. They were baby blue like the sky and still filled with innocence, despite the jaded exterior she put forward. "Wait. Would you? You mean you'd do that?"

Ryan sighed, wanting to help her all he could. No wonder she'd been in such a funk. She'd felt railroaded into a career that loomed ahead of her, and she wasn't even sixteen. "I can't make you any promises," he said. "But I'll do what I can. And anyway, Mads."

"Huh?"

"You can't be afraid to chart your own path. You will be an adult and on your own one day. It might feel like it's far away right now, but that future's honestly right around the corner for you."

She smiled, and he saw her childhood self again. The trusting little sister who'd looked up at him and had followed him around the house, pestering him with question after question about why butterflies had wings and how birds could fly. "You really think so?"

"I do think so."

"Is that what you did?" she asked him. "Chart your own path?"

"Yeah." His shoulders drooped. "And it wasn't always easy around Mom and Dad." That much was real. He'd gone ahead and done what he'd wanted anyway. Once he was in grad school and paying his own ticket, they didn't have much influence. He'd never turn back now. He just wanted his parents to be cool with the decisions he'd made.

She grinned like he'd let her in on a secret. In a way, he guessed he had. He didn't talk to many people about his parents' disapproval of his career. It made him feel lesser. Although it shouldn't. "Thanks, Ryan."

"Anytime."

After a beat, she asked him, "So. You and Evita? Where did you go?"

He gazed at her, hoping she wouldn't say anything to their parents. "Out for coffee."

She smiled, seeming to like that idea. "Don't worry," she said. "I won't tell."

The Machado family poured onto the beach in their bathing suits with Nanny and Quique scampering about like wild things. The children spotted Maddy and Ryan and raced toward them. Evita was busy hauling two coolers down from the deck. Robby went to help her with her heavy load. It looked like they were planning to have a picnic lunch on the beach like his family had done yesterday.

"Kids!" Kendra called, holding a brimming beach bag. "Come back here!"

Chachi was already trudging after them through the sand, but Nanny and Quique got to Maddy first. Their small faces glowed with curiosity and wonder.

"What are you doing?" Quique asked Maddy, staring at her macrame.

"Making a whale."

"Can it swim?" Nanny asked.

Maddy laughed. "Don't think so."

"Can you teach me to make one?" Quique asked next.

"Er. I don't know."

"Quique. Nanny," Chachi said, sounding stern. "What have your mom and I told you about staying on our side of the beach?"

"Why are there sides?" Nanny asked with big, sad eyes.

Chachi took her hand. "There just are."

Quique's eyebrows knitted together. "I don't like sides," he said. "I like whales."

Maddy covered her mouth and giggled. "I like whales too."

"Come on, you two," Chachi said, corralling Quique in front of him and herding his kids toward the Machado umbrella where Kendra had laid out a big picnic blanket. "Sorry," he said to Maddy and Ryan. Ryan watched Maddy's gaze trail them as they walked away, then both kids turned around and gave her a little wave.

Maddy bit her lip and grinned.

That evening after dinner, Evita's family sat around the firepit enjoying the warmth of the flames in the evening chill. Ryan's family were inside at the kitchen island, playing cards.

"What are they doing in there?" her dad asked.

"Playing bridge, I think?"

"Bridge?" Chachi said like that was weirdest thing in the world.

It did seem a little formal to Evita, but what did she know about the Hatfields? Maybe to them it was a casual game? Like poker or something.

Her mom took a sip of wine. "Figures."

Kendra stood up. "I'd better check on the kids to be sure they're really sleeping."

Evita suspected they would be. They'd been wearing themselves out on the beach, so appeared to have less energy for tormenting each other at night. In fact, this vacation seemed to be doing them good. It was nice seeing them interact with the greater family, and her parents adored them.

She'd noticed them talking to Maddy earlier, wondering what they'd said. She was also curious about Ryan's conversation with his sister and hoped it went well.

Robby and Eunice had just started to relax after putting Luisa down in her crib, then a whimper sounded through the baby monitor. Robby sighed, appearing deflated.

He raked a hand through his hair and moaned. "It never ends." He said it like he was joking, but Evita suspected there was a lot of truth in that.

Eunice looked like she wanted to cry. "She's already eaten a dozen times."

"Maybe it's just gas?" Evita's mom said.

"Or maybe she needs changing?" Evita's dad chimed in.

Robby and Eunice stared at each other like zombies, each waiting for the other to volunteer. Evita could almost hear their telepathic communications.

Please, please, please.

No you.

But I went last time.

I went the time before.

We're both so tired.

Ugh.

"Wait." Evita held out her hand. "I'll go."

"What? You?" Eunice asked in a daze.

"Yeah, me." Evita stood. "I know how to handle a baby."

"You did very well in the Suburban," Chachi ribbed.

"Funny, Chachi." Evita would not be deterred. Robby and Eunice needed a vacation. A real one. At a tropical resort somewhere that didn't allow kids.

"Are you sure?" Eunice asked, sounding grateful.

"No problem."

Robby's dark eyes sparkled. "Thanks, sis. We owe you one."

Ryan saw her come in the door and waved from the kitchen. Maddy seemed to be in a good mood. When he told some joke, she leaned toward him and laughed. It was maybe the first time Evita had heard Maddy laugh since they'd been here, and it made her heart happy.

Being a teenager was so hard. Even when you were outgoing and had lots of friends like she'd had. Maddy was more introverted, so it was nice to believe she and Ryan might be developing their sibling relationship. Evita didn't know what she'd do without her brothers. She loved their wives like family too. Their children as well.

She climbed the spiral steps to the bedroom where Luisa was winding herself up. Crying louder and louder, verging on hysteria. Evita quickened her strides.

"Come here, little one." She reached into the crib and held her. All softness and warmth, and bristling agitation.

She rubbed the baby's back and she let out a surprisingly loud belch, relaxing in her hold. Evita giggled. "Maybe your Tita was right," she said softly. "Maybe it was gas."

"I told you so!" her mom called loudly from the deck outside, her words drifting in through the partially opened French doors in the suite.

Evita sighed and shut off the baby monitor. *Prying ears. My family!* She changed Luisa's diaper while speaking soothing words, then swaddled her in a blanket.

She sat in the rocking chair in the corner and cradled Luisa in her arms, singing her a song about a mother hen and her baby chicks in Spanish. It was one her mom used to sing to her, and that her Abuela had sung to her mom before that. "*Los pollitos dicen pío, pío, pío...*"

The infant stared up at her with big bright eyes, almost like she knew and understood. This lullaby was a part of her. A part of her heritage and family's tradition. Her fussing became a soft cooing sound and then her eyelids drooped. First one and then the other. Finally both of them at once. Evita sang another tune, and then another. Wondering what it would be like to have a baby. Maybe not so bad when they were like this.

"You finally got her back to sleep, huh?" Ryan said with a husky whisper. He stood in the open doorway.

Evita smiled. "She dropped right off, after I burped her." She continued rocking as Luisa slept.

"Oh yeah, babies can have an issue with that."

She studied him curiously. "You remember from Maddy?"

"I do." He chuckled. "She was a bit of a fussy baby too, but she grew out of it." He shook his head. "And into a teenager."

Evita laughed quietly. "How did things go today when you talked with her?"

He sank his hands in his pockets. "Actually, pretty good," he said, appearing pleased. "Thanks for encouraging me to talk with her. That was the right move."

Evita smiled. He was such a good big brother. She knew what it was like having one of those. No, two.

Ryan leaned into the doorframe. "You're very good with her," he said, indicating Luisa. He surveyed the contours of her chubby cheeks and rich black hair. "She's a cutie."

"Yeah."

"Robby and Eunice are a little burnt out, huh?"

She chuckled softly. "Wouldn't you be?"

"Oh I'd definitely be," he said quietly. "Anyway. My family's turned in, and I'm pretty beat, so I'll probably say good night.

Maybe try to get some sleep." He cleared his throat. "Before Chachi and Kendra turn in."

She shifted Luisa in her arms. "Would you like some earplugs?"

"Earplugs?" he asked like she'd offered him the best kind of candy.

"Yeah. I didn't know my mom had brought them, but apparently she bought several after spending a week with Robby and Eunice—and Luisa—in LA."

She carefully dug into her shorts pocket, trying not to disturb Luisa's peaceful slumber. "She gave these to me before dinner once she realized that's why I'd been tired earlier. On account of Luisa. Well, and Robby."

"Are you sure? You need to get your rest too."

"That's the beauty of it," she said lightly. "My mom gave me two pairs."

He approached her with stealthy steps and took one set of earplugs. "Thanks," he whispered. "I'll wear them in good health." When he got to the threshold, he turned. "Thanks for going out for coffee with me. It was fun."

"It was fun," she said. She considered how warm and sweet he was. How much she enjoyed being around him. "We'll have to do it again." *Please say that you want to do it again.*

"Yeah." He laughed. "For sure."

Yes. Her heart cartwheeled. She wished that he'd say when, but when he didn't, she decided to bait him a little. "Now that you've got my number—" she teased.

He held up his phone. "Exactly." He slid his phone in his pocket like he wanted to say something more. After a beat, he pursed his lips. "If only our parents weren't so ridiculous."

"This is silly." She sighed. "We're too old to be this swayed by our folks."

"You love your family, Evita. You don't want to hurt them." Understanding dripped from his words. Resignation too. "Just like I don't want to upset mine."

"It's not Maddy who's the problem," she pointed out.

"No, she's cool. She saw us leaving today but promised not to say anything."

"Really?" Evita wasn't as much surprised as pleased. "That's good."

"Yeah. So it's not her we've got to worry about. Or your brothers and their families."

They both frowned. "It's our parents," they said sadly together.

A painful lump lodged in her throat. Then another truth occurred. Maybe—totally without meaning to—her family was hurting her by not allowing her to make her own choices, and Ryan's family was doing the same to him.

"I thought things were going so much better." He clucked his tongue at the lost opportunity. "But then today, with the music—"

Evita's heart clenched. "I know. That was my father." Shame swamped through her, but Ryan's face was every bit as red as hers felt.

He blew out a breath. "Mine too."

"I think everyone's settling in, anyway," he said. "Establishing a routine of sorts." He shrugged. "At least we're holding things together."

"Yeah." But in some ways, she felt the situation was combustible, about to blow apart. As much trouble as they'd had, she couldn't lie and say she wasn't glad to be here. She'd loved being around her family and the surprise opportunity to reconnect with Ryan too. "Do you think they'll ever get along? Our moms?"

He shook his head. "I wish I could say yes, but that somehow seems like a fantasy."

"I'll try talking to my mom again tomorrow," Evita said.

"Same." He raked a hand through his hair. "To my dad as well."

"Yeah. Me too." Evita sighed.

Ryan tapped the doorframe. "Well. Guess I'd better go."

"Good night, Ryan."

"See ya, Evita." She heard Robby's voice in the hallway.

"Ryan. Oh. Didn't know you were up here."

"Just saying good night to Evita."

"Oh yeah?"

"She's doing a great job with Luisa."

"I'm sure she is."

Robby poked his head into the room. "Everything okay in...?" His voice trailed off. "Looks better than okay." He smiled. "You've worked magic."

Evita scanned the baby bundle in her arms, thinking how easy it was to hold her when she was like this and not screaming her sweet, little head off. "She's precious, Robby. Really. You and Eunice are very lucky."

"Yeah." He sat down on the bed. "When we're not biting each other's heads off."

"I know it must be a bit overwhelming. Caring for Luisa and trying to work too."

"I thought Eunice was going to kill me for forgetting that breast pump. She asked me to grab it when we were packing up for the baby and, honestly, I thought I had. My brain is so fuzzy lately. Sleep deprivation. I don't know. I'm sure it's no excuse."

"Can you get another one here?"

Robby's cheeks sagged. "I ordered one online. It should arrive tomorrow."

"That should help things then." She tried to sound upbeat, but her brother still looked down, running his thumb along the piping on the bedspread. He seemed distracted and worn thin, maybe even like he was doubting himself a little. But there was nobody with more love in his heart for his daughter and wife than Robby. Evita didn't doubt that for a minute. She knew that Eunice didn't either.

"Eunice loves you very much, you know. She supports you too. Your writing." Evita smiled brightly. "She's convinced you're going to be a star."

He sat back on the heels on his hands, gazing up at the ceiling. "Don't know if I'll get one on Hollywood Boulevard, though."

"Rob-by," she chided, and he cracked a grin.

"Yeah, those are mostly for actors anyway."

Evita waved her free hand. "Doesn't matter about the star. You're already shining in Eunice's eyes."

"Just like she is in mine." He nodded. "I love and support her too."

Evita shifted the baby in her arms as her small body grew heavier and tiny puffs of breath escaped her plump lips. The little angel was now sleeping peacefully, and what a beautiful bundle she was. Evita glanced up at Robby. "I'm sure lots of new parents go through this."

"Probably." He gazed at her thoughtfully, summing her up in some new way. "When did you get to be so wise?"

She winked at him. "Might have learned a thing or two from my oldest brother."

"Aww. That's sweet." He surveyed Luisa. "Want me to take her? She looks ready to go back in her crib now. She'll probably sleep till morning."

"Just another few minutes, then I'll lay her down." Evita snuggled the baby close.

He studied her a moment. "So. You and Ryan? What's going on?"

"Nothing," she said, but her face burned hot.

"Nothing?"

"You know how Mom feels about Mrs. Hatfield."

"I wasn't asking about that," he said. "I was asking how you feel about her son?"

"Robby."

He held up both hands. "I know. I know. None of my business. But if it was." He cracked a smile. "I'd say you could probably do worse." He frowned. "Like Sebastian."

Evita gasped. "What? I thought everybody loved him." She remembered what Eunice had told her in the kitchen that first morning, and Chachi later outdoors. "Well, not everybody."

Robby set his jaw. "I didn't like how he was with you." So the evidence was building against her ex. Had everybody thought ill of him?

"What do you mean?"

"He talked down to you, Evita, like he somehow thought he was better." How had others seen this so clearly? She'd only caught on after their breakup. "And he wasn't, you know. Wasn't any better than you at all. He was inferior to you in many ways. He doesn't have your heart. Your sweetness. He didn't appreciate those things about you either."

"I guess it's a good thing we didn't get engaged then."

"A very good thing, yeah."

"Why didn't you and Eunice say something? Or Chachi?"

His eyebrows rose. "Would you have listened?"

"No," she admitted softly. "Probably not."

"You're too good a person to settle. Hold out for that man who worships you."

"Worship's a very high bar."

"Not for my little sister, it's not."

"Thanks, Robby."

"Don't stay up here too long," he said warmly. "We miss you down at the firepit."

"I won't."

Robby exited the room, leaving her alone in the shadows with Luisa and her thoughts. A lot of those thoughts were about Ryan. Going out for coffee had been nice. So nice. She liked spending time with him but didn't like the thought of them only being able to see each other in secret. Maybe tomorrow they could begin to break down the barriers between their families.

TEN

WHEN EVITA WENT DOWNSTAIRS THE next day, the Hatfields were gone. Her brothers and their wives and kids ate cereal and pastries at the dining room table. She glanced out at the deck, seeing it was empty. "Where's everyone else?"

"Mom and Dad are at the store. The Hatfields went into the Nantucket Harbor area for brunch," Chachi said. "And to do some touristy stuff."

She hid her disappointment at not seeing Ryan. It sounded like they'd be gone for a while. Maybe a lot of the morning. "Oh, well. That's good."

The front door popped open and in walked her parents, holding grocery bags. "Guess what's for dinner tonight?" her dad said with a big grin. "Carnitas."

Kendra's face lit up. "Yum!"

"I got a large pork butt to slow roast outdoors."

Her mom nodded, traipsing with her dad toward the kitchen. "We found a gas grill in the shed. There were even four bicycles!"

"Really?" Evita said, her cheeks warming.

Her mom gave her a curious look.

"The tires were all pumped up on the adult ones," her dad said. "Ready to go." Then he stared at Evita too and scratched his chin.

"Maybe the last people here used them?" Evita's mom said.

Evita took a grocery bag from her mom. "Here, let me help you put stuff away."

Chachi got to his feet. "More bags in the SUV?"

"Just a few," his dad said.

"I'll grab them."

"You didn't see a package on the porch?" Eunice crossed her arms in front of her while Robby held the baby. "We're expecting something."

"No," her mom said. "Nothing yet."

Her dad unpacked the pork butt and held it up. "Heh, heh. Just look at this beauty. I'm going to make a rub to coat it and let it roast for several hours."

"I'm sure it will be delicious," Robby said.

Their mom nodded. "Especially with your dad's chimichurri sauce." She pulled other items from her grocery sack. "Also having corn on the cob, melon, and cilantro-lime slaw."

"Mom," Chachi teased, bringing more grocery bags into the kitchen. "You're making me hungry."

Kendra rolled her eyes. "He's always hungry."

"Yeah. That's true," Chachi said good-naturedly. "But this meal sounds like the best. I can't wait." He unpacked the bags he'd set on the counter, stowing groceries in the cupboard, while the others restocked the fridge.

Evita finished helping her folks, then poured herself some coffee. "So. The Hatfields are gone for a while, I hear."

"Isn't this nice?" Her mom surveyed the room. "Having the place to ourselves."

"Oh yeah!" Chachi said to Kendra. "We could be eating at the kitchen island instead of here."

She shrugged. "Habit."

Nanny and Quique scooted out of their chairs and went to work on a puzzle that they'd started on the coffee table. "When can we go down to the beach?"

"Soon," Chachi told them. "Very soon." He folded up the empty grocery bags and handed them to his dad, who put them away.

"Um. Mom. Dad." They both turned and gave Evita their full attention. "About the Hatfields." She lifted a shoulder. "Do you think we can all try to get along?"

Her dad's brow furrowed. "We were getting along fine until Kirk turned off my music."

"And Daneen stole our umbrella," her mom added with a scowl.

Evita shook her head at her mom's bullheadedness. "It was technically theirs fir—"

"No, Evita." Her mom firmly pursed her lips, her platinum highlights shimmering around her youthful-looking face. "They must have switched the better ones for ours."

Evita's mouth fell open. "Why are you so mistrustful of them?"

Her mom set her chin and fine lines creased around her mouth and eyes. "Because. They've earned it."

Evita sighed. "Look. This week is almost halfway through. It would be great if we could enjoy the rest of our time here without drama."

"Hear, hear!" Robby said, raising his juice glass.

Eunice leaned over and kissed his cheek. "I'm sorry, honey."

"I know." He stared at her with love in his eyes. "Me too."

"Evita has a point," Chachi said. "Rather than fighting with the Hatfields, maybe we should try to include them?"

Her mom gasped. "Include them? How?"

Chachi shrugged. "By—I don't know—cooking out together?"

"With Daneen and her family? No."

Her dad frowned. "I don't like the sound of that either."

"Please, Mom and Dad, Ryan and I both want—"

Her mom's eyebrows arched. "How do you know what Ryan wants?"

Evita bit her bottom lip. "Um. He told me."

Her mom strummed her fingers on the countertop. "When?"

Her dad gaped at Evita. "Wait one minute. You didn't go out on those bikes?"

Evita shrank back but verbally held her ground. "We might have."

"*Ay dios mio*," her mom said. "Where?"

"Only to get coffee."

"*Coffee?*" she wailed like Evita had just said she'd eloped.

Chachi ducked out of the kitchen like he was fleeing an active missile range, scooting back toward the table and his breakfast.

Evita's dad fumed at her. "You're kidding me. You and that Hatfield boy snuck off together?" His voice rose. "Behind our backs?"

Evita exhaled and shut her eyes. She opened them, staring at her dad. "First off, Ryan is not a boy. He's a man. Full-grown and really accomplished. A college professor."

"But he's a Hatfield," her mom said. "One of them."

"Them?" Evita asked, gobsmacked.

"Entitled gringos, yes." Her dad frowned.

"Ryan's not entitled! He's not like that!"

Her mom threw up her hands. "Evita, please!"

"You're right, *querida*," Evita's dad said to his wife. "Based on what Daneen did to you in high school, I wouldn't trust any of them either."

Evita sucked in a gasp. "For crying out loud, Mom! High school was *ages* ago."

Her mom trapped her in her ebony gaze. "I never told you," she said, "because it didn't seem important, but maybe now you deserve to know."

Evita ran both hands through her curls. "Know what?"

Her mom tapped the toe of one of her sandals against the kitchen floor. "I worked very hard on that campaign, Evita."

"Seriously?" Evita moaned in frustration. "Are we talking about you being class president?"

"Yes, that." Her mom nodded curtly. "And I was all set to win, according to the early polls. But then Daneen's father stepped in with all his money."

Evita's jaw unhinged. "What?" She leaned into the counter, completely taken aback.

"He couldn't bear to see his daughter lose," her dad filled in with a disgruntled scowl. "So he threw a wad of cash toward the school."

Evita gasped. "I can't believe that's true."

Her mom huffed and set her hands on her hips. "Now you're

saying you don't believe me?" Her eyes fanned so wide Evita felt like she was staring down into the barrels of two huge cannons. Dark and dangerous ones, loaded with ammo.

"No, Mom. I—" Her head swam and her heart ached. "I just don't understand."

Her mom licked her lips. "My parents aren't rich. They never were. But they taught me to work hard and take pride in my accomplishments, and so I did. Working my way up through the student council. Daneen swooped in from out of nowhere! Her name just appeared on the ballot. She hadn't done the legwork or the time. She didn't know student government. But, oh yes. Her daddy had money. So he donated a bundle for a new football stadium, just in time to remind all the sports-crazy kids at our school about what a kind benefactor he was." She cleared her throat then said bitterly, "And that his daughter was running for class president."

Evita's stomach soured. "That's a horrible accusation."

Her dad held up a hand, as the others looked on stunned. "It's not an accusation, Evita," her dad said. "It's a fact."

Chachi leaned toward Robby and whispered, "Did you know about this?"

Robby shook his head. "No. Did you?"

"Nobody knew," their mom announced, "except for me and your father." She sniffed to collect herself when her eyes grew moist. "Well, my father too." Her family stared at her, and she continued, her voice warbly. "I ran home crying to your Abuelo after what Mr. Hatfield did, so sure it was all over. All my hard work down the drain. I'd wanted to be senior class president for years. Was hoping my being in student government would help get me into a good college. Any other perk—" She caught her breath and nearly broke down. But then her steady resolve returned and she squared her shoulders. "To even the playing field between the Machados and the Hatfields of this world.

"My dad understood, and he wanted to do something to help. But he didn't have a ton of money, just their small deli. They made dynamite pizza, though. So Dad had an idea. He'd bring pizza to the school on election day. Free for anyone who voted. Maybe if people understood our family for the good, hardworking people we were, they wouldn't be influenced by the Hatfields' money."

"And this worked?" Chachi asked, clearly amazed.

Evita's dad answered, "Your mom won of course, but she would have won regardless. She had the credentials and experience. Daneen didn't."

"But a football stadium?" Robby winced. "Yikes, I can see that was a lot to compete with."

"Everyone loves pizza, though," Chachi observed evenhandedly. "Especially teenagers."

Her mom sadly shook her head and walked into the great room. Evita followed her. "Did you know?" she asked her mom. "That Abuelo was going to bring the pizza?"

Her mom sank down on the sofa. "Honestly, no." She hung her head. "He surprised me by showing up at school on election day with his old white delivery van loaded up."

Evita sat down on the sofa with her. She knew her mom was proud and strong. She'd also probably been conflicted about Abuelo's unrequested intervention.

"I'm so sorry about that," Evita said to her mom. "All of it.

Really, I am." She gently rubbed her mom's arm. "But hey, look. The important thing is you did win. So Mr. Hatfield's manipulations didn't make a difference."

Her mom released a slow breath. "That still didn't take the sting out of the Hatfields' trick maneuver. Daneen was always that way, the rich girl getting what she wanted. Expensive clothes, a fancy car, whereas I still rode the bus to school with the younger kids at seventeen. Daneen barely ever said two words to me back then, like she was so superior somehow—wearing those pearls and that headband. And just look at her now. Nothing has changed."

Evita wondered about Mrs. Hatfield and how much she'd known about her father's plan. Maybe she hadn't known at all. Just like her mom hadn't known her dad was going to bring the pizza. She could tell her mom was hurting. Being looked down on by others never felt good. She laced her words in warmth, sensing how difficult the situation must have been for her mother. "But that's over now, okay? And honestly. That has nothing to with Ryan, or—"

Her mom's chin jerked up. "Is it over, Evita?"

Evita met her eyes. "It could be, if you and Mrs. Hatfield—"

"It's not up to me," her mom snapped. "It's up to her."

"Mom, please."

Her mom shook her finger. "Mark my words about Ryan! He's cut from the same cloth as Daneen." She wore an angry glare. "Or should I say designer fabric?"

Evita sighed and placed her hands on her knees. Then she stood wearily and muttered, "This is hopeless."

She rolled her eyes at her brothers, who wore sympathetic

pouts. Kendra and Eunice stayed quiet as church mice, not wanting to interfere in such touchy family business. Evita wished she could excise herself from it too, but she was in it. So deep. Because—there was no denying it any longer—she was starting to fall for Ryan again. Fortunately, the kids were oblivious to the adult conversation swirling around them. They stayed totally engrossed in their puzzle.

Evita strode toward the stairs, and her mom called after her, "We're just trying to help! Protect the family!"

"We don't need protecting," Chachi quipped, speaking up.

"Right," Robby said. "Us either."

"I wasn't talking about you, *hijos*." Evita glanced over her shoulder and at her mom's knitted-together eyebrows. "I was talking about your sister."

Evita paused at the bottom of the steps, pivoting to face them. She inhaled deeply, then blew out a hard breath. "Mom, Dad. Please hear me. I don't need protecting either."

Her parents' faces went slack with shock. "She doesn't know what she's saying," her dad grumbled.

"Of course not," her mom whispered to him. "She's confused."

Hurt welled in her throat that they still thought they could control her. The tender spot burned even more when Evita realized she'd let them. She balled her hands into fist when her fingers shook. It was time for her to take a stand. "That's where you're wrong, Mom and Dad." Evita raised her chin and confronted them both. "My head is clearer now than ever. My life is mine, okay? Not yours any longer, and if I want to see Ryan, then that's what I'll do."

"You tell 'em, Evita!" Chachi cheered.

Their dad wheeled on him with a steely look. "You. Stay out of this."

Chachi winced. "Okay. Sorry."

Kendra elbowed him and whispered, "You didn't have to apologize."

"Oh yes, he did," their mom said, overhearing. "It's one of the Ten Commandments. Honor your father and mother."

"Honor, yeah." Evita's skin flushed hot. "When they're being honorable."

Her mom huffed. "I don't know what's gotten into you. You weren't like this before." She glanced at the others. "This has got to be because of Ryan. He's a bad influence on her."

"What?" Evita said, horrified they'd hold him accountable when they'd been the ones behaving badly. "Why blame him? He's done nothing but try to smooth the waters on these choppy seas." She set her hands on her hips. "Just like I have."

Her dad spoke to her mom, joining her on the sofa. "I told you we were raising her to be too headstrong."

"The word is *independent*, Dad. And independence is good." She stared at her mom. "Maybe you should think of gaining some *independence* from your long-standing feud with Mrs. Hatfield, hmm?" Evita stomped up the stairs, and her mom called after her.

"She started it!"

Evita spun on the spiral staircase. "Really? Well, who's going to end it?"

Then she left the rest of them downstairs to think about that.

"Why is Auntie Evita mad at Tita and Tito?" she heard Nanny say.

"She's just not feeling well, *hijita*," her Tita answered. "We'll let her rest."

"Yes," her dad groused. He picked up a puzzle piece and studied it, then gave up when he couldn't instantly find where to put it. "Maybe she'll come to her senses." Evita huffed at them from the landing, then retreated to her room, shutting the pocket doors. Her parents had been impossible, but at least she'd made her point. Her brothers had clearly backed her too.

She felt bad for her mom and about her history with Mrs. Hatfield, of course. But that didn't mean that she and Ryan needed to have the sins of their mothers—and maybe their grandfathers too—visited upon them. Maybe, once her parents thought things through, they'd calm down and see that she was right. Or maybe not. She decided she'd better fill Ryan in, so he'd know what he was coming back to—just in case.

She texted his number.

Peacekeeping efforts did not go well.

Ryan checked his phone when it buzzed, then slipped it back in his pocket. Oh boy. Sounds like this was down to him. He had to make an effort anyway.

"So. Mom and Dad," he said as they enjoyed their omelets. They were at a cute little breakfast place near the docks and had plans to explore the historic district. Maddy was excited about seeing the Whaling Museum. "About how things are going back at the house—"

His mom rolled her eyes. "I know. The Machados are being impossible."

His dad threw up his hands. "The drinks! The music! The laughter!" Maddy smirked at Ryan. Right. Those didn't sound too bad. If you were any kind of normal person.

"And then," his mom said in hushed tones. "There was that underhanded move with our umbrella."

"We weren't using it," Maddy said in a bored tone.

"She's right," Ryan said. "I think you're being a little hard on them by presuming all kinds of negative motives."

His mom twisted up her lips like she'd tasted a lemon. "You're forgetting that Lissette and I go back forty years."

No. He hadn't forgotten that at all. Neither had she or Evita's mom. Apparently, that was the very big problem. "So what? This is all because you didn't win class president? Mom. Just look at you now. You've got a great job." He glanced around the table. "A nice family."

"I might have gotten into a better university if I'd had that on my high school résumé. Ivy League. Seven Sisters!"

Ryan set down his coffee. "Seriously? Who cares?"

She frowned. "My parents did. Quite a lot."

Ryan's heart sank for her; her parents' demanding expectations must have been a heavy burden to carry. "I'm sorry about that."

"I'm not sorry about how any of it worked out." His dad took a forkful of hash browns. "If your mom had gone to a different school, then I wouldn't have met her." His smile warmed the room. "None of us would be here." It was very unlike his dad to be sentimental. Maddy shot Ryan a side-eye.

"You see there?" Ryan said. "Things have worked out for the best."

His mom frowned. "Lissette only won because she was more popular. Outgoing and pretty with tons of friends. I was a lot shyer, and not nearly as glamorous as she was, but I worked hard nonetheless. Ran a tough campaign. I nearly caught up to her in the end, which is why she believes that I cheated. Which I did not."

"Why would Mrs. Machado even think that," Ryan asked, "if that's not true?"

His dad glanced at his mom. "There was that little issue with your dad's money."

"What issue?" Maddy asked, intrigued by a family conversation that might expose dirt.

"Kirk!" Her eyes flashed. "I've asked you not to bring it up."

"It's not like you did anything wrong," he said. "His donating to the school was legitimate."

"Donating for what?" Ryan asked.

His mom sighed. "Dad was big on football. Gave a huge wad to build a new stadium. They wanted to name it in his honor, but he declined."

"Whoa." Ryan thought on this. "Bet that made an impression on some of the students."

"The more sports-minded ones, yes. Your grandpa played college ball. Even got drafted by the pros but turned them down. In any case, he came to speak at the school when the stadium opened. A lot of the football players looked up to him as a legend. He probably shouldn't have said it, but at the end of his speech, he might have mentioned I was running for class president."

Maddy frowned. "Ick. Sounds like he was trying to influence the election."

"But I ran on my own merits!"

Maddy wrinkled up her nose and set down her sandwich. "Still."

In all these years, Ryan had never known the details of what had happened. "But Mrs. Machado won anyway."

"Of course she did." His mom rubbed the side of her nose. "Everyone loved bubbly Lissette, including her father. He brought free pizza to the school on election day. Passed it out at lunch."

"Oh, man," Ryan said. He shook his head. "That doesn't sound right either."

"It sure wasn't right." His mom tugged at her pearls. "Lissette—the daddy's girl—surrounded by swarms of her family. Her uncle was there. An older brother and a sister too, I think. It was actually highly embarrassing, the way they all flocked in."

Maddy set her elbows on the table. "Sounds like she had a supportive family."

"Supportive, ha!"

Ryan thought on this. "It's amazing the school let them all in."

"Oh no, our principal didn't." She released her pearl necklace and sniffed. "Lissette's dad parked his van in the parking lot, and the others handed out paper plates of pizza from there."

Ryan scratched his head. "To buy a vote for Lissette?"

His mom shook her head. "Not buy, no. Just to encourage voting. Period." She sighed, and her shoulders sank. "But seriously? What an enticement. It just wasn't fair."

Ryan's dad hugged his mom's shoulders. "I guess both of your parents were very interested in your young lives. Yours and Lissette's."

"Yes. But Lissette already had *everything*. The friends. The boys." His mom blinked and dabbed at her eyes with her napkin. She wasn't going to cry, was she? Ryan had never seen that happen, and he was hoping she wouldn't start today. Her voice quaked when she added, "The *family*."

"You had a family," Maddy whispered.

Their mom shared a wistful look. "No, sweetheart. It wasn't the same."

Ryan's heart ached for his mom, because he could see that she'd compared herself to Evita's mom and maybe wanted some of the things she'd had. It was possible that Lissette had envied his mom too. Either way, the past didn't have to be a prologue for both families. It was like history repeating itself all over again, and that's why history was important. You were supposed to learn from it, not repeat your past mistakes.

Ryan pursed his lips and spoke softly. "Sounds like there are a lot of parallels between back then and now." His mom shared a guileless look, so he continued. "Your dad," he said kindly, "and Mrs. Machado's were both overly involved."

"Way too involved," Maddy agreed.

Ryan nodded. "Sounds like one was just as bad as the other."

"No." His mom set her mouth in a hard line. "Her dad was worse. As evidenced by the fact that she won the election. If it hadn't been for that pizza—"

That didn't seem reasonable to Ryan, not given everything else he knew. "How do you know she wouldn't have won anyway?"

She blanched, her eyes growing wide. "Whose side are you on, Ryan?"

"I don't like sides," Ryan said. "I like whales."

Maddy pursed her lips.

"Whales?" his mom said like he'd lost his mind.

"Yeah, and so does Maddy. Don't you, Mads?"

She glanced at him unsurely. "Uh-huh. Yeah."

His mom took a sip of water, studying Ryan above the rim of her glass. "Where exactly is this going? It doesn't sound like you're talking about me and Lissette."

"The truth is... I'm not." Ryan cleared his throat. "You know what I think?" He leveled a look at his folks. "I think people should be encouraged to pursue the things they like without having their parents decide things for them." His mom's gaze swept over Maddy, like she suspected where Ryan was steering this conversation.

She set her chin, refusing to take orders from her son. "And others need guidance."

"You mean like your dad guided you?"

She scoffed. "You know that's not the same."

Ryan spread his hands on the table. "Look. I'm sure things were really tense between you and Mrs. Machado all those years ago. But time's moved on. Maybe you can both find a way to bury the hatchet. Put the past behind you."

"What?"

"If you won't do it for yourselves, maybe the two of you should think of your families."

"I'm always thinking of my family, Ryan. That's why I never wanted you to associate with that girl in high school. The apple doesn't fall far from the tree."

He raked a hand through his hair, having had just about enough of this. "Yeah, well. Your admonishments didn't always work."

His dad blinked. "Are you talking about when you were lab partners?"

Maddy stared at Ryan admiringly. "Cool. What class?"

"No. Not cool." His mom frowned. "Chemistry."

"I'm not talking about that," Ryan said. "I meant other things."

"Heaven's, Ryan." His mom slumped down in her seat. "This isn't about the prom?"

"Wait." Maddy touched his arm. "You and Evita went to the prom?"

"No." Ryan set his jaw and glared at his folks. "Because I never asked her."

His dad cleared his throat. "You don't know for fact she would have gone."

Maddy grinned from ear to ear. "Oh, I bet she would have."

"What's all of this about, Ryan?" His mom gasped. "You're not thinking of dating her now?" She stared at him wide-eyed, unable to continue.

"She seems like a nice girl," his dad ventured.

His mom cocked her chin at her husband like he'd landed from Mars. "Not you too, Kirk? Ganging up on me."

Ryan lowered his voice and said soothingly. "Nobody's ganging up, Mom. I just want us to be able to go back to that cottage and have a more peaceful time. Enjoy our last few days there without conflict. No more umbrella or music wars."

She smacked her lips. "I think you should tell that to them."

"Evita already has."

She crossed her arms. "So the two of you are in this together?"

"We're not together. But we have spoken, yes."

"Ryan may have a point," his dad said. "It would be nice to enjoy the rest of our vacation with less tension."

His mom's fingers fluttered over her necklace yet another time. "I don't know about us cooperating with the Machados," she said unsurely, but clearly she was outnumbered. "We can't do it all on our own. Lissette and her family will have to make an effort too."

"I'm sure that they will," Ryan said, only half believing it.

ELEVEN

EVITA'S DAD PROUDLY HELD UP his prepared pork roast in the kitchen before setting it in its roasting pan. "Ready to go on the grill." After her blowup with her parents, she'd come back downstairs, and no one had said anything further about it. That happened a lot in the Machado household. When someone had something to say, they generally said it, often really loudly. Then afterward, with the air cleared, people moved on. Sometimes things got resolved and other times, they didn't. But family was family, and the Machados didn't hold grudges with one another.

They appeared to reserve those for people on the outside. Only Evita was hoping her folks could finally put that aside. Maybe her mom was thinking about everything she'd said and would try to behave more civilly around the Hatfields. Her dad too.

Evita sat at the kitchen island drinking her coffee. She was in her bathing suit with shorts and a T-shirt on top. She planned to join the others down on the beach soon enough. Chachi and Kendra had taken their kids down, along with her mom. Robby and Eunice were still getting ready upstairs, so it was just her and her dad for the moment.

Evita smiled at her father, knowing he took pride in his grilling. "I'm sure the carnitas will be delicious."

"They should be." He washed his hands off at the sink and then dried them on a dish towel, wearing a frown. He looked up at her with all the sheepishness of a young boy who'd been scolded. "Evita," he said gruffly. "About what happened earlier when you told us to butt out of your business."

She pursed her lips. "I can see that Mom's still very upset."

"It wasn't just about the election, you know." His forehead rose. "But all the baggage that went along with it."

She studied her dad, who seemed uncharacteristically contrite. "Yeah, it's funny though. Mrs. Hatfield doesn't strike me as the mean sort. Not purposefully mean anyway. Could be there's more to her story than we know. Ryan said her dad was very strict."

Her dad glanced up at the ceiling, then he folded his arms. "I guess we all behave in different ways for different reasons."

Relief washed through her. She was finally getting through to one of her parents at least. "Yes. That." Evita set down her coffee mug. "All I'm asking is that you and Mom start thinking about the here and now, Dad. Living in *this moment*. Mom, especially. I hate seeing her trapped in that pain from all those years ago."

His eyes glistened, but then he set his chin. "You know, Evita." A muscle in his jaw flinched like it was difficult for him to say it. "You're right. This war between Daneen and your mom has gone on long enough. Having them compete against each other in business hasn't helped either. That merely added fuel to their fire."

Evita nodded. "Stoking the fire on the anger they'd built up in high school."

"I don't know what Daneen has to be angry about." He sighed. "She always got what she wanted."

"Not everything," Evita said. "Not class president."

"And so?" Her dad lifted a shoulder. "That was one small thing in her very comfortable existence. Why did it matter so much?"

Evita shrugged, because she honestly didn't know. "Like you said, I guess people have their reasons for acting how they do."

"Yes, but I have no excuse." Her dad uncrossed his arms. "For how I've acted around you." He walked toward her where she sat on a stool and stared down into her eyes. All at once, she sensed his pride and affection. "I understand where your mom is coming from, and—deep in my gut—I don't completely trust the Hatfields either, but I do know one thing. Your mom and I didn't raise our daughter to be any kind of dummy."

Evita blinked at his backhanded compliment. Still, she knew he was making an effort. "Just what are you saying, Dad?"

"Just that I—" He choked up a bit on the words. "I'm sorry." Hope bloomed in her heart. "I don't know about Ryan, but I do trust your judgment. And not just about that. In general."

Evita arched an eyebrow, needing to hear him say it. "Even though I'm not a boy?"

His rough chortle surprised her. "For heaven's sake, Evita. I know better than anyone that you Machado women can take care of yourselves."

She chuckled, thinking of her mom. "Yeah, I guess that's true."

"So what?" He held out his weather hands. "You forgive me?"

Evita leaped off the stool and threw her arms around him.

"You bet I do!" He gave her a big bear hug, swallowing her in his warm embrace, and for an instant she was a child again—safe and protected. But now she could protect herself, and her dad saw this.

He pulled back and held her arms. "Just be careful, eh?" His mustache twitched with the stern admonition, but then his face softened in a subtle smile. "And I know you will."

She hugged him again. "I love you, Dad," she whispered against his chest.

He gave her a firm squeeze. "I love you too."

Someone rang the doorbell just as Robby and Eunice traipsed down the stairs. Robby carried the baby across the living room while Eunice followed him wearing a pained expression on her face.

"I'll get it!" Evita said, walking toward the front door. Her dad picked up his pork butt in its heavy roasting pan and followed her. He'd made plans to hang out around the house and babysit his grilling project and already had the gas grill heating up in the drive.

Evita opened the front door, nearly colliding with the Hatfields who were coming indoors, laden down with grocery sacks. "Oh hi!"

Mr. Hatfield held a package in his hand. "Hello." He shot a curious stare at her dad's pork butt, then looked at Evita who had her hands free. "This was on the doorstep." He passed over the package. Eunice dropped her beach bag and raced forward, her arms crossed against her chest. "Finally!" She snatched away the package, then cut Mr. Hatfield a glance. "I'm about to burst."

Mr. Hatfield's whole face turned red, and Eunice scampered away upstairs with the package. "Meet you down at the beach!" she said to Robby.

Ryan sent her a silent signal of some kind. Ugh. She'd forgotten to check her phone. She'd go check it before she went to the beach.

Mrs. Hatfield marched into the house with her bags. "We're cooking outdoors tonight," she announced to no one in particular. "The kitchen is all yours!"

Evita's dad backed into the house, holding his pork butt. "Sorry?"

"We're grilling burgers," Ryan explained. He stared down at the pork butt. "Is that going on the grill?"

"It is." Evita's dad's mustache twitched. "That's why the grill is in the driveway and has been heating up for the past hour."

"Oh." Ryan shifted on his feet, and Maddy stared up at him.

"I think I'll, um, go somewhere else," she said, striding toward the deck and grabbing her canvas bag along the way. She followed Robby and the baby out the door and shut it.

Mr. and Mrs. Hatfield stood at the kitchen island, their arms halfway inserted into grocery bags. "What?" she asked in high, shrill tones. Then she seemed to temper herself. "What I mean is." She pulled her arm out of a bag, extracting nothing. "That's news to us."

"We didn't make a schedule for the grill," her husband told her.

"I made a schedule," Evita's dad said.

"Oh. Well." Mr. Hatfield blinked. "Maybe we can grill our burgers once you finish up?"

Her dad shook his head. "This stays on the grill a very long time."

"How long?" Mr. Hatfield asked.

Evita's dad's grin tightened. "Past your dinnertime."

Mrs. Hatfield's eyes flashed, but then she composed herself. "That's o-*kay*. We can grill our burgers another night. Can't we, Kirk?" She couldn't resist adding fake-cheerily, "Sacrifices must be made."

Evita's heart pounded. Oh no. This wasn't starting up again. Not now. Not after her dad promised. It seemed to take every ounce of control he had not to erupt at the Hatfields. But he did it. Her dad reined himself him, barely hiding his smirk.

"Thank you, Daneen," was all he said.

"I'll grab the rest of the stuff from the SUV," Ryan told them. When Evita was the only one looking, he dragged the back of his hand across his forehead.

She hid her giggle.

Yeah. Right. Close call.

She hunted around for her cell phone and found it on the coffee table beside the kids' puzzle. She scanned Ryan's text message.

He'd sent a thumbs-up emoji.

At least that was something—and she'd made inroads with her dad too. So that had been another step in the right direction. Maybe the two families would make more strides toward harmony today? Ryan saw her checking her phone and winked.

Her pulse fluttered. There was just something about him. Interesting. Fun. And she wanted to have fun with him without her parents standing in between them for once. "I'm heading down to the beach!"

"Okay," he said. "See ya!"

His mom shut her eyes but didn't say a thing.

A short time later, Evita greeted her mom and the others. "The Hatfields are back."

"That's nice," her mom said from behind her sunglasses with no hint of emotion in her voice. Evita saw Maddy had positioned her chair down the beach in the same spot where she'd been yesterday. Nanny and Quique were with her.

Evita jutted her chin in their direction. "What's going on there?"

Kendra spoke from her spot under the umbrella. "We told them not to bother her, but Maddy said it was all right." Robby sat beside her holding the dozing baby and appeared close to nodding off himself. Chachi and Evita's mom were soaking up rays.

Evita gazed at the kids, seeing they held their hands up in the air. Wait. They had macrame cord stretched between their spread-out fingers, and Maddy was showing them some kind of game. She demonstrated maneuvering her macrame cord and forming a teacup. Then another fun design. Oh! A star! Then a ladder! The kids eagerly copied her. Quique caught on first, but Nanny wasn't far behind him. From the joyful beams on their faces, they were having a great time. Maddy appeared relaxed and happy too. Evita never would have predicted this from their first day.

Eunice arrived and took the baby from Robby. "You look like you're ready for a nap yourself."

He sat up and blinked, pretending like he was wide awake. "Feeling better?"

She gave a huge smile. "Much."

Evita hadn't unfolded her chair yet, so she offered it to Eunice.

"Here," Robby said. "Why don't you take mine? I might go in with Luisa and rest for a bit."

"Okay," Eunice said, returning the child to his arms. "But when she wakes, text me."

"I can take a turn feeding her now."

Eunice sighed with relief. "Yeah, you can."

"You just enjoy," Robby said. "Seriously."

"Thanks, love," she told him.

He kissed her on the lips before leaving. "Thanks for being my wife."

"It's my pleasure," she answered in a flirty way.

Chachi and Kendra exchanged glances.

"Ah, Nantucket," Chachi said, leaning back in his chair. "A lovers' paradise."

The Hatfields arrived, and Mrs. Hatfield's gaze jerked toward Maddy.

She had a hushed conversation with her husband, then Ryan joined in.

At last, she took her seat.

Mr. Hatfield sat down too, and Ryan glanced at Evita.

She opted to make a bold move, carrying her chair to the imaginary dividing line they'd established on the beach. She plunked her chair right down beside it and looked at Ryan. He got it at once and moved his chair too. Planting himself beside her.

Evita's mom sat up, and Mrs. Hatfield leaned forward.

The moms locked gazes, then each one frowned, standing and walking toward each other.

"Evita," her mom said. "Get up."

"You too, Ryan," his mom commanded on the other side of him.

"What?" His eyebrows shot up. "No."

Evita crossed her arms and her mom huffed.

"What? Really?" She stared down at her daughter for a long while, but Evita didn't budge.

Neither did Ryan, hiding behind his sunglasses.

Finally, both moms gave up and strode away.

"Well, that was easy," Ryan said, deadpan.

Evita hid her giggle behind her hand. "Yeah, right." She was sure she and Ryan would both catch an earful about this later, but she didn't care. It was worth it. She settled back in her chair, savoring the warm sun on her face and the soothing sound of the waves.

"Do you think they'll ground us?" he teased her further.

Evita chuckled. "*And* take away the car keys."

"Good thing we've got bikes."

Evita gasped at a happy thought. "You know what else is in that shed?"

"Not the gas grill any longer." He frowned, but he was playing.

"No." She shared an impish grin. "Boogie boards."

"Great idea."

They glanced at their moms, who were distracted.

The Hatfields' umbrella had collapsed unexpectedly, and Ryan's dad and mom were attempting to shove it back up. Nanny and Quique had darted to their grandma and were showing her and the other Machados their new tricks. Maddy sat happily making a whale.

"Now!" Ryan said, peeling out of his chair.

Evita kept low to the ground sliding out of hers.

They hustled toward the steps as quietly as they could.

Evita and Ryan crept through the house. Her dad was busy in the kitchen with the blender, whipping up his chimichurri sauce and playing his music. Even though he and Evita had arrived at an understanding about Ryan, she didn't want to antagonize him into changing his mind. She and Ryan sneaked through the living area, bent close to the ground and trying not to giggle. Then exited the front door, shutting it gently behind them.

"This is going to be great," Evita said as they reached the shed.

He grinned. "Absolutely."

There were six boogie boards in the shed. Four were in better condition than the others. They grabbed two each, tucking them under their arms, then scurried back through the house, avoiding her dad's detection.

Maddy turned as they came down the stairs. "Boogie boards, cool!" she called from her far-away spot. Quique jumped up and down and tugged on Chachi's hand. "Dad! Dad! Can we?"

Chachi stared at Ryan and Evita then replied, "I think we must!"

Ryan handed one of his boards to Chachi, who thanked him, then he walked over to Maddy. She was already out of her chair and had packed up her macrame. It was the warmest day they'd had, and the water looked inviting, even if it was slightly on the chilly side. Ryan's parents stood.

"What's the meaning of this?" His mom's hands swept the beach as Chachi and Quique headed into the waves.

"We found them in the shed," Ryan answered.

She pursed her lips, but Ryan's dad said, "They're only boogie boards, Daneen. I mean..." He shrugged. "Why not?"

"Here, Eunice," Evita said, handing her a board. "Want one?"

She declined gracefully. "I think I'll sit this one out for now, but thanks."

Evita extended her second boogie board toward her mom.

"Oh no." She laughed. "Not me." She glanced at Kendra as Nanny gazed at her expectantly.

"Can we go too?" the child asked with a hopeful gleam in her eyes.

Kendra took her hand. "Sure. Let's do it."

Evita watched in surprise as Ryan's dad accepted a boogie board.

"Kirk!" his mom called as he raced toward the waves. "What are you doing?"

But he didn't answer. He just kept on going like a gleeful kid, skipping over the sand and hopping into the waves with a woo-hoo!

Maddy lay on her board, paddling through the shallows. "Da-ad?"

"What?" he asked from behind his seawater-speckled sunglasses. "I remember how to do this."

Evita stood beside Ryan on the shore. "Looks like we're all out of boogie boards."

"Doesn't mean we can't still have fun." He grinned and her heart thumped.

"Last one in's a rotten egg!" she shouted, racing ahead of him.

Ryan hollered and chased after her, and they both threw themselves into the rollicking ocean spray. Evita glanced back toward the beach where both moms observed the action.

Mrs. Hatfield shook her head and sat back down, burying herself in her book.

Evita's mom sighed and lowered her sunglasses, sinking down in her chair.

Both resigned.

"Auntie Evita!" Nanny called from an eddy. "Look at me!" She gripped on to her boogie board and kicked her small legs turning around and around in circles while Kendra stayed close by.

"And me!" Quique yelped, as Chachi pulled his board along, giving him a ride across the choppy waves.

"And me!" That was Maddy. Her face lit up as she caught a cresting wave, tucking her board under its fold. She sprang onto it and shot out like a rocket toward the shore, whooping at the top of her lungs.

Ryan's mom glanced up from her book but then continued reading with a dour expression. She was dead set against having fun, even if the rest of them were.

"Good one, Mads!" Ryan called as Maddy collected her boogie board and waded back out into the sea for another go.

"Thanks, bro!"

Ryan's neck colored and he got a sentimental look in his eye. "That's the first time she's called me that."

"Aww, that's sweet." Evita treaded water with her arms, relaxing in the water that wasn't much past her elbows. She sat back in the buoyant waves, letting them lift her in one rolling motion after the next.

"Yeah," he said warmly, "and so are you." Without warning, he pushed a huge splash of water her way and it hit her in the face.

"Oh, you!" she splashed him back, forcefully flinging water in his direction with both hands.

"Hey!" He stood in the waist-high water, dragging his arm across the surface and drenching her with a saltwater downpour.

She laughed and got him back. "Two can play at this game, hmm?"

He reached for her, but she ducked away then threw herself onto her belly, kicking and swimming toward the beach. He came after her but didn't catch her as she sprang out of the waves and darted onto the sand. "Ha ha ha!"

"Very funny."

She set her hands on her hips. "Guess I had the last splash. Ha!"

His heated gaze poured all over her, and her skin warmed. "I guess so."

Both moms loudly cleared their throats at nearly the same time.

Ryan reached for a towel and tossed it at Evita. She caught it, wrapping it around her shoulders as he dried himself off, his lean, muscled chest streaked with moisture and a smattering of sandy chest hair. Ooh, he'd toned up really well during these last ten years.

"Evita," her mom said, striding up beside her. "Do you think you could go and check on your father to see if he needs help?"

"Um." She glanced at Ryan. "Okay."

Ryan's mom waved him over to her umbrella. "I need your

help with this," she said, pointing to its drooping side. "The frame's bent again."

As Evita walked toward the steps, her mom whispered behind her, "Careful with Ryan, Evita. He's still a Hatfield, after all."

Evita sighed.

She didn't know what it would take for her mom to see the Hatfields differently.

Some kind of miracle, it seemed.

Ryan wrestled with his parents' umbrella, finally fixing the bent portion. At least well enough. His mom nodded in thanks, then met his eyes. "What was that out there?"

"Out where?" he asked obtusely, although he knew what she was hinting at.

"With you and Evita? Horsing around like you were teenagers."

"We were just having a laugh."

"Yes. Well, laughter can lead to other things." Her lips turned down. "And she's still a Machado."

"The Machados are a great family." He studied the beach where Chachi and Kendra played with their kids. "You can't blame their whole group for something that happened between you and Evita's mom when you were in high school."

She huffed. "Ryan. I said I'd do my best to accommodate your wishes. Be cordial enough. But you don't need to go pushing any boundaries."

"Pushing? What?"

His dad appeared at the umbrella, his hair all askew from the waves. "The water feels great, Daneen. Come and try it."

She stared down at her bathing suit sarong and sandals and clutched her book to her chest. "I'm perfectly happy here."

"Yes, but we're at the beach." He latched on to her hands, and she dropped her book. It slid off her lap when he pulled her to her feet.

"Kirk! No." She cast a sidelong glance at Evita's mom and Eunice, who were trying not to look but kept snatching peeks in their direction. "What are you doing?"

He impishly tugged on her hands. "Come in for a swim."

She blanched. "Not now." He tugged again and she stumbled, awkwardly shedding her sandals. "Kirk." She set her chin, looking fierce. "I said stop." She locked on Ryan's gaze.

"Dad. Maybe she's right."

"Of course she's right. Your mom is *always* right." His dad chuckled. "Except for when she's wrong."

He stunned Ryan by grabbing his mom under her knees and scooping her into his arms.

"Kirk! Whoa! What are you doing?" She kicked her heels but suddenly she was laughing. "Kirk! Stop right this instant!"

He took two long strides down the beach.

Her hat flew off in the wind, and the hem of her sarong whipped up around her husband's back. She pounded his shoulders, but he wore a devilish grin.

Maddy stopped playing in the water, standing and holding her boogie board. The Machados all froze watching too.

He was not going to do it.

Oh yes, he was.

"Kirk!" his mom wailed as they approached the roaring sea. "I said put me down!"

"All right." He leaned forward and kissed her, then hurled her into the waves.

"Ahh!" She sank like a stone then bobbed back up, gasping, her sunglasses pushed up into her hair. "Argh! You!"

She threw herself at her husband like a linebacker, knocking him backward. He roared with happy delight. "Now this is Nantucket!"

"Nantucket! Ha!" She splashed him with both her palms, then dragged herself out of the water, pausing briefly to straighten her sarong. Then she marched back to the umbrella, took her beach towel, and headed for the house.

"Daneen!" Kirk called after her. He waded out of the surf with upturned hands. "Come on, hon. It was all in fun."

She appeared anything but amused.

Ryan felt sorry for his dad.

As she passed Ryan, two bright-pink spots appeared on her cheeks. "Not one word."

No problem. He was speechless. So was Mads, apparently, since her mouth hung open.

Ryan's dad was quick on his mom's heels. "Daneen, sweetheart," he pleaded, following her up the steps. "Let's talk this over."

But his mom just kept going.

TWELVE

NEITHER OF RYAN'S PARENTS HAD apparently done much talking by dinnertime. The tension in the kitchen was so thick you could cut it with a carving knife. At least the meal was decent. They'd picked up fresh shrimp from the fish market in town and his mom had steamed it, since they'd had to put their burgers on hold due to the Machados' use of the grill. Ryan had prepared the baked potatoes, and Maddy'd made the salad. His dad had fixed the martinis, but his parents hadn't chatted over cocktails as usual.

His dad stayed at the kitchen island glued to his tablet and grousing over the day's stock market returns while his mom stepped out on the deck, trying to avoid Mr. Machado's curious gaze as he sat on a sofa. Evita's dad was supposedly working on a crossword puzzle on a folded-up section of newspaper, but he didn't appear to be having much luck filling it in.

Maddy peeled another shrimp and dipped it in melted butter. "Good shrimp," she said to no one in particular.

"Hmm, yes," his dad said. He peeled a few for himself and dunked them in cocktail sauce. "Nice and fresh." He continued speaking without looking at his wife. "Expertly prepared, Daneen."

She harrumphed and sliced open her baked potato, slathering on some sour cream. "Did somebody say something?" She peered around the kitchen and very purposely past her husband's shoulder.

Maddy rolled her eyes at Ryan, and he shook his head.

"Great salad, Mads."

"Thanks, bro."

His dad took a forkful of greens in creamy dressing. "It is good. My compliments. To you too, Ryan, on the potatoes."

Nobody said anything else for the longest while.

"How about those Red Sox?" Ryan joked in an effort to lighten the mood.

His mom and dad stared at him, and he winced. "You know," Ryan said. "I think I'm just about finished with my food." He glanced at Maddy.

She abruptly scooted back her stool. "Yeah! Me too."

They both got up, carrying their plates to the sink.

"But you haven't finished," his mom said.

Oh yeah, he had. Ryan was so past done with this.

Talk about an appetite suppressant. Watching his parents fight—but not fight.

"I was thinking," Ryan said to Maddy, sending her silent signals with his eyes. "We could go out for a bike ride?"

"Sure."

"Wait," their mom said. "Now?"

Maddy glanced over her shoulder. "We'll help with the dishes when we get back."

"From having ice cream," Ryan whispered to her as they scurried toward the door.

She raced outside ahead of him, breaking into giggles.

"I know." Ryan shook his head. "That was bad."

"I don't know why Mom's so mad," she said. "I think it was sort of cute and flirty what Dad did."

Ryan exhaled. "Don't think she views it that way."

Maddy's blue eyes widened. "Maybe she'll change her mind?"

"Maybe."

They passed the grill, which emitted mouth-watering scents.

"Wow, that smells good," Maddy said.

He unlocked the shed and they took out the bikes. "Yeah, but we'll make up for it with a double hot fudge sundae."

"Yum!"

He smirked. "I thought you didn't like ice cream?"

"Love it." She snapped the chin strap on her bike helmet. "Just don't like being treated like a child."

She was still his kid sister, but he got what she was saying. "You're not a kid to me."

"I know that now. Thanks." She hopped on her bike and took off pedaling. She didn't even know her way into town though. Luckily, he did. He put on his helmet and took off after her.

"Hey, Mads! Wait for me!"

Evita and her family didn't see much of the Hatfields after their episode on the beach. They had an early dinner and had cleared out of downstairs by the time she finished her shower.

Except. Wait. Was that Mr. Hatfield standing in the foyer with a hangdog look? He leaned into his suite's door with one hand and knocked lightly with the other. "Seriously, sweetheart," he said in hushed tones. "I said I was sorry."

Whoa. She'd locked him out? Poor Mr. Hatfield. How humiliating. Especially with them all sharing this one cramped cottage.

Evita's dad rolled his eyes at her from the sofa. Since he'd been in here the whole time, Evita guessed he'd witnessed a bit of Hatfield drama. He set down his crossword puzzle and got to his feet. "I think I'll go check on that pork butt," he said aloud but more to himself. He crossed through the foyer, and Mr. Hatfield stepped aside with an embarrassed frown.

"Roses always work for me." He tossed his gruff comment into the air as if it had no intended target, but it very strategically landed on Mr. Hatfield's ears.

"Roses? But where—?"

Her dad motioned to the front door, and Evita hid her giggle.

What was this? Her dad was helping Mr. Hatfield?

But why? Because he couldn't stand to see another husband in the marital doghouse, she surmised. She was dying to know what would happen but couldn't stand here staring a moment longer. When she returned from changing into her clothes, the outcome was clear.

Mr. Hatfield was no longer in the hallway, and a few tell-tale flower clippings sat on the countertop and in the kitchen sink.

Her dad arrived with his pork butt which looked—and smelled— cooked to perfection. They would be eating late tonight, and Evita's brothers and their families mingled on the deck, holding piña coladas and admiring the blood-orange and purple-streaked horizon.

Nanny and Quique had been tasked with shucking the corn

into paper grocery bags and seemed to be taking their jobs seriously, their foreheads furrowed in concentration.

"That looks fantastic," she told her dad about his masterpiece.

"I hope it will be."

"Want some help?"

"Maybe with cutting the melon?"

"Sure." She took the honeydew from the refrigerator and located a cutting board, rinsing the fruit and getting to work. "Saw you talking to Mr. Hatfield earlier."

Her dad was busy pulling the pork butt apart using two large forks. Savory scents wafted toward her on a warm cloud of steam. "Hmm."

"That was nice of you."

"Nobody likes to be locked out of their bedroom." He said that like he'd had experience with the situation himself, but she was not about to pry. Just thinking about her parents—ick. She scrunched up her lips. No. She wouldn't go there.

"So. Ryan and Maddy aren't around. I guess they turned in early?" She sliced the melon in half, seeding it and cutting her wedges into cubes, while depositing them in a large salad bowl.

"They didn't turn in." His eyebrows knitted together as he gently tugged the pork into shreds. "They took out the bikes."

"Oh nice." It was fun to think of Ryan and his kid sister doing stuff together. They'd probably not had lots of opportunity for that in the past.

Her dad shook his head. "Wasn't so nice the way it happened."

She finished with the melon and washed her hands. "What do you mean?"

Her dad looked up and sighed. "Their parents had a fight at dinner. Something about Daneen being embarrassed, and then Kirk claiming she'd embarrassed him with her reaction."

Evita twisted the dishtowel in her hands. "Uh-oh."

"That's why their kids skedaddled out of here."

Evita frowned. "I almost feel sorry for Mr. Hatfield."

"Oh. I don't know about that." He stared at the ceiling, evidently recalling something happy. "Making up can be *very sweet.*"

Evita gasped and shoved his shoulder. "Dad!"

He chuckled at her reaction. "There may be snow on this roof, but there's still fire in the hatch, Evita."

Okay. Well, good. She didn't want to dwell on that. Ick. Ick. Ick. Or on Mr. and Mrs. Hatfield either. Ahhh. Nope.

"In any case." He finished with the pork and set his forks aside. "Ryan and Maddy probably won't be gone much longer." He glanced out the window. "It will be dark soon."

That was good because Evita was dying to talk to Ryan. She still didn't know what had been said during their brunch and wanted to congratulate him for making strides with Maddy.

"Don't be too obviously interested in Ryan's whereabouts," her dad warned. "You know how your mom feels about that, and she's still coming around."

"Yeah, but—"

"Cordial is fine," he said. "Romantic? Not so fine. Not yet, Evita."

Evita bristled at his interference. "But you said you trusted my judgment!"

"I do." He lowered his eyebrows. "Which is why I trust you not to antagonize your mom." Right. Which meant Evita needed to have a talk with her mom, just like she'd had with her dad. As soon as possible too. Whenever she could find a private moment for the two of them in this ultra-crowded house.

"Gee, Dad," Evita hissed in low tones. "It's not like I'm angling to get *romantic* with Ryan."

His eyebrows arched, and Evita licked her lips.

"Okay," she said on a breath. "But not anytime soon."

Liar. If he asked you out, you'd go in a heartbeat.

No. No. Not in a heartbeat.

Her heart beat double-time.

Okay, yeah. Maybe.

Her mom walked into the kitchen, looking fresh and pretty after her shower. "Pablo, your pork smells amazing." She took a small pinch in her fingers and popped it in her mouth. "Mmm! Tastes amazing too!" She reached back into the pan, but Pablo playfully swatted her wrist.

"Stop that, Lissette. You'll have to wait along with the others."

She kissed his cheek. "If I must." She turned to Evita. "What's left to do?"

"Not much and besides," she said, because this had been the prior agreement between her dad and her siblings, "tonight is your night off."

"Most definitely." Her dad reached into the freezer for his pitcher of piña coladas. "Let me pour you a drink."

She preened like a princess. "That would be lovely."

Her dad held up the pitcher. "Evita?"

"Yes, please!"

By the time Ryan and Maddy returned, Evita and her family had all sat down to dinner in the dining room and dusk had fallen outdoors. "How was your bike ride?" Evita asked them.

Maddy answered first. "Really fun." She yawned and covered her mouth. "But I'm whipped. I think I'll head upstairs." Evita knew she had a TV in her room. All the bedrooms were outfitted that way, except for Quique and Nanny's since Chachi had removed the cable as a proactive measure. Otherwise, the kids might have stayed up all night watching things, some of which might not have been suitable for their young eyes.

Evita had the impulse to ask Ryan to sit down and join her, even though he'd clearly eaten. Just to enjoy a drink and conversation. But things weren't yet to that level in this house. A slow thaw had begun between the Hatfields and the Machados, but there hadn't been a total ice melt by any means. Besides that, her mom might not appreciate her inviting Ryan to sit down at their table. This was her special night off, and Evita didn't want to make waves.

"Yeah, it was nice," Ryan answered. "Good ride." His gaze roved over the table. "I think I'll head on up too. You all enjoy your meal."

Everyone said good night, and Ryan followed Maddy upstairs, pausing briefly on the staircase. He glanced over his shoulder at Evita and she raised her eyebrows at him. But she guessed there wasn't much he was going to say in this public venue. So he just waved and turned away. Evita's heart sank. She'd hoped to spend time with him tonight. Get a chance to talk in private. She took her phone out under the table and dashed off a quick text.

Meet up later?

"Evita," her mom said. "I hope you're not texting at the table?"

"No, uh." She deftly put away her phone. "Just checking the weather."

"And?" her dad asked her.

"Tomorrow's another beautiful day!"

Thunder clouds boomed, rousing Ryan from his slumber. He removed his earplugs and was greeted by the clatter of rain against the roof and gusts slamming the windows. What a storm. He checked his phone for the time. It was nearly midnight. Wait.

There was a text from Evita. She'd sent it hours ago, but he'd missed it. Great. That probably meant she thought he'd seen it but ignored her. Which he was not inclined to do. He hadn't been able to get the woman out of his head since first seeing her on Saturday.

He set his feet on the floor and switched on the light. Maybe she was still up? If she wasn't though, he didn't want to wake her. Ryan raked a hand through his hair, his gaze skimming the earplugs on his nightstand. She'd be using those too. So if she'd gone to bed, his text wouldn't disturb her.

Sorry. Just saw your text. Still up? He stared at his phone, willing a response to materialize, then he saw the tiny typing dots. *Yes.*

Yeah.

Everyone else in bed? he queried.

Evita's text lit up Ryan's phone. Think so. The house is quiet. A split second later. Apart from the wicked storm.

He decided to go ahead and ask. Midnight snack?

It didn't take her long to answer. Sounds good.

Nice. He offered to go downstairs first. I'll check it out and text an all-clear.

Hurry! My battery's dying. Left my charger in the dining room.

Right. He had to move fast. Ryan crept to the pocket doors. Holding his breath, he knocked lightly then waited a beat before sliding them open. Chachi and Kendra spooned together under the covers, sleeping soundly. Ryan tiptoed past them in the dim glow of the nightlight streaming in from the bathroom. Then, gripping his phone, he slipped out the door and into the darkened hallway.

Winds howling up from the beach slammed against the house, and rain sliced sideways into the big glass windows as he eased down the spiral stairs.

The great room stood in shadows sweeping eerily in from the tumultuous sea. He scanned the kitchen and then the dining area. The front foyer too. Empty. He texted Evita, then waited. No response. He waited some more, pacing between the two seating areas while gripping his arms at the elbows. The storm raged outdoors, thrashing the ocean this way and that, creating enormous, angry-looking waves.

He stared down at his phone. Still nothing.

Then he saw Evita's charger on this side of the dining room table plugged into an outlet in the wall. Argh. Her phone had to have died before she'd gotten his last message. Maybe she'd chance it and come down anyway? Or maybe she'd worry that her parents were up and out here, after being awakened by the storm?

He was wide awake now himself. And she was probably up there waiting for his signal.

He studied the spiral staircase on the side leading up to Robby and Eunice's suite. He couldn't really go up and walk through their room. That would be creepy, and Robby might wake up and slug him, believing him to be an intruder.

A pail of seashells sat under the covered porch portion. They didn't belong to anyone here, as they'd been there when he and his folks had arrived at the house. So some other family had forgotten them or intentionally left them behind. He had a decent throwing arm and had pitched some ball in high school. Maybe if he hit Evita's window just right, he could get her attention? The screen would prevent it from breaking. It was worth a shot. He'd need to get a few shells first and then leave through the front door since her room faced the drive.

Ryan grabbed his rain jacket from the coat closet and slid it on, then headed for the deck.

THIRTEEN

"PSST. RYAN? WHAT ARE YOU doing?" Evita wore shorts and a baggy pink sweatshirt that said "Blooming." It had the stenciled outline of a rose on it. She'd been so stealthy in her descent he hadn't heard her coming down the stairs.

He stood there barefoot in his sweatpants and T-shirt feeling awkward about it. "I was just going to get you."

She reached the ground floor and her eyebrows arched. Winds ripped across the deck, dragging along sheets of rain that splashed into the firepit and sent furniture scuttling. "What?" She scrunched up her nose. "Out there?"

He tugged at his rain jacket. "I figured your phone had gone dead. So." He nodded through the glass door, and she spotted the bucket of seashells. "I was going to send you a signal by 'shelling' your window." Her eyes sparkled in the dim light appearing bigger and browner than ever.

"You were ready to brave the elements for me?" She appeared pleased.

Thunder boomed, and lightning crackled across the sky, startling them both.

"Ah, yeah." He shrugged out of his rain jacket. "Maybe a good thing you saved me from that."

"Yeah. Maybe so." She nearly tripped over her phone cord walking toward him. "Ah. Here it is." She had her phone in her hand and plugged it in, setting it on the dining room table.

His text message popped up on the screen.

All clear!

She giggled and stared out at the storm. "Maybe all clear down here but not outdoors."

"I know." He shoved his hands in his pockets. Being alone with her in the darkened room felt personal. Intimate. "I didn't think the bad weather was coming until later."

"Guess things are a little unpredictable out here, huh?"

She got that part right. He couldn't have predicted how hard his heart would beat just looking in her eyes. He glanced toward the kitchen, and so did she. "So. Want to grab that snack? Maddy made some cookies."

"Did she?"

He nodded. "Chocolate chip."

"Yum." A grin lit up her face, and those dimples settled. "I'm in."

Warmth spread through his chest. He was in too. So much deeper than he knew. But did she feel the same about him?

They crept into the kitchen, and she switched on an under-the-cabinet light. Its warm glow cast a deep-gold hue across the room, framing the center island.

"Where are the cookies?" she asked, opening the pantry.

"Square tin. Top shelf."

Evita found it and carried it over to the island, grabbing a stool.

"Milk or wine?" he asked, reaching for some glasses.

"Let's do milk."

He opened the refrigerator and took out the Machado gallon and the smaller half-gallon carton that belonged to his family. He held each one up in a hand. "A fitting representation."

"Yeah." She nibbled on a cookie. "Ooh, Ryan." She sighed. "I'm going to have to compliment Maddy. These are so good."

He lowered his voice in a confiding manner. "I'd never tell Mom this, but Maddy's more skilled in the kitchen." He poured them glasses of milk and carried them to the island, returning the containers to the refrigerator.

"How about your dad?"

Ryan shook his head, joining her at the island. "He's good at grilling a few things. Burgers. Steaks. Salmon. But doesn't do much with a stove." He helped himself to a cookie as well and took a bite. "These are really good, you're right."

She nodded. "How about you? You cook?"

"Enough to feed myself, but nothing gourmet. How about yourself?"

"I cook gourmet," she said. "I just don't have enough people to cook for."

"No?"

"I make big batches of food and freeze and save for later. Makes things easier for me during the busy work week."

"Yeah, that makes sense." He hesitated before asking, but he was dying to know. "So, you're not seeing anybody then? I mean, I know about Sebastian. Since him?"

She locked on his gaze and his heart pounded.

She was not a stupid woman. Far from it. She knew exactly why he'd asked and what he was asking. "I'm not seeing anyone. No." She took a sip of milk. "How about you?"

The tops of his ears burned hot. "No. Um. Not currently."

Her eyebrows arched. "Currently?"

"I've done some of the dating apps since my last girlfriend. But it's so hard out there."

"Abysmal. Yeah." She frowned like she was remembering something, maybe lots of somethings.

"You never really know about people, you know what I'm saying? Everyone tries so hard to present their best selves—"

"Meaning they sometimes make stuff up," she said, cutting to the chase.

"Yep." He shook his head. "I went out with one woman who used profile pics from at least ten years ago. Possibly fifteen."

"Ew. What?" Evita grimaced. "She was cougaring you?"

His eyebrows rose. "Not sure if that was her goal, but yeah. It was pretty evident when I saw her in person that she was a lot older than she'd said. Then she got a call from her daughter. Her twenty-year-old daughter, who turned out to be a student in my class."

"Oh no!" Evita gasped. "So did you tell her? About her daughter being your student?"

"I did."

"What did she say?"

"Some glib line about how you're only as old as you feel. If I'd like to go back to her place, she'd prove it."

"Holy cow! Forward."

"Right? I said thanks but no thanks as politely as I could and left some cash on the table to pay for our drinks." He groaned at the memory. "She flipped me off when I was leaving."

"Some people."

"I know. It wasn't like I was in the wrong."

Evita sighed in sympathy. "I'm sorry, Ryan." She shook her head. "I've had men fudge their ages too. What's up with that?"

"No clue. I mean, why even go there?"

Evita groaned. "Such a waste of time."

Ryan got it. "Don't get me started on the married people acting like they're not," he said, taking a sip of milk.

"What? Women do that too?"

"Sure they do. When I call them on it, they often have stories about open relationships or the 'trial separation' they are going through."

Evita smirked. "Yeah, maybe without their husbands' knowledge. It's so hard to know what's real anymore, and who is on the level."

"Seems it's better to be honest and let those chips fall where they will. Especially with so much searchable on the internet these days and everyone on social media." He liked sharing things with her. It reminded him of their bond in high school. Only this was better with them both all grown up. He heaved a breath. "Isn't it weird how people sometimes don't sound how you think?"

"From their photos? Yes!" She giggled, leaning into their conversation. "There was this big bodybuilder-type guy with all the tats, and when I met him, his voice was higher than mine. I mean, totally not his fault. I know. But it was such a surprise. He was nice, but I—just couldn't get past it."

Ryan chuckled. "I went out with this one sultry-looking woman who I thought might talk all husky, like one of those old movie starlets, but she spoke in this super-high falsetto like a little girl. Or like she'd inhaled big-time from a helium balloon."

Evita burst out laughing. "Oh no!"

"Oh yeah. I maybe should have had compassion, but honestly? It kind of creeped me out."

"Oh man." She dabbed at her eyes with her napkin because she'd been laughing so hard. "Poor woman," she said, but then she cackled again. "You mean like Donald Duck?"

"More like Daisy."

Evita roared and held her sides. "Stop!" she joked. "I'll toss my cookies." Then she winced and glanced toward the stairs, probably realizing how loud she'd been.

The rest of the house was quiet, except for the sound of the rain.

He liked having this effect on her. Making her laugh and smile. "Then there's the professor thing." He said it wearily like it was such a burden. This piqued her interest, just as he'd hoped.

"Oh yeah?" Her eyebrows rose. "What professor thing?"

His face felt hot. Maybe he was oversharing. "Some women have an—interest."

She searched his eyes. "In?"

Okay. He was definitely oversharing. What was he trying to do? Make himself out to be a player? Which he clearly wasn't.

"Never mind." Although it was true. Certain women were oddly turned on by his job. Maybe it went back to early teacher crushes.

"What?" she asked in a singsong way. "They want to play school?"

Heat surged from his neck to his temples. He'd definitely stepped out of his depth. "Um." He winced. "Maybe?"

Evita roared with laughter again. But it really wasn't that funny.

She caught herself and glanced toward the stairs for the second time in the last ten minutes. "Oops. Sorry. I know we should keep it down, but oh. Ha ha!" She slapped the kitchen island. "With you of all people."

Wait. What did that mean? "What?" He didn't mean to sound hurt, but he was slightly injured. "Some women find me..." He swallowed past the burn in his throat. "Hot."

"I'm sure they do." Her cheeks turned red. "But that wasn't my point."

"What was, Evita?"

"You're just so..." She studied the ceiling, hunting for the right words. "Good. Kind. Considerate." She squared her shoulders. "Upstanding."

"Way to wound a man."

"Stop. You know what I mean."

"You're saying I'm a nerd."

"No." She lifted her chin. "A gentleman."

"And that would be—"

Her eyes danced. Her very dark and beautiful eyes. "A good thing."

"Yeah?"

"Yeah." Her smile filled his soul with sunshine. She licked her lips and they glistened. If they were on a date, he'd be tempted to kiss her. "I couldn't say that about a lot of the men I've met."

"I'm sorry about that." He took her hand on the island, needing to touch her and make a connection. She locked on his gaze and gave his hand a squeeze.

"Yeah." The word came out breathy. "So am I."

The seconds ticked by, and rain splashed against the window panes.

Evita's grip relaxed in his hand but she didn't let go, and he was glad.

"So about your last girlfriend?" she asked.

"Oh, Ciara?"

"That sounds sophisticated."

"My mom had her for lunch. I meant that figuratively and in the worse possible way."

"What?"

"I made the mistake of bringing her home, and my mom wouldn't let up. Asking about her education, her background. What did her parents do... That kind of thing."

"She couldn't take it?"

"Most women can't take my parents, Evita. Especially my mom. She makes them feel—inferior. Even when they're not." He hung his head, conceding he sometimes felt inferior around his parents too, even though he had no business thinking that way. He was good at what he did and out there making a difference. It shook him to think that was maybe how his mom had always felt around *her* dad. Maybe, in some twisted way, that's how she'd been taught to care. To love. Tough love. Too tough, in Ryan's book. But sometimes it was hard to know better when all you knew was where you came from.

"I'm not afraid of your mom. Your dad either, for that matter."

He viewed her admiringly. "Yeah. I got that."

"Are you afraid of my folks?"

"Truthfully? I used to feel intimidated, by your dad and your brothers. Maybe a little by your mom."

"But now?"

He shook his head. "Not since this week. It's different, you know. To see them as real people versus only how you imagined them in high school."

"Yeah, I think that about your family too. Your parents have their quirks, but you know." She lifted a shoulder. "Don't we all?" She smiled softly. "And Maddy's cool. Very sweet."

Her perfumy scent washed over him, and in that instant he was a goner. "Evita." He tugged her closer with his hand, and she let him. His heart pounded in his throat. If he kissed her now, would she want that?

She blushed and jerked away her hand.

Apparently not.

The sudden motion rocked him on his stool. He gripped the counter, trying to act like his pulse wasn't pounding in his ears. That his heart wasn't beating wildly. What an idiot he'd been. Thinking this attraction was brewing on both sides.

"So!" she said, selecting another cookie. "Tell me about Maddy!"

He experienced an odd burst of relief. They'd been teetering on the edge of a romantic involvement. And—definitely—a kiss. Maybe it was good she'd pulled away. Getting involved now would be complicated with both of their families filling the house. That didn't mean that they couldn't get along and enjoy each other's company in a platonic way. Now that they'd nearly crossed the line though, it was hard to think of her as just a friend. But he could get his head in that space. He'd done that all through his junior year of high school.

She held up her new cookie. "How did your talk go? Excellent, I'm thinking?"

He savored her bubbly warmth. Evita was basically always upbeat, which made him feel happy too. "Thanks to you," he said about Maddy.

"Not thanks to me." She chewed while covering her mouth, enjoying her cookie. "Thanks to you and whatever you said to her."

"I was really surprised to learn she's not into the cello like everyone thinks."

"I thought she was some huge virtuoso?"

"She's talented. It's not that. It's more like she doesn't want our parents picking her career for her. She'd like the chance to explore other things too."

"Like?"

"Art. Stuff she can make with her hands."

Evita nodded. "I've seen her doing macrame on the beach. She seems to like it."

"She does. She also doesn't necessarily want to go to Julliard."

Evita frowned. "That's going to be tough news for your parents."

"No joke. Especially my mom." He lowered his eyebrows. "I suppose I've failed her expectations too."

"You?" Evita blinked. "But you're teaching college."

"She'd like it better if I were at Wellesley."

Evita shook out her hair, and her dark curls bounced. "Wellesley's not for everyone."

"No. That's true." He thought of his brunchtime conversation. "Hey, I finally found out about our moms and what happened way back when between them."

Her eyes shone with interest. "And?"

He told her the entire story about them facing off for senior class president and about how their dads had slickly tried to sway the election.

Evita set down her milk glass, which was half empty. "Wow. I heard the same story, only differently."

He gently touched her arm. "Differently how?"

Her forehead creased. "More from my mom's perspective, I guess. I don't think she completely understood the pressure your mom was under. Or that your grandfather had broadsided her. She didn't even know about Abuelo, you know. He never told her he was going to bring pizza. He just did it as a show of support."

"What is it with our moms?" He sighed. "Only wanting to believe the worst about each other?"

Sadness glimmered in her eyes. "Maybe they've been conditioned that way?"

"Conditioning can be changed though." He cleared his throat. "But that does take time and effort."

She pursed her lips and nodded. "By both parties." She took another sip of milk. "Not just one."

She was right and he knew it. But it somehow seemed impossible to traverse this monstrous chasm between. "Nutty, huh?" He hung his head. "That they can't move past this?"

"They did a little better today." He looked up and met the hopeful glimmer in her eyes. Evita was just that way. So positive. Determined. Sadly, sometimes determination wasn't enough. Especially when it was being forced upon unwilling parties from the outside.

"Sure," he replied. Ryan rolled his eyes to try to make light of it. "Until my dad pulled his prank on the beach."

Evita giggled. "But that came out okay, right? I mean, they *did* make up?"

He shrugged. "By the time Mads and I got back from our bike ride, they'd gone to bed. So, who knows? Hope so." Ryan set down his milk glass. "If only we could think of a way to get our two families together, you know? Focused on something other than their differences."

"I think we should try a group game," Evita suggested.

He winced. "I'm not sure if my crew will go for it."

"Come on, why not?" She shared an encouraging grin. "It will be like—team building!"

"Team building, yeah," he said, clearly not convinced but hesitant to disappoint her. He gazed at her sitting there in the shadows, wondering what kind of team the two of them might make. They'd been a dynamic duo as lab partners and conflict mediators. But dating? He'd definitely felt a mutual tug earlier. Unless that had just been wishful thinking on his part.

There'd been other moments though, and he recalled each one in detail.

So this couldn't be one-sided on his part.

"Ryan," she said sweetly. "This has been so good. Really great spending time with you."

Yes. He knew it!

Okay. Hoped it.

"I know, Evita. I feel the same."

"If it weren't for our families," she said. "If we'd met some other way."

"Like through one of those dating apps?" His voice went husky in spite of himself.

Color swept her cheeks. "Exactly."

"I wouldn't have been disappointed by you." The truth oozed out of him before he could stop it.

Her eyes twinkled warmly. "Me either."

He got swept up in her current. It tugged at his soul, pulling him nearer.

Luisa wailed and Robby stumbled down the steps, gripping the railing with one hand and clutching on to her with the other. Ryan and Evita sprang apart, sitting up on their stools. He'd come so close to kissing her. And he'd been desperate to, despite the complications.

"Robby!" she said, capturing his attention. "What's going on?"

He jostled the whining baby on his shoulder and lumbered toward the kitchen, wearing dark circles under his eyes. "The storm," he said. "It woke her."

"Oh gosh." Thunder boomed and lightning blistered the sky. "I'm sorry."

Robby stared at the island. "Are those cookies?"

"Help yourself." Ryan held the tin in his direction, and Robby shifted Luisa in his hold.

"Here," Evita said, standing. "I'll take her."

Robby passed her the baby without complaint and bit into a cookie. "Okay," he said, waving it in the air. "This was worth getting up for." He studied their glasses of milk. "Great idea," he said, going to pour himself a glass.

Evita shifted from one foot to the other trying to soothe Luisa while rubbing her back. But she was cranky and stiffened like a bowed board arching forward. "Poor baby." She glanced at Robby. "Does she need to eat?"

He shook his head. "Eunice fed her a little while ago, then fell right back asleep."

Evita tried a little dance, but nothing seemed to work.

Luisa's face pinched up like an angry prune.

Robby shook his head with a haggard look. "Here. I'd better—"

"No," Ryan said. "Let me."

Evita stared at him in surprise when he held his arms out for the baby. "I did this a time or two when Mads was small." He glanced at Robby, who was eagerly devouring another cookie like it was his last meal. "If it's okay with you?"

"Sure. Sure." He took a swig of milk, then rubbed his eyes. "Thanks, Ryan."

Ryan accepted Luisa and held her naturally, cradling her in

his arms. "Yeah, yeah," he said softly. "I know it's bad. Big bad tummy ache, huh?"

She sputtered a cry, but he kept talking to her, dropping his voice to a low rumble.

He swayed her gently, then took bobbing steps around the room, each one a bit springy but gradual. "It will be okay, little one," he said. "All okay."

He glanced back toward the kitchen and caught Evita eying him with wonder.

Her smile lit up his soul. "You're a natural."

"A little rusty." Luisa's head sagged against his shoulder, proving he wasn't rusty at all. Then the weight of her settled in his arms, and he could tell she was falling asleep.

"Rusty!" Evita said softly. "Ha." Her eyes twinkled, then she darted a look at Robby. He'd set an elbow on the island while sitting on a stool. His chin was in his hand and his eyes were closed.

She gently nudged him. "Robby?"

He didn't move.

She nudged a bit harder and he opened his eyes. "Oh! What?"

"You should probably go on to bed."

"The baby."

"We've got her." She nodded toward Ryan and Robby's forehead rose.

"Nice." He covered his mouth in a big yawn.

Evita pushed at his arm. "Why don't you go upstairs?"

"Okay." He stood on wobbly legs and made it as far as the sofa, which seemed to grab him. He collapsed down on it and rolled onto his side, shoving a pillow under his head. "Mmm," he said in a daze. "Good night."

Evita giggled and held up her hands.

Ryan motioned toward the sofa blanket.

"We can't just leave him down here?" she whispered.

Ryan considered Robby, who was roughly his size. "I don't think we'll be carrying him up the stairs either."

Evita nodded. "Right." She lifted the sofa blanket and draped it over her brother.

He didn't budge, but then he began to snore.

"Guess he's down for the night." Ryan viewed Luisa. "That makes two of them."

Evita approached him and opened her arms. "I'll put her up in her crib."

"I'll clean up."

He gave her the baby. "Thanks, Ryan."

He fought the very strong urge to lean over and kiss her on the lips, like they were a couple. But they weren't. And Luisa wasn't their baby. If they were to become involved though, they might eventually get married and someday have a child of their own. The thought shook him to his core.

He wasn't ready for that. Was he? Babies? Marriage? No. He couldn't even. Although with Evita, he was beginning to imagine. And that unnerved him.

Emotions swamped through him, tumbling over each other. "You're welcome," he said, as she took Luisa upstairs. "Good night."

Evita lay Luisa in her crib, her heart pounding. The way Ryan had looked at her just now. He'd taken her breath away. It was like he'd been thinking... She didn't know what he'd been thinking, but she could guess. And hope. That maybe he'd been thinking about the two of them having a future.

She'd had no clue he'd be so good with babies, or Luisa in particular. But of course his history with Maddy made sense. Evita and Ryan had that in common. They valued their families, even though their moms could be a little misguided at times. Okay. A lot misguided when it came to this ridiculous family feud. Evita was ready to put an end to it, and so was Ryan.

She walked on quiet footsteps toward her sitting room and slowly shut the pocket doors. Having cookies and milk with Ryan had been fun. She'd gotten a kick out of his dating app stories. It had felt like they were back in chem class again, trading high school gossip. Only that exchange was about themselves and the similar dating experiences they'd had. It made her feel like she had a friend, someone who understood.

As much as she adored Josie, Josie was so caught up in her engagement she could barely recall being single anymore, and Evita's other girlfriends were married, some of them with babies already. It really was murder out there and so hard to find the right one.

Her pulse thrummed. Maybe she and Ryan hadn't clicked with other people because they'd been waiting on each other? To circle back around from their flirty friendship in high school by taking things one step further? If ever there was a right time, it was now. Now that they were adults and finally solid enough in themselves to stand up to their families.

She placed a hand on her heart, telling herself not to get carried away. She didn't need a boyfriend to make her life whole. She knew that. But that didn't mean she couldn't dream a little.

FOURTEEN

THE NEXT MORNING, EVITA FOUND her mom in the kitchen. No one else was around.

"Hi, Mom. How you'd sleep with the storm?" Rain pinged against the plate-glass windows and speckled the deck, but the torrential downpour had subsided along with the loud claps of thunder and lightning bolts that had cut through the sky.

"Good. You?" They both fixed their coffees and carried them to the sofa in the great room.

"I slept all right."

Her mom's eyebrows arched. "All night through?"

"I. Er." Evita bit her lip.

"Because when I came down first thing to start the coffee, Robby was on the sofa." She scanned Evita's eyes like she knew something. "And there were three empty milk glasses in the sink."

Evita blew out a breath. "Yes. Okay. I was down here too."

"With Ryan?"

"Robby was with us."

Her mom sipped from her mug. "But not the whole time, I'm guessing."

Evita frowned. Would this Hatfield animosity never end? "Well, no. But, Mom? Please listen. Ryan is a very good guy. He's always been."

Her mom's shoulders sagged beneath her red bathrobe. "I'm sure you're right. That's what your dad says too."

Evita couldn't believe her ears. "What? He talked to you?"

"About Ryan, yes," her mom said. "I've also seen how Ryan is with his sister. Caring. How somebody treats their family says a lot about a man." She shook her head. "But, Evita." Her expression was weary. "Daneen and I—"

Evita touched her mom's arm. "That was so long ago. And anyway. Could it be that you're both somewhat at fault? Not for then, but for how you're behaving now?"

Her mouth hung open. "Evita. I'm your mother."

"I know you are, and I love you. So, so much. Which is why I hate to see you carrying this for so long. Ryan told me his mom's side of the story about the election."

"Daneen told him about her father and how he manipulated things?"

"Mom. Abuelo brought pizza."

She squared her shoulders. "That was only to encourage voting, not any particular kind of vote."

"Right."

Her complexion reddened. "I'm stunned you'd think that of me, Evita. That I'd cheat."

"I didn't say you cheated, Mom. Honestly, I don't believe either you or Mrs. Hatfield did. You both just had—overeager parents. Dads who believed they were helping their daughters in their own ways." She shot her mom a look. "I know what it's like having an overinvolved parent."

"I am not overinvolved when it comes to you."

"You seemed very eager to have me marry Sebastian."

"But, baby, that was different. He seemed like such a good catch. Established." She playfully lowered her eyebrows. "Handsome." She clucked her tongue and scowled. "But that was before I knew he was a Don Juan."

"It wasn't just about Liliana, Mom. Sebastian was a jerk to me in other ways. Maybe more than I saw at the time. But Chachi saw it, so did Eunice. Robby and Kendra too."

She set down her mug. "They said something?"

"Yeah." Evita exhaled sharply. "They didn't like how he treated me, like he was superior."

"Superior to you? No way." She frowned and was silent a moment. After a beat, she sighed. "I didn't tell you this the other night when we had our talk, but your dad had his misgivings too."

"What?"

"He always said, 'There's something about that man I don't like,' but I told him, 'Pablo, we have to respect Evita's choices.'"

Evita latched on to that opening. "I'm so happy you feel that way!" She hugged her mom's shoulders.

Her mom pulled back like she'd walked into a trap. "It's different with the Hatfields."

"No, it's not. At least, it shouldn't be." She met her mom's eyes. "Look. I like Ryan. I really do. I've liked him for a long time, since all the way back in high school."

She looked panic-stricken. "Does this have to do with chemistry class?"

Evita laughed softly. "Maybe, in a way."

Her mom slapped her forehead. "*Ay.*"

"So, we had chemistry together," Evita teased lightly. "I suspect we still do."

"Evita!"

"Mom! I'm a twenty-eight-year-old woman and old enough to make up my own mind about who I do—and don't—hang out with. If I want to hang out with Ryan during the rest of our time here, then I will."

"You're being very defiant."

"No. I'm being assertive."

"Yeah? Who taught you that?"

She set her palms on her mom's cheeks, cradling her face in her hands. "You did."

Her mom's dark eyes glistened.

Evita dropped her hands. "You taught me to be strong and to know my own mind. To stand up for myself and for my life. I never would have opened that flower shop without your support—yours and Dad's—and you know it."

"It's very embarrassing to be dressed down by your daughter."

"I'm not dressing you down." Evita patted her mom's hand. "I'm building you up." She shrugged. "And anyway. I don't need a man to complete me."

"Of course not, but—"

"There is no 'but.' I've got my shop. I love it. I've got other plans too."

"That community garden of yours?"

"Yeah. And, you know, some day? If I find the right person? Great. I'm not opposed to company or to eventually having a family. But I learned something important from Sebastian. That I was rushing into a serious relationship because I thought I needed to compete with Chachi and Robby on so many levels. The house. The spouse." She sighed, thinking of her adorable nieces and nephew. "The kids."

"You don't want those things?" Her mom sounded distressed.

"If they come along in the right order? Sure."

"And what order is that?"

"First, I'd have to find someone I love and who loves me back, organically." Her cheeks warmed when she remembered Robby's comment. "Maybe even worships me."

Her mom held Evita's chin in her hand. "Worships?" Her eyebrows arched. "Just as long as it's mutual, hmm? It's not good for only one to put the other on a pedestal. That only sets up a fall."

"Yeah."

Her mom got a dreamy cast in her eyes. "Your dad and I do worship each other, it's true. Even after all these years."

"Aww. That's sweet." Butterflies flitted around in her belly. She and Ryan would never go that far. Surely? Last night, as she drifted off to sleep though, she'd been thinking about that. Wondering what if? In so many ways. Her imagination painted all sorts of different scenarios.

Her mom sighed. "So, you want to what? Date him?"

It was clear she was speaking of Ryan. "I don't know where that's going to go," she replied honestly. "But I do know I'd like to get through these last few days without more fireworks. Ryan would like that too." She shrugged. "Maybe everyone would. And Mom?"

Her mom cocked her head.

"Maybe it's time you and Mrs. Hatfield think about burying the hatchet?"

Mrs. Hatfield strolled out of her suite wearing a sunny grin. "Hel-lo! Good morning!" She practically sang out the words like she was walking on air. "Sorry I'm late in the kitchen." She stared at Evita and her mom. "Would you mind if I grab some coffee to take back to Kirk?"

In their bedroom? Whoa. Evita's mom shot her a look and she tried not to giggle.

Guess that make-up session had gone well.

Ew. No. Put that out, out, out of your mind!

"Go right ahead, Daneen," Evita's mom said graciously. "Be my guest."

Mrs. Hatfield pranced past them in her white satin robe with a little spring in her step. Her slippers had wedge heels and fluffy white feathers across the top. She was not wearing her pearl necklace for once—or her headband—making her appear years younger. Or maybe it was that rosy glow on her face.

She fixed two mugs of coffee in the kitchen, then traipsed back through the living room, shooting them a smile. "Ta! See you!"

When her bedroom door shut, Evita's mom gasped. "Maybe she and Kirk did try the shower?"

"Mom! Gross!" Evita said, but she was laughing.

"Don't knock it until you try it." She bit her lip. "Not that I'm suggesting you try it with Ryan." She flushed. "Ever. And certainly not here."

"You have nothing to worry about." Evita held up her hand in a pledge. "Promise."

Her mom considered her a moment, affection flooding her gaze. "I love you, Evita."

Evita hugged her. "I love you too."

"Good morning!" her dad said, stepping into the foyer with a happy grin. He stared at his wife and daughter. "Okay. What did I miss?"

Evita and her mom filled him in on Mrs. Hatfield and her effervescent appearance.

"Must have been the roses," he said with a knowing grin.

"Roses?" Her mom's eyebrows shot up. "From where?"

"Out there, *querida*." He gestured at the front door. "It's not like there's a shortage."

She stared at the foyer. "No, I guess not."

Evita hoped Mr. Hatfield hadn't clipped from some obvious spot, leaving a big, gaping hole in the fence somewhere.

The rest of the Machados materialized soon. Eunice bounced into the kitchen beelining for the cookie tin. "I heard there were cookies!" They were still on the island.

"Wait!" Evita called but it was too late.

Eunice opened the tin and grabbed one, sinking her teeth into it. "Yum!"

Oh well. It was just one little cookie. "Robby told me about these." She nibbled, then poured herself some coffee. "Said they were to die for."

Nanny and Quique scrambled down the stairs in their cute pajamas. Hers had teddy bears on them and his showed an array of cartoon action heroes. "Cookies! Yay!"

Kendra was right on their heels. "Not right now."

She followed them into the kitchen, eyeing Eunice's remaining morsel. "Ooh, those do look good."

Eunice smacked her lips. "Nothing like cookies for breakfast."

Chachi reached around Kendra and nabbed a cookie from the open tin. He held it up like a prize. "Mrs. Fields is in the house!" he cried, referring to the famous brand of cookies sold in shopping malls.

"Chachi, wait!" Evita strode toward him, but he gobbled it down in record time.

Kendra slipped one to each of her kids. "Don't let it spoil your breakfast." Quique dragged his tongue across his cookie like it was a lollipop. Evita gasped.

Nanny copied him. "Yummy!"

Chachi rubbed his belly, chortling at the kids. "Mmm! Who made these?"

"Maddy, all right?"

Chachi tried to make a joke. "I said Mrs. Fields, but it was more like Miss Hatfield! Ha ha!"

Evita snatched away the tin, which was distressingly almost empty. There'd been a lot more of these last night. "Stop pigging out, everybody." She swatted Chachi's hand when he went after another. "These are for the Hatfields."

"What? Oh." Kendra covered her cram-packed mouth. She stared down at her kids. "Maybe you should, uh, put those back."

They frowned and Quique said, "Dad ate his."

Nanny nodded at her mom. "So did you."

Kendra held out her hand, demanding the cookies' return.

"No!" Evita said. "They've already licked them."

Evita's dad and mom swarmed the kitchen next. "What's all this about cookies?" He squeezed past the others and lustfully viewed the remaining treat. Where had all of them gone? Her mom was right beside him.

"Ahh. Chocolate." Her mom sighed. "And pecans?"

Evita pulled back the tin. Her mom and dad were *not* going to eat the last cookie.

Maddy descended the stairs dressed in shorts and a baggy top, and wearing one earbud. The other earbud dangled from the looped cord around her neck and she held her phone.

She stared in the cookie tin. "Whoa. Just one left?"

"Yes." Evita's mom practically drooled out the words. "It looks amazing."

Maddy chuckled. "You can have it if you want it, Mrs. Machado."

"Oh no, I—"

Evita's dad reached for it. "I'll take it then."

"No, you won't!" She grabbed the cookie and beamed at Maddy. "Thank you."

Maddy scratched her head. "I thought I'd made two dozen?" She glanced around the room at their guilty faces.

Kendra and Eunice shrank back from Maddy's perplexed stare.

"We might have had one or two." Chachi winced. "They were delicious."

Nanny and Quique chomped away as fast as they could, their small cheeks bulging out.

"Mmm-hmm," Quique said, barely understandable with his mouth full.

"No worries." Maddy closed the empty cookie tin, putting it away. She beamed at everyone. "I'm glad you liked them." She glanced over her shoulder at the others. "Okay if I grab some cereal? I know I'm a little late."

Evita's mom waved a hand, salivating over her cookie. "Don't worry about that silly schedule. Yum. These are fabulous."

"Were fabulous." Evita's dad frowned.

"Okay, Pablo, here," she said, chuckling. She held out her cookie. "Take a small bite."

He took a big chomp and she shouted. "Not the whole thing!"

Maddy served her cereal, plugging in her errant earbud. She observed the drenched deck and the rain that was still coming down from the sky. "Guess I'll sit in the living room."

Ryan sauntered down the stairs, still looking sleepy-headed in an adorable way. His hair stuck out every which way, and his eyes held the faraway gaze of a man needing coffee.

"Oh no," Evita said. "Did we wake you?"

He watched her curiously. "It sounded like a lot was going on down here."

Her heart fluttered because of how he looked at her. "Yeah. Sorry." She shrugged. "I'm afraid my family might have eaten all the cookies."

"What?" He laughed in surprise. "All of them?"

Eunice pursed her lips. "Robby said he had a few more when he woke up this morning."

"Way to blame the man who's not there," Robby said, descending his set of steps while holding Luisa. He blinked at the group. "Wait. Seriously? The cookies are all gone?"

Luisa started whining like she didn't like that either.

"Auntie Evita?" Nanny tugged at her hand. She was precious in pigtails and small gold earrings. "Where does this one go?" She held up a misshapen square.

"Ahhh." Evita studied the puzzle on the coffee table and pointed. "How about there?"

Nanny tried it and yelped with glee. "Yay! It fits!"

Quique handed her another piece. "Do this one!"

Evita loved indulging these kids. "Okay. I'll help you. But first." She glanced briefly at Ryan, who shot her a grin. "More coffee."

"Coffee," he agreed groggily. "Yes."

Nanny stopped him when he was halfway to the kitchen. "Will you help too?"

Ryan lifted his chin. "Of course I will." He hesitated and stared at Chachi and Kendra, then at Evita's parents. "If it's okay?"

Evita's mom sighed, savoring the last bit of her cookie. Evita had never seen anyone take so long to consume a treat. She nodded her assent.

"But don't feel like you have to," Kendra said.

"Sounds like fun." Ryan winked at Evita and her face warmed. "I love puzzles." He was so easy to be around and wasn't daunted by her family, even though her parents kept sneakily watching him like hawks.

Her mom tried to act cool, but she clearly couldn't help herself from interfering.

"Evita, why don't you sit on that side of the coffee table on the sofa with Nanny? Ryan can sit on the floor next to Quique."

Ryan's forehead rose, but only Evita saw it before he turned away to fill his mug. "The floor sounds great!" he said, speaking into the air. He came back to the living area, nodding good morning at Maddy, who waved. She'd finished her cereal and had begun a new macrame of another whale. She seemed to be making loads of those.

Ryan sat down on the floor with his legs crisscrossed and surveyed the room. "My mom and dad aren't up yet? Huh. That's weird."

Evita glanced at her parents.

They both pursed their lips.

"No. Um." Evita's skin burned hot. She was not going to go into details. Much less allude to anything. "They seem to be sleeping in."

FIFTEEN

AFTER A WHILE, THE MACHADOS made themselves an informal lunch by piling their plates with yummy leftovers, which was Evita's favorite kind of meal. Her mom had encouraged everyone to eat up so she wouldn't have to take a ton of food home. Ryan and Maddy sat at the island with their potato chips and sandwiches. It felt weird segregating them, especially without their parents present. Her folks looked squirmy about this too.

"Ryan and Maddy?" Her dad gestured to the dining room table and his plate. "You're welcome to come sit over here with us."

Evita's mom nodded. "Yes, of course," she said. "We can pull up more chairs."

Ryan dipped his chin. "That's very nice of you. Thanks. But we'll just stay put."

Evita joined her family at the table, and guilt gnawed at the pit of her stomach. This was really wrong. While it had seemed like an okay idea at the time, this whole house division was seriously messed up.

Mr. Hatfield emerged in the foyer. "Good morning, all."

Mrs. Hatfield stepped up behind him and whispered with an embarrassed grin. "It's afternoon, darling."

Darling? What?

Chachi and Kendra raised their eyebrows at each other while the rest of Evita's family exchanged looks around the table. Maddy and Ryan gaped at each other. That was definitely not like the Hatfields to be lovey-dovey.

Mr. Hatfield straightened his tropical shirt collar. It had bright-green palm trees and colorful dolphins and seashells on it. Super shouty for Mr. Hatfield. His wife, though, was back in her headband and pearls.

"Already having lunch?" she said to her kids.

Ryan nodded at the refrigerator. "Want me to make you guys sandwiches?"

"No thanks," his dad said. "We'll do it."

Mrs. Hatfield reached into the refrigerator and took out some lunch meat and condiments. "You know what I can't wait to have?" She turned to her daughter. "One of your homemade cookies for dessert."

Evita's mom dropped her fork.

Then the room grew silent. So quiet they could hear the wind whistling outside, sweeping away the remnants of the storm.

"Did I say something?" Mrs. Hatfield asked, looking around.

"No," Evita's dad said.

Chachi hung his head, chowing down on his food. "Didn't hear anything."

"Mom?" Maddy said.

Evita held her breath.

"Yes, sweetheart?" her mom asked, slathering a piece of bread with mayonnaise.

Maddy's forehead rose. "I'm not sure they came out well. A lot of them were burnt."

"Burnt shmearnt. I'm sure they're delicious. I can't wait to try one."

"Okay," Maddy said. "But maybe later?" She tried to avoid glancing at the Machados. "Like when I'm not around?"

Mrs. Hatfield rolled her eyes at her husband and then at the group in the dining room as if she were sharing a secret. "Teenagers," she said like they were some huge mystery she'd never figure out.

Was it her imagination, or did all of her family seem to eat more quickly? Maybe to get out of there before Mrs. Hatfield went for dessert? Her mom wore a polite smile leading the rest of them across the living area. "We're just going to deposit our plates in the kitchen."

Mrs. Hatfield nodded, nibbling on a potato chip. "Go right ahead."

Good. This was good. Everyone was getting along. So far.

And trying to keep their distance from the island where the Hatfields sat munching on their food. Ryan raised his eyebrows at Evita, and she got it. The cookie revelation was not going to go well.

"I've been dreaming about those cookies the whole trip," Mrs. Hatfield said to her husband. "I don't know why we didn't break them out sooner."

"I did!" Ryan said. He lowered his voice to a normal range. "What I mean is, I ate a few." He cleared his throat. "Last night."

His mom stared at him. "Last night?"

"Yeah, I—had trouble sleeping. With the storm."

She frowned. "Sorry about that. Well! At least there are plenty more."

Evita and Chachi bumped into each other scrambling for the dishwasher. Robby was in the way too. "Just go," Eunice said, taking his dishes. "Get Luisa ready for the beach."

The sun hadn't exactly come out, but the rain had stopped, so they'd all decided to go down after lunch. They'd been cooped up enough this morning.

Kendra scooted past Robby herding her kids up the spiral steps. "We'll go change into our swimsuits."

"I might have had a cookie too," Maddy said, after observing the action.

Evita waved a hand. "Er. So did I."

Mrs. Hatfield frowned. "You?"

None of the rest of the Machados fessed up though.

"I offered her a few last night," Ryan explained hastily.

"Wait." His mom narrowed her eyes. "What were—?" Her mouth twitched. "Oh no."

Robby turned on the spiral steps, holding Luisa. "I was here too!" He blinked when she gawked at him. "Chaperoning."

Chachi held up his finger and improvised. "It's a Latin tradition!"

Latin? What? Evita sighed. From maybe a hundred years ago.

Mrs. Hatfield got to her feet as Evita's mom shut the dishwasher. "As long as nothing happened."

Ryan's face reddened. "Of course not, Mom."

"And we still have cookies!" She reached for the tin in the pantry and Evita's heart stilled. Her mom was halfway out of the kitchen, but seemed frozen in place.

Mrs. Hatfield shook the tin. "This feels very light." She surveyed Ryan. "How many did you eat?"

"Uh." He sent Evita a panicked look. "Almost all of them?"

"Ryan," she said cajolingly. "You couldn't have." She pulled back the lid on the tin. Her face fell. Then she looked up. "What? Empty?"

Maddy grimaced. "I threw away the burnt ones?"

"I don't recall any being burnt," Mr. Hatfield said. He stared sheepishly at his wife. "I might have had one last night when I was cleaning up after dinner, but there were plenty left."

"Then how?" Mrs. Hatfield glanced around the room. Evita's brothers and their families hightailed it the rest of the way up the stairs. Her dad had reached the foyer, but he eased back a few steps under the loft so he could keep an eye on his wife in the kitchen.

"Wait." Mrs. Hatfield's gaze settled on Evita's mom. "Did the rest of you eat these?"

"Maddy offered!" her mom said.

Mrs. Hatfield frowned. "Maddy is also a child."

"I'm not—"

"Who also made the cookies," Ryan pointed out.

Maddy gaped at her big brother.

"Plus, she's not a little kid," Ryan added hastily. "She's in high school now and very mature."

"Mature?" His mom stared at him like she didn't know where this was coming from.

"Yeah," he said. "Smart enough to make up her own mind. Start deciding things like what classes she should take."

His dad spoke up. "Now, Ryan, let's not get carried away."

"What do her classes have to do with this?" Mrs. Hatfield shook the empty cookie tin. She pulled a face at her daughter. "You what? Want to be a baker now?"

Maddy shook her head. "No, Mom."

"A pastry chef then? Something culinary?"

Maddy set her chin. "I just don't want to play the cello, okay?"

Mrs. Hatfield stumbled, grasping the counter. Her face paled like she might faint.

"I think emotions are running a bit high," Mr. Hatfield said. "Over these cookies."

"My thinking too," Evita's mom said, trying to make her escape.

Mrs. Hatfield grabbed her sleeve. "What do you have to do with this, Lissette?"

"Me?" She shook off Mrs. Hatfield's hold. "Maddy's classes? Nothing."

Mrs. Hatfield set the empty cookie tin down and it clattered. "I meant the cookies?"

"I, uh." Her mom gazed at her dad.

"Come on, Lissette." He held out his hand. "Let's go."

Mrs. Hatfield blocked Evita's mom with her arm. "Did you eat any?"

"I—" She glanced out the window. Low-lying dark clouds hugged the sky. "Might have had one." She glanced at Maddy. "It was delicious."

"There was only one left—" Maddy started to explain.

Mrs. Hatfield's eyes grew huge. She wheeled on Evita's mom. "You ate the *last cookie*?" She sounded remarkably distressed.

"I told her she could," Maddy said, but her mom didn't hear her.

Mrs. Hatfield sent her an icy stare. "Who would have thought you'd stoop so low?"

"Stoop?"

"What is your family? A pack of hungry wolves?"

"Hang on!" Evita's dad stepped forward. "I don't appreciate that wolf reference." He stroked his mustache, then puffed out his chest. "Although in some ways it's not so bad." He frowned and mumbled something to himself about being leader of the pack.

"Yes, it's bad," his wife said. "Horrible." She squared her shoulders and stared at Mrs. Hatfield. "I demand you apologize."

Mrs. Hatfield set her chin. "Apologize for stealing our cookies."

"We. Did. Not. Steal."

Evita held up her hands. "Please!" The moms spun on her and her shoulders sank. "Everything was going so well."

Ryan stood beside her and in between their mothers. "Evita's right." He spoke to his mom. "Can't we please just move on?"

She bit her lip. "Fine." She lowered her eyebrows at Evita's mom. "Just keep your family from raiding our part of the pantry—again."

Evita's mom placed a hand on her hip. "We did not raid."

Ryan's mom shot a look at the kitchen clock. "And this is *our time* in the kitchen."

Evita's mom backed out of the room with a bow, dragging Evita along with her. "It's all yours, Daneen."

Daneen spoke in clipped tones. "You! Stay on your side of the house!"

Her mom's cheek flinched. "You! Stay on your side of the beach!"

Ryan shut his eyes.

Great.

"And," Evita's mom added, getting cranked up, "keep your son away from my daughter!"

Evita gaped at her. "Mom. We had a talk." She couldn't believe her mom had erased all that so easily. It was only because she was mad at Mrs. Hatfield. Anger clouded her judgment.

"Ditto, Lissette! Keep your daughter away from my son!"

Ryan raked both hands through his hair. "This has got to stop. Both of you please."

"Yes," his dad said. "I agree." He glanced at Evita's dad for solidarity, but he froze like he'd been caught in headlights. "Pablo, tell them."

"I think"—he shoved his hands in his pockets—"we should all just keep our heads—and our distance. We only have two more days left."

"Two and a half days, Pablo," Evita's mom corrected.

"During which," Mrs. Hatfield said, "we'll be cookie-less."

Evita's mom tsked. "What do you want me to do, Daneen? Go out and buy you some more?"

"No thanks." Mrs. Hatfield cleaned up her lunch plates, setting them in the dishwasher. "Just stay out of our way."

"Gladly." She spun and hooked on to her husband's arm. "Come on, Pablo."

"Your side!" Mrs. Hatfield shouted after them.

Evita dragged a hand down her face. Right. Another long day. This morning, she'd felt like her mom had heard her. That things were going to change. Until all those cookies crumbled.

———————

The rain picked up again after lunch, forestalling people's escape to the beach. So the Machados went to the historic district to explore the sights, leaving the house to the Hatfields. It had seemed cold and empty without Evita and the others there. The gloomy weather hadn't helped Ryan's spirits. That blowup over the cookies had been the final straw breaking their fragile peace. He got that his mom wasn't as upset over the cookies as she was about the rest of them ganging up on her over Maddy. Okay. She probably was a little ticked that Evita's mom had gotten that last cookie too. It wasn't just about chocolate chips. It was symbolic. In her mind, Lissette Machado always came out on top. But that was an impossible thing to believe of anybody. No one was perfect.

He and his parents and Maddy had more or less reverted to their former vacation mode, all doing their own thing and turning in early to separately watch television, while he viewed shows on his laptop in his room. Ryan clicked his bookmark for the Wellesley application, thinking it wouldn't take him too long to complete it. Easy enough to attach his CV. He'd need references though, so would have to reach out to his dean and a few former professors.

He heard car doors close in the drive and shut the application window. It was Evita's family coming back from dinner. The kids scampered up the stairs, then the suite door popped open. Chachi and Kendra. He put his earbuds in and turned up the volume on his movie, his heart thudding in a dull ache. Wellesley didn't feel right.

Neither did hanging out all evening long without Evita.

He snapped up his phone and sent her a text.

How'd the day go?

She answered quickly.

Okay. Nobody talked about it.

He decided to tell her the truth.

Missed having you around.

This time the delay was longer.

Missed being here too.

SIXTEEN

THE NEXT AFTERNOON, RYAN SAUNTERED down the steps to the beach carrying folding chairs and his parents' beach umbrella. They were behind him, and Maddy trailed after them. The Machados had hit the beach even before his family got up. They'd been down here all day. So his folks had stayed up at the house. Finally, his mom had said this was ridiculous, she intended to enjoy her remaining time at the beach and would not be "trapped" in the cottage. Ryan failed to point out that it had been a self-imposed sentence. What was the use?

He and Evita needed to separate themselves out from their families' problems. If there was any way, and he had faith there was. He spotted her on the beach with her brothers and Kendra. They appeared to be setting up a bocce ball game while Evita's parents and Eunice sat under their umbrella with the baby. The sky was overcast, but the sun was predicted to come out later. Best to be prepared.

Quique and Nanny spotted Maddy and charged her. "Maddy! Maddy!" Nanny said. "Can you play?"

"What? Now?" Still, she seemed pleased that the little kiddos idolized her.

Quique nodded. "Can we make a sandcastle?"

Maddy cut a glance between her folks and Mr. and Mrs. Machado. "Uh. I'm not sure—"

Evita's mom lowered her sunglasses. "Maybe build one right there." She pointed to a spot in the sand where they'd drawn the imaginary line dividing the beach on the first day. "We can still each be on our sides." Ryan knew it wasn't Maddy and her grandkids Mrs. Machado was concerned about keeping apart. It was him and Evita.

Okay. She also didn't want his mom all up in her face either. He still couldn't believe the huge deal she'd made over the cookies and was embarrassed by it. He'd added fuel to the fire by bringing up Maddy's music then too. Bad move.

Ryan's mom blew out a breath, weighing the situation.

"They're only kids," his dad told her.

He met her gaze until she gave in.

"Okay," she said to Maddy. "But stay right there."

"Yay!" the kids called, dashing to the designated spot.

Kendra called out, "Don't be pests, now!"

"We won't!" they chimed in unison, dropping to their knees.

Maddy deposited her things beside the umbrella Ryan was in the process of putting up.

Quique and Nanny kneeled in the sand and scooped clumps of it into their hands, trying to form walls, which kept collapsing.

"I've got a better idea," Maddy said, joining them. "How about we make a drip castle?"

"What's that?" Nanny asked her.

"It works really great with wet sand," Maddy said. "You drip it from your fingers like this." She dug a hand into the sand and held up the wet sludge, letting it seep between her splayed fingers in clumps. She formed a small pointy tower and then another.

Quique's dark eyes shone. "Cool!"

Evita's dad seemed to approve. "It will look just like the Sagrada Familia," he said, mentioning the whimsical cathedral by architect Antoni Gaudi in Barcelona, Spain.

Evita's mom patted his hand. "That's right."

"Ryan, hey!" Evita said, when he finished with the umbrella.

He nodded. "Evita. What's that you all are playing?"

"Bocce ball."

He wanted to join in but wondered if now was the right time to push that envelope. Maybe he should let tempers cool further first. "Looks fun."

Evita pointed to the beach, indicating he could join them, but he decided to pick his battles carefully today. "Maybe in a bit!"

He caught his mom watching him with a triumphant look and he bristled.

Ryan was not going to make a big scene now, but he also wasn't going to be told what to do. He picked up his beach chair, carting it right to the imaginary line in the sand and set it down a few yards back from where Maddy worked on her drip castle.

Evita said something to her brothers and Kendra and strode to her parents' umbrella, picking up her collapsed chair.

"Evita?" her mom asked.

She didn't turn to look, just kept striding to her destination, plopping her chair in the sand beside Ryan's. "Hello, there," she said softly.

A smile tugged at his lips. "Evita."

She dropped her beach towel in her chair and returned to the game.

Mrs. Machado appeared at Ryan's side in an instant. "Ryan," she said, hoisting Evita's chair into the air. She lifted her chin and carried it back to her umbrella.

Evita's mouth hung open. "Mom!" She strode back to the umbrella and grabbed her chair. Her mom tugged, but she tugged harder.

"Evita, stop!"

"No, Mom. You stop." She softened her tone. "Please. You promised."

"I know," her mom hissed. "But his mother drives me so nuts. You don't want to have children with him; they might turn out like her."

"Shh! That's not nice."

Ryan overheard their comments, and his neck burned hot. Him and Evita making babies? No. He sat with the idea a second, warming to the idea, which actually wasn't totally terrible. In the far distant future. Some day. Assuming things worked out.

Evita plopped her chair back in place beside Ryan's with a determined scowl, then she shot him a wink before strolling away.

Evita's dad tugged down his hat, sinking lower in his seat, and obviously taking a pass on this confrontation.

Meanwhile, Ryan's mom angled forward, seeming to have enjoyed the show. She stood and approached Ryan. "Lissette has a point—for once." She apparently couldn't help adding the dig. "You shouldn't be sitting here either. Come on, Ryan. Please move your chair."

"My chair? But Maddy's right—"

"Ryan." His mom grabbed his seatback.

A muscle in his jaw tensed. "I like being in the sunshine."

She looked up at the sky. "It's cloudy."

"The sun will come out."

"Tomorrow, tomorrow!" Nanny sang in a surprisingly great voice. "I love ya, tomorrow!"

Quique joined in, belting out, "You're always a day away!"

Ryan's mom blinked. "How?"

"Children's Theater!" Chachi said proudly.

"Oh. Well." His mom looked positively thrown.

Ryan had no idea those kids could sing. That was cool.

"Your kids are very talented," his dad remarked to Chachi and Kendra.

They preened, and Kendra said thank you.

Ryan stared at his mom, who was still waiting for him to move.

"I'm sorry. I love you. But—"

"But what?"

"I'm staying right here."

Her eyebrows arched and she waited. Then she waited some more.

Finally, she turned around. "He wasn't like that before," she complained to her husband. "See what being around Evita has done to him?"

"We heard that!" Mr. Machado said.

"Yes." Mrs. Machado leaned their way. "We're very proud of our daughter. If she's been any sort of influence, it's been a good one, no doubt." Ryan read Evita's surprised look, but then she flushed happily.

Ryan's mom sat down in her chair and opened her book. His dad started reading too. Ryan took out his e-reader, but his eyes were on Evita. She wore her emerald swimsuit under a tank top and shorts and painted such a pretty picture standing on the beach with the others. They were close enough for him to hear their conversation between the wisps of wind.

"I can't wait to learn how this works," Evita said to Kendra.

"Easy peasy," Kendra said. "You'll catch right on."

Robby pointed to a smaller white ball by his feet. "That one is the jack or the pallino. Someone throws that first, and the others try to land their ball close to it." He swept his hand across the grouping of eight balls. Two were red, two green, two blue, and two yellow. "Each team gets four. You score by having your ball land nearer the jack than the others."

Evita glanced up to see Ryan watching her. Her grin took his breath away. No matter what was going on, she had a sense of self, a confidence, that couldn't be robbed away by any circumstances or their warring families. He wished he could be more like her in standing up to his parents. Then he saw that he had made headway this week. Not enough probably, but some. Before long he'd be telling them to stop talking about Wellesley and to start honoring all the decisions he made. He kicked himself for even starting the Wellesley application. That's not what he wanted deep in his soul. Maybe Evita's influence had been good. She made him want to trust in himself and his instincts the way she unfailingly believed in hers.

"All right." Evita rubbed her hands together. "Let's play."

Robby addressed the others. "How about the boys against the girls?"

Kendra rubbed her hands together. "Sounds good to me."

Evita lifted a ball into her hands, evaluating its heft. "Look out, boys! No mercy." She stepped up to the line and tossed her green ball underhanded, landing it very close to the white one.

"Nice going, Evita!" Chachi shouted.

"We'll have to look out for her," Robby teased. He tossed his ball, which overshot its mark.

When it was Kendra's turn, her ball landed next to Evita's.

The boys whistled. "Uh-oh," Chachi joked. "Prepare for a crushing."

Kendra winked at Evita. "We've got this."

Ryan saw Maddy periodically glancing at the bocce ball game. It probably looked like fun to her too. The others played a few rounds, then Robby caught Maddy's eye. She and the kids had just finished their drip castle. "If you'd like to play," he whispered and motioned to their makeshift court in the sand.

Maddy glanced at her parents, but both had dozed off in their chairs. She giggled and got to her feet, dusting off her knees. "Sure," she said. "For a sec."

"Maddy!" Evita beckoned her forward with a grin. "Come on and join us girls."

"That leaves us outnumbered." Chachi raised his forehead at Ryan.

Ryan stood unsteadily from his chair and walked toward the group. Eunice and the baby were napping, and Evita's parents had gone back in the house to grab some snacks, but they could come back at any minute. "Maybe I'll just watch for now."

"Come on, man." Chachi elbowed him lightly. "You can't just stand there on the sidelines all the time. Sometimes you have to dive in."

Ryan met Evita's eyes. Her cheeks turned pink and his neck burned hot, both of them intuiting the veiled message in Chachi's words.

"He's right, you know," Robby said.

Evita raised her chin. "My brothers need help. So?"

Ryan got to his feet, unable to deny her request. The truth was, he wasn't sure he'd be able to refuse anything Evita asked him to do. "All right," he said. "I'll try it."

He learned to play the game, and it was fun.

But not half as much fun as spending more time with Evita beside the roaring sea. Gulls squawked above them, then darted for the waves as breezes blew. Then the scattered clouds parted, allowing for rays of sunshine. Ribbons of light shimmered through Evita's curls, igniting a pretty glow in her eyes. "I think I'm getting the hang of this," he said, evening up the score.

Evita tossed the final ball. "Not quite," she teased, winning the match for the girls.

Maddy whooped and jumped around in the sand, forgetting herself and being too loud.

Her mom's eyes popped open and so did her dad's.

She quickly dropped down on the sand, sitting casually beside the drip castle.

"What? Oh." Ryan's mom looked around, and Evita's folks came down the steps carrying coolers.

"Evita!" her mom said, seeing them standing close together.

"Ryan!" his mom called, sounding all uppity about it.

Ryan turned to Evita. "Want to go for a walk?"

"Run!" She giggled, racing down the beach. He ran after her, chuckling.

Quique shouted, "Yay! It's a race!" He sprang into action, but Chachi caught him.

"Just for your Auntie Evita and Ryan."

Nanny pouted. "Can we race next time?"

"Ryan! Come back here!"

He glanced over his shoulder to see his mom standing in a frustrated pose. Evita's mom wore a frown.

"They'll never catch us," Evita said, hurrying along. She wore that impish grin he remembered from high school. It said she knew she was breaking the rules but wasn't sorry in the least. He wasn't sorry either. Far from it.

He laughed and caught his breath, then kept running. "Probably not."

They found a patch of sandy dune that had partly dried out from the sun, which rose high in the sky now, bathing the beach in its warmth.

"We're going to be toast when we get back," Evita joked.

Ryan held up a finger. "Biscuits."

"You're getting the marmalade side." She rolled her eyes and sank back in the sand. "What a wild week this has been."

"I know. Challenging, right?" He hung his head. "Look. I want to apologize—about yesterday and the cookies."

"It's not you who needs to apologize, Ryan. My family ate them. Or most of them anyway."

"Doesn't matter," he said. "My mom didn't need to react the way she did."

Evita sighed. "Neither did mine."

"So your day out? It was good?"

She nodded. "Dinner too. It was yummy. But the kids. Well." She chuckled and he got it. It probably was a challenge with the three of them in a restaurant. "What did you have for dinner?"

"Potpie." He grimaced. "With the leftover chicken."

"Oh no. I saw you struggling through that." She winced. "Oops, sorry. Didn't mean to diss your mom's cooking."

He laughed. "It's all right."

Her forehead rose. "Was it any better? The potpie?"

He shook his head. "I'm afraid not."

"Ooh, sorry."

He stared out at the horizon. "At least we're all in one piece still."

"Yeah," she agreed. "We've made it this far." She glanced at him. "Now, if we could just make a bit more progress. You know, find a way to all come together. Like by playing group games, like I mentioned earlier."

He frowned. "Somehow I can't imagine our families playing group games, though."

"What?" She ran a hand through her curls. "Ryan, it's our last hope." She wryly twisted her lips and said, "I haven't given up." She shoved his arm. "You shouldn't either."

He grinned, appreciating her sunny optimism. "Which games are you thinking about?" How could he not support her? He had to, and he wanted what she wanted as well.

"I suppose we can see what we find back at the house." She shrugged. "There's always charades."

He drew up his knees, wrapping his arms around them. "I'm not sure my folks know that one."

"Come on. Everyone knows that one."

He shook his head. "We never played when I was growing up."

She frowned sympathetically. "Maybe because it's harder to play with just four?"

"Maybe." He stared out at the waves, rising and falling majestically, thinking about his family and hers. With Evita's brothers and their wives around, their gatherings always felt like a celebration.

"Do you really play bridge?"

The question surprised him. "What? Oh yeah. Cards? Sometimes. Sure."

She wrinkled up her nose.

"What's wrong with that?"

"Nothing, really. Just sounds a little stuffy."

He chuckled. "Yeah, I'm sure you're right."

She leaned her shoulder against his. "You're not stuffy though. You never were."

Her eyes glimmered in the sunlight.

"Maybe you're just easy to be around."

"Unlike Layla Petroski?"

Her again? A sly grin tugged at his lips. "So you were jealous, huh?"

She made a pinching motion with her thumb and forefinger. "Just a little."

A warm rumble filled his chest, laughter combined with joy. "I was jealous of Craig."

"Craig?"

"Craig Johnson. They guy who took you to the prom instead of me."

"Oh. Him," she said like it was no big deal.

"Both years."

She blushed and hung her head. "He was sweet, but we never dated."

"No? But I thought—"

"We were just friends."

"Like you and me?"

She met his gaze and held it. "No. Not like you and me."

His heart hammered and his face heated.

"I definitely liked you more."

"Yeah, well. I liked you more than Layla." He rubbed the side of his neck, embarrassed by his admission.

She gasped, leaning into him. "What?"

"It's true, Evita." His voice was all husky.

"We were star-crossed lovers then." She tried to say it lightly, but it struck a chord.

"Hmm, maybe so." He studied her pretty face, knowing they couldn't have made it work. Not back then and at their ages. The resistance between their two families had been too strong.

"Well. Anyway." Her eyebrows arched. "Now, here we are."

"Here we are." He stared back at the sea, unsure of what to say next.

She built a bridge for him. "Where do you see yourself in five years?"

His lips twitched. "What's this? An interview?"

"Go on." She pressed into his shoulder again, and her warmth seeped into him. For an instant, he found it hard to breathe. Then the breeze picked up, and the scent of her perfume called him home.

"Ah yeah. So. In five years?" He searched the sky. "I'd like to be promoted, I guess. Hopefully tenured."

"At Smithburg?"

"Yeah." He hung his head. "I can't believe I even considered it."

She stared at him. "What?"

He gritted his teeth together before saying sheepishly. "Wellesley."

"Wait." She cupped a hand over her mouth. "What do you mean? You were going to teach there?"

"Nothing guaranteed." He gave a bitter laugh. "Boy, wouldn't my mom have loved that."

"But no?" Evita's eyebrows arched.

"No," he said firmly. "I looked at an application though. Even started it. There was a job opening, and I thought about it. But then you know what I decided?"

She waited for him to continue, as wind raked through her curls.

"I decided I wanted to be more like you."

"Me?" Evita thumbed her chest. "I don't understand?"

"Yes, you, Evita Machado. Someone so sure of themselves. Following their dreams. Look at you and Coming Up Roses. Your own shop! So impressive. And I want to be impressive too. But not just to anybody. And not necessarily to my folks." He sighed.

"Although that would be nice, that's not the most important thing to me."

"No? What is?"

He placed a hand on his chest. "That I feel impressed with myself. Satisfied in myself, the way you are with your life."

She shot him a cockeyed grin. "You've just impressed me."

"Have I?" He swallowed past the tender knot in his throat. "Well, good." Ryan wrapped his arms around his knees, staring out at the ocean. Somehow, it had felt really good to say that, and he was glad he'd shared that with Evita. It was almost like a dress rehearsal. He'd give that talk to his parents next. He might not have been able to do that a week ago, but he felt fully capable now.

She nudged her body against his. "That's great. What else?"

He thought of his kids and how great they were. "I'd like to still be coaching youth soccer too."

"What?" Admiration flooded her gaze. "I didn't know that you did that."

He nodded. "The kids on my team are all pretty amazing. Some of them have parents at my school. That's how I got recruited into coaching. This is my second year, and I love it."

She studied him appreciatively. "I remember you were a soccer star in high school."

His neck warmed. "I don't know about the star part, but yeah, I played a bit."

"Not in college though?"

"No." He shrugged at the truth. "Probably wasn't good enough. I also wanted to focus on my studies. Had my eye on grad school and all that."

She nodded. "That's cool, Ryan. Maybe someday you'll have a kid of your own on the team?"

He closed his eyes, trying to imagine that. Weirdly, the boy that he saw had curly dark hair like Evita's, and dimples. His heart thudded and his eyelids flipped open. "Don't know. Maybe." He brushed that thought aside. "I'd also like to have most of the work done on my house by then. Although with those kinds of projects, the work is never really done."

"Projects like what?"

He was happy to share about his dream. "I want to buy an old farmhouse and fix it up. I saw Andrew Wyeth's place once and it inspired me."

"The artist's home in Pennsylvania?"

It amazed him that she knew. "Yeah."

"I've been there and to the museum too. The house was very cool. Basic. Rustic."

"Right." He pursed his lips. "I'm thinking a little less rustic than that. Bigger too. With room enough for a family."

"Big family or small?"

He shrugged. "Medium."

She laughed, apparently liking the sound of that. "You always were good on compromise."

His forehead rose. "We're compromising?"

She pushed back on his chest with her hand, as they sat side by side. "Sure. Why not? We're only just talking anyway." She sighed and sat back in the sand, supporting herself on the heels of her hands. "The farmhouse sounds nice. Romantic." He warmed at the word. "With land?"

He nodded. "A few acres at least. Minimum five."

"So, a mini-farm then?"

"Yeah."

"Horses?"

"Maybe not. I wouldn't mind a dog though."

She sighed. "I've always wanted a dog."

"Yeah?" Then he remembered her talking about this in high school. "That's right. You couldn't have them because of Chachi. He's allergic."

She nodded. "To cats too." She stared out at the ocean. "We had fish and turtles, but it wasn't the same."

"You volunteered at the animal rescue."

"Still do twice a week."

He beheld her admiringly. "But you've still never gotten a pup?"

She shrugged. "I'm in an apartment now. But some day, when I have a house, yeah, I'd like to."

"What kind?"

"Any kind with four legs and a tail. I'd take a three-legged one too, if he needed a home."

He viewed her warmly. "I bet you would, and he'd be lucky to have you."

Intensity flickered between them, and she blushed, looking away.

When she turned back to him, she said, "Maybe I'd like a beagle. Like Snoopy!"

"A beagle would be sweet, but those bay a lot, you know."

"As if I'm not used to commotion in a house." She rolled her eyes, and it was like she'd sent an arrow straight through his heart, overwhelming him with her charm.

"Fair point." He smirked and then asked, "How about you in five years? What do you see yourself doing?"

Excitement lit up her face. "I'd like to have my community garden up and running by then."

"Oh yeah?" That sounded like a worthy goal. "Where do you plan to start that?"

"In my grandparents' neighborhood, I hope. I've had my eye on a vacant piece of land for a while now. I'd have to reach out to the owners and investigate permits and such, but I've been doing research on how to get one of those off the ground."

"I love the sound of that."

"Yeah, me too. It could be so cool. So great for that neighborhood, give the younger families something to invest in and the older retired people, like my Abuelo and Abuela, something beautiful to do."

"Sounds like a win all around. You've always had a green thumb, that's for sure."

She gave him a thumbs-up, appearing dreamy-eyed. "I'd like to involve the local schools too. Have kids come and plant things, and maybe older ones contribute to the upkeep. They could earn community service credits."

"Oh yeah." He grinned. "Like you and I did in all those outreach clubs in high school."

She sighed a happy sigh. "Exactly."

"I think that's fantastic. You should definitely do it."

She beamed up at him. "You should definitely buy your farmhouse."

"I think I will."

"In the meantime." She cocked an eyebrow. "I've got a plan for tonight."

"Really? What?"

"It's about the group games and how to get everyone engaged."

"I'm listening."

"Remember how we talked about team building?"

"Team building, yeah."

"I've got uniforms." She bit her lip, looking impish.

"Uni-what?"

"Remember those T-shirts with the whale on them?"

"For Nantucket? Sure I do."

"When I went into that shop to get them, I didn't buy ten, Ryan. I bought fourteen."

"You didn't." He grinned so big it hurt.

"Even a tiny little one for Luisa. They all match." Her grin matched his. "You think your parents will wear theirs?"

He wasn't so sure about that, but he didn't want to burst her bubble while she was on a roll. "I'll sure wear mine. I'm betting Mads will wear hers too." He couldn't believe she'd been this thoughtful. But that was so like her. It also proved she'd believed in a chance for whole-house harmony since then, maybe even before.

"You're a pretty special woman, Evita. Thank you."

Her eyes danced. "You're a pretty special man."

The mood shifted between them, becoming intense and romantic. Wind raked through their hair and rippled their clothing. But they were in their own world. A certain kind of paradise.

He leaned toward her, and she held his face in her hands. His spirit keened toward her light.

She spoke softly but with a determined edge. "We're going to make this work."

She wasn't just talking about their families getting along. She was hinting about the two of them being together. His throat went tender and raw, because that's what he wanted. Both things. He lowered his mouth toward hers. "I'd like that."

"I'd like that too," she whispered. "A lot."

Her breath brushed across his lips and current crackled through him. Then softly, tenderly, he pressed his lips to hers in one lingering kiss.

It seemed to go on forever, lifting him up through the clouds and high above the Atlantic. Blowing him out to sea where he floated on the wind. Then, suddenly, it was over.

Her eyes glistened. "That was nice."

He stroked her cheek with his thumb. "Yeah. Just like I knew it would be." And he had imagined it so many times. Only reality exceeded his fantasies.

"Me too." She sighed and kissed him again. Tenderly and just once on the lips, a silky sweep of butterfly's wings.

He wanted to ask what was next, or talk about how they could work this out around their families, but the moment was so special, he didn't want to ruin it. So he just wrapped an arm around her shoulders and held her close, wishing with all his might that he could kiss her like that again. But not yet. Not now. Someday though. Yeah. Absolutely.

She snuggled into the crook of his arm, and they both watched the ocean waves cresting and pounding the shore, as their hearts kept time to the steady rhythm.

And, for this brief moment, this was all he wanted. Just being here with Evita as the sun sank low in the heavens, the crimson colors of twilight painting the sky.

SEVENTEEN

EVITA AND RYAN WALKED BACK to the cottage along the shore, watching the night close in. It had grown chillier, and they wrapped their arms around themselves, strolling along the sand while staying out of the waves. It felt so natural being with him. Perfect. And his sweet, tender kiss had blown her away. Her heart fluttered just remembering the gentle pressure of his mouth on hers, wispy soft, and warm. Tingles raced down her spine. Sebastian hadn't kissed like that. He'd been more aggressive. She sensed that Ryan could up his game, but that he'd taken things slow on purpose. She appreciated that. Any more right now would have been too much.

"How you doing?" His eyes sparkled, and her stomach flipped. He was so amazingly handsome and kind. Just all around—she sighed—everything. She hadn't known about him coaching soccer, and that only added another layer of niceness to him. He'd always been a good person. Someone who cared about others. Now it seemed he was starting to care about her in a romantic way. Her heart thumped. At least that's what she was hoping.

The breeze picked up, sending chill bumps down her arms. "A little cold."

He wrapped his arm around her as they moved along and warmth pooled in her belly. "We're almost there." His voice was husky below the wind, and she enjoyed the feel of his body pressed up next to hers. He wasn't a bulky guy. More like lean, but solid.

She glanced over at him as they walked along, their bare feet sinking in the chilly sand. "We've been gone a long time."

His smile warmed her heart. "So maybe a long time was what we needed?"

"It *was* good to get away from all the shellfire."

He blew out a breath. "Boy, was it ever."

"I learned some things about you." Her tone was flirty as she tossed her curls.

The tips of his ears turned red. "I learned what you're going to name your dog."

"Stop. You know what I mean. Serious stuff. Like about that farmhouse."

"You do seriously want a dog though." He lightly squeezed her shoulder. "I could tell that part." Winds whistled past them, somersaulting off the waves as they strolled along in tandem, each one effortlessly matching the other's steps.

"True. And the community garden."

"Both things will happen for you," he said tenderly. "I feel it."

She waited for him to mention the kiss, but he didn't. She hoped it wasn't because he was sorry about it, but she didn't think so. He stared out at the sea with a faraway look, and she could tell he was stewing over something. If it was about the two of them, he wasn't sharing. Ryan was usually pretty open, so maybe that was a bad sign. Pain seared through her gut.

No, Evita. Don't overreact. He's probably just processing like you are. Give him time. Maybe she needed time too. "So, game night," she said after a lull. "We're in? The Hatfields and the Machados?"

"I'll do my best with my crew," he said. "But I can't guarantee anything."

"I understand."

They reached the spot where their families had set up their separate camps on the beach. Everything had been packed up, including the bocce ball. Ryan frowned. "I probably should have helped pick up."

She paused at the bottom of the wooden steps. "I'm sure they'll forgive you this once."

He chuckled at her choice of words. "I'm not so sure I'll be forgiven at all." The twinkle in his eyes said he wasn't sorry about it though. He leaned toward her and kissed her cheek. Her face warmed. "But I'll deal with it."

She stared up at him, wishing they could stay down on the beach, just the two of them. But she knew they had to go and face the music. They had just a few more days to get through, and hopefully they'd be more peaceable ones. "Okay." She drew in a deep breath. "Here we go."

He held up crossed fingers. "Here we go."

They climbed the stairs and found Ryan's family sitting at the picnic table in front of the kitchen window hunkered over their food while wearing light jackets. Their plates were loaded with burgers and fries.

His mom's eyes went wide as she surveyed her son.

"And—where—were you?" She sat beside Maddy and Mr. Hatfield had his back to them.

He peered over his shoulder. "Could have used your help with the grilling tonight."

"Yeah. I know. Sorry." He addressed his mom. "We went for a walk."

She studied Evita and frowned. Evita waited for some kind of tirade to escape her, but she miraculously held her tongue.

"I'm going to go—check in with my family," she said, hurrying past them and toward the French doors. Just because Mrs. Hatfield hadn't said anything to her straight-out, that didn't mean that she wouldn't, given further opportunity.

As she left, she heard Ryan tell his dad, "How about if I make it up to you by cleaning the grill?"

His dad grumbled. "Sounds good."

"There's food warming for you in the oven," his mom said. "Better grab it before the Machados get after it."

"Mom."

"What? They've been known to forage our food."

Evita turned to say something to defend her family, but then she thought better of it. Why bother? Plus, she didn't want to antagonize the Hatfields. She wanted them in her corner for tonight.

"Did you want something, Evita?" Mrs. Hatfield asked when she caught her staring.

"Um, nope! Just wanted to say—those burgers look great."

She stepped into the house, greeting her family. Her mom raised a cocktail glass. "And where were you?" She and Mrs. Hatfield were speaking in stereo.

Evita ran a hand through her curls. "Walking with Ryan."

Her dad frowned. "Long walk."

"Nothing happened, okay?" It was just a little white lie and honestly none of their business. She didn't know where things would go with Ryan after this week, or even after tonight. Her heart twisted. Maybe nowhere at all. His kisses had been sweet, and so had he, but that didn't necessarily mean anything for the future. He hadn't mentioned them seeing each other once they left Nantucket. To be fair, neither had she. She'd been almost afraid to bring it up, fearing an answer she didn't want to hear.

Her mom stared at her swimsuit and shorts. "You'd better shower and clean up. Dinner's in half an hour." She considered Evita carefully, like she suspected something about Ryan. After Evita's talk with her this morning, she had a right to wonder.

Evita also had a right not to discuss it. She was still sorting through things herself.

"I'll be ready!" she said, dashing for the stairs. She passed Robby coming down on her way up. His eyes held a knowing gleam.

"So, you and Ryan?"

"No," she whispered.

His eyebrows knitted together in a playful manner. "You sure?"

"Robby, shh!" She pinched his arm and squeezed past him.

"Ow!"

"Ow what?" her dad said, looking up from the sofa, where he'd gathered with the rest of the group. Quique and Nanny had started a new puzzle, and Eunice sat on the floor holding the baby and helping them. Chachi and Kendra sipped drinks while making token efforts at the puzzle, but they seemed way more interested in each other. They'd been that way this whole trip.

Robby glanced down at his hand. "Just got a splinter or something."

"But the banister's wrought iron," her mom said. She glanced at Evita as she slipped away.

———————

Ryan fixed his plate and joined his parents at the picnic table. By the time he went inside, Evita had already disappeared to go shower. He'd do that after he ate and cleaned the grill.

"Good burgers, Dad," he said, taking another bite.

"Ryan," his mom said, "about that 'walk' of yours."

"It was just a walk, Mom."

Maddy stared at him like she knew something, or maybe just suspected it.

His dad wiped his mouth with a napkin. "Well, we won't have much longer for walks on the beach, will we?"

Maddy frowned. "I've kind of liked it here. I hate to leave."

"We might have enjoyed it better." His mom pinched up her mouth. "If we hadn't had company."

His dad took a sip of beer. "Won't be much longer for that either."

Okay. He should do this. Now.

"Which is why," Ryan said, "we should make the most of these last two nights, right?"

"Most?" His mom tugged on her pearls. "How do you mean?"

"I was talking with Evita—"

She grumbled. "I'm sure you were."

His dad cocked his chin at her and she forced a pleasant expression.

Ryan cleared his throat. "Like I said, I was talking with Evita, and we both thought it might be fun for our two families to play some group games?"

Maddy's eyebrows rose. "I'd be down."

"I was hoping you would," Ryan told her before glancing at his folks.

"What kind of group games?" his dad asked.

Ryan shrugged. "There are a bunch of them in the storage closet in the laundry room."

His mom finished eating and pushed aside her plate. "I don't think we need to go getting cozy with the Machados."

"What do you mean by cozy?" Maddy asked.

"It's not like we're going to be all on top of each other," Ryan said. "Come on. They're just some games. Like maybe Pictionary or charades."

He could practically see the mental stop sign go up in his mom's brain. His dad looked like he was thinking about it though.

"Mom," Ryan cajoled. "You said you wanted us to bond."

"Yes, but as a family. Over a dignified game like bridge. Not with other people."

Maddy rolled her eyes. "I think we should do it." She wore a stubborn pout. "Why not?"

His mom arched her eyebrows at Maddy. "You're being awfully assertive."

"She can state her opinion," Ryan said. "And should be encouraged to." Maybe now was a good time to finish their earlier conversation. There didn't seem to be a great one. "Like about her playing cello."

His mom's mouth fell open, then she closed it—three times. She looked a like a fish. With blond bangs and nice jewelry. She stared at her daughter. "Does this have to do with what you said in the kitchen earlier?" The color drained from her face. "I thought you were being dramatic."

Maddy heaved a breath. "Okay," she said. "Here's the deal." She shot Ryan a look and he nodded, showing his support. "I don't want to go to Julliard," she said to her parents.

His mom appeared gobsmacked. "What?"

Maddy squared her shoulders. "At least I don't think I do. Not for cello anyway. What I do know is I want to do something different."

"But you're so good at the cello," her mom said like that meant everything. "First chair!"

"That's another thing," Maddy said. "I'm tired of playing in the orchestra. It's boring."

Ryan's dad rubbed his forehead. "I'm sorry that you feel that way, Mads. We had no idea."

"That is a shame," his mom said. "But it's probably just a phase," she said to Ryan's dad. "She'll get over it."

Maddy's cheeks went pink. "It is *not*. A phase. Okay?"

Her gaze bore down on her daughter. "After all the work we've put in? The top-tier instrument, the private lessons—"

"I didn't ask for any of those things!" Maddy protested.

Their mom pursed her lips. "You begged us to play."

"To try it, yeah! Not to make it my life!"

His mom turned to him. "Did you put her up to this, Ryan? We've noticed you two having a lot of secret conversations, your dad and I."

"It's not Ryan's fault." Maddy rushed to his defense. "He was just trying to help me."

"Sure," his mom said. "By filling your head with nonsense." She shook her head at Ryan. She was disappointed in him. Again. Of course she was. She didn't have to say it.

Hurt burned through his chest, lodging a lump in his throat. "It's not nonsense, Mom. Maybe you should listen to Maddy."

"A fifteen-year-old? Right."

"Daneen!" his dad said. "That's enough."

She stood as if to close the conversation, speaking to Maddy before she left. "I will not have you throw away years of effort on some seaside whim." She picked up her plate. "This discussion's over."

His dad stood. "I'm sorry, kids." His eyes shone dimly like all the light had gone out of them. "I'd better go and talk to her."

Maddy hung her head, and Ryan set his hand on her shoulder. "The worst part's over," he said, hoping that was true.

"But Mom said—"

"I know. I heard, and Dad heard too. That's a good thing, huh? I saw it in his eyes. He gets you."

"Oh great, sure. And what's that mean?"

"He'll talk to Mom. Get her to—"

"What? Change her mind?" Maddy huffed. "Like Dad's going

to do that. Stand up for me." She spat out the words. Her face had gone from pink to deep red. Tears glistened in her eyes. "He's never done that a day in his life." She slid out of her seat and walked past the firepit.

"Mads! Wait! Where are you going?"

She answered without turning. "On a walk."

"Want company?"

She sniffed and dragged her arm across her face. "No thanks."

Ryan's shoulders sank. He knew how she felt. His dad had never intervened on his behalf either, and he'd had thirteen additional years to do that in Ryan's case. Which was why Ryan needed to own his life and stand up for himself. He also pledged to do better by Maddy and be there for her. He was not backing down on this. No matter how many roadblocks his mom put up. Maddy deserved to chart her own future, just like he did. Whether their parents approved or not.

He shut his eyes and let cool winds whip across his face and tug at his T-shirt.

Finally, he pulled out his phone and texted Evita.

Did not go well.

By the time Evita and her family sat down to dinner, she'd convinced them to play group games with the Hatfields. Her brothers and their families had been all-in. It was her parents who'd taken some nudging. They couldn't very well fight everyone, and since the rest of her family wanted to participate, they reluctantly agreed to as well.

Whether the Hatfields would join in was another story. Ryan's text had worried her. She'd written back asking what happened, but he didn't reply. He'd been outdoors cleaning the grill and now passed through the great room wearing a distracted look and headed for the stairs. She caught his eye, and he smiled sadly without saying a word.

Maddy wasn't anywhere around, and his parents were having an after-dinner drink by the firepit. Mr. Hatfield kept waving his hands and then stopping, his mouth moving at the same time as his hands. Mrs. Hatfield wasn't seeming to let him get a word in edgewise. After a bit, he hung his head, nursing his cocktail with a frown.

Evita sat up straighter in her chair, determined not to give up. She'd bought everybody those T-shirts, and she planned to share them after dinner, once Ryan and Maddy were back. Maybe that would break the ice? Who could resist cute T-shirts?

"I have a surprise for everyone after dinner."

"A surprise, Evita?" Her mom looked pleased. "Wait. This doesn't have to do with—?"

"No!" She stopped her before she could say Ryan. "This is something fun for everyone." She stared at Quique and Nanny. "The little ones too."

"Fun! Fun!" Nanny kicked her heels under the table.

Quique pumped his fist. "Yes."

"That was sweet of you, Evita," Kendra said, and everyone agreed.

Eunice held Luisa upright, rubbing her back as the baby's tiny eyelids grew heavy.

Evita grinned. "I got something for Luisa too."

"Aww," Eunice said. "Thank you."

Robby rubbed his chin. "Then it can't be taffy."

They all laughed.

"Fudge either," their dad joked. "No candy for infants! Ha ha! No teeth."

Her dad had the goofiest sense of humor. Still, they all loved him.

"Is it bigger than a breadbox?" Chachi's dark eyes sparkled. "Come on, sis. Give us a hint."

Evita giggled. "All in good time. You'll have to be patient." She dug into the *piñon* her mom had prepared ahead of time and frozen to bring to the beach. It was like a Puerto Rican lasagna made with ground beef, plantains, and cheese, and it was delicious served with rice and small peas. The taste was sweet yet savory. It reminded her of home.

"Delicious dinner, *querida,*" her dad said, taking another bite.

"It is so good," Kendra said, scraping her plates. "I can't believe how hungry I've been on this trip."

Chachi gave her a sultry grin. "We've been getting plenty of exercise."

Ew.

That was the other thing about her family. Everybody talked about everything. Even personal things. In some ways, her sisters-in-law were still catching on to this. Evita was more used to it. That didn't mean certain topics didn't make her feel squirmy though.

Kendra flushed and changed the subject. "You're looking good, Eunice. Rested." She stared at Robby, who at last appeared a bit more rested too. "Both of you are."

Robby ran a hand through his hair. "It's hard to rest with a baby, but having family around has been a big help. Thank you everybody for pitching in."

"With our kids too." Chachi nodded at his parents, chewing on his food. He scanned the deck. "Maddy's been great, hasn't she? Is she around?"

"I think she went for a walk on the beach," Eunice offered. "I saw her go down the steps after her family had dinner."

"I hope she didn't go far," Evita's mom said. "It's already dark out there." Just as she said it, Maddy came up the steps and onto the deck. When she walked past her parents, she seemed to be avoiding their gazes, especially her mom's.

Evita called to her as she came indoors. "I've got something for you after dinner!"

Her face brightened from her previous down expression. "Oh yeah?"

Evita nodded. "It's a surprise. I hope you'll like it."

Emotion washed over Maddy's face. Like she wasn't used to receiving surprises, or kind gestures of any sort from relative strangers. "Thanks. I'm sure I will."

"We're looking forward to our group games later," Chachi added. They'd all nearly finished up, so the games would be starting before too long. Evita couldn't wait. She had faith in her plan and wanted it to go well. If the two families could at least have one good laugh together, that would be such a huge step.

Maddy darted a glance at the deck and turned to Evita's family. "Yeah," she said. "Me too." She looked around like she wasn't sure what she should do next. "I—think I'll head up to my room and watch some TV. Can someone come get me when we're ready to play?"

"You bet," Evita told her.

"She seems a nice girl," Evita's mom said, once she'd gone. She dropped her voice in a whisper. "At first I thought she was spoiled. Now, I see she's just moody." She embellished further, "*A teenager.*"

"She's not that moody," Eunice said quietly. "I was worse."

Evita's dad's eyebrows shot up. "What? You? But you're always so even-tempered?"

He was apparently giving her a pass for her new-parent spats with Robby. But he was right about Eunice. She typically was very chill.

"I wasn't with my Umma and Appa, trust me. I gave them tons of grief."

"At least you've outgrown it," Robby teased.

"Yes." Evita's mom nodded. "Now you have experience for when Luisa's older."

"Oh gosh!" Eunice gently swayed the baby, rocking her to sleep. "I hope she's not like I was."

"What goes around…" Robby smirked. They all laughed, the tempo in the room rising.

Their dad waved his full fork at his oldest son. "You weren't perfect either."

Chachi chuckled, nearly spilling his wine. "None of us were."

"Except for me!" Evita claimed.

"Of course." Her dad nodded. "You were our little princess."

"I want to be a princess," Nanny said. Her dark eyelashes fluttered. "When I grow up."

"I want to be an astronaut!" Quique announced excitedly.

Evita's mom addressed her grandchildren. "You can be anything you want to be."

Kendra spoke to Chachi under her breath. "Royal's going to be a stretch."

Evita's mom overheard this. She leaned toward Nanny. "Never give up on your dreams, hmm?" She wiggled her eyebrows at the others. "You never know."

Nanny grinned from ear to ear. "With a tiara," she said, pivoting her head from side to side. "And everything."

Her Tito mussed her hair. "A crown would suit you very well."

Robby sat back in his chair. "Isn't this great? All of us here together?" He was so sweet. Always sentimental.

"Amazing," Chachi said. He toasted their mom. "Thank you for winning this week."

Her dad chuckled, apparently enjoying his wine. "She wasn't the only one."

"Pablo!" her mom scolded. "Stop!" But she was chuckling too. "*Ay.*" She rolled her eyes. "What a vacation."

"We've done okay," Evita said, because in many ways they had. Despite the uncomfortable circumstances, she and her family had managed to have a good time. She'd also reconnected with Ryan. Her heart fluttered. In a very personal way. It made her nervous to think about next week, and her life going back to normal, because a lot was uncertain. So she willed herself not to focus on that and to savor the here and now.

"That's because we stick together," her dad said, acknowledging her statement about their vacation's success. He puffed out his chest. "We're family, and family's what counts, hmm? When the chips are up!" He lifted his glass, and his wine sloshed sideways. "And when they're down." He lowered the glass so abruptly, Chachi grabbed his wrist to steady his hand. He turned to Chachi. "What?"

Chachi gently released him. "Nothing, Dad. Your speech was great."

Kendra raised her glass to her father-in-law. "Absolutely. Right on."

"A toast!" Robby raised his wineglass, and the others followed suit. "To family!" His eyes twinkled as he surveyed Eunice and Luisa, who'd dozed off on her shoulder.

Eunice blew him a kiss, and he looked like he'd floated to the moon.

"Wait." Her mom stared into her empty wineglass. "I need a drop more."

Kendra refilled her glass, then they all prepared to toast again.

Evita perused the room and the circle of glowing faces, understanding she was blessed. Warts and all, she'd take them. And keep them. Through thick and through thin. They were all so different, but everyone fit together so beautifully. No one was out of place.

"To family!" her parents sang together. "*Salud!*" Love filled the room from the floor to the vaulted ceiling, echoing off the walls—and above the tenor of the ocean.

"*Salud!*" the rest of them said. They clinked glasses and turned at a sound. Mr. and Mrs. Hatfield had just shut the door.

They blinked at the dining room table, like they'd invaded a private moment.

"We're sorry," Mr. Hatfield said.

"It's okay." Evita's dad gave a cheery grin and motioned them forward with his hand. He was *really* enjoying his wine. "Come on over and join us!"

Mrs. Hatfield looked like he'd asked them to jump off a cliff.

"No thank you." She forced a strained smile. "We were just passing through."

An awkward silence settled at the table. Evita's mom's gaze trailed after the couple and her dark eyes glistened. And, for the first time during this trip, Evita knew her mom wasn't angry with Mrs. Hatfield or in competition with her. She now felt sorry for her. The truth was, Evita did too. And not just for her. For everyone in Ryan's family.

But maybe they were okay and that's just how they were? More buttoned-up? None of them seemed happy about it though. Where was the joy? Where was the love? Rooted down in there somewhere; it had to be. Otherwise, how could she explain Ryan, as wonderful as he was?

Her mind snagged on the memory of Mr. Hatfield carrying his wife into the waves. So Mr. Hatfield did have a playful spirit. Evita suspected he would show that side more often if his wife didn't have such tight reins on him.

"Okay," her mom said, standing. "Who's ready to help me clear this table so we can get our surprises from Evita?"

That spurred everyone into action, including Nanny and Quique, who quickly scooted out of their chairs. Evita picked up her empty plate and a few other items from the table. When she turned and looked up, she saw Ryan standing in the loft, almost appearing paralyzed. He'd evidently showered in the hall bath and changed into shorts and a T-shirt. She didn't know how long he'd been there, but she guessed long enough to witness the toast.

EIGHTEEN

"OKAY." RYAN RUBBED HIS HANDS together, examining the stack of games he'd set on the coffee table. "We have Pictionary. Apples to Apples. Telestrations. And—"

Nanny frowned on her side of the room. "Do we have to read?" She sat on Kendra's lap on the sofa.

Kendra jostled her in her arms. "The grown-ups will help you. Or we can play in teams."

"I like the idea of team games," Evita said, carrying a shopping bag down the stairs.

After a quiet discussion in the foyer, Ryan's parents joined the others, striding into the living area. His stomach soured recalling what his mom had said about him earlier and how hard-hearted she'd been about Maddy. He wasn't thrilled by his dad's response either, but he wasn't sure what he'd expected him to do. Maybe speak up a little more during the conversation, rather than afterward.

He hadn't talked to his folks since dinner and neither had Maddy. They needed to have a chat, all of them in private. But for now, his parents appeared ready to pretend that everything was normal between them, which was really okay. Ryan didn't want to air their dirty laundry in public, especially in front of Evita's family, who seemed so comfortable around one another. Their toast at the dining room table had been heart-melting. Just like a touching scene out of a movie. If he had a family of his own one day, he hoped it would be a lot like theirs.

"I have something for you too, Mr. and Mrs. Hatfield." Evita's eyes sparkled in the lamplight as she approached them. She was calm and collected, taking charge of the situation like a pro. With polite firmness and a smile that showed off her incredible dimples.

"That was thoughtful," his dad said. "Thank you."

His mom shrank back, almost instinctively. "That's really—not—necessary."

"I know," Evita said, grinning around at the group. "But sometimes what's not necessary turns out to be the most fun."

"So true!" Chachi agreed.

His mom's eyebrows drew together like she was trying to figure Evita out. Ryan had never seen anyone handle his mom that way, with so much pleasant confidence. It was like she didn't know what to do with Evita's poised approach, or how to respond.

His folks awkwardly bumped into each other while taking their seats on the sofa.

Maddy was in an armchair.

"We might have to mix the seating around a little," Evita said. "Once we split into teams."

Mrs. Hatfield held up her hands. "Oh no. We're not playing." She picked up her book from the coffee table and waved it in the air.

His dad leaned toward her. "But I thought—"

She leveled him a look like they'd discussed this. "Just the kids, yeah?"

His shoulders sank. "Yes. Fine." He picked up his book too, and Evita pursed her lips.

Ryan saw the disappointment written on her face. She'd convinced herself she'd be able to get everyone to participate. That showed her sunny optimism. Knowing his parents like he did, he'd had his doubts.

She regrouped quickly, making the best of the situation. "No problem," she replied sweetly to his folks. "It's great to have spectators for our sport."

"And *here* are our uniforms." She glanced around the room, growing happy and animated. Her enthusiasm was contagious. It was hard not to get swayed by her energy. You'd have to be made of steel. He glanced at his parents and sighed. They were the only people here not smiling.

Evita dug a hand into her shopping bag and pulled out a T-shirt. She examined the size at the collar. "Large." She handed the T-shirt to her father. "Dad, this one's for you."

He rose briefly off his sofa to grab it. He unfurled it with a flourish, splaying it against his broad chest. "Nantucket," he said. "I love it!"

"Oh my gosh," Maddy swooned. "It's got a cartoon whale."

Evita sorted through her bag. "I've got one for you! What size do you think you are?"

Maddy shrugged. "Medium?" Evita gave her a shirt and she pulled it on, tugging it over her glittery top. It was a bit snug, but it worked.

"It's very cool, Evita," Maddy said. "Thanks."

"I'm a medium too," Kendra said.

Eunice got into it. "Have you got a small?" Robby was upstairs putting Luisa to bed, but he'd be down shortly.

Evita doled out the shirts, then produced a tiny one. "Small and extra-small." She handed the set to her sister-in-law. Everyone oohed and ahhed over the infant-size T.

"This is so sweet," Eunice said. "I'll have to put it on Luisa tomorrow." Her eyes lit up. "I know. Maybe we can take a group picture?"

"Yeah," Chachi said. "All of us in our shirts!"

Ryan's parents looked petrified, but thankfully said nothing. They didn't need to be in the picture if they didn't want to. Besides that, Eunice had probably only been thinking about the Machados and not the two families together. Like that would ever happen.

"What about me?" Quique asked with pleading dark eyes.

Nanny jumped out of Kendra's lap. "And me!"

Both kids raced toward her, and Evita tried to calm them. "There's one for everyone, okay? Just a minute."

She handed a T-shirt to her mom, who made a big fuss over how lovely it was, and then surveyed Mrs. Hatfield. "Medium or small?"

His mom's face colored. "Oh! I don't need—"

Evita shrugged. "But it's a gift," she petitioned with a smile.

"Yes, but—"

"I believe she's a small," Mr. Hatfield filled in.

She turned to him. "*Kirk.*"

"What? You are. I know it from birthday purchases and such."

Evita set a small T-shirt on the coffee table in front of his mom. She stared at it. "I, uh—"

"Just take it home," Evita suggested. "A souvenir."

His dad nudged his mom and she blinked. "Thank you."

"You're welcome," Evita answered in bright tones.

Ryan's dad had no such reservations. He accepted his gift graciously. "Thanks so much." He shook it out and held it up against his chest, and for a second Ryan thought he was going to slip into it then and there. Instead, he glanced at Ryan's mom and neatly folded the garment in a square, setting it on the coffee table beside hers.

"This was a fun idea," Ryan whispered to Evita a few minutes later. He wiggled into his T-shirt, and she already wore hers.

"I'm so glad everyone likes it," she whispered back.

All at once they were a team again, just him and her. They could do this. Bring their two families together. They were all gathered in one place amicably now, weren't they? Okay. His parents weren't laughing and joking around like the others, but at least they were here. For them, that was huge. Baby steps.

His folks would come around, he knew they would. He just needed to present things sensibly and in a confident manner like the one Evita displayed. Tell his mom he was good with where he was. Happy. That Maddy deserved to have some happiness too. Being a teenager wasn't easy. She and his dad didn't have to make it harder.

Evita gave T-shirts to her brothers and then to Nanny and Quique, who tugged them over their pajamas and danced around the room. "I'm a whale!" Quique shouted. "Roar!"

Maddy giggled. "I don't think whales roar."

He stopped and raised his fingers like fangs in front of his face. "Grrr!"

The grown-ups laughed.

"My whale isn't mean." Nanny patted her T-shirt, rubbing the design in a circle. "She's got a baby in her bump like Mommy!"

A hush fell over the room, followed by happy gasps.

"Kendra?" Mrs. Machado said. "What?"

Kendra's warm brown complexion deepened a hue. "Nanny," she whispered. "It was supposed to be a secret."

"But Tita says secrets are bad."

"Not all secrets, hey?" Chachi tousled her hair. "It's okay, Nanny." He smiled proudly around the room. "We were waiting to tell you until the last day."

Kendra nodded shyly. "I'll be past my first trimester then."

"Oh my gosh!" The Machados leapt to their feet and shouted with congratulatory exclamations and hugs. Ryan had never seen such a swirl of excitement, with everyone rushing at the expectant couple. Mr. Machado almost tackled Chachi, going for a bear hug.

Eunice's eyes held a knowing gleam. "I wondered about you skipping those piña coladas," she said liltingly to Kendra.

"Yes," Mrs. Machado said. "Me too." She spoke to the rest of her family. "I also noticed her toasting at dinner—but not drinking." She embraced Kendra with a motherly grin. "I'm so happy for you! For all of you!"

"What? Seriously?" Evita set her hands on her hips, but her face glowed. "I had no idea!" She leaned toward Ryan and giggled. "Guess I was clueless."

"You're far from clueless, Evita," he whispered back. Because honestly, she was one of the brightest, most astute people he'd ever met. The pregnancy clearly came as a surprise to most of them. A welcome surprise. The Machados were wildly happy about it.

Robby came down the stairs holding a baby monitor. He goggled at the commotion. "Hang on. What did I miss?"

"It's Kendra and Chachi!" Mrs. Machado's joy bubbled up in her voice. "They're going to have a baby!"

"What?" Robby grinned with delight. "Another one?" He pumped his brother's arm, solidly shaking his hand. "Congratulations!" He squatted low to high-five Quique. "You get to be a big brother again. You'll be just like me. The oldest of three."

Quique crowed happily. "Will I have a mustache too?"

This brought chuckles.

Robby's eyes sparkled. He clearly adored his nephew and niece. In fact, all of the Machados seemed super fond of one another. "I suppose if you'd like." He winked at the child. "You'll probably have to grow older first." He hugged Nanny next. "And you get to be a big sister! Go you!"

"I'm still going to be a princess," she declared.

Robby gently held her chin. "Of course you are."

"This calls for champagne!" Mr. Machado said, walking toward the kitchen.

"Wait." Ryan's mom said. "You brought champagne?"

"We always have champagne." Mrs. Machado chortled happily. "You never know when you're going to need to celebrate."

Evita frowned momentarily before forcing a brighter

expression, but Ryan caught the downcast look. "Is everything okay?" he asked quietly.

"Oh yeah, yeah. I just think—"

"What is it?" He glanced at his parents, but they weren't paying attention to him and Evita. They were too shell-shocked by the boisterous goings-on to do much more than gawk at the bouncing and jumping—sometimes cheering—Machados peppering Kendra and Chachi with questions. Did they know the baby's sex yet? *No. We've decided to wait and be surprised.* Have they picked out any names? *Not yet. We'll work on that later.*

Evita bit her bottom lip. "I mean, it's true," she said softly. "Mom and Dad always keep champagne on hand at home—in case. But this time—" She paused and drew in a small breath. "I think they might have brought it to the beach for me."

"You and ?" He pieced it together. "Sebastian?"

She sighed. "We were supposed to get engaged when he got back from Mexico. Everybody knew it. It was public information. He'd even talked to my parents about his intentions."

Ryan's gut tensed. Wait. People still did that? Obviously, in the Machado family they did. His heart ached for Evita. He'd never gotten that serious about anybody. Not close-to-marriage serious. The breakup had to have come as a blow. He grimaced. "Sorry. Sounds rough."

"It was for a bit. But"—she stood up a little straighter—"I'm over it."

"Are you?"

She dove into his eyes and his heart pounded. "Yeah." He didn't think it was because of him, but he was glad she'd gotten there. This Sebastian guy didn't sound worth hanging on to psychologically. What an idiot to toss away Evita. Ryan regretted her pain, but he couldn't lie and say he was sorry it hadn't worked out with Sebastian. She deserved better.

Mr. Machado dug into the back of the refrigerator and pulled out two bottles. "Success!"

"Where did you hide those?" Ryan's dad asked him.

Mr. Machado explained breezily. "Crisper drawer. Behind the celery and apples."

"We brought some too!" Chachi chimed in.

Maddy glanced at her parents, a hopeful expression on her face.

His mom shook her head.

"Don't worry, Maddy," Kendra said. "You can have some sparkling cider with me."

"And me!" Eunice announced brightly.

"Right," Chachi said. "We brought some of that too."

Nanny jumped up and down on her heels. "Is it pink like last time?"

Chachi laughed. "No. That was when we were celebrating Luisa. This sparkling cider is yellow like apple juice."

"I'm glad it's not pink," Quique said. "Yellow's better."

"Pink's a nice color," Kendra said kindly. "For everyone. Girls and boys."

"Yeah," Nanny said. "Tito wears a pink shirt!"

"It's true." Her granddad told her. "It's my favorite guayabera."

"Congratulations," Ryan's dad said to the Kendra and Chachi. "That's really great news."

"Yes," his mom added. Still, her smile was stilted. "Very nice. Congrats."

Mr. Machado poured the champagne, and Robby helped him pass it out.

Chachi headed to the kitchen to pitch in. "I'll grab the cider for the others."

Robby handed a glass of champagne to Ryan's mom. "Oh!" Her expression screamed trapped. "Oh. Well. Okay." She took a tiny sip. "Thank you."

His dad took a glass too, and Maddy got her cider shortly afterward from Chachi.

Once they were all served, Mrs. Machado raised her glass. "To Chachi and Kendra and their growing family!"

Everyone cheered and said, "Hear, hear!"

NINETEEN

RYAN'S GAZE FELL ON EVITA standing beside him. Her face held a happy glow. "Cheers!" She raised her glass to his, and he clinked it.

"Here's to the great news, yeah."

Her eyes sparkled, and he caught his breath. Earlier on the beach when he'd kissed her, he'd been swept away. Helpless like a shell dragged out by the tide. At the same time she made him feel powerful too. Like he could be his strongest and best self around her. She made him want to be better than he was. To be able to stand up to or tackle anything. He wanted to see himself the way she saw him. As someone capable and good. In charge of who he was.

She motioned toward the pile of games with her champagne. "So, should we pick one?"

Ryan held up the choices one by one, but every selection had at least one detractor. With people gleefully settled in with their champagne, nobody wanted to learn something new, and too many of the games presented learning curves for more than one individual. The crowd seemed to be getting restless. Even Maddy had put her earbuds in, excusing herself from the discussion and saying whatever everyone else wanted was fine.

Ryan feared if they didn't get started soon, people would start to peel away. His parents weren't playing, one way or another. They'd set their champagne glasses on the coffee table and had buried their noses in their books the moment the game-picking discussion began.

"How about charades?" Evita said. "That's easy?"

Ryan liked that thought. Anything to get the ball rolling.

"I love charades!" her dad said. Everyone agreed that was a stellar idea.

Quique and Nanny said "Yay!" even though they were yawning by now, but trying to conceal it. Ryan wasn't sure they even knew what the game was. They just wanted to be part of the adult action. Which was cute. At their age, Ryan would have been tucked into bed by now. The Machados seemed to operate on a somewhat later and looser schedule, or maybe it was just because they were all on vacation.

"So." Evita looked around. "How should we divide? Count off by twos?"

Mr. Machado held up a finger. "*Uno!*"

His family laughed and Evita rolled her eyes. "Good," she said fondly. "We'll start with Dad. He's on Team One." She went around pointing to people as they said their number. Ryan and Evita landed on different teams. He was on Team Two with Mrs. Machado, Robby, and Kendra. She was on Team One with Maddy, her dad, Chachi, and Eunice.

Everyone agreed that Quique and Nanny could "float"

between the groups and try to guess, because a lot of it would be above their heads anyway, although they didn't say this expressly to the children. They were charged with being little helpers. Their main job was to decipher: book, song, or movie. Chachi ran them through a drill with the pantomimes, and they caught on right away.

Ryan and Evita passed out cut pieces of paper and pens and pencils, and each person wrote down the name of a book, song, or movie, folded their paper closed, and dropped it into a bowl. The teams exchanged bowls, and Chachi was tasked with going first. Ryan was glad he hadn't been picked to get started. He wanted to watch a few others before him and get the hang of it. He'd played as a kid at camp, but it had been a while.

Chachi stared at his paper and sighed. "What?" His forehead wrinkled up as he read it again. "I'm not sure I—" He scratched his head. "Is this something very old?" He glanced at his mom who was on the opposing team. "I think I know the handwriting."

She marched over to him and snatched away the paper. "Come."

They turned their backs and mumbled to each other.

Finally, Chachi said, "What? Ooh. What? It is? Huh. No. But yeah. Okay." He pivoted back around, and Mrs. Machado returned to her group.

Chachi straightened his whale T-shirt around his thick belly. "I think I've got it."

He lifted his right hand in a reeling motion and the kids shouted out, "Movie!"

"Very good!" Mr. Machado said, grinning below his thick

mustache. He took a sip of champagne, looking happy and relaxed around his family. Ryan's dad, by contrast, sat nearly ramrod straight on the sofa reading his book, his body posture tense. Then again, he was almost always that way, and Ryan's mom's stance matched his. He saw her look up—very briefly—when the kids shouted "Woo-hoo!" But she just as rapidly dropped her gaze to her book.

They'd rearranged the furniture and dragged over a few dining room chairs, so each team had their own space in which to convene. Maddy sat on a dining room chair near the Machados' sofa on the other side of Eunice's armchair. Evita was on the sofa between her dad and the empty spot that belonged to Chachi.

Mrs. Machado was in the other armchair near the French doors, and Ryan had dragged over one of their armchairs and set it beside her for Kendra. Robby and Ryan had dining room chairs next to those with their backs to the deck, completing their arc.

Chachi stood in the middle of the room in front of the Machados' coffee table, facing his team. He rubbed his chin, thinking. "Okay." He held up his arms like he was about to make some kind of motion, and the baby monitor on an end table wailed.

"Oh no." Robby frowned at Eunice as Luisa's cries grew louder. They had Ryan's sympathies. It had to be rough, never catching a break. Still, he was sure it was worth it.

"Let me go." She stood from her spot in her armchair. "It's my turn." Luisa cried louder, and she hurried toward the stairs. "Besides! Our team has five and yours four! So I'll just sit out for a bit."

"If you're sure?" Robby called after her. Relief flooded his face when she nodded, reaching the upstairs landing. "Okay, thanks!"

They heard Eunice's soothing tones as she entered the bedroom, then the monitor clicked off.

Evita's dad raised his champagne glass and took a sip. "Okay, where were we?" Evita loved being around her family when they were having fun, which was basically almost always. She remained hopeful that the Hatfields would find the fun contagious. Even though they'd declined to play, it was hard to ignore the action that was unfolding in the center of the room.

Chachi gulped from his glass before resuming. He set it down on the coffee table.

"Okay." He nodded. "Here goes!"

Evita couldn't help chuckling at Chachi. What was he doing with his arms? Jiggling them up and down, and up and down while flicking his wrists? "Chachi? What?" But she knew he couldn't explain.

"He's dancing," her dad said.

Chachi shook his head and moved his arms more dramatically, bouncing up and down on his legs. Maddy burst into giggles. So did several others in the room. Except for Mr. and Mrs. Hatfield, who hid behind their books, pretending not to watch. But Ryan caught Evita watching them as they snatched glances at the game, and he sent her a secretive thumbs-up. Chachi started to move, skipping around and waving his arms out in front of him. He raised one up high and mimicked cracking a whip.

"Zorro!" Quique shouted.

"No wait." Maddy screwed up her face. "I think he's riding a horse!"

Chachi nodded eagerly and pointed to his butt.

Kendra roared with laughter. "Chachi! What?"

Evita covered her mouth with both hands. Chachi was hilarious. He shook his head and clip-clopped around the room again, evidently holding imaginary reins. He dropped them, then leaned over and opened a door.

Evita's dad tweaked his mustache. "Look!" he said as Chachi climbed out of his imaginary vehicle. "He's in something!"

Chachi spun and pointed behind him. Then he did the horse pantomime again.

Evita stared at Ryan, who had his arms crossed in front of him. He was chuckling so hard, his face was going red. She loved that he was having a good time, and she was loving being around him. Their talk on the beach had been so special, and his kisses—wow.

"A wagon!" Maddy guessed as Chachi kept bouncing along.

Chachi shook his head and motioned for her to keep guessing.

She bit her lip. "A sleigh?"

"No," Evita's dad said. "A chariot!"

Evita locked on his gaze. "Chariot?" What made him think of that?

"Yes!" Her dad's eyes gleamed when Chachi nodded. He jumped up and shouted, "*Ben-Hur!*"

"Ben who?" Maddy asked.

Chachi shook his head, and Evita's dad frowned, sitting back down.

"Chariot—" Evita started. But nothing else came to mind. She glanced at her mom, who giggled. This probably was a very old movie. She was a little stunned it wasn't *A Walk in the Clouds*.

Chachi rubbed his cheek, at a loss. Then he held his arms straight up above his head, pressing his palms together. He wiggled his hips from side to side.

Robby snorted champagne through his nose and grabbed a napkin. "Ha ha ha! What are you doing?" Evita couldn't believe Ryan's parents weren't rolling on the floor like the others. What were they? Made of stone. And she saw they were watching, sneaking little peeks from time to time.

"You're not guessing," his mom corrected. "It's Chachi's team."

Maddy's mouth hung open. "Are you a—hula dancer?"

Chachi shook his head no and swayed his arms above him still keeping his palms pressed together.

"A genie?" Evita guessed.

No.

Her dad chortled. "'I'm a Little Teapot'?"

Chachi gaped at him. "What? No! That's a song!"

"Chachi, shh!" his mom admonished. "No talking! It's charades!"

He blew out a breath and hung his head, raking both hands through his hair. He looked up and raised a finger.

"Good." Evita's dad leaned forward. "An idea."

Chachi nodded and dropped down on the floor.

He rolled onto his back and held up his arms and legs.

"What?" Kendra burst out laughing. "Chachi!"

RIGHT GIRL, WRONG SIDE 301

"Dog?" Maddy said. She glanced at Evita. "Down dog?" She gasped. "Play dead!"

Evita's dad tugged at his mustache. "No. This has to do with a chariot."

Evita's mom doubled over in hilarity, nearly spilling her champagne. Robby took it from her and set it down, but he was laughing too. So was Ryan, his eyes wide.

Ryan's parents though. Wait! Mrs. Hatfield had been watching, peering over the top of her book. Mr. Hatfield was watching too, sneaking cagey glimpses of the action from time to time. His mouth twitched. Seriously. This was hilarious.

Chachi stayed on his back motioning to his team, like come on, come on.

But Evita had absolutely no idea.

Kendra held up her cell phone that she'd been using as a stopwatch. "Time!"

Chachi sighed and rolled onto his knees. "Guys! Fire! I was fire!"

All their faces went blank except for Evita's mom. She cackled and gripped the arms of her chair. "Chachi! *Ay dios mio!* That's fire?"

"Yes!" He stood and brushed off his knees. "I was a campfire. Burning."

Everyone groaned and shook their heads, roiling with laughter.

"And before?" Robby asked. "With the?" He mimicked Chachi's hula dancer move, and everyone roared.

Chachi scowled, but it was all in fun. "I was a candle, okay?"

"A candle?" Evita hooted. "What was this?" She placed her

hands above her head, her palms pressed together, imitating his crazy dance.

"My flame." He shook his head in exasperation.

Evita's dad snapped his fingers and moaned. "*Chariots of Fire!*" he proclaimed. "I might have known."

"What's that?" Maddy asked.

"It's a movie," Evita's mom explained. "About running."

"Running?" Evita shook her head. "From what year?"

Her mom chuckled again. "Can't remember."

Evita playfully rolled her eyes at Ryan. "Figures."

He seemed to be enjoying himself a lot. Maddy too.

Ryan's dad lowered his book. "I was going to guess that when you all said chariot."

Mrs. Hatfield elbowed him.

"What?" he complained to her. "I was."

Evita tried to encourage the couple. "It's not too late to join in, you know?"

Mrs. Hatfield raised her book. "We probably won't be up much later anyway."

Evita sighed and Ryan's shoulders sank. He held up his hands like *What can you do?* She couldn't do much more than she had, it was true. And the fact was his dad, at least, had been paying attention and, in her opinion, enjoying Chachi's acting.

"Okay," she said. "Who's next?"

"I think we should make Mom go," Chachi said, reclaiming his seat on the sofa. "Get her back for that."

The others chuckled, then Evita's mom got to her feet.

"I'm not afraid to go," she said. She strode haughtily to her team's bowl on the coffee table and pulled out a piece of paper. She read it and her face fell. "Oh no."

Evita's dad hooted. "No backing out of things now, *querida.*"

TWENTY

AN HOUR PASSED BEFORE THEY knew it. Evita was so glad they'd tried this. Everyone was having so much fun. Well. Everyone except Ryan's parents, who kept trying not to look, but sneakily watching anyway. They had to be getting into the fun. It was impossible not be swept up in the Machados' energy. Evita knew that firsthand. Eunice crept back down the stairs without Luisa, saying she'd gotten her back to sleep. She had the baby monitor and set it on a side table. "Sounded like you all were having a blast down here."

They told her about Chachi, then made him demonstrate his moves.

He did, and Eunice burst out laughing.

Mr. Hatfield hid a chuckle behind his book, and even Mrs. Hatfield seemed amused, while attempting not to show it.

"I'm sorry I missed all the fun," Eunice said.

"Not all," Robby told her. "Maddy found a new game."

"A new *old* game," Maddy said. "It looks super retro."

Evita's mom nodded. "Very old. We played that at slumber parties when I was young."

Mrs. Hatfield lowered her book. "Twister? Us too."

"I do remember that game," Mr. Hatfield said. "Funny."

Evita shot to her feet. "I think we should try it."

Maddy flipped over the game, looking at the back, then she opened the box, hunting for directions. "Does anyone remember how this goes?" She pulled out a plastic mat with lots of colored circles on it and handed it to Evita, who opened it and shook it out, laying it on the carpet.

Evita's mom shook her head. "Not exactly."

"Wait," Maddy said. "Here." She held up a small leaflet and scanned through it. "Cool! I can be the referee if you want? Who wants to play?"

People started chanting. "Cha-chi! Cha-chi!"

He laughed. "If you insist." He glanced at Kendra, and she held her belly.

"No. I'd better not."

"I'll just watch too," Eunice said.

"I'll play," Robby said, standing up.

Evita's dad shook his head. "I'm too old."

"No, you're not, *mi amor*," her mom chided.

His forehead rose. "Are you going to do it?"

She grinned. "Of course."

He grumbled and got to his feet. "If I break something, Lissette—"

"Oh stop, Pablo. You won't."

Ryan's parents went white with shock. "You're actually going to play Twister? You're in your fifties."

Evita's dad huffed. "Yes. But not dead yet."

Evita glanced at Ryan. "What do you think?"

He shrugged. "I mean, sure. But how many can play at a time?" He directed his question at Maddy.

"Four. But maybe four little people, not grown-ups. Could get tight."

Quique and Nanny would have jumped right onto the mat, if they hadn't dropped off to sleep on the sofa during charades, even in the midst of the laughter. Chachi and Kendra had carried them up to bed.

"There's no reason we can't play in two rounds," Maddy said.

The first round was hilarious with Chachi bumping into his mother and father.

The idea was that Maddy called out a circle color and body part like hand or foot, and everyone had to claim their spot without knocking the others over. Anyone who fell down or touched the ground with their knee or elbow was out.

"Chachi!" Evita's mom said. "Get your butt out of my face!"

"Sorry, Mom. I—" He struggled to keep his balance raised up like a bridge facing the mat with his hands and feet far apart. His dad's foot was between his two hands. "Dad. You're kicking me."

"I am not. Kicking." He gasped, trying to maintain his balance. "I'm trying not to fall—ohhh!" And he was down, taking Evita's mom with him when he crashed into her arm.

"Pablo!" she scolded, but she was laughing.

Chachi stood victorious, holding up his hands like he gripped a trophy, displaying it this way and that. Everybody clapped.

Ryan's mom huffed behind her book. "Really," she quipped to her husband. "Adults acting like children."

Mr. Hatfield patted her arm.

Maddy straightened the mat, having a great time leading the game. "Who wants to go next?"

Kendra and Eunice shook their heads as Evita's parents struggled back into their chairs. They'd been good sports, but maybe it had been a lot for them. All that bending and twisting. The falling down especially.

Robby frowned and set his hands on his hips. "Somebody's got to play with me." He stared at his sister and then at Ryan.

"Okay." Evita glanced over her shoulder, and Ryan stood up too.

Mrs. Hatfield leaned forward and set down her book like she wanted to stop them, but Mr. Hatfield gently held her back.

Maddy spaced them all out on three sides. Evita across from Ryan, and Robby across from her where she stood as referee. "Ready?"

They nodded and the game was on.

Robby blundered on his second turn, hitting the mat with his elbow. "Oops! I'm out!" He held up a hand acting guileless, but Evita suspected he'd done that on purpose, leaving just her and Ryan in the game. But that was okay. This was just Twister. Some goofy game from her mom and dad's day. "Yellow, left hand!" Maddy called. "Red, right foot!" In a few moves, she and Ryan were a jumble of limbs.

"Ah, hi there," she whispered, tucking her head under Ryan's fully extended arm and reaching for a circle. She tried not to topple forward, but her chest was pretty close to the mat.

"Hi." He grinned, his face tawny pink, and she felt like she wanted to die. This was so embarrassing, so intimate—but still. Just a silly game.

Maddy announced another move, and each attempted to maneuver around the other, but it was no use; they were so twisted up. They collapsed in a heap. Evita's heart thumped, and Ryan landed on top of her. "Ugh. Sorry!" He rolled right off, and she flipped, and they were somehow in each other's arms.

Evita's family roared, clapping. "Woo-hoo!" Robby cheered.

"Good try!" said Chachi.

Evita's parents clapped like the good sports that they were.

Mrs. Hatfield shot to her feet. "I think that's enough."

"Daneen." Mr. Hatfield reached for her arm, but she jerked it away.

She stared down Evita's mom. "Is this what passes for fun in your house, really?"

Ryan and Evita scrambled off the floor, and he approached her. "Mom, it was only a game." His dad stood up too.

"I saw what it was pretty clearly."

"It wasn't anything lewd, Mrs. Hatfield." Chachi held open his hands. "Come on."

She blinked at him, then wheeled on her husband. "I think it's time we turned in." She glanced back at her daughter. "Maddy too."

"Me?" Maddy thumbed her chest. "Why me? What did I do?"

"We should never have agreed to this," Mrs. Hatfield said to her husband. She sounded drained and distraught, like the whole evening had been a chore.

Evita's mom crossed her arms, offended. "After all the efforts we've made toward you. We asked you to join us. Join in the fun."

"We gave you champagne," her dad embellished.

Robby frowned at their empty glasses. "You drank it."

"Is nothing enough for you, Daneen?" Evita's mom questioned. "Nothing at all?"

"I'll tell you what will be enough. Having this vacation over."

Maddy gawked at her. "Mom! You're being so rude."

"Don't talk back to me, Maddy."

Ryan blinked. "Maybe you need talking back to."

She blanched. "What, Ryan? You too." She stared him down. "This is all on account of Evita. You weren't like this before this week. I think we should all go to our rooms. Call it a night. Take a breather."

Ryan's neck turned red and then his whole face. His ears too. "I think you should apologize to the Machados first," he said, standing his ground.

"Apologize? Me?"

Evita's mom piled on, springing to her feet. "Yes, you! Try listening to your son. At least he has manners."

Steam practically rose off her. "*You* don't talk to me about my son."

"*You* don't bad-mouth my daughter."

"She's been bad for my son."

"Your son is a man! He knows what he's doing!"

Kendra raised her hands. "I'm sure if we all calm down—"

"Stop talking about Ryan and me like we're not here!" The words rushed out of her before Evita could stop them. Silence rained over the room.

"Evita," her mom said. "Stay out of this."

"I can't! Not when you're both so wrong."

Her mom's eyebrows arched. "Who's wrong?"

"You and Mrs. Hatfield."

Evita's mom rolled her eyes toward the ceiling. "Unbelievable."
She stared at her husband. "And there I was defending her."

She was? Oh wait. It had sounded really shouty though.

"Pablo. Do something."

He sighed heavily and stood. "I'm going to bed."

"Good idea," Mr. Hatfield said. "Me too."

Maddy folded up the Twister mat and placed it the box.
"Good night, everybody." Her face was all pink. "Thanks for the
games. They were fun."

"Come on, honey." Robby wrapped his arm around Eunice,
and they retreated too.

Chachi grabbed Kendra's hand and nodded toward the stairs.
"Baby, let's go."

Evita's mom stomped off after her dad and into their suite and
banged shut the door.

The Hatfields entered their suite, and Mrs. Hatfield slammed
their door too.

Ryan and Evita stared at each other. His eyes held a glossy
sheen, and warmth built up in hers till she felt they were bursting.
If she were a weaker person, she'd be crying buckets right now.
But she rarely cried, and she wasn't starting now. They'd only be
tears of frustration anyway. She and Ryan had tried so hard to
make this work. Then, it had all blown apart. *Kaboom!* At the
very last minute. What a total disaster.

She stared at Ryan, wondering what to do. She didn't feel like
turning in. The last thing she'd be able to do now was sleep. She

also wasn't ready to part with Ryan. Not with so much churning around in her heart and in her head.

"Want to have a drink?" she asked him. "Something stronger than milk?"

His eyes twinkled. "Yeah."

Evita and Ryan sat on the steps leading down to the beach from the deck, their toes in the cool sand. They'd left off the outside lights to allow for the moonglow. It was a beautiful night, only slightly chilly, with light breezes blowing and the moon lifting off the water. The inky-black sky blanketed with stars.

Evita sadly tilted her short glass toward Ryan's. They drank scotch on the rocks. Ryan's dad had brought some high-end brand. "Think your parents will ever wear those T-shirts?"

"Don't know." He blew out a breath. "It was really nice of you to buy them." His smile was melancholy. "Maddy loves hers." He sipped from his drink. "So do I."

She leaned back against the stairs behind her, resting her elbows on a higher step. "You know. Call me a fool, but I'd really thought this would work."

"I'd never call you that, Evita." His gaze washed over her in the moonlight as waves pounded the shore. "You're probably the smartest woman I know."

She swelled with pride. That meant a lot coming from him, a college professor, someone who worked around really smart people all the time. Plus, he was no slouch in the IQ department. He'd graduated valedictorian of their high school class.

"Thank you, but I think this time…" She shrugged. "Maybe I was too optimistic."

"Your optimism's one of the things I appreciate about you."

She sat up on her step to look at him more squarely. "Yeah?"

"Yeah." His eyes danced, and tiny shivers tore through her. She wished he would kiss her again, because his kisses seemed to help the rest of the world melt away. The bad things in the world anyway, like the things she didn't want to think about or waste energy on. His mom and hers and their differences key among them.

"You're very sweet," she told him.

His voice grew rough. "I'm sweet on you." The old-fashioned expression made her heart flutter. It was so retro. So Ryan. He leaned forward and kissed her. His lips landed like satiny pillows against hers. Luscious and warm. Her pulse fluttered. "I hope you like me too?"

She nodded and her face heated, her chest too. Maybe a few other parts. Lower.

Suddenly wearing two layers felt way too hot. She peeled off her whale T-shirt, setting it on the step beside them. He stripped his off too. "It's getting warm out." He chuckled. "Or maybe it's just us." His neck and ears were crimson.

She giggled. "It's probably just us."

He held his wadded-up T-shirt. "Yeah. Well, I'm hanging on to this forever. I mean, what a souvenir."

"I'm keeping mine too." She smiled. "It will remind me of this week. Of Nantucket."

Of you.

"Still, I hate this." She frowned. "Hate it about our moms. It's like, as much as we've tried, this whole week long, we haven't been able to fix it. This feud between them."

"Maybe that's just it." His eyebrows rose. "Maybe it's not up to us to fix?"

She wondered if he was right. Maybe they had this role-reversal all wrong. Playing the parents to their folks, who were behaving like children. It wasn't her job to be the grown-up in her family, and it wasn't Ryan's to be the adult in his. The best they could do was be as mature as they could in their own lives, and careful in their choices.

Winds ripped off the ocean, combing through her hair and cooling her off. Even though sharing the beach house had been complicated, she wouldn't change this week if she could. The Hatfields were quirky, sure. But so were the Machados. She'd learned more about Ryan by getting to know his family, and now understood him better. And the more she understood him, the more she liked him.

He was an incredibly attractive guy. Not just physically. Though he had that too. It was his kindness that meant so much. He wasn't self-absorbed like Sebastian. Ryan shone his bright light on others. He wanted to help. He wanted to teach. And coach. The goodness oozed out of him, and she admired him so much. For who he was and the things he stood for. What he valued in life.

He set his chin and gazed out at the sea. "I'm talking to my mom tomorrow. Talking to both my folks." She could tell he'd been thinking about this.

"Really? What are you going to say?"

His Adam's apple rose and fell. "Things I probably should have said a while ago." He shook his head. "There's a lot going on. Some of it goes way back. I almost wonder"—he turned to her—"if my mom being the way she is has to do with her dad. My granddad." Ryan reflected a moment. "He was very strict. Held high expectations."

"Like your mom?"

Evita's family held high expectations too. She knew her grandparents had been that way, both sets. Her mom's folks in Lexington and her dad's parents in Puerto Rico. Her parents had always insisted she and her brothers do their best too. But maybe that was different. They hadn't told any of their kids who, or what, to be. They'd all landed in vastly different careers.

"Hmm. Maybe." He clinked her glass with his. "In any case, I'll talk to her. There are some things I need to say, and not just about me, about Maddy."

"That's good of you to look out for your little sister."

"My dad needs to hear some things too."

She grimaced. "How do you think they'll take it?"

"Don't know." He took a big swig of scotch. "But I'll sleep better for having said it. I need to get on with my life."

She wasn't totally sure what he meant by that. "Get on?" She held her breath. Move on from her? No. That's not what she wanted.

He shrugged. "By doing what makes me happy."

Her tension eased. She nudged his shoulder with hers. "Of course you should do that. We all should. Life is too short."

She fell into his gaze, lost in the moment and him.

"You're right, it is."

He kissed her again, and this time his kiss lingered. Delighted tingles tore through her. He smelled so good, still fresh from his shower.

The pressure of his mouth tantalizingly warm. He tasted of scotch, and heat. Smoky peat and fire. So sexy. He was torturing her with this slow burn.

But he was working through stuff, she could sense it. Very serious stuff for him. Now wasn't the time to push for more. Plus, pacing herself could be good. She'd rushed in headlong with Sebastian without thinking. And look where that had landed.

"Tomorrow," he said, looking up at the stars. They twinkled like a billion glittering lights above them. "I'm going to suggest we go out for coffee. My parents and Maddy and I. Maybe to that cute place where you and I went in 'Sconset Village."

She got what he was saying. He didn't want to talk here with her whole busybody family blustering around, and more chances for their moms to spontaneously combust around each other. It didn't seem to take much. Each was like a powder keg just waiting on the other to strike a match. Then—poof! Any progress that had been made was undone in a flash.

He met her eyes. "I'll let you know how it goes." He took her hand, and she held on tight, enjoying his nearness and the sound of the ocean. The shimmer of the moon upon the water.

"Thanks, Ryan. I'll be rooting for you."

"I know. You always have." He kissed the back of her hand, and warmth coursed through her. Despite the battle raging between their moms, being with Ryan made her feel settled. Whole. In a good place with herself and in the world.

They sat there with their thoughts, the surf gobbling up the sand.

Then they stayed a while longer because neither one wanted to go.

Evita laid her head on his shoulder and watched the waves cutting shadows against the darkness. "This is nice," she said, her voice breathy.

"Yeah." He squeezed her hand. "It is."

"Ryan?"

"Hmm?"

"Thanks for being who you are, that's all."

TWENTY-ONE

WHEN EVITA WALKED INTO THE kitchen the following morning, Chachi and Robby were at the island together, drinking coffee. Both wore ratty shorts and T-shirts and were barefoot. Robby had stubble on his chin. Chachi hadn't shaved in three days, and it showed.

"That was some game night," Chachi said, raising his coffee mug.

"Right," Robby said. "Particularly at the end."

"Ha. Ha." She sashayed her way across the kitchen, homing in on the coffee pot. "Where is everybody?"

Robby shrugged. "Still sleeping."

Chachi shook his head. "Probably worn out from the big blowup."

"What is it with Mom and Mrs. Hatfield?" Robby asked.

Chachi drank from his mug. "I think it's worse on Mrs. Hatfield's end."

Mrs. Hatfield strolled into the kitchen, wearing her robe and surprising them all.

Robby and Chachi jumped off their stools. They were in

Hatfield territory, and this house was still very much divided. Evita finished pouring her coffee and issued a tentative greeting. "Good morning."

Mrs. Hatfield gave a perfunctory, "Morning," while she grabbed a mug. Her smile didn't reach her eyes.

Evita didn't dare ask if she'd slept well. She definitely didn't have that rosy glow she'd worn while prancing into the kitchen in her bathrobe the day before. Evita scooted out of the kitchen as fast as she could, joining her brothers outside on the deck. They settled in Adirondack chairs overlooking the water on the far side of the firepit so they had a full view of the beach.

"Ah, this is nice," Chachi said. "A little slice of heaven."

Robby quipped, "Last night, it felt a little like hell."

"Come on," Evita said. "Not all of it."

"True." Chachi's eyes gleamed. "I did put on an Oscars-worthy performance." He waggled his eyebrows at Robby. "Hey! Maybe you can write me into one of your screenplays?"

Robby laughed and shook his head. "As what? The comedian?"

Chachi pulled a face, looking hurt. "No, as the romantic hero."

"You, Chachi? Romantic?"

"Just ask Kendra." Chachi wiggled his eyebrows. "There's a reason we've got number three on the way."

Robby's mouth twitched, and Evita held up a hand. "Enough information."

Chachi rolled his eyes at Robby. "Our baby sister is such a Puritan."

Evita gasped. "That's not true!"

"You just wait until you're married, hmm?" Chachi said. "Nothing is sacred after that."

She didn't know what he meant and didn't choose to believe it. Of course things were sacred after marriage. There were rules about honoring and loving each other.

"Yeah," Robby warned. "No modesty allowed in the delivery room."

"What?" She mentally blocked any images of her sisters-in-law giving birth. Ick.

She knew it was natural of course. People lived through it. Although she didn't need to imagine all the body fluids and screaming while enjoying her coffee.

"Look at her," Robby teased. "She's gone all pale."

"Have not." Although her face did feel cool and drained.

"You think you'll ever get to use the bathroom again in private?" Chachi challenged. "Or take a shower in peace?"

Robby guffawed. "So that's what you were doing out here?"

"Guys, really."

Chachi sighed. "Everything changes after you have kids."

"Yeah, well." Evita spoke from above the rim of her coffee mug. The brew was hot and tasty, warm steam filling her nose. "I suspect a lot of things change for the better." She stated that like she knew something about it, which she technically didn't. She could only hope. Otherwise, why did so many couples go there? Her parents seemed happy; so did her brothers and their wives. They were just pulling her leg now like they loved to do.

"Oh sure." Robby staged a big yawn, stretching an arm over his head. "Like getting so much beauty rest."

Evita tsked. "What are you two trying to do? Dissuade me from having a family?"

"No." Robby's dark eyes sparkled. "We're preparing you."

"Forewarned is forearmed," Chachi said.

"Yeah," Robby teased lightly. "Maybe we should tell all this to Ryan too?"

Evita pinched his arm.

"Ow!"

"Don't you dare."

Robby glanced innocently at the sky. "You came in very late last night. Eunice and I didn't even hear you."

"Same with Ryan." Chachi nodded. "Who knows what those two were up to, downstairs in the dark—and all alone."

"Very funny!" Evita shoved Chachi's chest, and coffee sloshed out of her mug. She jumped back, avoiding getting hit, but a big splash landed on the deck. "We were just talking, okay?"

"I'm sure you had a lot to talk about," Robby said. "After the 'Mommy Wars.'"

Evita sighed. "This really has to stop."

"It will," Robby assured her. "We leave tomorrow bright and early."

Evita's chest tightened.

As difficult as things had been, she didn't relish the thought of going home. It would feel awful to leave things hanging. In some ways, the tension between her mom and Ryan's seemed even worse than before, after all the bickering they'd done here. Robby laid a hand on her shoulder, noting her frown. "Cheer up, Evita. Life's not that bad."

"He's right," Chachi said. "Things have a way of working out the way they're meant to. If you're meant to see someone again," he said very intentionally, "then I'm sure that will happen too."

"Yeah," Robby said. He acted all dreamy. "Love conquers all."

Chachi waggled his finger at his brother. "Spoken like a true romantic."

"I am a romantic, aren't I?" Robby rubbed his chin. "That's why I write *romantic* comedies."

"Oh, Robby!" Evita rolled her eyes, but she already felt better. About this beach week and everything. She didn't know what she'd do without her brothers. She loved them and never doubted that they loved her. Now, here they were hinting about Ryan. Unusual for these super-protective guys.

The ones who hadn't had much use for Sebastian, apparently. "So," she said as casually as she could. "About Ryan then?" Her eyebrows rose. "You what? Approve?"

Chachi brought his fist to his mouth and snickered at Robby like they'd caught her red-handed. "I knew it," he said. "She really likes him."

Evita groaned. "Okay, okay, but shush!" She giggled. "Just a little. Don't tell anyone."

Chachi stared at Robby, and then she understood. Everyone else already knew. At least the people in her family. Not only that. Ugh. They'd all talked about it. And her. And Ryan. And her with Ryan and where they thought that was going. She sighed.

When had all this happened?

It really didn't matter.

They always found out one way or another, and it was much harder to hide things from them with her and Ryan being right under their noses.

Family.

———————————

Ryan sat in the small coffee shop with his folks and Maddy. The vibe wasn't as cozy as when he'd been here with Evita. But that was okay. This time, his goal was different. He wasn't here to impress a woman. He was here to set things straight with his family by finally finishing the conversation he'd never been able to finish before.

"This was a nice idea," his mom said. "Getting out of the house for a bit and coming into town. This village is so quaint." She clearly had no idea what Ryan's plan really was. His dad looked uneasy though. Like he suspected something. Maddy too. She darted glances at him from where she sat beside him in the booth. She also toyed with her discarded straw wrapper, twisting it around in her fingers until it made a tight spiral. She'd ordered a frappe whip something or another. The rest of them had straight coffee.

"How did you hear about this café?" his dad asked. "Find it online?"

"Uh, yeah," Ryan answered because he had initially. He decided to toughen up and not avoid the subject. He was heading in that direction anyway. "I also came here with Evita."

"What?" His mom set down her paper cup and frowned. "When?"

"A few days ago." He shrugged. "When we took a bike ride." He gestured with his chin out the front window. "She got all those T-shirts at the shop over there." He'd noticed Maddy was wearing hers. His parents weren't. No surprise.

"A few days ago…" His mom set her lips in a thin line. "When you were 'too tired' to be down on the beach?" She shook her head. "Really? Inventing excuses? Sneaking around? I'm very disappointed in you, Ryan." What else was new?

"I know you are." He met her eyes, determined to stay strong but calm. "That's one of the things I brought you here to talk about."

Her jaw unhinged. "Talk?" She stared at his dad. "Did you know anything about this?"

He shifted in his seat. "No." He addressed Ryan. "What's this all about?"

Ryan heaved a breath, gathering his courage. "It's about this week truthfully, but not just that. Other things too."

Maddy raised her eyebrows with a pleased expression. His mom caught the exchange.

"If it's a grown-up conversation, you shouldn't have brought along your little sister."

Ryan shook his head. "Look, I think it's okay that Maddy's here. Some of this conversation concerns her too."

His mom fiddled with her pearls. "Yes, and so?"

Maddy's posture tensed. She gripped her tall plastic cup without drinking from it. The whipped topping was starting to melt. He decided to get Maddy's part over with. It would be kinder to her to get that out of the way first.

"How does this involve Mads?" his dad asked, paving the way.

Thank you.

"It's about her playing the cello."

His mom spread her hands out on the table. "Please, Ryan. Not that again."

Maddy spoke up. "He's right though. It's not fair to make me do it if I don't want to." She frowned. "That goes for Julliard too."

His mom paled. "This has really gone too far. Kirk." She turned to him. "Tell her. We're the parents. We decide."

His shoulders sank. "You know, Daneen. Maybe they're right?"

She gasped. "Kirk!"

"I mean it though." He spun his coffee cup around in his hands, staring down at it. When he met her eyes, he said, "We shouldn't make Maddy do something that makes her miserable."

"She's not miserable."

Maddy pursed her lips. "Yeah, Mom. I kind of am."

"But, sweetheart—"

"I tried to tell you yesterday," Maddy said. "This isn't a beach whim or whatever you called it. I've felt this way since last summer, and every month it kept getting worse. Do you know how much school stuff I had to miss because of cello? Dances. Football games."

Her mom blinked. "Football games?"

"Yeah, sure."

"Regular stuff," Ryan said. "Things that kids do." Maddy snapped him a look. "Not that Maddy's a little kid."

His mom tugged on her necklace like it was choking her. For as long as he remembered, she'd worn those pearls, even when they seemed overly formal for the occasion. "Naturally there've been sacrifices."

"But I've sacrificed friends." Maddy's chin trembled. "Do you know what it's like to be the cello geek? The 'prodigy who's going to Julliard'? The one the teachers talk about and that people make fun of behind your back?"

His dad's eyes misted over. "Sweetheart, that's terrible. Your mom and I—" He glanced at her. "We didn't know."

"But you do now," Ryan said. "That's just the thing."

"You can't quit in the middle of summer orchestra." His mom looked alarmed. "You have performances coming up."

Maddy pushed aside her plastic cup. "I could quit after."

"How about taking a break?" her dad said. "Rather than chucking it altogether?"

This actually sounded like a decent plan to Ryan. As mature as she liked to think she was, Maddy still had lots of growing up to do. She was gifted at cello. Could be she'd miss it once she stopped. "You mean like taking a semester off?" he asked.

His dad nodded and stared at his wife. "Daneen?"

"I suppose that sounds reasonable."

Maddy surveyed the group. "I think it sounds good too. But only if you let me be the one to decide about going back to it." She sat up straighter in her seat. "Or not."

"We can't make her be someone she doesn't want to be," his dad said softly to his mom.

His mom pursed her lips for a long while, a dimple forming

in her chin. "All right," she finally said. "But one semester. One semester *only*. Then, we'll talk about it."

The rest of them exhaled.

"Cool!" Maddy beamed around the table like she couldn't believe it. Then she picked up her drink and drained a third of it in one long swallow.

His mom swept back her hair, adjusting her necklace. "So." She gazed at Ryan, appearing weary. "You said there were other things?"

He decided to tackle himself next, since they were on the topic of family. "I'm really glad we got that out there—about Maddy. Thank you both for hearing me." He glanced at his sister. "For hearing us, most especially her. Because it is her life, and even though I know you only want what's best for her, she's the one who has to deal with the consequences."

"Or glory," his mom couldn't resist adding.

"Yeah, that's true." Ryan licked his lips, which suddenly felt extra dry. He took a sip of hot coffee, but that didn't really help. "Here's the thing. A lot of the same could be said for me."

His mom's forehead creased. "You?"

"I'm afraid I don't follow, son," his dad said.

"It's simple," Ryan said. "Maddy's her own person, and so am I. What she chooses to do for a career going forward should ultimately be up to her."

His dad picked up his cup. "But you've already chosen."

"Right," Ryan said. "And, Mom and Dad, I love what I do. Not just a little. A lot. The students I teach are amazing, all of them work so hard. They're dedicated. Driven."

"Not half as driven as those in the Ivy League." His mom shook her head. "Or in the Seven Sisters."

He frowned. "Mom, I'm trying to stay polite about this, but I really need you to stop doing that. Knocking down my job." She blanched like he'd gotten that wrong. But, oh no, he hadn't. "It's like every opportunity, at every turn, you can't keep yourself from wishing I was at Wellesley."

"And saying it out loud," Maddy added.

"But you could have taught there," she insisted. "Maybe still could. Better yet, Harvard."

"I don't know about that."

"What?"

"My degree is from a great school, a Public Ivy, sure, but I haven't published in big journals. I've published in small ones. And you know what? For me that's okay. I research topics that interest me. I love history, I do. But I love working with people more. That one-on-one experience, like tutoring a struggling student or coaching kids' soccer."

Maddy stared up at him and her eyes glimmered. "You coach? Cool."

Ryan nodded.

His dad wore a proud mug. "I think that's great."

"Of course," his mom said. "Charity work is excellent, but you don't have to do charity for a job."

"Mom. Look at me." He stared straight into her pale-blue eyes. "Oh yes, *I do*. I do because I want to give back, need to give back. To me that means something. More than fancy accolades or awards, or being at a ritzy nameplate university. I'm good, Mom and Dad." He included his father because this speech was for him too. "Good with where I work and good with who I am, and I won't have you questioning that any longer. That goes double for who I date."

"Ahh." His mom sighed. "So this *is* all about Evita."

His dad crossed his arms. "Sounds like a bit more than that, Daneen."

Ryan ignored his mom's comment and kept going. He was on a roll, flexing his spiritual strength, and it felt good. "Look, I'm the first to admit that this whole week came as a surprise—for everyone. But it wasn't the Machados' fault or ours. So we opted to make the best of it. Fair. Only things haven't been fair between us; there's been constant warring on either side."

"Because of Lissette and Pablo."

"Not only because of them." His dad wore an embarrassed frown. "I'm afraid we've been guilty too."

His mom messed with her necklace again, adjusting it behind her.

"Is something wrong, Daneen?"

"This darn thing just keeps catching somehow. I don't know." She met her husband's eyes, then viewed her kids. "Maybe the sailing has been a little rough in Nantucket, but it's almost over now, isn't it?"

"I think the Machados are cool," Maddy said. "They've all been really nice to me."

"They are a nice family," Ryan agreed. "And do you want to know a sad truth?" He decided he might as well spill it. "When I saw them toasting together last night at dinner, for a split second I got an ache right in here." He pressed his hand to his heart. "And you want to know why that was? It was because I was wishing our family could be more like theirs."

His mom frowned. "Loud?"

His dad laid a hand on her arm. "I think you know what he's saying. And so do I."

"The Machados might be loud," Maddy said. "But here's one thing you know just by looking at them. The people in their family, they love each other."

Ryan's mom's face went pink and her eyes glistened. "We. Love. Each. Other." She choked on the words. She turned to his dad, then spoke to them all. "Don't we?"

His dad took her hand. "I love you, Daneen." He gazed at Ryan and Maddy. "And I love you, even though I haven't always shown it in the right ways." He avoided his wife's eyes. "And might have let you down in others."

Maddy squirmed because this was getting so emotional, and the Hatfields didn't do emotional. At least they never had, until now. "Yeah. I wasn't saying that we don't love each other. I was just meaning it's not as obvious with us."

"You don't have to put it all out there on a billboard to feel it," his mom said in warbly tones. "Not everyone's demonstrative." She yanked on her pearls and they broke apart. "My necklace!" Small white beads bounced onto the table and rolled onto the floor. "No!"

The four of them sprang to the floor on their hands and knees, recovering the rolling orbs as they scurried away. Other customers stooped down to help, and a barista joined them. At last, all the pearls were accounted for, and his mom stared down at them in her hands as they sat back in the booth. Both her palms were full, and the necklace had clearly been destroyed. But at least she hadn't lost any of the pieces.

"We'll get it fixed," his dad said. "I know a good jeweler."

Her face was slack and bedsheet white.

"Daneen, honey?" he repeated. "I said, we'll fix it."

"It's not that." Her voice shook like she might full-on weep. "It's—" She gave a small sniff. "This was from my father." Ryan was surprised she'd never mentioned this.

"Wait? What?" Maddy said. "It was?"

She nodded. "He gave it to me when I was about your age," she said to Mads. "When I turned sixteen. It was such a grown-up gift." Her smile drifted like she was far away. "I really felt like I'd made it in my dad's eyes." She laughed sadly. "And that wasn't easy. If I got an A minus in a class, instead of saying congrats, he'd ask me what the minus was for."

His dad patted her shoulder, seeming to have heard this story before.

"He was very tough."

"He was tough," she said. "But he loved me. I know he did." She transferred the pearls to a pocket in her purse and wiped back a tear. "Even though he never said it. My parents were old-school that way. Very stiff upper lip. When I wore those pearls, I felt bigger. Bolder. Like I could conquer the world. I sailed through my eleventh-grade year, earning only As. No minuses. Maybe a plus or two."

Heat burned in Ryan's chest. He'd never seen her cry.

Maddy's eyes brimmed with moisture too. Their mom was such a powerhouse normally. Seeing her softer underbelly was upsetting somehow. It was terrible to hear about the pressure she'd been put under. She had been pushy about Ryan and Maddy's choices, in her mind trying to steer them the right way. But she'd never berated them over grades.

"I'm sorry about your pearls, Mom," Maddy said. "Is that why you never said they were from Grandpa? Because the memory made you too sad?"

"In a way, yes." She blew her nose on a napkin, collecting herself. "The pearls were meant to be part of a set," she told them. "They came with beautiful pearl earrings."

Ryan had never seen her wear those. "Do you still have them?"

She shook her head. "My dad, he"—she blinked back more tears—"believed in strong motivators. So. He"—her voice shook—"showed me the earrings on my sixteenth birthday, telling me that's what I would have to work for. Once I got into Bryn Mawr..." She bit her lip, unable to keep going.

Ryan knew she'd never gone to Bryn Mawr, or to any of the Seven Sisters schools for that matter. She'd gone to a state university. "So he never gave them to you?" That seemed incredibly callous of his grandfather to withhold the present. Cold. Unfeeling. It sounded like his mom had done her best. Worked super hard in school.

Her eyes glistened. "He said I needed to pad my student résumé. Run for leadership positions. He was *so disappointed* when I lost the class president position to Lissette Machado. Almost like it had been my fault. Like I hadn't wanted to win.

And maybe I hadn't? Deep inside. I was never very outgoing. The thought of making speeches unnerved me. I had the worst time with the campaign. I'm surprised I came as close to winning as I did. It must have been on account of that football stadium."

Maddy frowned. "The one your dad helped build."

"Yes. My dad always said that maybe if I'd made class president, I'd have gone on to bigger things. He was sure I would have gotten into Bryn Mawr. I suppose he convinced me of that too, because that's what I used to believe."

"And now?" Ryan asked her.

She hung her head. "I'm not so sure."

"What about when Grandpa died?" Mads asked. "Didn't Grandma give you the earrings?"

"No. My dad had given them away by then, or returned them. I don't know."

"And then Grandma died a few years after him." Mads frowned, recalling the story. "Here's what I don't get," she told her mom. "If your dad was that hard on you, why did you still want to wear the necklace? I mean, even now?"

"It was his one stamp of approval." She sighed at her admission. "I guess I always wanted to please him. For him to be proud of me. In some strange and silly way, I still do."

"Maybe it's okay," Maddy said. "Just to be proud of yourself?"

Out of the mouth of babes. Ryan nodded. "I'm proud of you, Mom. You've built a really great career. With or without Bryn Mawr."

His dad's eyes twinkled. "And an excellent family."

"You're right. I have." She scanned their faces, and for the first time in a long while—maybe since he was a young boy—Ryan felt a glimmer of affection. No. Something deeper. "But I haven't done any of it on my own."

"Yes. So." His dad hugged her shoulder. "Maybe certain things in the past are no longer so important? Hmm?"

"You know what they say." His mom sighed. "Life goes on."

"It sure does," his dad said. He glanced at his son. "Ryan, thanks for thinking of the coffee. Maybe we did need to get out and clear the air."

His mom nodded. "Yes, and I'm sorry. I only wanted the best for you and Maddy. Because you're both so bright and capable. I thought maybe you could accomplish things I couldn't, if you only put your minds to it."

"But if their hearts aren't in it, Daneen…"

"Yes, yes. I know. I'm sorry, kids. Really I am. I hope you can believe and forgive me."

"We all want different things," Ryan told her gently. "What's right for you and Dad is different for me. And what I want is 100% going to be different from Maddy."

She nodded. "I understand that better now." For the first time in forever, Ryan felt like she did.

A lump welled in his throat. "Thank you."

"Thank you, Ryan. I'm sorry that you've never felt like you had our respect."

"You've certainly earned it," his dad said.

Warmth spread through his chest. "Thanks, Dad."

"Gosh!" His mom moaned and wiped under her eyes where her mascara had run a little. "This has been an exhausting coffee."

His dad released a weighty sigh. "It has been wearing, hasn't it?"

"Maybe we can go get some ice cream?" Maddy suggested as they left the booth.

Her mom stared at her empty drink cup. "You're still hungry?"

Maddy giggled. "Not right now. I was thinking we could take some back for dessert?"

The day was gorgeous and balmy when they stepped outside.

"Great idea," Ryan's dad said. "Maybe the Machados would like some too?"

His mom nodded. "We can buy extra."

The clouds parted in Ryan's soul, and rays of sunshine poured in. He glanced at his mom, wondering about her and Mrs. Machado.

"I'll talk to Lissette sometime tonight," she said. "I promise."

TWENTY-TWO

EVITA SIGHED AND DROPPED HER cell phone into her beach bag. Ryan's text message was better than she hoped. Was it impossible to believe the two archenemy families could spend their last night together in harmony? That would be a game changer for everyone, especially her and Ryan.

"Good news?" Robby asked.

Evita smiled at her oldest brother. "Hope so!"

They were enjoying their last afternoon on the beach and would head inside to wash up for dinner soon. The boys were going out for pizza to make everything easier. People had packing up to do to get ready for tomorrow. First though, they were going to have their Machado family beach party with cocktails and appetizers. Yay!

"Auntie Evita." Nanny tugged at her hand. "Will you dance with me before dinner?"

"We'll all dance," Evita promised her. "It's your Tita's favorite thing."

"Your Tito's too," her dad said, tugging on the brim of his sun hat.

Quique busily built another drip castle. Nanny had been helping him and her hands were all grainy, covered in sand. Luisa slept in her carrier under the umbrella between Robby and Evita, while her mom and dad took in some sun. Chachi and Kendra played bocce ball with Eunice. It was wonderful being with her family, but the Hatfields' absence oddly left a big, gaping hole. She knew that this was how her family had pictured the vacation initially. With it being just the ten of them.

Now that they'd been fourteen for the week, only ten people felt weirdly lonely. She thought of how things would have been for Ryan's family if it had only been the four of them here in this big house. Would Maddy and Ryan have had their breakthrough? She didn't know. She didn't take credit for that exactly, but she did feel glad Ryan had talked to her about it, and that she'd encouraged him about being closer to his little sister. Ryan had interestingly granted her courage too. She'd generally been pretty direct with her parents, but not nearly as solid as she'd been when speaking to her mom about Ryan. Adulting felt good.

She checked the angle of the sun. Ryan and his family had been gone for an awfully long time. Too long for just having coffee. They must have stayed in town to do other things. She missed having Ryan here and wished he would return. She was dying to hear firsthand about how that talk went. She also hoped he'd tell her more about what the topic was, if he was comfortable sharing. In high school, they'd told each other everything, even personal things, and they'd only been at-school friends.

Chachi grabbed one of the coolers and went up to the house for more beer. "Anyone want anything?"

"No thanks," their mom said. "I'll probably head in soon."

"Me too," her dad said. "Have to get started on those frozen daquiris." That was their announced cocktail of the night.

"Good thing we picked up more ice," Robby said. He and Eunice had run to the store earlier to get more diapers for Luisa and had grabbed a few fill-in groceries while they were there. They didn't need much since they were leaving in the morning, but Robby and Eunice also wanted to make sure they were supplied for their plane trip back to Los Angeles.

Evita scooted out of the shade of the umbrella to soak in some rays one last time. She leaned back in her chair, enjoying the cool ocean breeze and the warmth of the sun kissing her face. It was hard to think about going back to work on Monday, but at least her work was fun and she loved it.

She had so much to tell Josie. She'd thought of filling her in by text, or even sneaking in a quick phone call. But the landscape seemed to change here daily, and she wanted to get a better sense about her and Ryan before she said anything. Josie would be blown away to know the two families had shared the one beach house together. Evita was still wrapping her head around that herself.

Chachi returned with his cooler. "The Hatfields are back," he said to Robby and Evita as he passed them. "They brought ice cream."

"Oh, nice," Evita said. "For?"

"For all of us," Chachi said. "For dessert."

Evita's heart pounded. That had to be a good sign. Otherwise, why would they make the gesture of sharing food? After their huge falling out last night, someone was going to have to break the ice. "How were the Hatfields?" she asked. "Ryan's parents. How did they seem?"

Chachi shrugged. "Normal."

Normal, right. "Not chatty. Or conciliatory?"

"Mr. and Mrs. Hatfield aren't the chatty sort. Not sure what you mean by conciliatory. Did they apologize for anything? No. But I doubt they would to me. Maddy was busy putting away the ice cream. Ryan said hi, but he looked distracted. Like he had stuff on his mind."

She had to see Ryan. She couldn't wait. Evita hurried up to the house.

Ryan met her coming down the stairs. "I was just coming to look for you."

"And?"

Small lines tugged at the corner of his eyes. "I think it's good news." He cracked a slow grin, and her heart fluttered. "My mom's talking to yours tonight."

Evita's gut clenched. "That's good news?" she asked uncertainly.

"I believe so." He set a hand on her cheek.

Her face warmed. "I hope you're right."

"Ryan!" his mom called from the deck. He dropped his hand. "Can you come help with the umbrella?"

"We want to hit the beach one last time," he told Evita. "You staying?"

"No. I, uh…" She glanced over her shoulder. "I promised my mom I'd help with some stuff. Making a crab dip."

"Crab dip sounds delicious."

"Yeah, you're welcome to some."

"Thanks. We might take you up on it."

"We?"

He winked. "Keep the faith," he whispered.

Her heart skipped a beat, and then it beat harder. What on earth was he saying? That everything was fixed? It wasn't fixed on her parents' side, as far as she knew. Not completely. Her parents were not at all happy by how things had ended last night after the games, with Mrs. Hatfield exploding and her mom erupting as well. She claimed she'd had no choice since "Daneen started it." That was always her excuse. What were they, five? As hard as it was to believe, in some ways, Quique and Nanny behaved better.

Ryan went to get the umbrella, and Evita passed the rest of the Hatfields coming down the stairs.

"Evita." Mrs. Hatfield nodded, but her expression gave nothing away.

"How was the beach?" Mr. Hatfield asked pleasantly enough.

"Oh, er. Good! Really nice." She smiled at Maddy, who held a boogie board. "Have a fun time riding the waves."

"Thanks!"

She turned and watched them. Maddy dropped her canvas bag and ran straight into the water. Quique and Nanny squealed and followed her. Kendra dashed after them. Ryan passed Evita, carrying the umbrella. "Do you want any help?" He almost looked hopeful. "With that crab dip or anything?"

"No, that's okay," she said. "Go on and enjoy the beach. It's our last day."

He held her gaze. "Yeah. I know." For an instant he looked

melancholy, but then he turned upbeat. "I have a feeling it's going to be a good one too."

There was so much she wanted to ask him, but that would have to wait until later, she guessed. When they could grab a moment, just the two of them.

"So." She shifted on her feet. "See you later then?"

"You betcha," he said with a heart-melting grin.

Later that evening, Ryan's parents sat on the deck having their final-night martinis. He had one too, and Maddy had bottled water infused with berries.

"At last." His mom sipped from her glass. "A night of peace and quiet."

Evita and her family were inside showering and prepping snacks in the kitchen. His dad was grilling surf and turf for dinner: steaks and lobster tail. He couldn't wait. He also couldn't wait for his mom to settle things with Mrs. Machado, but he didn't want to push her. That might backfire and cause her not to make any gesture at all.

They'd only had brief exchanges with Evita's family since returning from having coffee. He wouldn't exactly call them friendly. Her parents did say hi, but they'd seemed more withdrawn than normal, like they preferred keeping their distance. Ryan didn't really blame them after his mom's display during the games.

His dad raised his martini glass. "Here's to an eventful week at the beach."

"I think the Machados made it more fun," Maddy told them. "If it had just been us, it would have been boring."

"Boring?" But Ryan could tell his mom wasn't seriously mad. More like perplexed.

Maddy rolled her eyes at Ryan. "At least we didn't have to watch British television."

He chuckled. "No." Not that he would have minded, personally. Even at Maddy's age, he was interested in stuff like that, but that was him, not Mads. Or probably most teenagers. Maybe he was a bit of a nerd in some ways, but that was okay. He liked the nerd he was, and apparently so did Evita. Each time they were together, he felt that buzz between them. Today on the steps it had been stronger than ever.

He was going to see her after Nantucket, if that's what she wanted. Even though he didn't live in Lexington any longer, his home wasn't that far outside it. They could make it work if she was interested too.

He knew their families didn't have to make peace for that to happen. He'd made clear to his parents he intended to see whoever he wanted. Knowing Evita, she'd said just as much to hers. But having their families at least not on hating terms would make everything so much nicer.

"This house is beautiful, and the views—oh my." His mom studied the ocean and took another sip of her cocktail. "But in some ways I'm glad this vacation is over. It's been..." She sighed heavily. "Stressful."

Maddy glanced at Ryan, like *Yeah, stressful because of you.* But Ryan knew the tension wasn't all on their mom. Mrs. Machado had played her part in it too. She was headstrong like Evita and didn't like being challenged. His mom was bullheaded too, but in a different way. He really wanted them to settle this.

Music cranked up indoors. Loud music. And people cheered. "What on earth?" His mom spun toward the house. The rest of them looked too.

The Machados were spread out all over the living room and definitely not sticking to a side. They were doing some sort of line dance, even Quique and Nanny joined in. Right hand to left shoulder, left hand to right shoulder. Touching both sides of their heads. Then their hips. Hip swivel then—whoa—a big jump.

"What are they doing in there?" his mom said, aghast.

The chorus went up with the next big jump with them lifting their arms and shouting, "Hey Macarena!"

His dad leaned in for a better view. "I think that's the Macarena."

"How do you know about the Macarena?" Maddy asked him.

"I remember it from—back in the day."

"I've only seen it in GIFs." Maddy giggled. "Not done live."

The music continued with a heavy base beat. *Boom-dada-boom, dada-boom, dada-boom! Boom-dada-boom, dada-boom, dada-boom!* "Hey Macarena!"

"That's *very* loud." She reached for her pearls, then tapped her fingers against her neck when she remembered they were broken.

His dad seemed intrigued. "I wonder how they learned all that?"

"It's not hard," Maddy said. "Just a series of steps, then everything repeats."

The line of Machados jumped again. This time their swaying backsides faced the windows. Evita was between her niece and nephew, urging them along. A few more turns and they were facing the sea. Evita was prettier than ever, wearing a big grin and a warm glow on her dimpled cheeks.

"They look silly."

Actually, they looked like they were having a blast.

"Mom." Ryan chuckled. "It's just a dance."

She sat back in her seat. "I think I need another one of these." She held up her martini glass.

His dad set his hands on his knees and stood, taking her glass. "Be right back."

The music seemed to go on forever, then it finally stopped.

His mom heaved a breath. "Thank goodness."

"Once more!" Chachi shouted. The other Machados chorused in. "Again!"

Boom-dada-boom, dada-boom, dada-boom!

His mom rubbed her closed eyelids. "Seriously?"

Maddy laughed. "The Machados sure can party."

Uh-oh. Here they come.

The French doors flew open, and Mr. Machado led the group in a conga line of sorts. Music blared through the open doors as they laughed and hollered. "Hey Macarena!"

Ryan's mom froze in shock when the group snaked around the firepit. Chachi was second in line, then Kendra and Eunice and Robby. Quique came next, then Evita and Nanny. Mrs. Machado brought up the rear, swishing her large, curvy hips and grinning to beat the band.

Wait! Ryan blinked. His dad followed Mrs. Machado out the door, hanging on to her shoulders. He'd joined the line!

TWENTY-THREE

RYAN'S MOM BLANCHED. "KIRK. WHAT are you doing?"

He laughed and shouted, "Hey! Macarena!"

Boom-dada-boom, dada-boom, dada-boom!

Maddy shot to her feet. "I'm going too."

"Maddy, what?" Her mouth fell open so wide, her chin nearly smacked the deck.

"Come on, Ryan," Mr. Machado said as he danced past them.

Ryan glanced at his mom. "Sorry. I'm going in."

She sat there looking lost and pale. Ryan held out his hand. "Why don't you come too?"

"No, I—" She recoiled and stroked the empty spot where her necklace had been. "I'm good here."

Ryan shrugged and latched on to Maddy's shoulders, completing the line as it wound into the house. *Boom-dada-boom, dada-boom, dada-boom! Boom-dada-boom, dada-boom, dada-boom!* They all formed a large circle encompassing both sofas and went through one last pass with the song, cycling through the moves. By his final jump, Ryan had it.

"Hey! Macarena!" Everyone threw up their hands and

whistled and cheered. The room roared with laughter bouncing off the high ceiling.

"Oh, ha ha!" Maddy held her sides. "That was crazy fun."

"It was crazy fun, wasn't it?" Ryan had somehow landed beside Evita when the conga line broke apart and the circle formed. He stared down at her flushed face and warm brown eyes and his heart flipped.

"Glad to see you and your family getting into the spirit."

He got swept up in her gaze. "Me too."

"Well!" his dad said. "I'd better mix those martinis."

"You can have a daquiri if you'd like!" Mr. Machado said. He held up a pitcher in the kitchen. "We have plenty."

Ryan's dad looked tempted. "Thanks. But maybe another time."

Evita's mom whispered to her dad as she pulled the crab dip from the oven. "At least some of Daneen's family knows how to cut loose."

Mr. Machado chuckled. "A happy surprise."

After things had ended so badly last night, Ryan was surprised the Machados had been gracious about his family joining their dance. Maybe that's how they were? They could come on strong, even blow a fuse occasionally. But then they got over it and went back to their jovial selves. It was a different way of being. Expressive yet accepting in the end. The crab dip smelled delicious, its savory scent with hints of Old Bay filling the room.

"Evita!" her mom called. "It looks ready."

Evita excused herself from Ryan. "Let me go get the crackers to go with that." Her eyebrows rose. "Want some?"

"I'd love a taste if there's enough."

"Come on." He followed her to the stovetop where her mom had left the hot dip. "Can you grab the crackers from our shelf in the pantry?" she asked Ryan, while taking a platter out of a cabinet.

He found two different kinds and brought the boxes over. "These?"

"Yeah, thanks."

Mr. Machado was back in the living room with his sound machine. He selected a different soundtrack, and trumpets wailed while maracas shook in the background and guitars strummed. It sounded like what he'd been playing on the deck when he and Ryan's dad had gotten into it. Mrs. Machado stood by him, and they both nursed their daquiris. They were engaged in quiet conversation, shooting occasional looks outdoors at Ryan's parents.

Evita set her platter on the island and arranged the crackers around the hot dip dish she'd moved over.

"Ooh! Crab dip!" Chachi was the first to filter into the kitchen. Soon, more Machados flooded the room, loading up crackers and making appreciative noises. So many hands reached for the dip, it looked like a game of Twister with wrists and elbows overlapping.

"Delicious, Evita," Robby said.

Kendra agreed. "World's best!" She made a couple of crackers for her kids, who scarfed them down in record time.

"Yum-my!" Nanny proclaimed.

"Can I have another?" Quique pleaded, a dab of crab dip on his chin. Kendra wiped it clean with a napkin.

"Just one more," Chachi said. "We don't want to ruin our appetites for the pizza."

Ryan noted Chachi was on his fourth cracker himself.

Eunice chomped on a cracker loaded with crab dip. "So tasty!"

Ryan took a bite, and it was so cheesy and good. He nodded at Evita. "This is great stuff."

Evita smiled and made a cracker for herself. "Thanks."

Through the window he saw his dad hold out a fresh martini for his mom. She drained it in one long swallow and set down her glass. She stood and walked to the French doors, cracking them open. "Lissette," she said. "Can I have a word?"

Mrs. Machado's eyebrows arched, and she glanced at her husband.

He nodded toward the door like she should go and see what Ryan's mom wanted.

She passed him her daquiri glass to hold. "I'll be right back."

Ryan's dad came into the house, evidently wanting to make himself scarce on the deck. If it were Ryan, he wouldn't have wanted to be within earshot of the two moms. Or shouting distance either. "Is that crab dip I smell?"

"Yeah," Evita said. "Come and try some." She made room at the island, stepping away, then herding Ryan closer to the window. "What's going on out there?"

He stared at their two moms having a heavy conversation by the railing.

Both wore frowns.

"I hope my mom's apologizing," he whispered.

Evita nodded. "Hope my mom is too."

They watched while trying not to be obvious. "Want something to drink?" she asked him without taking her eyes off the deck. He was too enthralled to look away himself.

"No thanks. I think I'll wait for a bit."

"Yeah. Me too." She peered out the window, straining to see. His mom fluttered her fingers against her throat where her pearls had been. "Wait. Where's your mom's necklace?"

Ryan kept his voice down. "It broke at the café earlier. This whole story unfolded about her dad and how he'd given it to her. Pretty sad really. Sounds like he was not an easy parent to have."

Evita frowned. "Like—"

"No, Evita. Not like our moms. Worse. I think it scarred Mom, honestly. I also think it has a lot to do with what went on between our moms back in high school."

"I don't understand."

He turned his back to the others in the kitchen, shielding their hushed discussion. "Her dad was pretty furious with her for losing that class president election."

"You're joking. That wasn't her fault."

"No, but he made her feel like it was. He'd promised her earrings to go with the necklace he gave her, but only if she got into a certain high-level college. He made her believe that holding an elected office in high school would make her a shoo-in for admission."

"How horrible. The pressure."

"Exactly." He frowned. "And when she didn't get accepted—"

She gasped. "This all circles back to my mom?"

He pursed his lips. "I'm afraid so."

"What happened to your grandfather? Is he still around?"

He shook his head. "He died some years ago. My grandma Wilkins not long after."

"Ryan," she whispered. "Look."

Evita's mom braced his mom's arms in her hands and she nodded. His mom hung her head.

Then the impossible happened.

Mrs. Machado pulled his mom into a hug.

She looked up a second later to see Ryan and Evita spying on them. They quickly spun away, walking into the kitchen.

"Looks like their talk went well," Evita whispered.

"Yeah," Ryan replied, stunned. From the great room, he saw Mrs. Machado leading his mom toward the door. She pulled her inside by the hand and raised their linked hands together, like prize fighters after a match. "Another round of the Macarena!" she announced.

You could have knocked the whole house over with a feather, the room was so still.

Robby and Chachi were in the foyer with their keys ready to go pick up the pizza, but they returned to the great room.

Evita's dad chuckled and opened an app on his phone. "Of course!"

The obedient speaker blared. *Boom-dada-boom, dada-boom, dada-boom!*

People cheered. "Hey, Macarena!"

Ryan's dad took a long sip, then put down his martini glass. "Great song." Then he brought himself up short, checking his watch. "But—I should turn the grill on."

"Grill schmill!" Evita's dad waved his hand. "Save your steak and lobster for home. Have pizza with us tonight."

Ryan's parents exchanged glances.

"We have plenty of ice for your coolers," Mr. Machado said. "We're happy to share."

"Not having a big cleanup would be nice," Ryan's mom agreed.

"Then it's settled." His dad wore a big happy grin. "Thanks."

The music played on with its rhythmic beat.

Boom-dada-boom, dada-boom, dada-boom!

"Come on, Mom," Maddy directed, showing off her smooth moves. "Like this!"

His mom was a little stiff, but Chachi encouraged her too, telling her she was doing great.

"That's good." He did a wide hip swivel, demonstrating. "Stay loose!"

She reddened and moved her torso, her frame rigid like a board. She looked like a wooden spoon rotating in a cooking pot. But at least she was trying.

Ryan pursed his lips and Evita giggled. She nudged him. "Let's dance."

They joined in the party with everyone hooting and hollering and swaying to the music. Ryan had never participated in a multi-generational rager, but he now understood their appeal. It was fun, and Evita was stunning, with those dimples settling deep and her grin big and wide. He couldn't believe how lucky he was to have found someone like her—twice in a lifetime, and this second time around was so much better.

Evita glanced toward the kitchen, speaking above the music. "Want to grab something to drink?" she asked, noticing that Chachi and Robby had each paused to grab a beer from the refrigerator. But Ryan didn't need any alcohol. He got all the buzz he needed looking into Evita's heady dark eyes. And a question was burning inside him so hot that it would scorch him from the inside out if he didn't ask her.

"I have a better idea," he said, grabbing on to her hand. She laughed and followed his lead as he dragged her across the great room, weaving through the dancers.

"Wait! Where are we going?" she shouted when the music blared again. Ryan didn't know how many times her dad could play the same song, but he guessed he was going for a record.

"I've got something to ask you!"

Ryan's mom saw them heading to the door and stopped gyrating. She cut a panicked look at Evita's mom. "It's all right, Daneen. Let them go."

She nodded and focused on her dance moves. Right hand to left shoulder. No. Hip. She started over. Everybody jumped and turned, leaving her behind. His mom did a giant bunny hop to catch up. By the next jump she was with them.

Ryan glanced over his shoulder, tugging Evita out the door. She was laughing so hard she could barely breathe.

"Ha ha ha! Oh my gosh." She chuckled, closing the door behind her. "Your mom! Ryan!"

"I know." He took one last peek inside and his mom was smiling. Not any old smile either. A genuine one. Like someone had opened up a pressure valve, releasing eons of pent-up angst.

She looked years younger. "Come on," he whispered huskily to Evita. "This way."

————————————

Evita was still laughing as they crossed the deck. She couldn't believe Mrs. Hatfield's moves! She couldn't believe their moms had made peace. Whew! "Whatever your mom said to mine worked."

"Yeah," Ryan agreed. "So crazy. Seeing them together like that. Hugging! Dancing!" He chuckled. "Can you believe it?"

She shook her head. "Things will be better now. They have to be." All that negativity had been released. Their moms would always be competitors in their jobs, but that didn't mean they couldn't get along personally. Nobody was saying they had to be best friends. Anything other than enemies worked for her. She was sure it also worked for Ryan.

Her heart pounded because of how he looked at her. She wasn't positive about what he wanted to tell her, but she hoped it concerned the two of them. And if he didn't say it, she intended to. What they had was too good to forget about after this week. They owed it to themselves to give it a try. She believed that in her gut.

She skipped down the steps beside him, and they reached the sand, still holding hands. Sea foam spread across the beach, and ocean waves towered high, crashing down with force and kicking up spray. It prickled their faces and arms with chilly sprinkles as they neared the water. The moon sent a shimmering glow across the ocean as it heaved and moaned, sloshing around their bare feet and numbing their toes and ankles. The shock of the water was icy cold, but neither one minded. They were too high from what had just happened indoors.

Ryan let go of her hand and brought his arms around her waist. "We did it." He set his chin. "We survived the week."

"I *know*," she said. "Who would have thought?"

His gaze washed over her, bathing her in happiness and warmth. "This has been the wildest time."

She giggled, remembering the tug-of-war. "Oh my gosh. The umbrella!"

He shook his head. "Your dad's music."

She lowered her eyebrows. "The *shower*."

He laughed out loud. "The cookies."

She rolled her eyes. "And Twister!"

He jiggled her in his arms. "And yet, somehow, we made it."

She sighed. "Yeah. Somehow, we did." She considered his handsome face. His slightly imperfect nose and his shaggy golden-brown hair, his very dreamy brown eyes. "You know, I think you were right. It wasn't up to us to fix it. Our two moms had to go there themselves."

"True. But, in my mom's case, she needed a little nudging."

Evita laughed. "My mom probably needed encouragement too." She'd been wondering about something. "What else did you guys talk about during your coffee?"

"Maddy," he said. "About her not wanting to play the cello." His expression lit up his face. "My folks are letting her take a semester off to see if that's really what she wants to do."

"Oh Ryan, that's fantastic."

"Yeah, it was a good compromise, because Maddy, you

know." He shrugged. "She's fifteen, so could change her mind. She's also very, very good."

"I bet she could be good at lots of things."

"I'm sure you're right."

"It's great that you had that talk then."

"That wasn't all." He grew more serious now.

"No?"

Then a smile, affectionate and warm. Loving.

He held her a little closer. "I talked to them about me. Told my parents to back off in criticizing my career and other choices."

"Go you. What did they say?"

"I think they were surprised at first, but then it sank in."

She scanned his eyes. "How do you feel about things now?"

"Totally awesome."

She chuckled warmly. "I'm so glad."

"Yeah. Me too. I guess I'd been dreading that conversation for a while. Now that it's over, I'm really glad we had it."

"I had a talk with my mom too."

"Did you?"

She nodded. "About similar things. Not that I need my parents' approval, but sometimes it's easier without their resistance, if you know what I'm saying."

"I definitely do."

"It wasn't about my job," Evita said. "She and my dad have always supported that, but it was about my choices."

"Like who you date?"

She blushed. "Yeah."

"That's good, because I'd like to date you."

"Oh yeah?" She grinned, incredibly pleased.

"I mean," he said a bit awkwardly. "If you want that too?"

She stared into his eyes, seeing all sorts of amazing possibilities with him, like a happy relationship built on friendship and trust. History. Respect. And, okay, okay. Hints of building lust. Because it was true. He was such a sexy professor. "I'd like that too."

He pulled her closer, resting his forehead against hers. "A wise man once told me," his voice was husky below the wind, "you can't just stand there on the sidelines. Sometimes you have to dive in."

She smiled softly. "Chachi."

"I love your family, Evita."

"I like yours too." And she did, she really did. It said a lot about Mrs. Hatfield that she could admit she'd been wrong. Mr. Hatfield had his interesting side too, an undercurrent of warmth that could be brought out under the right circumstances. And then there was Maddy, so sweet and just wanting to belong. To have people accept and understand her for who she was.

"I think we can do this," he said firmly.

"Date?"

He nodded. "And this." He ran his hands through her hair, his fingers threading through her curls. Her face heated. "And this." His lips brushed over hers, so silky and warm. Her pulse fluttered. "And *this*." He did it again, and warmth pooled in her belly. He pressed his mouth to hers in the sweetest kiss. All her senses came alive, tuning her in to her surroundings. The briny scent of the sea, the roaring crash of the waves, the beating of her heart against his.

She wrapped her arms around his neck and held on tight, kissing him back with all her might. He moaned and pressed her to him, deepening his kisses, again and again. Her world turned upside down, and she felt like she was sailing out to sea, carried by the rippling tide, pulling harder and harder until she had no choice but to give in—and ride that wave.

Whoosh!

And then another.

Whoosh!

He could definitely up his game.

"Oh, Ryan. I—"

"I know," he rasped, kissing her again. "Me too."

"Should we go back?" Her breath shuddered. "The pizza?"

"It can wait."

"Our families."

"So can they."

He was right and she knew it. This was their time, his and hers. Just for now it was only them, the moon and the stars...and the wild, wind-tossed sea.

Nothing else mattered.

TWENTY-FOUR

THE NEXT MORNING, ROBBY STEADIED his cell phone against the pop-out shelf on the grill with his travel container of coffee behind it to keep it upright. He'd flipped the camera to face the group, tweaking it gently. "Almost selfie time!"

Both families gathered in the driveway in front of the cottage, their vehicles packed to go. They'd risen early, everyone operating in lockstep. No time for leisurely coffees on the deck; they had cleaning up to do. Putting the grill back in the shed would be their final chore in checking out of the cottage. They'd run through a checklist and left all the dirty laundry in a pile in the foyer as directed. Trash was out too. Dumpsters pulled to the curb. Dishwasher loaded and running. Several of them had checked all the rooms, making sure they'd been cleared. Refrigerator and pantry emptied. Wall outlets scanned to catch any forgotten chargers. Not even nine o'clock, and it felt like eleven. Evita was slightly hungry for lunch. She'd probably eat the sandwich she'd made for the trip before leaving the island.

Everyone wore their Nantucket T-shirts, Ryan's parents included. Evita's heart was full to bursting. This had been such a great trip—in retrospect. She'd stayed down at the beach savoring Ryan's hot, sexy kisses until the pizza went cold. She'd do it again in a heartbeat. From the look in his eyes, so would he. When they came back to the house, a party was in full swing with people eating bowls of ice cream and slurping after-dinner drinks.

She'd tried to join in the conversation, but her mind had been totally elsewhere, wondering about what the coming weeks would bring. She and Ryan didn't make a display in front of the others, or any kind of statement. Her family seemed to know they were together, and so did his. Nobody said anything about it though, and maybe that was for the best.

Ryan stood beside her with his parents on the other side. Robby was trying to line people up for their pic, but not everyone was cooperating.

Robby studied the camera preview on his screen and motioned to Evita. "Move over that way. Hide the gap in the flowers." She looked behind her, seeing a big chunk of roses had been excised. Oh no! She giggled and covered her hand, glancing at Mr. Hatfield.

He flushed and stared at his feet.

Ryan saw the hole in the fence too. His forehead rose like he had no clue what had happened. "Was that one of the kids?"

"No," she said softly. "Your dad."

"What?"

"Shh." She giggled again. "I'll tell you later."

Eunice was on Evita's other side holding Luisa. The angry little munchkin in an infant T-shirt could not be consoled, no matter how much Eunice coddled and soothed her. There was an empty spot for Robby beside Eunice.

Evita's parents stood by their SUV arguing over who would drive. Her mom hated driving over water for whatever reason, but her dad claimed he'd done a lot of partying last night so deserved a break.

"I didn't tell you to make all those Kahlúas and whatevers."

"You didn't have any trouble drinking them."

She huffed. "Because they were good."

Ryan's mom spoke quietly to his dad. "Those Kahlúa drinks were delicious."

"Mom! Dad!" Robby yelled, getting their attention.

His dad held up a hand telling Robby to wait.

Poor Robby. This was an impossible task.

"It's only a ferry ride, Lissette, not a bridge."

"I'll get seasick!"

"The Suburban won't be moving."

"Oh yes. It will."

"Fine." He set his hand on his hips. "I'll sit behind the wheel when we get on the boat."

Robby waved to his brother. "Chachi, hey! You need to stand right over there."

But Chachi was busy trying to peel Quique away from Maddy. "Will you come visit?" the kid asked the teen. "You can see my astronaut stars! They're on the ceiling!"

"You're welcome any time," Chachi said graciously. "Once you start looking at colleges, there are lots of good schools in New York."

Kendra had her sticker board ready. "Good behavior in the car," she said. "You'll earn your bronze star."

"Bronze means video games," Quique said to Maddy. "But I like drip castles better."

Maddy chuckled and glanced around. "Where's Nanny?"

"Oh my gosh!" Kendra clutched her sticker board to her heart. She shrieked, looking wild-eyed when Evita's niece was nowhere in sight. "*Nanny!*"

"Wahhhh!" Pounding came from inside the house. "Tita locked me in!"

Evita's mom gasped, her hands on her cheeks. "*Ay dios mio, no.* What?" She glared at her husband. "You said everyone was outside?"

"They were! I counted. Fourteen!"

Kendra and Chachi stormed the porch.

"Don't touch the keypad!" Evita's mom warned. "You'll freeze it!"

"Oh, great." Eunice groaned, staring down at a spot on her T-shirt. "I've sprung a leak."

Evita turned to her, and Eunice shoved off the baby. "Here! Can you take her?"

Luisa kicked her heels and wailed. Evita rubbed Luisa's back, but she was making those gurgling noises again. The bad kind. Okay. Not good. She didn't even have a burp cloth.

Eunice scampered toward the Suburban.

"Eunice!" Robby called. "Where are you going?"

She waved her burp cloth like a flag then pressed it to her chest. "Where are the breast pads?"

There are breast pads?

"Diaper bag!"

Ryan's face turned bright pink, and his folks grimaced at each other.

Maddy had her earbuds in and was swiping through her phone.

Evita's mom was on her phone with someone and standing by the door. "No. I said right now. I need that new code pronto, please. You don't understand, my granddaughter's locked inside." She sounded like a commando. She could be like that, Evita's mom. Tough and assertive. She'd have that code in an instant.

"It's okay, honey!" Kendra called to Nanny. "Mommy's coming!"

"Wahhhh!"

Chachi peered in a window. "Maybe one of these is loose?"

"Chachi, no!" his mom hissed. "We can't break in!" She nodded, talking into her phone. "Yes, yes. Got it. Thank you." She announced a series of numbers, and Chachi punched them into the keypad. The dead bolt slid open, and Kendra cheered.

Nanny leapt into her arms, tears streaming down her cheeks. "Mommy! Mommy!"

The baby chortled in Evita's arms. "Wait!" she screamed. She had this weird premonition she'd have to dart inside. But if they locked that keypad again.

"Don't close the do—"

Blurp!

Oh, nasty. She was never having babies. Never. Ever. Ever. Ew, ew, ew. Ick. Ick. Ick. It was all over her face and in her hair.

Eunice returned, adjusting her T-shirt. "Oops! Sorry, Evita." She took back the baby. "Maybe you should, erm—go wash up?"

Evita sighed and glanced at Ryan. She expected him to be horrified, but instead, he smiled. "You look just like that first day. Beautiful."

Talk about a litmus test.

No one looks good in baby barf.

But he thought she did. Aww, her heart sighed. Okay, maybe she'd have a baby or two. Someday. Butterflies flitted around in her belly. If it was with someone like him. Her heart pounded. *He'd make such a good daddy.*

Not today though. No. "Be right back," she said, beelining for the stoop. She would kill for soap, hot water, and a washcloth.

Was this really her life? Yeah. She guessed so.

Still. She wouldn't change it.

"Hurry!" Robby hollered. "We'll miss our plane!"

Kendra was still consoling Nanny. "Oh honey." She hugged Nanny's shoulders. "What were you doing inside? I told you to wait out here with Quique."

"I had to go pee-pee."

"Okay."

"The potty flooded."

"*What?*"

"All over the floor."

Kendra grabbed Nanny's hand, speaking to Chachi. "I'd better go and—check things."

"Not you too!" Robby yelped, his cry hollow. "Kendra!"

"We'll just be a minute!"

There's nothing like a family vacation.

TWENTY-FIVE

"IT'S AMAZING ROBBY GOT THE picture," Josie said, staring down at Evita's phone. Evita had spilled the whole story the minute she and Josie walked into the shop on Monday morning. All Josie had to say was, "How was your beach week?"

"It's amazing that Robby and Eunice didn't miss their flight."

"Love the Nantucket T-shirts." Josie chuckled. "Looks like you're all on a team."

Evita laughed. "We were on opposing teams at first."

"No kidding." Josie enlarged the photo. "Ryan's handsome. You're right. A real hottie." She peered closer. "Aww, you two look cute together."

Evita's cheeks warmed. "He's so great, Josie." She booted up her computer, checking the online orders that had come in over the weekend. The shop was only open half a day on Saturday and closed on Sunday. It was going to be a busy day, but busy was good. "Really sweet and kind." Her pulse fluttered when she remembered his sexy kisses. "Smart and funny."

Josie looked up from punching in her register code. "Ever wonder what would have happened if you'd started dating in high school?"

"You mean if he'd really gone ahead and asked me to the prom?" Evita giggled. "I don't know. Maybe it wouldn't have lasted. I don't think either of us had the maturity to stand up to our families back then. Plus, maybe the timing wasn't right." She hunted around in a storage cabinet for the right vase for her first project.

"What can I do to help?" Josie asked her.

"Pink and yellow tartan ribbon."

Josie walked to the large spool mounted on the wall and began unraveling a length of ribbon. "That's really sad about his mom and that necklace."

"Yeah," Evita said, selecting flowers and greenery from a refrigerated case.

Josie returned to the workstation the same time as Evita, laying the ribbon on its surface beside the vase. "Do you think she'll ever wear it again?" she asked about Mrs. Hatfield's pearls.

Evita looked up from her floral arranging, wondering about that herself. "Mr. Hatfield said he was going to get it fixed."

Josie frowned. "Mrs. Hatfield's dad sounded totally overbearing. That whole election thing!"

"Yes. Well." Evita stopped messing with her flowers a moment to stare at Josie. "My Abuelo wasn't exactly a saint."

"Sounded to me like he was being clever, trying to encourage people to vote. I don't think that would have swayed things. I'm sure the votes were secret."

"True."

"I'm glad your mom and Mrs. Hatfield finally worked things out."

Evita smiled and retrieved some baby's breath from a container of dried flowers. "We're all glad." Josie admired Evita's handiwork as she finished off her arrangement and tied it off with a bow.

"Someone needs to nominate you and Ryan for some kind of peace prize."

"It wasn't all us." Evita placed the card holder in the vase, prompting Josie to return to her register and print the note card out. "Our moms had to seek their own resolution."

"Sounds like the others helped," Josie said as the printer whirred.

"They did." Evita smiled, thinking of her brothers and sisters-in-law, as well as her nieces and nephew. Maddy too. The dads naturally had to side with their wives, but they'd grown weary of the tension too, periodically trying to diffuse things in their own way. Except for during certain episodes. Like with the music speaker and the umbrella. "I think having more people around served as a buffer. And Maddy's sweet. Quique and Nanny loved her."

"I love that you all made up with a dance party at the end." Josie inserted the gift card in its envelope and handed it to Evita. "That sounds very Machado."

Evita laughed, attaching the card to its holder. "You should have seen Mrs. Hatfield doing the Macarena!"

Josie's face lit up. "I wish I could have."

"Mr. Hatfield too. He actually has rhythm."

Josie winked. "Maybe that's where Ryan gets it from?"

Evita's cheeks burned hot. "I never said anything about—"

"Didn't have to," Josie teased. "It's written all over your face."

"Josie!"

"What? I was talking about his dancing."

She smirked. "Sure you were."

Josie picked up the finished arrangement and carried it to the refrigerator case for outgoing deliveries. "You have to have kissed him at least, during one of those romantic times on the beach—when it was just the two of you," she said in a knowing way.

"Okay, all right!" She sighed, going all dreamy. "He is a great kisser, it's true." Evita hung her head to hide her blush.

Evita began collecting supplies from the bins for her next project and setting them on her workstation. "So! Tell me about the wedding planning and how all that's going?"

"Really great." Josie grinned. "We're almost set for September. We just have to give the caterer our final numbers once the rest of the RSVPs come in."

"I love fall weddings. It's such a pretty time of year, especially up here."

Josie's eyebrows arched. "Think you'll bring a plus-one?"

Evita smiled, liking that idea. "If things go well."

TWENTY-SIX

SIX MONTHS LATER, EVITA STOOD at her workstation completing her last project of the day. Snow drifted outside the front window, dotting the darkness with dancing white flakes. December snow was always magical, and this snow was no different. Holiday decorations filled her shop, with potted poinsettias lending an extra pop of color. She and Ryan had been nearly inseparable since their return from Nantucket, seeing each other as often as their work schedules allowed. Ryan had been her plus-one at Josie's wedding in September. He'd outshone everyone wearing that tux. And she'd caught the bouquet, which had been very strategically aimed at her by the bride.

They'd had lots of fun dates and had gone on some road trips, even once on a lark back to Nantucket in early October—just for lunch. They'd set out at dawn, taking the high-speed passenger catamaran and leaving their car in Hyannis. That saved an hour and a half in travel time over the traditional ferry, giving them more daylight hours on the island, which they explored on bikes.

They'd returned to the small café in 'Sconset Village for coffee and rode past the rental cottage where they'd stayed with their families, chatting and laughing about that week. A gardener had attempted to fix the gap in the roses by moving some vines around on the fence. They would have loved to take a peek in the house, or sneak around to the beach, but a vehicle was in the drive—maybe the owners'—so they'd biked right by, not wanting to intrude.

She and Ryan had made so many great memories in and around Lexington since June. They'd picnicked in the park and gone to fun pubs. A fancy restaurant or two, as well, and Evita had cooked for Ryan tons. She'd toured his college and been introduced to his students, later cheering his team on in soccer games. She'd met his friends, and he'd met hers, including of course Josie and her husband, David. They'd even had a few family dinners at her parents' house, and at his folks' place, though the two families hadn't yet gathered together.

It had been such a whirlwind of happy times, and the more she got to know Ryan, the more she loved him. She suspected he loved her too, but they'd yet to speak the words. She'd meant to say them a couple of times, but something always held her back. She wasn't sure what. It had seemed the same for him. Like the words had been on the tip of his tongue, but he'd not been ready to say them. But she wasn't worried. She was happy. Chachi was so wise. Things worked out how they were meant to. She had faith in that.

She arranged the pretty selection of Stargazer lilies in a tall, narrow vase. The beautiful crimson petals had thin white borders and dark freckles splashed across them. The bouquet smelled like heaven. It had been special ordered by a husband for his wife's birthday, and she was basically guaranteed to love them since they were her favorite flowers and these were gorgeous. Evita strolled to the giant spools on the wall, hunting for the perfect shade of purple ribbon. Violet? No. Magenta? Hmm. Maybe yes. The red undertone for Christmas, coming later this month. Josie tapped her shoulder.

"Sorry to bother you, but would you mind checking an order?"

Josie almost never needed her work double-checked. She didn't prepare orders herself normally, but filled in when things got busy, and she never made mistakes.

"I'm sure it's fine." She measured out a length of magenta ribbon visually and cut it.

"But," Josie pursed her lips, being strangely persistent, "this one's important. I want to get it right."

Evita turned, seeing a long white box had been set on the workstation. The kind they used for dozens of long-stemmed roses, which was probably their most romantic gift option. Big sellers at Valentine's and for special couple's occasions. Sent once in a while just to say I love you. Evita's heart warmed. She adored her job. It was all about people being thoughtful to each other. Caring.

"That's funny," she told Josie. "I didn't see that one come in online?"

"It was a phone order," Josie said. "Last minute."

Evita nodded, wondering why Josie hadn't mentioned it. She generally commented on phone orders during their casual chitchat around the shop. "Must have been very last minute," Evita joked, walking toward the workstation.

"It was!" Josie disappeared into the back room. "The customer should be here any minute." Since buying a car, Josie had taken to parking behind the shop. But she couldn't be leaving already?

"Josie, wait!" That was weird. Evita checked her phone. It wasn't even six o'clock? Just five forty-five. So, no. She probably just went to grab more supplies. A few of the bins were low. Maybe she'd thought of restocking. Josie was always one step ahead. Extremely competent. So Evita had no clue why she'd fret over some random order.

Evita approached the workstation and tied a pretty bow on the lilies, garnishing them with the card Josie had printed out earlier. Then she set them in a floral cooler, leaving them ready to go for tomorrow. The delivery was scheduled to go out around nine.

She studied the outside of the long-stem rose box. It had been wrapped so prettily in a glossy red ribbon that she hated to disturb the packaging.

But she was skilled at this.

Josie—she was sure—had no cause to worry. Evita could guess the arrangement was pristine judging by how much care had been taken on the outside.

She lifted one end of the box and gently slid the ribbon forward, nudging it off the box. It dropped daintily to the woodblock surface in a silky coil.

The back door clicked shut.

Evita looked up. "Josie?"

Seriously? She'd left without saying a word? What was up with that? Her fingernails found the ridge on the underside of the lid, and she removed it slowly, inspecting the contents of the box. The perfect bouquet—it held twelve exquisite russet-red rosebuds attached to elegant forest-green stems wrapped in wispy tissue and ribbon.

A pretty handwritten note card sat on top of the bouquet.

Marry me?

Evita's heart jumped, and then it pounded so hard.

No. Wait. She stared around her empty shop and then down at the rose box.

This couldn't be? It wasn't for—?

No. That didn't make sense.

"When a man loves a woman, he should say it with roses." That voice! It was Ryan's! Heat flooded her face and her body, shimmying down to her toes. She spun toward the back of the shop, and there he was, the shoulders of his field coat and his shaggy golden-brown hair speckled with snowflakes. "Hello, Evita."

His eyes twinkled, and her head felt light. "Ryan? What?"

He nodded toward the roses. "I hope you like them."

"They're gorgeous, but—"

He walked toward her and pulled something from his pocket. It was a ring box. Unmistakable in its shape.

"I've waited a while to say this because I wanted to get it right." He gave her a lopsided grin and her heart flipped. "Wanted to find the right way, the right words, to tell you. And then I thought, what better way than with roses?"

Her eyes burned hot. "Oh, Ryan. Was it your dad who said that thing about giving women roses?"

He nodded and stepped closer. "He heard it from your dad, he said, so it has to be true."

Her pulse raced. Was he really saying? And the roses? A ring box?

"I love you, Evita Machado," he said in husky tones. "I really do. I've loved you for so long now, I can't even remember when it started." He chuckled warmly. "Maybe back in high school."

Her heart danced. Yeah, maybe she'd loved him then too. But not like she did now. Oh no. This love. This feeling that was bursting out of her.

"It took that week in Nantucket," he said, "for one thing to become crystal clear. You're the woman for me, and I'd never want another. You're fierce and strong and so, so beautiful in a way that"—he paused, getting choked up on the words—"makes my heart sing."

Oh my goshhh.

She was melting.

"You and I?" His voice tore apart. "I feel it. Believe it. Way down deep in here." He patted his chest. "Call it destiny or karma or anything you want. I just know that we're meant to be together. So, beautiful—"

He got down on one knee.

Her breath quivered. Okay. This was really happening. She wanted to shout with joy. Run into the street and do the Macarena. But she wasn't going anywhere right now.

"Please say you love me too." His brown eyes shimmered, and she went all tingly inside.

"I do," she whispered. He held her hand.

"Then let's go build some dreams together. Buy that farmhouse, get a dog, start a community garden." He became surer as he talked, emphasizing every word. "Love. Live. Laugh. Give back."

She grinned. "Have babies too?"

His smile lit up the room. "I'd like that."

"So would I." Her cheeks warmed. "And if they're colicky?"

He smiled so warm and tender. "I'll love them twice as much."

He flipped open the ring box. "Evita Machado," he said. A stunning solitaire diamond engagement ring sparkled on a glistening white pillow. "Will you marry me?" His forehead rose, his heart out on a limb. She tugged him to his feet and into her arms, determined not to let him wait a second longer.

"Yes! My answer's yes!" She pressed her hands to his cheeks and kissed him with all her might. "I love you too, Ryan Hatfield. So, so much." He chuckled with joy. "To the moon and back." She sighed.

"Well, that's a relief!" He nodded to the ring box. "How about you try it on?"

She didn't care if it didn't fit. She knew they could get it sized. And it was amazing, a truly perfect diamond, a testament of his love. And she loved him for it. For planning this out and working so hard to make it right.

"This ring is *gorgeous*," she said in a gasp.

He slid it on her ring finger, and it settled below her knuckle just right.

She stared up at him in surprise. "It's perfect."

His blond hair tumbled over his forehead. "Your mom told me your size."

"My mom?"

He nodded. "I did the old-fashioned thing." His neck reddened. "I talked to your parents about my intentions."

Her eyebrows arched. She couldn't believe it. What a sweetheart.

"Which are—good!"

She laughed with delight, her heart so happy. "Oh, Ryan! You didn't?"

"I did."

She didn't even know how he'd thought to do that, but she'd ask him. Later. She threw her arms around his neck, holding him close. Brr! He felt like a snowman. "Your coat!" She giggled and shook out her damp hands, wiping them on her shop apron. He was so chilly and wet.

"Oh, sorry." He removed his coat, taking her in his arms and holding her close. His warm brown eyes shone with love and affection. Admiration and longing. A sizzling touch of *heat*. She caught her breath. Thinking of the scotch and those fiery-hot kisses, and all the others that had come along since.

"I think we can do this, Evita."

"Marriage?" She believed that too, agreed with everything he'd said. "Yeah, so do I."

He nodded. "And this." He ran his hands through her hair, his fingers threading through her curls. Her face heated. "And this." His lips brushed over hers, so silky and warm. Her pulse fluttered. "And *this*." He did it again, and warmth pooled in her belly. He pressed his mouth to hers in the sweetest, softest kiss. She closed her eyes and all her senses came alive. Suddenly, she was back in Nantucket.

The briny scent of the sea, the roaring crash of the waves, the beat-beat-beating of her heart against his. Her world turned upside down, and she felt like she was sailing out across the ocean, carried by the rippling tide, pulling harder and harder until she had no choice but to give in—and ride that wave.

Whoosh!

And then another.

Whoosh!

"If you keep kissing me like that I—" she said all breathy. "I'll—"

His eyebrows rose. "You'll what?" He had the tenderest look in his eyes. Loving and sweet. It made her want to ravage him with kisses.

He was going to be her husband! They were getting married!

She and Ryan. A Hatfield and a Machado.

Wonders never ceased.

She pulled him in for a kiss. "I'll make you do it again."

EPILOGUE

Five Years Later

EVITA HANDED THE TOY SPADE to the towheaded toddler. His hair was golden-brown like his dad's but curly like hers. It was mid-April, and Oliver had just had his second birthday. He sat on the ground in baby dungarees and a little jacket, helping her work in the garden. Today they were planting squash. "Like this," she said, digging in the dirt with her trowel. "See?"

Oliver grinned, showing off his deep dimples. He patted the dirt with his plastic shovel, then scooped some into his bucket. "Dig! Dig!"

"Dig dirt." She patiently demonstrated again.

"Dig dirt!"

Evita clapped her hands. "Good!"

She took his loaded bucket, and he watched her turn it upside down, creating a mound in their designated plot cordoned off by railroad ties. "Now we have our little hill."

"Hill!" he said, but the *H* was garbled, sounding more like *gill.*

"Now's the fun part." She held out her hand, and he watched her. "Open like this." She pried apart his pudgy, balled-up fist, dropping a small collection of seeds in his palm. Then she slowly moved his arm by the wrist like a lever. "Now drop!"

"Drop!" He let go of the seeds, and they landed on the mound. She covered them with more soil so the seeds were buried an inch deep. She leaned forward and kissed the top of her son's head.

My son. Her heart sighed. Hers and Ryan's. What a wonderful five years this had been.

Oliver chortled happily, digging up more dirt. "Dig! Dig!"

"In the bucket," she said. "That's right."

Abuelo wandered over. His snowy-white hair matched the mustache that barely hid the deep dimples etched into his cheeks. Evita's mom hadn't inherited his dimples, but her Tia Margarita had, and Evita had gotten the gene. "Our roses are going to be beautiful."

Abuela joined him, wearing a cheery grin. She stripped off her garden gloves, her dark eyes beaming. Her salt-and-pepper hair was in a loose bun that was becoming undone. "We have them all in the ground."

"That's wonderful."

"This is wonderful." Abuela swept her hand around the garden. It was right in the center of their neighborhood, and they'd volunteered as team captains to help keep an eye on things.

"Thanks, Abuela."

Abuelo twinkled at Oliver with dirt smudged on his cheeks. "I see he has a green thumb."

"Like his mother," Abuela said.

Evita hugged Oliver's shoulders. "He's a natural."

It was a sunny springtime day with puffy white clouds dotting a bright-blue sky. Fluttering butterflies and songbirds flitted through the garden, exploring the landscape.

A boys' club was growing pumpkins. Some younger couples, various kinds of peppers. An elementary school had registered to grow cherry tomatoes. And then there was her favorite. The wildflower garden. People could pay tribute to a lost loved one by paying to have their name installed on a garden plaque. In exchange, they were given a packet of mixed wildflower seeds to distribute in a designated area in honor of their deceased. People had memorialized friends and relatives. Even pets. It really was very special, and the funds additionally helped support the garden.

Mrs. Hatfield had given a donation in honor of her late parents and had seemed to make peace with old issues with her father. Ryan's dad had repaired her necklace. Then, that first Christmas after Nantucket, Kirk had given Daneen beautiful pearl earrings to match. Ryan said it was only the second time in his life he'd seen his mom cry.

She wore the set proudly, even when she was dressed casually. Evita understood that more perfectly now. Daneen and Kirk were awesome grandparents, considering this was their first time at it. They were also great in-laws who could dance a mean Macarena. Okay. Kirk was gifted at it. Daneen, not so much. But what she lacked in grace, she made up for in effort. Two-hundred percent.

Evita's parents were obviously experienced grandparents. They adored Oliver, along with the rest of their clan. The Machados did a big family get-together with the Hatfields at a state park every Fourth of July, bringing both families together to reminisce over Nantucket and share about their lives.

Robby and Eunice were still in LA with Luisa, who'd taken up ballet—and karate. Eunice's film editing job was still going well, and Robby had finally gotten his big break. He'd rewritten one of his rom-com scripts, giving it a new twist. It was about two families who'd been at odds with each other, and who were forced to share a beach house. One family's son and the other one's daughter fell in love. The film was bought and produced! It made huge box office sales, skyrocketing Robby's career. He and Eunice had bought a bigger house, and Ryan and Evita had visited. They could see the Hollywood sign from the pool deck. It was so amazingly cool.

Robby ran into an old friend of Evita's and Ryan's from high school, Layla Petroski, on the studio lot. She'd evidently decided she liked being behind the camera better than in front of it and worked as the top assistant to a show runner now. Layla was married with three kids and lived in Burbank. She sent Evita and Ryan her best regards, pleased—but not surprised—to hear they'd married.

Chachi still worked as a school counselor and Kendra as a child psychologist in Brooklyn. They had a precious four-year-old son, Javier, who played air guitar with ambitions of being a rock star. Nanny was ten now and gifted at art. She'd given up on becoming a princess, saying she might want to be a veterinarian instead. Quique, twelve, wanted a career as either a race car driver or a biologist. Chachi and Kendra supported their dreams, well aware of their ages and the fact that dreams can change.

After some deep soul-searching her junior year, Maddy had taken up the cello again, and then gone to Julliard—her choice.

Chachi and Kendra had her out to Brooklyn often for dinner. Sometimes they took their kids and met her in Manhattan for lunch. They made a point of attending a number of her performances too. So they'd grown closer with Kirk and Daneen, who appreciated their caring involvement.

Maddy also ran an Etsy shop online, selling her macrame wares. Her most popular design was those Christmas tree ornament whales. She'd gifted each of the Machados with one after Nantucket: her folks, Chachi's family and Robby's, as well as Evita, and had made some for her parents and Ryan. Evita and Ryan were the lucky to have two to hang on their tree. Each year at Christmas, they were reminded of that fateful summer that had brought their two hearts together.

"There's my boy!" Ryan said, walking up to them. He wore his soccer coach shirt and had their dog, Snoopy, on a leash. Snoopy tugged at the lead, nosing his way toward Oliver on his wobbly old joints.

"Doggie!" Oliver called. He wrapped his chunky arms around the hound's neck, and Snoopy slurped his tongue across the kid's face. The senior beagle mix had big brown eyes with white rings around them. His darker markings were graying too. Oliver gurgled and clapped his hands. "Doggie! Kiss!"

Ryan grinned down at his son. "How ya doing there, fella?"

"Dad-dy!" Oliver held up his arms, and Ryan picked him up, passing Snoopy's leash to Evita. Evita patted the dog's head. He was an old boy when they got him, a rescue. But he'd been a sweet and gentle companion in their home.

"Come to Abuela," her grandma commanded the dog. "*Ven!*"

The dog obeyed. *"Siéntate,"* she said, and Snoopy sat alertly with his ears perked up.

"He's very smart." Abuela said. "Who says you can't teach an old dog new tricks?"

Abuelo chortled. "I'm still learning."

The others laughed, but Evita was aware he'd also learned belatedly about all the trouble his high school pizza party had caused during her mom's class president election. He'd apologized for that sincerely, saying he'd never asked anyone to cast a particular vote, and Evita's mom and the rest of the family believed him. That was just Abuelo's way. He had a big heart, but sometimes inserted himself way too much in his family's business.

Sort of like. Well...Evita's and Ryan's moms had done.

She scooted off the ground and stood beside Ryan. Sunlight glinted in his hair, making it appear a golden, buttery brown, the same as Oliver's. "Looks like you're taking off here," Ryan said, perusing the garden.

"Yeah, it's going really well."

"I'm so glad." He smiled mysteriously. "I heard back from our agent."

Evita's heart pounded. "No. Seriously?"

They'd been searching for over two years for just the right property, but it had been so hard to find. Ryan wanted the chance to restore their house, lovingly with his hands. Since his recent promotion and his securing tenure, they had a little more money for that too. They wanted a fixer-upper but not a total dump and didn't really have the cash to bulldoze someplace completely and start over from scratch.

They'd found a charming mini farm last week with a 1920s farmhouse that—thank goodness—had indoor plumbing installed, although it was antiquated and had no closets. It sat on five acres, and the land around it was lush and beautiful with picturesque views through its old-timey beveled windows. It had been love at first sight. They'd put in an offer at once. But there'd been competing bids.

On a prayer, Evita and Ryan had submitted a letter to the sellers, saying how much they loved the property and yearned to make it their home. For the two of them and Oliver and their sweet elderly adopted dog. Their agent said the note might not make a difference. Their down payment hadn't been as hefty as another potential buyer's, since they'd deferred some funds to put into the community garden, but neither of them regretted their decision.

Evita stared up at Ryan, her heart hopeful. "And?"

He grinned broadly. "We got the house."

Evita squealed and hugged him, her embrace surrounding Oliver too.

"House!" Oliver said.

Snoopy jumped and barked, sensing the excitement.

"Guess what, buddy boy?" Ryan said to the dog. "You're going to have a new home."

"Where you can run and play in the country," Evita added.

Ryan nuzzled Oliver's nose with his. "So are you."

Snoopy bounced around on his paws, springing up and down like a kid on a pogo stick. Then he started to bay. Howling so loudly others in the garden turned their way.

"We got the farm!" Evita shouted happily.

"How wonderful," Abuela said.

Abuelo smiled. "Congratulations!"

Others around her cheered and shook their fists in signs of victory. She'd told everyone here who would listen everything about the farm since last Sunday.

Oliver looked at his mommy and daddy and grinned. "Happy!" He clapped his little hands together, his dimples huge.

Evita's eyes warmed. "Yes," she said, hugging her husband and son. "Happy."

"Happy doesn't even begin to describe it," Ryan said, holding them tight.

Evita's heart sighed, loving her family—large and small.

Everything was coming up roses.

The Holiday Mix-Up

One Week Before Christmas

KATIE SMITH PAUSED WITH HER coffee pot held mid-air and stared at gorgeous Juan Martinez. "Wait. You want me to do what?" Her heart skipped a beat. She'd probably misheard him. He wore a starched white button-down shirt below a charcoal-colored suit jacket with no tie. His slacks matched his jacket. Juan Martinez was always dressed to a *T*, and his sturdy build filled out his business clothes expertly.

"Pretend to be my girlfriend"—he shrugged sheepishly—"for Christmas dinner?" He sat at the counter on his customary stool eating a piece of gingerbread cheesecake. Beyond him, a Christmas wreath adorned the door and swags of fake greenery dripped from the cracked plaster walls. It was slow season in wine country and a dead time of day at the diner. Only one other patron sat in a booth, waiting on his late lunch and reading his tablet. Tiny Castellana, California did its fair share of tourist trade three-fourths of the year. From December through March though, not so much.

Katie's mind whirled as she refilled Juan's coffee cup. She'd crushed on him for the past three months, which was approximately how long he'd been coming in for coffee. When he'd begun asking for her advice, she'd secretly hoped their quasi-friendship would lead to something more. Like a real date, not a fake one. Although beggars couldn't be choosers. Not that she was begging, exactly. He was the one who seemed borderline desperate.

He dropped his voice into a whisper. "Remember when I told you about my Titi Mon coming from Puerto Rico for Christmas? Well." He winced. "She's already here, and my great-aunt takes her double role very seriously."

Katie returned the coffee pot to its warmer. "Double role?"

"She's also my Godmother. And, as my *madrina*, she feels a certain obligation to find me a 'nice Latin girl.'"

She didn't exactly fit that profile. What with her extremely Anglo roots, light brown hair, and basic brown eyes. At least she wasn't *that* pasty—when she wasn't wearing makeup. Only medium pale.

Juan leaned toward her and continued. "Last year was such a disaster. She had three poor women lined up. One for Christmas Day. Another for New Year's Eve. And a third for Three Kings Day."

"Three Kings Day?"

"The Spanish tradition of the wise men bringing gifts to Jesus. In our house they brought presents to us kids, Mateo and me, when we were small. Last year, my Titi Mon invited her best friend's second cousin's grand-niece to my parents' house for dinner to meet me. I don't think she was much interested in being there, though, because she stayed glued to her phone."

Katie laughed when he pulled a face. "Oh no. But why would these women even agree in the first—?"

She looked at Juan and bit her tongue. Because. Why wouldn't they? Nearly every living, breathing soul in Castellana wanted to go out with him once they'd seen his picture. Katie had to pinch herself to believe she might actually get a chance. She dropped her chin when she blushed. "Never mind."

"I can't figure out why they'd do it, either," he confided huskily. "I think mostly as a favor to their moms, or grandmothers, or great-aunts... Or"—His eyes sparkled—"maybe their *madrinas*." He shook his head. "Seriously. If not that, then probably on account of my connection to the winery. I mean, come on, the place is beautiful. What's not to love?" He laughed self-effacingly. "I don't think it's because of me."

She appreciated that he didn't have an ego. At least not as big a one as he rightly could own, with his deep brown eyes and his nearly black hair. Juan was very handsome and accomplished. He also had somewhat of a checkered dating history. Katie had read about that online. None of his relationships ever lasted very long, but that was likely because he kept dating flighty jet-setters. Maybe if he settled down with somebody stable and ordinary, things would go differently.

"Well, if you don't want her to fix you up—"

"Katie," he said smoothly, and her mouth went dry, because he looked so helpless, and ooh, how she wanted to rush to his rescue—with open arms. "There's no talking to my Titi Mon. She's trying to set me up this year with Adelita Busó."

"Who's Adelita Busó?"

He sighed. "Only her grand-niece's second cousin's cousin—by marriage."

Katie winced. "That sounds complicated."

"It is complicated—by the fact that I don't even know her. She supposedly lived in Castellana years ago and has recently returned to town. So what if she's the CFO of some mega media company that she now works for remotely? Fact is, I'm not interested.

"But it's hard getting through to Titi Mon, especially with Abuelo on her side. The two of them are always going on *and on* about how I don't value my culture." Juan's family had owned Los Cielos Cellars for generations.

She hesitated and then asked. "Do you?"

"Sure I do." Juan took a sip of coffee. "I also value my independence. So think I should be able to make up my own mind about who I do—and don't—see. Don't you agree?"

"Well, sure." That sounded reasonable enough.

His expression oozed sincerity. "Look. You're a nice woman. Kind. Genuine. Once my family sees me with someone like you, they'll finally back off."

"Back off how?"

"By letting me lead my own life." Juan squared his shoulders. "I'm thirty-two. A man and not a kid. Old enough to make my own choices."

Over the past few months, he'd told her about some of those. While the rest of his family lived at the vineyard, Juan owned a fancy modern condo in town. He also followed his industry and was keen on modernization. Always up on the latest trends.

Her heart beat harder when she imagined herself trending with him. Juan was active on social media and pretty much every single woman in Castellana followed him. Maybe a few of the married ones too. What if fake led to forever and they actually coupled up? She bit her lip, knowing that was a stretch, but still. A girl could dream.

Katie had never had a serious boyfriend. Well, not since Wes in high school. He'd been smart and ambitious and had gone on to do other things. He was an entertainment lawyer in Los Angeles now. He also had a girlfriend. Katie stalked him once in a while on social media. Members of their old friend group too. It was hard to believe she'd once been one of them. But that was before her life had taken a different turn.

"I don't know, Juan." She frowned. "I mean, I get what you're saying—"

"Then please, say yes." He pleaded with his eyes, and Katie found it impossible to resist him. Why would she turn down an opportunity like this? The diner was closed on Christmas Day, and it wasn't like she had tons going on in that lonely little house of hers anyway. Last year, she'd opened a can of jellied cranberry sauce and slapped that and some turkey lunchmeat between two pieces of white bread, calling it Christmas. She hadn't had a happy Christmas in forever. So maybe she'd get to experience a real heartwarming holiday now? Plus, she'd get to meet Juan's family.

The family that wanted Juan to date someone *not like her*.

Her stomach clenched.

Maybe this was a bad idea.

But no, Juan would be there with her—holding her hand. Possibly even literally. *Yes.*

"Just for Christmas dinner?" she asked, acting like her cheeks weren't burning so, so hot.

He grinned reading her expression, which must have looked goofily giddy.

Gah.

"So, what?" His face lit up. "You'll do it?"

Katie pursed her lips. It was only for a couple of hours and, maybe after doing him this favor, she'd stand a chance with him for real. Assuming she impressed him enough. She'd also have to win over his family. This last thought filled her with dread. She was a simple person and the Martinezes were—well, the Martinezes, with their beautiful winery and all that land with so much history behind it. She'd never been there, but she'd seen Los Cielos Cellars written up in area wine magazines and online blogs. She'd bookmarked all the pages that had photos of Juan on them. Embarrassingly.

"Okay, yes," she agreed. "I'll do it." She peeked at him shyly. "If it will help you out." And *helping* was a good thing. *The right thing,* especially to do at the holidays.

"Great!" His cell dinged and he took it from his pocket, scanning an incoming message. "Ugh, sorry." He texted back, engaged in a fast exchange, then set his phone down by his plate, grinning at her.

"Thanks, Katie," he said. "You're awesome." He winked and her stomach fluttered. "I won't forget this. Just promise me one thing."

"Huh?"

He lowered his voice. "Don't breathe a word about this being fake to my family. This has got to be our secret." He glanced over his shoulder, but there was nothing behind him but the coat rack, holding the lone other customer's jacket. "None of them would understand."

Katie swallowed hard. "Okay. Sure."

Panic gripped her when she realized she had nothing to wear. But that was fine. She had a whole week to think on it. Which was a lot more time than she'd had to prepare for some of her last-minute dating app meet-ups, none of which had ended well. Maybe she was being too picky, but she wanted someone she was comfortable with and whom she could talk to. Someone like Juan.

Although, technically, when Juan was here, he did most of the talking and rarely asked her about herself. Okay, not rarely. Never. But hey, that would change now. He'd have to get to know her at least a little better, before bringing her home for Christmas dinner, if they wanted to convince his family they were really a couple. They'd need to put their heads together and plan. That could be fun.

Juan finished his cheesecake and set down his fork. "This is delicious. Can I take a piece to-go?"

Katie nodded and boxed up the slice, setting it beside Juan's coffee cup. This was going to be good. No. *Amazing.* She was going out to Los Cielos with Juan! She wiped her damp palms on her apron and her cell phone jiggled in its pocket. Too bad she didn't have someone to text with her stellar news. Like Jane. Or Lizzie. But she'd lost touch with those girlfriends so long ago, it would be weird reaching out to them now. All of a sudden and over something like this.

"Order up!" The diner's cook, Mark Wang, spun from the griddle, setting a plate on the high metal shelf beside Katie. His dark eyes gleamed, offsetting his amber skin. "BLT with a side of fries." Mark was in his forties and married with two kids. He was also a secret romantic and forever ribbing Katie about her private crush on Juan, goading her to do something about it.

So there! Now, she was.

Mark sent her a sly look, rolling his eyes toward Juan, like he suspected something was up. Katie smugly set her chin, deciding she could tell him later. She couldn't wait to tell Daisy first.

"Sorry." She glanced at Juan. "Duty calls."

"Sure." He stood and grabbed his overcoat from the stool beside his, sliding it on. He held his cell phone in one hand and lifted the pie box in the other. "Thanks for this." He smiled. "And thanks especially about Christmas."

She picked up the lunch order and delivered it to the other customer, who asked for more coffee. When she turned around, Juan was already at the register, and her boss, Daisy, was ringing him up. Before he left, Juan said to Katie, "We'll work out details tomorrow."

She couldn't wait. "Sounds good!"

As soon as he'd gone, Katie scuttled over to Daisy, dying to share.

"Juan's invited me to Christmas dinner," she said in an excited whisper. She had to stop herself from squealing.

Daisy's forehead rose, the creases in her dark complexion

deepening. "Is that right? My, my." Daisha Santos had come to Castellana from Panama and still had a bit of an accent. Everyone knew her as Daisy, as that's the name she'd given her diner.

Katie nodded, beaming.

This was really happening! She was going out with Juan!

Sort of.

"Well, congratulations. I'm glad the boy has finally seen the light." Daisy shared a motherly smile and Katie wanted to hug her, but she didn't. Daisy and Mark were the closet things to family she had, but they each had families of their own. So Katie kept her relationships with them friendly but distant, because distance was what she knew best.

She sighed, hoping that Daisy was right and that Juan really would come around. She didn't tell Daisy that her Christmas date was just pretend, because that part didn't matter so much. The important thing was that she'd been legit invited to Los Cielos.

By Juan.

Who knew what would happen from there?

Daisy's eyes twinkled. "You know, if Juan hadn't asked you to his parents' house, I would have invited you to Christmas dinner myself. You'll always have a place at our table."

Daisy was so kind. She'd invited Katie home for various holidays before, but Katie had never been able to let herself cross that line. Daisy already had five kids and a husband, plus multiple grandchildren. So, Katie typically invented excuses, saying she'd made other plans. She never mentioned those plans involved eating sandwiches alone while working online crossword puzzles, because—even to her—that sounded a little sad.

"Thanks, Daisy."

Daisy glanced at a spot in front of the register and frowned. "Oh no."

Katie saw what she was staring at. Juan's wallet.

"He set it down to check his phone," Daisy said. "It kept buzzing."

Who'd been texting him like crazy?

Maybe his mom or his Titi Mon?

Katie's pulse stuttered. What if he'd already told them about bringing her home for Christmas dinner? Maybe he had and they were going ballistic.

Stop being so negative and paranoid.

Or—maybe he had, and they were super happy?

Sure, that could be it. Think positive!

It's Christmastime. Good things happen.

It was true they very rarely happened to her, but now she had a date for Christmas. So things were looking up.

Katie grabbed Juan's wallet and dashed for the door. "I'll catch him!"

Luckily, Juan hadn't gone far. He had paused at a crosswalk and stepped into the street, carrying his pie container in one hand. He held his cell phone in the other and was one-handed texting. If he wasn't answering his family, maybe he was caught up in some business deal.

"Juan! Wait!" she called, but he was so absorbed in his messaging he didn't hear her.

Katie hurried toward the crosswalk, moving faster. "Juan Martinez!"

The lights changed and a large white van screeched around the corner, driving way too fast. Katie's heart lurched.

No way. It was heading right for him.

"Juan!"

He startled and his eyebrows shot up.

Next, he saw the oncoming van.

But it was too late.

The van driver hit his brakes.

Tires squealed and the van slid sideways, a two-ton lightning bolt of metal streaking in Juan's direction. Katie shot into the street and shoved his arm with all her might, pushing him out of the way of the oncoming van, which slammed past them and into a lamppost with a thundering *crash*.

Juan tumbled backwards toward the curb, and she tripped and fell.

People called out and a woman screamed.

Then everything went black.

ACKNOWLEDGMENTS

Thanks to the many individuals who helped make *Right Girl, Wrong Side* possible, starting with my fabulous agent, Jill Marsal, who championed my work, and talented senior editor, Christa Désir, at Sourcebooks Casablanca, for believing in this story and giving me free rein to write it. I adored getting to know Evita Machado and Ryan Hatfield and their respective families, who demonstrate that—though the world may pull us apart—love and acceptance can bind us together. A huge nod of appreciation to Christa Désir for bringing out the best in these characters during their dynamic, poignant, and interesting journeys.

Special thanks to copy editor Meaghan Summers and editorial trainee Samantha Bustillos for ensuring I dotted my i's and crossed my t's, while italicizing my *ay dios mios*. Art director Stephanie Gaffron has my deep gratitude for delivering a stunning cover that captures the lively and romantic mood of the story. I'd also like to thank assistant editor Rachel Gilmer, editorial assistant Letty Mundt, editorial assistant Jocelyn Travis, content editor Susie Benton, and production editor Shannon Barr for their valued roles in seeing this project through to completion. Added thanks to marketing director Pamela Jaffee, author liaison Madeleine Brown, and royalty associate Jessica Castle for their important contributions.

This book couldn't have been written nearly as easily without the full support of my thoughtful husband, John. Thanks for the many delicious meals and enabling countless writing sessions by supplying homemade chocolate chip cookies. I love your laugh, and your smile, and those *very blue eyes* my mom could never get over. You know your way to my heart, and will dwell there forever. Big hugs to our kids, and their spouses and significant others, for standing by me, as well. I couldn't have asked for a greater cheerleading squad from you or our extended family. I'm still shocked (and secretly touched) when you brag to one of your friends that your mom/stepmom/sister/relative...writes books. My heart warms at your sweetness.

Thanks to my late parents, Irma Aboy Turner and Elbert Daymond Turner Jr., for giving me roots and wings, and teaching me to fight for my dreams. I wish you'd been here to see this book published. I have a hunch you would have loved it, but perhaps in some happy way you know. I'm so glad you met and fell in love in Puerto Rico during World War II, and that Mother survived the torpedo attack on the SS *Carolina* as an infant many years before. If her family had moved to Brooklyn as planned, rather than returning to San Juan, many chapters in our family's history never would have been written. Thanks for being bold and daring to be different, though you faced resistance in bringing two opposing cultures together. It's been a beautiful mix.

Lastly, thanks to my readers everywhere for selecting this book and giving *Right Girl, Wrong Side* a chance. I hope it moved you and lightened your heart, just as it did mine, helping you believe in happy endings.

Warmly,

Ginny

ABOUT THE AUTHOR

New York Times and *USA Today* bestselling author Ginny Baird writes wholesome contemporary stories with a dash of humor and a lot of heart. She's fond of including family dynamics in her work and creating lovable and memorable characters in worlds where romance is a given and happily-ever-afters are guaranteed. She lives in North Carolina with her family.

You can visit Ginny Baird at ginnybairdromance.com and facebook.com/GinnyBairdRomance, as well as on Instagram @ginnybairdromance and on Twitter @GinnyBaird.